Witches' Brew

Wylfheort Magical Mystery Books
History Fantasy
Est. 2010

L. J. Hutton

ISBN: 978-1-7396943-4-0

Published by Wylfheort Books 2023

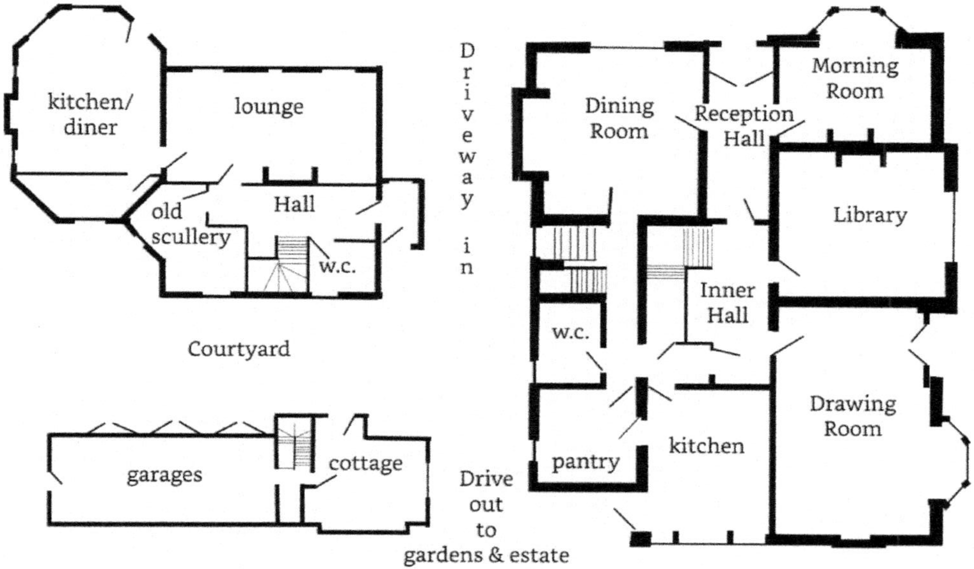
kitchen/ diner
lounge
Hall
old scullery
w.c.
Courtyard
garages
cottage
Driveway in
Dining Room
Reception Hall
Morning Room
Library
Inner Hall
w.c.
pantry
kitchen
Drawing Room
Drive out to gardens & estate

Chapter 1

"Angelo Vance has bought a library," Mr Harris, head of Restorations, Valuations, & Cataloguing at *Miller, Bronson & Carter* announced to his audience, "and it needs sorting and cataloguing."

A collective groan rippled through the assembled team of twelve, because Angelo Vance was a nightmare of epic proportions. His father, James 'Jacko' Vance, had been minor rock and roll royalty for the few years before he died, although careering off an embankment in Birmingham and embedding a Ford Cortina into a power pylon, while pissed as a rat, lacked the tragic allure and musical significance of Marc Bolan's similar demise some years earlier. A short, chunky, aspiring Ozzy Osborne, complete with the same accent – although in fairness because he came from Birmingham too – he'd failed to hit similar heady heights.

However, while Jacko Vance had only managed to be a one-hit-wonder with his own band, somewhere along the line he'd managed to write half a dozen songs which still kept getting covered by much bigger name performers with considerable success, and as a result large royalties had kept coming in decades after Jacko's death. Couple that with Angelo's mother being a minor countess used to handling money, and who'd been having her wild fling with 'a bit of rough' until getting what her family must have hoped for as a 'proper' husband – though Jacko had never lived long enough for any separation or divorce to become necessary – and the money had been managed well by professionals, rather than vanishing in epic rock and roll booze and cocaine binges on the road. And so by the time Angelo was old enough to start spending his inheritance, it had grown into a substantial investment; which had then been used by Angelo to create an online presence, proving that blogging could be big business, and making himself into one of those celebrities who are famous simply for being famous, rather than any specific talent.

All of that made him into the archetypal thirty-six-year-old spoilt playboy in personality. But what made him into *Miller, Bronson & Carter's* headache, was that although he did the typical thing of dashing out and buying whatever took his fancy – just because he could – Angelo nonetheless had a good eye for an investment. Last year he'd stumbled across a collection of old china up for sale, which had been dug out of an attic by a Chinese family who had made it big in the restaurant trade, and were moving into a high-tech chrome and steel conversion in the heart of the city, where such old reminders of where they'd come from weren't wanted.

None of the conservators could work out whether Angelo was simply born lucky, or whether behind the vacuous façade there was actually a brain at work, because that collection had turned out to have some incredible pieces in it, including some minor pieces of Ming. And, of course, as the valuations had progressively turned into something more than their usual kind of assessments – such as granny's favourite teapot or vase – so their fees for their services had increased. Therefore there was no question of turning down Angelo's demand for someone to come and sort out his latest acquisition, because huge commissions like that didn't just fall from the sky for regional/county companies like theirs. Even big names like Sotheby's might think twice about declining a job when such eye-watering sums could be made from it, particularly once auctioneer fees were added in for those pieces sold on.

Consequently, everyone turned to look sympathetically at Lucy and her two assistants, Carrie-Ann and Fleur, who were the ones who dealt with books and papers, Lucy asking,

"What do you mean, he's bought a library? Just the books or a whole building?" Nothing was out of the question where Angelo's whims were concerned.

Mr Harris sighed and pinched the bridge of his nose under his specs, a sure sign that he was already getting a headache just thinking about this. "You all remember that he decided to take over his maternal grandfather's old Herefordshire mansion after his grandfather died?" That had been another commission none of them would forget, when the furniture experts amongst them had had to go in and decide what was worth keeping before the building restorers went in, and the current contents got packed up or sold off. The place had been on a long lease as a hotel up until then, and so not everything in it had been original or valuable. "Well it seems there was once a considerable library there, not that you'd have known it by what we last saw. The books were sold to pay off part of the inheritance tax back when the great-grandfather died, and empty shelves weren't of any use once it became a hotel, so they went and a bar and small ballroom went in."

Harris heaved a weary sigh. "Last year Gascoigne House in the West Country went to auction, and Vance bought the library, fittings and all." Another sigh. "You know that I hate it when beautiful old houses get ripped apart like that, but apparently Gascoigne House was one step short of falling down anyway – something to do with water seepage into the foundations – so I suppose it's better that as much of it gets saved as possible. Since then, Vance has had a team of specialist carpenters reinstalling that library shelving into his mansion, and now that they are all ready and waiting, he wants the books brought out of storage, catalogued, and put back onto the shelves."

"Oh God, I hate that man," Fleur said bitterly. "He's probably never read a book in his life. What does he want us to do, artistically arrange a job lot of book markers in them while we do it, so that it looks like he might have actually picked one or two of them up?"

Carrie-Ann giggled, "Leave one or two pulled just that bit forward as if recently read? Maybe add in an old envelope as a marker, to add that 'authentic' touch? I wouldn't put it past him! Once he's put the photographs up on TikTok, Instagram, or wherever, that's all he'll ever be interested in them for."

Harris smiled faintly at Carrie-Ann's withering sarcasm. "I'm sure you're not far from the truth," he admitted.

"I don't suppose there's any chance of him being away on something like *I'm a Celebrity*… is there?" Lucy asked hopefully. "Film festival in Outer Mongolia, maybe?" And when Harris sadly shook his head, groaned, "Oh well, looks like it's back to the *Fox & Hounds* for us then, girls."

The three who dealt with china and glassware had virtually lived at the nearest pub for weeks on end during the unpacking of the Chinese collection. And if the menu was chips with everything, at least they'd been spared stopping at the mansion, or on the estate, thanks to Angelo preparing for and then holding some major launch party in what were then the habitable bits on the ground floor. Lucy had ended up at the pub, too, because of some of what the china was wrapped in – which had turned out to be of considerable importance in its own right – but with Fleur as the newbie, only Carrie-Ann had gone down there with Lucy except for on the day when they'd brought a load of stuff back to be conserved.

However, Harris was now looking positively sick as he waved a finger in their direction. "Not all of you, just Fleur."

"Me?" Fleur yelped. "Why me?"

"Because he specifically asked for you," Harris told her apologetically.

Fleur was aghast. "But you did tell him that although I'm the oldest of us three, it's because I went to university late? That I'm actually the most junior and least qualified of us all? Has that sunk in with him? That it's Lucy who has all of the technical knowledge, and I'm still learning?"

Fleur had only been with the firm for three years, and that after going to university as a very mature student to take her master's degree in conservation at Northumbria University. Moreover, she'd suffered the mature student's problem of being considered too old for the usual internships that others on her course had naturally progressed into, and so she'd been incredibly grateful that Mr Harris and Lucy had offered her a full-time job. And that, even more than random encounters with Angelo Vance, was why she didn't want to go into this job under false pretences. One genuine mistake by her might harm more than just her own reputation.

"It's because he's learned you're a divorcee," Carrie-Ann teased with a wink. "Thinks he might be onto a good thing! Not like with us two married ladies – as if he'd get anywhere with Lucy anyway!"

At which Lucy threw back her head hooting with laughter, but also showing off her glorious mane of auburn hair. Her stunning good looks had men swarming around her, but then going off totally disconcerted when she introduced them to her wife. Carrie-Ann, on the other hand, was the part-timer because she had two young children at school, and needed to work her hours around them. However, Fleur wasn't as amused.

"I am not staying in his house!" she declared firmly.

And Lucy, sobering up fast, backed her. "God! I should think not! Come on, Harry," a nickname only she and a few other senior staff ever dared use, "you know that Vance is bloody predatory! It's not exaggerating to say that it's little short of dangerous to send *any* woman into his den alone."

However, Harris was already throwing his hands up to fend her off. "A point I've already made to the directors, Lucy. I told them it was not a good idea to send anything less than a team of three in. But it seems Vance is insistent."

"Then I want it put down in writing that we, as a team, object to Fleur being put in this position. I'm serious, Harry. You know full well why our rivals won't touch him with a barge pole after they got sued by one of their own."

The collected teams were nodding vigorously in agreement with her. A bigger rival company based down in Cheltenham had rued the day they had ever given in to Vance's request for one of their staff alone. She had subsequently accused Vance of rape, but also sued the pants off her employers for knowingly sending her to Vance's townhouse in Cheltenham, when others had already complained of being groped by him. She'd won her case, too, and received such a large settlement via the court that it must have knocked out most, if not all, that they had earned from the commission.

Harris was looking faintly green around the edges as he nodded in agreement. "And I've told the directors that as well," he said plaintively, "but they're not convinced that the woman wasn't partly to blame."

"Partly to blame?" Lucy screeched. "Look, we all know that Angelo Vance has drippy girls wilting at the sight of him. One flash of his 'baby blues' and there's always some kid barely out of her teens ripping her knickers off for him. It's a bloody awful trick of fate that he's got the looks to go with his money, and there'll always be someone daft enough to believe that they're the one to tame the wild boy.

"But don't forget, I knew Claire! She was a sensible lady of forty-two, not one of his acolytes, and I'm telling you, in court she was a wreck. She's been scarred for life by what happened to her there. She took that payout from the court and fled to the west coast of Scotland, living miles from anywhere now, with the kind of security system you normally find on big houses in places like London. You don't do that because of some silly scare."

"I know," Harris sympathised. "What I have managed to do is insist that Fleur be given somewhere of her own to live. I did my best to get her booked in at the *Fox & Hounds*, if only because we could then have asked the landlord and landlady to ring us the moment she didn't get back when expected. But of all people, it was Vance's mother who objected and offered one of the cottages on the estate."

"Then please tell me that Mrs Vance is going to be around," Lucy demanded.

Angelo's mother was still fit, glamorous, and a force of nature, despite being in her mid-sixties, and she was the one person who could bring Angelo to heel with just a single word or a look. Herself the daughter of an Italian countess and the then heir to the estate in question, Claudia Vance was the source of Angelo's stunning good looks, but she'd also inherited the 'Italian mama' mindset and temperament, and it was rumoured that she wasn't beyond administering a good slap – even now – if she felt he needed it.

"I can't say for certain that she'll be there," Harris confessed, "but her objection to the pub was that these days, there's quite a rowdy crowd of young men who go in there, and she didn't think it would be wholly safe for Fleur on her own. So if she thinks that, I can only pray that she has the wit to think the same when it comes to her son as well."

"I bloody doubt it," Carrie-Ann muttered darkly, turning to Fleur and adding, "I've got some pepper spray that my cousin in the States sent me, back in my single days when I was working in the City. I know you're not supposed to have it over here, but I've got a couple of canisters, and I'm going to insist you have one of them!"

"And I'll take it gladly!" Fleur said. "I never had to use that self-defence class I took while living up in Newcastle, but I'm damned well going to go home and brush up on what they taught me now! If Angelo Vance thinks he's going to start pawing at me, he's in for a shock – I'll make him eat his nuts if he pushes me!"

"Oh Christ," Lucy heard Harris softly moan, guessing that he was envisaging a whole other kind of lawsuit coming their way. "I told them this wasn't a good idea, I told them. …Said we should never have agreed to this."

"Well then they'll learn to listen the next time, won't they?" she snapped back at him, equally inaudibly to the rest of the team, who were busy commiserating with Fleur. "It's on Fleur's personnel record that she had to get a restraining order against those mates of her ex-husband's, and what happened when they ignored it. You don't go through the kind of shitty divorce that she had without toughening up a lot. Just because she's a nice, polite, and clever lady here with us, it doesn't mean she's a doormat type. If anything, I'm glad that Vance picked on her, not Carrie-Ann, because if it comes to Vance getting physical, Carrie-Ann would wilt – Fleur won't! You've put her in a position where she could end up with her back against the wall, both metaphorically and literally, and if she does, she'll come out fighting."

At the word 'fighting', Harris let out another groan, but only because he knew just how competent Fleur was after hearing her talking in the staffroom during lunch breaks about her unarmed combat classes. She hadn't been bragging, just passing on some useful tips to one of the secretaries who had somehow picked up an unwanted shadow on her walks home, but even that had been enough to kill Harris' appetite simply listening to her. It seemed her instructor had been a former member of the Special Forces, and having realised that her divorce had included some rough pals of her ex-husband's trying to frighten her into not making the court appearances, had taken a personal interest in making sure she was more than equipped to handle any further incidents.

All of which meant that if threatened, Fleur would not be standing in the street going through some archaic, oriental combat, pre-emptive move called something like 'duck farting on the temple steps', but would be snapping fingers and crushing testicles with a vengeance. And the thought of Angelo Vance in A&E, and being told that his chances of fathering a dynasty had just vanished over the horizon, was enough to have Harris breaking out into a cold sweat, and wishing that the days of having a bottle of decent malt whisky in the bottom desk drawer had not long gone in the company's wave of political correctness.

Meanwhile, Fleur was saying to the others, "I can't imagine why the silly sod wants me! I'm not one of his silicone implanted twinkies. My hair colour is my own, even if it isn't exactly inspiring, and I could do with losing a few pounds these days. I'm not even remotely going to see thirty again, let alone twenty-one, and that's the age group he usually chooses his companions from, going by what we saw the last time and in the press. So the only woman of around my age we know he's had anything to do with is Lucy's friend Claire – and when it comes to what happened to her, I believe Lucy one hundred percent! So, is he some kind of nutter, who every so often feels the need to knock the living daylights out of a mother substitute, and then rape her? Because if so, he's not just spoilt, he's a bloody menace and should be in the nearest psychiatric hospital, not wandering loose and a danger to others."

"And if he wants the job done with any speed and accuracy, he should want the whole team," Carrie-Ann sympathised. Then clarified, "I don't agree with what you said about being the least of the team, either. You've worked damned hard to get up to the standard of the rest of us. I'm talking simply about how much longer it's bound to take with just one person doing the work of three. It doesn't make sense. Angelo Vance normally has the patience of a moth diving at a candle flame. I can still remember the whining we had to put up with when we were unwrapping the china, and he couldn't see all the pieces fast enough! *Sheesh*! All those snotty little messages he kept leaving about the place for us! Nearly drove us insane! So what's he thinking? What's that nasty brat got planned that we don't know about?"

A little while later, Lucy, Fleur and Carrie-Ann were clustered around Lucy's computer trying to look online to see if they could get any sort of clue as to what the Gascoigne House library had been like or contained, when Fleur quietly asked,

"Why didn't Vance do time for rape, Lucy? He didn't, did he? Yet surely the court could see how traumatised your friend was?"

She didn't want the whole team within the open office they all shared chiming in, and it getting into the inevitable slagging off session of their most hated client, but Lucy's more insightful point of view.

Lucy sighed and leaned back in her chair. "He didn't do time because it came down to him having an alibi for the night – a rather dodgy and questionable one, but an alibi nonetheless."

Both Fleur and Carrie-Ann looked at her worriedly, Fleur asking, "What kind of alibi?"

"Well, it seemed that Vance had been in London during the day, and rather visibly so, too. People there could certainly place him in a high-end restaurant in the late afternoon. So it all came down to how fast he could have got back to Cheltenham."

She winced. "Claire was attacked around six pm, just as she was packing up for the night, and she was found by a passer-by distraught and with her clothing torn after she managed to escape out into the street. But the trouble was, nobody called the police in for another hour or so until after she'd been seen at Cheltenham hospital. It took that long for Claire to be coherent enough for them to get the story out of her, you see.

"They sent someone around to the townhouse, but it was all locked up and as quiet as the grave. Not a soul there. And then there was the delay as they had to get permission to go in and look for evidence – couldn't really bash the door down since there was no sign of a perpetrator there to arrest, and all that. Angelo Vance rolled in the following morning off the London train, demanding to know what all the fuss was about, and he kept that profession of innocence up right the way through the trial.

"Even I found him shockingly convincing on the days I managed to get there to support Claire! But then there was the testimony of a passer-by, who came forward and said that he'd seen Claire through one of the windows pushing an unseen person away, and hands reaching out and pulling her to them. Unfortunately, the Vance house is one of those with an area basement, so the ground floor rooms are that bit higher than street level, and so once Claire and the unknown person were away from the window, the man couldn't see anything more.

"He, poor bloke, was really upset when he saw the state Claire was in. He kept apologising, saying he'd thought it was just some domestic tiff, which was why he hadn't come forward earlier as he hadn't connected what he'd seen with a violent rape. Apparently, the traffic had been noisy enough at that time of night that he'd not heard her screaming, either.

"But all of that meant that in terms of identifying Claire's assailant, it came down to her word against his. Nobody doubted that Claire had been badly attacked – you couldn't see her and not believe that. No, it was whether it was actually Angelo Vance who did the deed, or some unknown man who'd got into the house, and who in her terror Claire had assumed was Vance."

"Blimey!" Carrie-Ann gulped. "Poor Claire! What an awful mess."

However, Fleur was thinking fast and asked, "I know I'd only just joined you all then, so I don't remember much, but did nobody question whether Vance could have caught the train to Cheltenham and then returned to London? For heaven's sake, it's not the longest train journey in the UK, is it? People regularly commute to and fro, though I wouldn't want to, but it's more than possible."

Lucy nodded. "Yes, the police looked into that, but the CCTV at the Cheltenham end had no sign of Vance anywhere near the station until the morning when he got off the train as he said. The guards on the late-afternoon and evening trains were questioned, and nobody saw him on what had turned out to be a rather quiet time in terms of passengers on the few trains which ran. It all built up to a lack of solid evidence."

"Not even DNA?" Fleur was surprised. "Surely to God someone did a rape kit on her? They didn't just sluice her down and leave her to be patched up? That would be incompetent beyond words these days!"

"Oh, they did one," Lucy said with a grimace. "Unfortunately, what they got was surprisingly inconclusive. The technical witness said that there had been abnormally little semen, and that they'd struggled to process what evidence Claire had had under her nails from where she'd tried to defend herself – but then that was another thing! Vance appeared with not a scratch on him! He ought to have been looking like he'd been clawed by a wild cat, and he didn't. But then some aggressive bloody barrister defending Vance managed to convince the court to confront Claire with Vance, and the way she fell to pieces, screaming the place down in terror wasn't faked either, so although that backfired on them it wasn't enough to secure his conviction.

"In the end, the court went with Claire being attacked by a person unknown for want of any better evidence. She then got the settlement from her firm through a separate civil suit she brought against them – or rather her switched-on barrister did –

because she'd gone on record as having been pestered by Vance on previous days and within view of other colleagues, albeit with them downstairs and her up on the first-floor landing. So on that dreadful day, when they told her to go back and wrap things up alone, she put in a written complaint and copied it to her union rep even before she set out. That's what nailed her the compensation – what had gone on before and them deliberately sending her back into harm's way, since nobody could have known that Vance *wouldn't* be there that day; that and her undoubted assault, albeit not necessarily by Vance himself. Somebody in the house, whether Vance or a person unknown masquerading as him, had raped Claire subsequent to her repeatedly telling her bosses that she felt threatened there, and that turned out to be enough. Personally, I think that the judge in the civil case believed her that it was Vance, but couldn't override the previous judgement."

"What an awful mess," Carrie-Ann said with a sigh. "You be doubly careful, then, Fleur, because that mansion of his is miles from anywhere. There won't be any convenient passers-by to come to *your* rescue out there!"

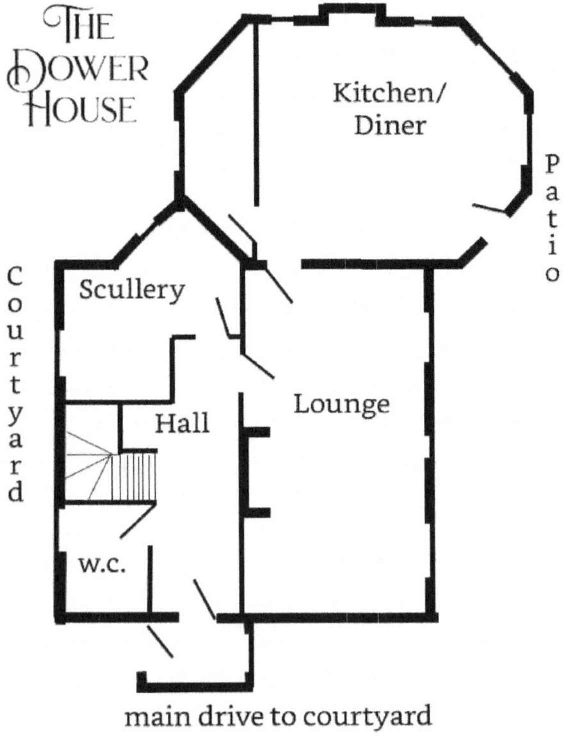
THE DOWER HOUSE
Kitchen/
Diner
Patio
Scullery
Courtyard
Hall
Lounge
w.c.
main drive to courtyard

Chapter 2

Fleur was feeling no better about the whole process as she drove her battered Ford Fiesta up the long drive to the Vance property. In her bag was the canister of pepper spray from Carrie-Ann, and every other kind of personal alarm she had managed to get her hands on as well. Forewarned and forearmed was going to be her motto with this job.

As she reached the house, she had no choice but to drive between the two parts of the frontage and into what amounted to an inner courtyard, the old stables at the back now forming garages, and the space in front of it the only place where there was room to park. Already feeling rather hemmed in, as she got out of the car it was with some relief that she saw the elegant figure of Mrs Vance coming out to greet her. Angelo was nowhere in sight, thank heavens. That didn't make her feel much better, though, and she decided to be fairly blunt about how she regarded these arrangements.

So as Mrs Vance smiled and held out her hand, saying, "Hello, Fleur, I'm so glad you've arrived," Fleur took the hand but said very firmly,

"I want you to know that I'm here under protest."

That made Mrs Vance's immaculate eyebrows rise in surprise, and Fleur decided to press on while she had the advantage.

"I'm sorry to say that your son's reputation precedes him," she said, keeping her tone polite and controlled. "So I am very uncomfortable about being here alone without my colleagues. I also have no idea why you would ask for me alone when Lucy Collingwood has far more expertise and experience, and when the three of us would get this job done with far greater speed and efficiency. Therefore I'm letting you know right now that I have put my objections into writing with the company, and have left a copy with my solicitor. You will not want to hear this, I'm sure, Mrs Vance, but if there's so much as a hint of your son trying with me what he did to Claire Marshall, not only will I sue him for every penny he has, I am also well versed in self-defence techniques and I won't hesitate to use them."

Mrs Vance was now looking horrified. "Oh! …Oh dear! I had no idea that you would be so hostile to the idea of coming here. I thought you would welcome the chance to take the lead on a job like this."

"It's not the job," Fleur clarified, still keeping her tone even. "I always enjoy working with old books. It's the arrangements around the job that I'm less than happy with. I will do the job to the very best of my professional ability, have no fear on that score. But I wanted you to know right from the start that it's the high-handed decisions about me personally that I object to."

Mrs Vance appeared mortified, and had clearly had no notion that the demands and arrangements would be so distasteful to Fleur.

"I think you had better come inside and let me explain things a little better," she said with more concession than Fleur had expected. If anything, she had been praying that Mrs Vance would take umbrage and send her off to the *Fox & Hounds* after all. Fleur would rather have sat in her room every night to avoid the drunks for a few hours than be stuck on the estate all week. But now there wasn't much that she could do other than follow Mrs Vance inside.

This section of the house lay to the right of the drive as you approached the buildings, while the main house, known as *The Rookery*, lay on the left. However, this was the first time that Fleur had seen *The Rookery* all in its full glory, because the previous times she had been here it had been swathed in scaffolding while the restoration was in full swing. Even Angelo Vance's infamous party had had to be held in part under a marquee attached to the house because of the ongoing work. And so looking at it now for the first time as a whole, she had to admit that it was a beauty of a building and probably as old as somewhere around the 1750s, going by the then fashionable Dutch gabled ends, and the patterns in the brickwork. The part she was about to go into wasn't quite that old, but was probably still as old as the early 1800s, and made out of the same lovely old red bricks with cream stone lintels, sills, and edging around the windows. It was a very pretty house, which made it such a shame that it carried such a nasty reputation with it, otherwise Fleur would have been thrilled to be stopping close by and able to explore the extensive gardens. Currently, however, the scale of those very private gardens just gave her the shivers.

They entered the other building from the side, and Fleur found herself in an elegant hallway and then turning right into a large lounge, which had three generous windows looking out onto a front garden filled with flowers.

"Please, have a seat," Mrs Vance said, waving Fleur towards the comfortable-looking sofas and armchairs which faced the windows. "Would you like tea or coffee?"

"Whichever you're making, I drink both," Fleur said with a half-smile, realising that when Mrs Vance was doing her best to be hospitable, it would be bad manners to carry on as good as accusing her son of rape. She had said her piece. Now it was time to be professional about things, both for her sake and the company's. "This is a lovely room," she complimented, and meant it. Everything was in elegant creams and golds, with just enough floral prints to give it that faded English country style in perfect taste.

"Thank you," Mrs Vance's voice came from the room beyond, and hearing the sound of running water and then cupboards being opened, Fleur's curiosity got the better of her. Leaving her bag by the chair, she got up and strolled to the doorway, not having to fake her delight as she exclaimed, "Oh wow! What a lovely kitchen!"

The room was an unusual shape, and Fleur realised that it was within an octagonal shape at the end of the rectangle of this part of the house. A glass door led out onto a small patio and the front garden, and the warm terracotta of the floor tiles and the colour of the walls reminded Fleur of a Tuscan farmhouse she and some friends had rented for a week one summer, back when she had been free and single and without a care in the world.

She hadn't realised that she'd said as much out loud until Mrs Vance turned with a beaming smile of pleasure and responded with delight, "You can see it! Oh, I'm so glad! My mother's family have a *castello* in Tuscany, which my uncle was the lucky one to inherit, but I spent a lot of time there as a child, and I still go back as often as I can. I've tried to recreate that atmosphere here, but you're the first person to notice it, and I wasn't sure if it was just wishful thinking on my part that I'd achieved it."

There was such wistfulness in her voice that Fleur couldn't help but warm to this woman. Whatever kind of monster her son was, his mother was a very different kind of person, and there was no mistaking the longing for Italy in her voice.

"I adored Italy," Fleur confessed. "I loved the way that you could just sit and eat outdoors in the fresh air, and the way that families all mingled together over food. The few times I managed to get over there, I couldn't help but think that they had a much better life-work balance. Simply being able to come home and sit out in the fresh air and watch the sunset, and eat fresh food …it's just so much *healthier* in every respect. People must switch off from the stresses of life that much easier, and I feel so sorry for the kids over here when they don't have that experience of sitting around the dinner table with their family and just talking."

Mrs Vance looked at her as if she had just descended from the heavens with words of magical comfort. "Did you have that, too?" she asked, as if almost unable to believe that someone in England would even remotely understand.

Fleur smiled. "Oh yes! But then my paternal grandmother was from Greece, so she too had the continental attitude towards family, and my parents picked it up from her. We *always* sat around the table together, and after my dad died in an accident, mum and my sister and I moved in with gran and granddad as something of a financial necessity, so I got a very European upbringing. It was only once I was grown up and away from home that I found out how rare that was for most people of my generation."

"I knew there was that special something about you," Mrs Vance said with what sounded very much like relief, and Fleur realised how genuinely shocked she had to have been to realise that someone might dread coming to this house.

The coffee had now bubbled up in the Moka pot on the hob, and with two delicate mugs of coffee which could have whisked Fleur to paradise on the smell alone, Mrs Vance offered Fleur a seat at the kitchen table, looking out onto the garden. Given that it conveyed a much more relaxed atmosphere, Fleur was glad to accept, hoping that if Mrs Vance was more at ease, she might give more information up without Fleur having to dig too hard for it.

In that she was right.

"This is the Dower House, you know," Mrs Vance began, waving a hand at the building in general. "It was built for my father's however many times great-grandfather's mother in 1805. So it's quite a bit younger than the main house. I hope you don't mind, but I'm going to have to tell you something of my family's history in order for you to appreciate what I need you to do with your job."

"Of course, go ahead." Fleur was already intrigued as to how this lady could have ended up with Jacko Vance, and was more than prepared to listen.

Mrs Vance smiled, and began, "My father met my mother at the end of the Second World War, and theirs had to be a fairly long courtship because he was sent back to England to be demobbed. But eventually they married early in 1955 and he brought her here to *The Rookery*. She always told me that she hated the main house. There was an unpleasant atmosphere about the place, she said, something nasty lurking in the dark corners.

"After she miscarried their first child later that same year, my father decided to let her move into here instead, once she'd threatened to go back to Italy and not come back. I think he was terrified of losing her and the next child she carried because she was getting so stressed by being in the main house. Even so, my mother wasn't prepared to have her confinement here, and so she returned to the family home in Tuscany for the last months of her pregnancy, and I was born there. Of course, it was made possible because his own mother died while my mother was in Italy having me, and so this place was vacant once more – which it hadn't been when they first came here to live."

That was a bit convenient, Fleur thought, and then chastised herself for her cynicism. She really must stop seeing conspiracies and danger at every turn or else she'd be jumping at shadows the whole time. And Claudia Vance was continuing,

"I'm told that my father was already struggling to pay the death duties on the estate, because his father had died a few years before I was born, and so around that time he agreed to let the whole place out to someone who wanted to run it as a hotel. He dealt in stocks and shares, you see, and divided his time between an apartment in London and Tuscany with his family, so my younger sister was born there too."

"Lucky you! That must have been idyllic," Fleur sighed enviously, only for Mrs Vance to rock her hand and say,

"Not entirely. My sister had a difficult birth, and as she grew it became apparent that she had suffered brain damage because of it. She wasn't terribly disabled, you understand, but it became clear that she wouldn't cope with going to boarding school, as I did, for instance."

Bloody hell, Fleur thought, *this is too spooky for words,* before telling Mrs Vance, "I know just what you mean. My own younger sister was born with mild Down's Syndrome. Again, just like yours, she wasn't that bad, but she couldn't cope with the hustle and bustle of holding down even a simple, ordinary, full-time job, for instance. She helps out a couple of days a week at a local café in the village where she and my mum live, but the people who run it are very protective of her, and never expect her to work on the busy weekends. It gives her a bit of a sense of independence, but the reality is that she's very reliant on my mum seeing to everything in the way of bills and things. I don't think she'll ever be able to live fully independently. Modern life is just too fast and complicated for her."

"Good gracious!" Mrs Vance gulped. "I had no idea that you had had that same experience. …Well I never. …In that case you'll understand more than most why the peace and tranquillity of the Tuscan countryside was far more suitable for Romana, and why most of my school holidays were spent there with my mother's family.

"In the mid-seventies the people running the hotel here went bust, and once again my father was looking for someone to lease the house. This time, though, he found someone who only wanted the main house. For heaven's sake, that has nine bedrooms all by itself! So if you are marketing a place as a boutique hotel, you don't really want many more than that. But that suited my father, too, because he'd set up his own business by that time, and had created an office in Cheltenham. That meant that he could use the townhouse the family had been letting out, and get rid of the London apartment, which fetched even more than the townhouse would have on the market at that time."

"Was that the first time you spent much time here, then?" Fleur wondered, revising her assumption that this had been Mrs Vance's childhood home, and that had been why Angelo Vance was so keen to keep it for her.

"It was. By then I was a young woman, and I wanted more nightlife than Tuscany had, so I was glad to have somewhere to come to more in a town like Cheltenham. I spent most of my time at the townhouse, of course, but from there it was far easier to come over here to Herefordshire for weekends. And as the daughter of the owner, it meant that I had access to the hotel swimming pool that had been put in out the back, for instance, and that made me very popular with my friends!" She had the grace to roll her eyes in despair at her younger self's naivety. "All the *wrong* sort of friends, of course! The ones who just wanted to freeload on the girl with a rich father, but then I learned that lesson pretty quickly."

"At least you learned," Fleur said sympathetically. "I've known some who never seemed to catch on to the fact that they were being used."

"But that was the attraction with Jacko, you see," Mrs Vance confided. "He didn't want me *for* anything. He just loved *me.* When I brought him down here for the first time, he didn't want to raid my father's cellars for the fanciest and most expensive wines, he was happy to just go to the pub and chat to the locals, and that was so refreshing. He was a man who was happy in his own skin, as they say, quite content to be himself – an unreconstructed lad from the back streets of Birmingham."

Blimey, Jacko, what a breath of fresh air you must have been! Fleur thought. *No wonder she fell for you. And it sounds as though she still misses you. Clearly you had hidden depths that never came out in all the publicity drivel!* All she could say, though, was, "He must have been nothing like anyone your parents were expecting."

Mrs Vance laughed. "You can say that again! My father loathed him, but I think Mother understood the attraction. She had loved my father dearly at one time, but his constant demands to keep up appearances when in this country she eventually found horribly wearing, and by the time she died they were as good as separated. But his conservative morals are partly why it's come as something of a shock when I found what had been stored up on the top floor of this house. This is not as large as across the way, but there are still what must once have been four attic bedrooms which the servants would have used, and they were all sealed away behind a heavily locked door on the staircase, and full to the brim with boxes.

"Of course, when I came here as a girl, I knew that the top floor was locked up – of course I did. But my father told me it was just old furniture up there, and to be frank, I was never here for long enough to get bored and want to explore. It was perfectly logical to keep this place securely locked up when Father or I weren't here, given that there was a constant stream of strangers about the place from the hotel, and dusty old furniture holds little allure for a teenage girl. And then once I'd met Jacko, we were off travelling all over the place. Jacko had loved it over there. He was even talking about buying a place and setting up a music studio out there. But then he died after he and I had returned to England, and although I had little choice but to remain in England when Angelo was born – he came prematurely, you see – once he could travel, it was easier for me to go back out to Tuscany where I had the support of my family, at least until Angelo was old enough to go to school."

An odd expression accompanied that last statement, and Fleur had the impression that this had been a very tough time for Mrs Vance, and that possibly this wasn't anything like the whole story. However, Claudia seemed to shake it off and was carrying on with,

"At that point I made the townhouse my own, because it was both convenient to get Angelo to and from primary school, and because my father had retired and was living in this house full time, and going across the way to have all of his meals in the hotel. He liked to be waited on hand and foot…" those last words coming out with considerable bitterness, giving a Fleur the impression that Claudia Vance had thoroughly loathed her father for some reason. Whatever wealthy upbringing she had had, Mrs Vance had not been her rich daddy's little girl, spoilt and only having to stamp her foot to get anything she wanted out of him. Indeed, Fleur did a quick mental recap and realised that Mrs Vance had effectively said that if her father was here then she was at the townhouse, and when he'd been at the townhouse, she'd been off travelling or visiting the dower house.

However, Fleur dared not pry, even if she was getting more and more curious about the whole Vance family setup, instead asking,

"So is it what you found behind that locked door that you wanted me to look at?"

Mrs Vance gave her brilliant smile again. "Yes! Very much so. You see, when Angelo and I actually got into that space, it wasn't furniture at all. It was piles and piles of boxes. We hadn't really ever explored any of these properties before, you see. My father died five years ago, but Angelo was able to pay what death duties were required, not least because my father had sold off most of the land and farms that once belonged to the big house anyway. So it was a much smaller estate to inherit. And the lease on the hotel only had eighteen months to go at that stage, so we just waited until it expired because we knew the hotel owners didn't want to renew."

"Ah!" said Fleur. "And that's when you had our team come in and assess what was worth keeping. I wasn't with the company then, so would I be right in thinking that at that time they only dealt with the contents of the main house?"

Mrs Vance nodded. "We thought we knew what was in here, you see. My father wasn't exactly a cultured man," and Fleur thought she saw a hint of shudder at the mention of him personally again. "He had terrible taste, and all we did was make sure that the drawers and cupboards in the various pieces of furniture were empty after your team had removed the ones of value, and then called in a house clearer. Angelo and I carried on living in the townhouse while the restorers and decorators were completely stripping this side and making it habitable again. And then I moved in here with my own choice of fresh furniture. If we thought anything of the attics here, it was that there might be some smaller pieces stored up there from the main house which could be used in the lesser rooms. So it was only when those were ready to be furnished that we thought to unlock these attics."

"What was in the boxes, then?" Fleur asked, gripped in spite of herself by Claudia Vance's stories.

"Well, a particularly fine and complete set of early Royal Doulton china, for a start, which I'm keeping – so no need for assessment of that for anything other than insurance. And some rather grand vases and decorative bits, but again they can be assessed once Angelo has the house complete and we're looking at insurance for the whole place. What we weren't expecting to find were eight large boxes of books, and very old books too."

Fleur knew she was hooked, and that her eyes were probably lit up like Christmas trees as she asked, "What sort of books?"

"To start with, a very old family Bible, in which all the generations of my father's family have been recorded – they had this place built, you know, so it's stayed in their hands all the way down the centuries. But what we weren't expecting was to find that they had been more than a little secretive. They hid their Catholicism very well in the years when it was dangerous to openly worship – that's not that unusual – but what shook me was to find that even that was a cover for something else."

"Really?"

"Yes. I unexpectedly find myself with rather a lot of ancient witches' grimoires!"

Chapter 3

"Grimoires?" Light dawned for Fleur. The only conversation she could ever remember previously having with Mrs Vance was when she had been here last, and had had her sleeves rolled up, revealing her triskele tattoo. In Fleur's case this was of three hares conjoined by their ears, but Mrs Vance had recognised the style if nothing else, telling Fleur that a triskele was the emblem of Sicily where her mother's grandmother had come from. They had shared a brief chat about how it was also the Isle of Man's, though in both those instances it was three legs joined at the centre. Fleur had also shown her her other tattoo, which was of a pentagram with a rose entwined, and obviously Mrs Vance had remembered that Fleur was paganly inclined.

Mrs Vance's smile broadened as she saw how Fleur had sat bolt upright, eyes shining, and repeated, "Grimoires," quite firmly, adding, "and some very old tarot decks!"

"Wow!" Fleur gasped. "Do you have any idea how old they might be?"

"That's what I was rather hoping you could tell me. All I can tell you is that the books, and the additional notebooks which seem to be with them are written in very old-fashioned English, which I can scarcely understand, and on that thick, almost fabric-like paper that you only get with really old books."

"Rag paper," Fleur said immediately. "Yes, years ago they used to use the fibres from old rags in papermaking, so you're right, they will be old, but rag paper was only made for the first time in 1800, and really only mass-produced so that you'd get it in notebooks from the 1850s onwards."

She saw the disappointment in Mrs Vance's eyes and hurriedly added, "But what you thought of as just ordinary paper might actually turn out to be older in that case. We were making paper in England – rather than using parchment – in larger quantities from roughly 1600 onwards, so that could theoretically push a date back another two hundred years. But in terms of just the paper, you could be talking even earlier if they originated on the continent. The further east you go, the earlier the potential date. And anyway, the rag paper books surely coincide with the building of this house?"

That stunned Mrs Vance into temporary silence as the full significance of that settled in. Fleur allowed her time to think, guessing that there were connections here which she was totally ignorant of.

"How many generations back do you think we're looking at here?" she finally asked Fleur, who could only reply,

"Won't the family bible have the answers?"

In response, Mrs Vance hurriedly got up and vanished out of the door into the lounge, Fleur then hearing her footsteps going upstairs. It took a few minutes, but then Mrs Vance reappeared cradling a truly huge old bible in her arms, resting on a cloth to save her immaculate ivory coloured sweater from dust marks.

"Good grief, what a monster!" Fleur said with a grin. "You know that they used to cure ganglia by hitting them with a family bible?"

Mrs Vance put the bible down on the table with a thump. "Ganglia?"

"Yes. These days they're better called cysts, but they're a particular kind of cyst that forms because of inflammation in joints, so they tend to be a swelling filled with a jelly-like fluid. Massage is often used nowadays to get rid of them, and they can just go down of their own accord, though if they're related to rheumatoid arthritis, they can require surgery. But the Victorian method was to wallop one with the family bible – especially if one was on somewhere accessible like a wrist or elbow!"

"Good God!" Mrs Vance gulped, looking at the weighty tome she had just put down. "I wouldn't want to be hit with this thing! It weighs a ton!"

"Quite!" Fleur laughed. "It'd be a toss-up which was more painful – the complaint or the cure!" She had got up and come to stand beside Mrs Vance. "So, I presume the family entries are in the back?

They usually are if there are a lot of them, but some families do have them in the front."

"Front and back with Father's lot," Mrs Vance said with a sigh. "They did have awfully big families – even bigger than ours over in Italy, but then our family over there were only going through the motions of deferring to the Church."

Again, Fleur laughed. "The biggest communist party outside of Russia is in Italy, so I'm not shocked at that. It must have something to do with familiarity breeding contempt when you have the pope and the Vatican right on your doorstep."

"I suspect you're right, and my great-grandfather William's family do seem to have been going through the motions of being devout, because they even turned out the occasional monsignor for the Church. …Look, you can see one here …Monsignor Alberto Fitzpatrick."

Fleur put her glasses on and scrutinised the page. "Hmmm… Born right at the peak of Prince Albert's popularity, so no great mystery in his name. Looking at the fact that there was an Arthur and a George and a William in the same generation, albeit not brothers, it looks very much as if they were trying to be as conventionally English as possible – at least in terms of names." She was scanning through the names at the back of the bible, then carefully turned it over so that she could look at the front. "My goodness, you've quite an archive piece with this alone. It's not many family bibles than go right the way back to the Restoration as this one does."

Mrs Vance pulled a face. "My father was always so damned proud of the fact that his family got given this place in compensation for having supported the king during Charles I's reign and the Civil War. You'd have thought that they'd single-handedly tried to stop the king's execution to hear him talk."

Her tone made Fleur dare to say, "You sound like me when I'm talking about my ex-husband."

"You're divorced?"

"Yes, and what a bloody divorce it turned out to be! Carl was a nice lad when we met, and he was still a nice enough chap when we got married," Fleur admitted, hoping that this revelation of her own would ensure that Mrs Vance didn't clam up on her. "But then he lost his job in an office, and the only thing he could get was retraining as a trucker. And that was when he changed. It was okay for a bit, but then it was long hours, and he was getting pretty drained, so we were living fairly heavily on what I earned. Then some evil sod gave him some pills to help him keep going, because he just wasn't used to physical work, you see. Well, he had a bad reaction to them, as people can. It seriously changed him mentally, and he became paranoid and violent. He'd never even offered to lift his hand to me before that, and I certainly wouldn't have married him if there'd been even a whiff of anything like that.

"But after eight years of being a fairly normal young couple, he all of a sudden started lashing out at me. I told him he needed to get some proper help, but he just took it as criticism that he wasn't being the man of the house and bringing in more money than me. I stuck it out for three more years, trying everything I could, even to persuade him to give the job up and get some therapy, but what I didn't realise until I told him I was leaving, was that he was being tugged in the opposite direction by a bunch of Neanderthals at work. That all came out when the divorce hearing came up, and I found myself being threatened by them."

"Threatened?" Mrs Vance was aghast.

"Oh yes, and quite physically, too." Fleur gave a shudder. "For the whole of the time the divorce was going through, I didn't dare go and visit my mum and sister, because I was never sure when one of those animals was following me. I mean, you don't know every truck that follows you along the road, do you? And they took to using the cabs that they hook the containers up to just on their own; but again, you see a lot of those on the road after they've dropped off a load, or on the way to pick one up, and these guys worked for an agency, so they were never in one company's livery."

"You couldn't see your own *mother*?"

"I wouldn't risk it after the first time I got surrounded by three of them, and they started pushing me around. They never did more than shove, push and pull, but it's bloody intimidating when you have three men, all bigger than you, right up close and manhandling you. …I was never sure whether it was going to become more than that, either. Looking back, I can now see that they were smart enough to not leave bruising on me, or anything I could have used as proof in court, but it was frightening at the time, and I was terrified of how distraught my sister would be if they ever did something like that to her. She would never have recovered."

"No, I totally understand." Mrs Vance was all empathy, and again there was something in her expression that hinted that she might have had something similar happen to herself – she was too affected by it for it to only be general sympathy. Yet Fleur also got the impression that whatever abuse Mrs Vance had been through, it wasn't with Jacko but possibly with her father. Whichever it was, she didn't know her anything like well enough to press the matter out of nothing more than her own curiosity. Instead, she thought it better to steer the conversation back towards the matter in hand.

"Anyway," she said brightly, "to get back to your tarots and grimoires, I was being specific when I was talking about the earlier dates for the paper. What I really need you to be aware of is that unless you have an amazing find of international significance hidden away in those boxes, it is *highly* unlikely that you'll have either books or cards going back to even the Tudor period, let alone anything earlier. The very first surviving tarot deck we have –

and it's not complete – is the Visconti di Modrone deck which dates to the early 1400s."

She saw Mrs Vance's eyes light up and swiftly added, "But those very early decks are very different to any modern tarot you would know. For a start off, the court cards for each of the four suits each had a male or female counterpart, so there were six – not four – court cards for each of the four suites, with the addition of a dame to mirror the knight, and a maid to mirror the page. These days we only have a king, queen, knight, and page per suit. And what you'd know as the major arcane also have differences too, so if you've looked at the decks and they seem familiar, I want you to be aware that we're not talking about anything remotely as old."

She saw the disappointment written on Mrs Vance's face and tried to soften the blow. "There's nothing to say that you don't have an Early Modern replica of a Renaissance deck. I just want you to have reasonable expectations of what I might find. There is another and slightly more complete deck known as the Visconti-Sforza deck, dating from the mid-fifteenth century – so about forty years after the Visconti di Modrone deck – but that is split between major museums, it's that significant! The Visconti di Modrone deck is held by Yale University, by the way, so you see how rare it would be to find any deck of that age."

Fleur dug deep to try and recall something, anything from her thesis, which would give Mrs Vance a more realistic view of what she might have.

"The first deck to be made available commercially was the Tarot de Marseilles, which was made by French and Swiss playing card makers from about 1700 onwards. Now that doesn't mean that they didn't use earlier designs from back in the seventeenth century, but in the eighteenth century you got decks being manufactured in Italy and France. It's therefore much more likely that the earliest potential deck you could have is from then, because with the whole Enlightenment Movement and the Age of Reason, a great many people were deprived of the solace they had previously got through the Church, and so there was a reaction against all that science and reason which led to Romanticism. By the start of the nineteenth century, you had a handful of occult movements, which I think I'm right in recalling started in France, but had spread to as far afield as America by then, and you also have the rise of a fascination with Eastern religions, which triggered the unfounded beliefs that tarot cards originated in Egypt or other parts of the East, or even had Kabbalistic origins."

Mrs Vance smiled faintly. "My word, you do know your stuff, don't you."

Fleur laughed. "Sorry! I didn't mean to go all academic on you. It's just that after a couple of years in this job, I've come to realise that most lay people have no idea of what time scales they are looking at with their treasured possessions, and can be absolutely crushed when they discover that the thing they thought was going to go back centuries is a copy from, say, the nineteen-twenties. It's much better to hand out the warnings first, and then if something does go back further than expected, it's an unexpected bonus."

Claudia Vance had the grace to give a sigh but then smile. "I see. Well thank you for at least warning me that I might not have quite such a treasure trove as I had anticipated."

"Oh, it's a treasure trove, alright!" Fleur responded without hesitation. "I've never heard of someone having quite such a large collection away from modern times – by which I mean the folks who nowadays collect dozens of decks as much for the lovely artwork as anything. So all by itself, that makes what you have noteworthy. I just didn't want you to think that individually the decks and grimoires would be worth vast amounts of money. If they turn out to be valuable, it's more likely to be if they show the handing on of a tradition through generations of a family. I can truthfully say that I've never come across that situation even being mentioned, much less seen it myself, and I think you might have interest from a museum, for instance, if that was the way you wanted to go to ensure that the collection stayed together. It's just not going to buy you a new yacht!"

Then Fleur added, "And I think I need to get your decision on something else, as well. As far as I'm aware, it's your son who is paying my employers for me to catalogue the library, and I think it might get me into trouble if they then find that I've been spending time during working hours looking at your things. Are you okay with me dealing with these after I've finished for the day? Because if not, I think you need to get in touch with *Miller, Bronson & Carter* and ask them for a separate bill for the work I'll do."

"Oh, Angelo won't mind," Mrs Vance said with an airy wave of her hand, but Fleur wasn't having that.

"No, I'm very sorry, Mrs Vance," she insisted, "that won't do at all. It has to be in writing! Either I do the research on your things in the evenings, and in my own time – which I'm quite prepared to do because of the personal interest it holds for me – or you get a separate quote from *Miller, Bronson & Carter* for me to do the work as the focus of several days."

Claudia Vance looked at her rather askance. "My word, you're very forceful when you want to be," making Fleur groan inside.

She didn't want to alienate Mrs Vance, especially in case she needed her help to keep a rampant Angelo at bay, but at the same time, she couldn't afford to go off-piste from her employers either.

"I don't mean to come across as dictating terms and conditions," she apologised. "It's just that I know how these things work. If this was just me in a one-person business, then it would be very different. I could decide what I would and wouldn't do for a client. But these aren't my decisions to make. I'm only an employee of *Miller, Bronson & Carter*, and a very junior one at that, not one of the directors. I can't dictate what I will and won't do when I've been given a specific job. I'm making you an offer to do the research in my own time, but if that's not what you want, then I really will have to defer the decision to my bosses."

Fleur could see Mrs Vance stiffening at this refusal to do just whatever she wanted her to do. It was almost like watching a switch being flipped inside her with the way she physically stiffened and her expression became far less friendly. Clearly there were two very different sides to Mrs Vance, and she had better watch out.

"I must say," Claudia Vance declared, aggrieved and not a little annoyed, "I don't normally have to negotiate with people when I've already employed them."

"I'm sure you don't," Fleur conceded, "but it's not me you've employed or ought to be negotiating with, is it? It's your son who is paying, and *he's* employed *Miller, Bronson & Carter*. He and they are the ones who did the negotiating, not you and me. They've gone along with the request to have just me come here ...but was that him, or was it you? Because if he's the one footing the bill, then you see he could refuse to pay us if the job isn't done as he specified."

"Angelo won't do that! He's left me in charge!"

Fleur sighed. Clearly, she was getting nowhere, and Mrs Vance was determined to have things her way, but Fleur resigned herself to the fact that she wasn't the one to argue the point with her.

"Very well, then, Mrs Vance. I'll make a start on the cataloguing for now. Could you show me to where I'm going to be staying, please? I'll drop off my bags and then make a start."

Rather less warmly than her initial greeting, Mrs Vance led the way back out of the Dower House, but to Fleur's horror, went only as far as to the other side of the courtyard to where a small cottage backed onto the former stables.

"Here you are," she said, opening the front door with a flourish. "I'm sure you'll be comfortable here. It's much more convenient than that pub for you. The main house is unlocked. I'm sure you can find the library. All the boxes of books have been taken to there by the movers."

With that she turned on her heels leaving Fleur standing there at the door, and thinking, *it may be convenient for the library, but it's also far too close to the house if Angelo Vance turns up! Thank heavens I've got that pepper spray*!

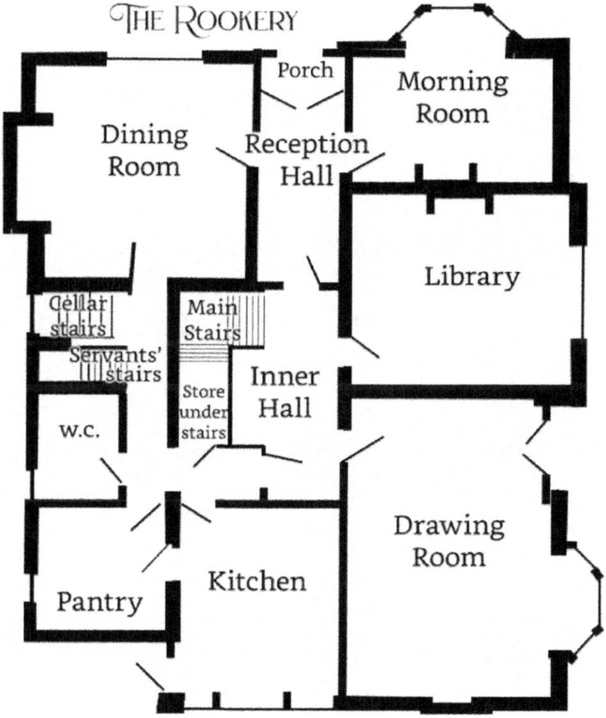
THE ROOKERY
Porch
Morning Room
Dining Room
Reception Hall
Library
Cellar stairs
Main Stairs
Servants' stairs
Inner Hall
Store under stairs
W.C.
Drawing Room
Kitchen
Pantry

Chapter 4

The first thing that Fleur did after going and getting her case from the car was to call in to work on her mobile, making sure that Mrs Vance was nowhere where she could overhear what was going to be said.

"This is already turning into a bloody nightmare!" she told Mr Harris, and went on to explain Mrs Vance's plan to have her dealing with her own heirlooms – or whatever they were – as well as the cataloguing.

"Oh dear!" Mr Harris groaned. "No, you were quite right to refer this back to me, Fleur. I think it was most generous of you to offer to look at these other items in your own time. But if Mrs Vance wants you to make them any sort of priority, then we shall have to take the matter back to Mr Vance. We can't afford for there to be any confusion over what he's paying for. If necessary, we can offer Mrs Vance a separate invoice, but you've done nothing wrong and everything right in telling me about this."

Lucy must have been close by, because he then said he would hand Fleur over to her.

"What's up?" Lucy immediately asked. "I didn't expect to hear from you quite this soon."

"Oh, you wouldn't believe it!" Fleur growled, and proceeded to tell Lucy both about the extra work, and about how close she was to the main house in the cottage. "I can't even see a decent bolt on the inside of the cottage door!" she finished fuming with. "If he's got a key to this place – and why wouldn't he as the owner – then he could just waltz in here at any time! I'm not happy about this, Lucy, I'm really not!"

"I should bloody well think not!" Lucy agreed. "Is there anything you could drag across in front of the door once you're inside?"

"There's a couple of sturdy kitchen chairs. I could put one in front of the door. But the trouble is, the latch is quite high, so I couldn't wedge one underneath it. All it will do is make a racket if someone opens the doors not expecting it to be there."

"Bloody hell!" Lucy swore. "I'm going to pass this on to Harry as well, and I'm going to make a written report of what you've said right now, timed and dated, and I'll take it personally up to the directors' secretary. You be careful, Fleur! I want you to call me first thing every morning, then again at lunchtime, and again at night. Don't text me. I want to hear your voice! That way there's no chance of someone sending a text pretending to be you. I don't like this. I don't like it at all."

"I'm none so keen myself," Fleur said to the

empty room as she rang off. And it was with great trepidation that she got her special cotton gloves and other kit out and went in search of the library.

Entering through the kitchen door almost opposite to where she was, she found that the doors into the corridor beyond, which she hoped would lead into rooms, instead only went to two separate staircases. Or rather the cupboard under one broad, upwards one, which presumably got accessed from the main hall; and a dual one going downwards one way to the cellar, or going by the size of the house possible several cellars, and one upwards which was presumably the servants' stairs. This back end of the house was quite a maze, and when she had followed the corridor onwards past the cellar stairs door, she found herself in a room which she guessed would be the dining room.

But now she was at the front of the house and looking out onto the front garden. There was a second door out of this room which presumably led to the front door, and when Fleur went through it, as well as the front door there was a door opposite her which gave onto a lovely smaller room with a bay window also looking onto the front. However, this wasn't the library, and the only other door besides the front door off this corridor looked as though it went back into the servants' area.

Sighing in frustration, Fleur went back the way she had come through the dining room and back around to the staircases and through another door, discovering that as she had thought, the main stairs went off a new inner hall, the flight making a quarter turn to the left to create the cupboard beneath which she had already found. When she went through the door directly opposite to where she had come into the hall by, it turned out to be a very grand room, with French windows leading out onto the more substantial side gardens and a rustic patio. This must have been where Angelo Vance had held the infamous party of a couple of years ago.

"Very nice," Fleur muttered, "but where the hell is the library?"

Again, she closed the door on that room, and walked down this inner hall to try the next door off it, also on her right. This time she struck lucky, finding herself in a square room with ceiling to floor bookshelves, and a couple of low ones under the window, as well as low ones backing onto a huge desk which sat in stately splendour in the middle of the room. Or rather it would have had the floor not had box upon box stacked on it, making negotiating the room something of an obstacle course.

"Bloody marvellous," Fleur groaned as she looked at the uppermost boxes, none of which had anything written on them which might give a clue as to what was inside of them. It was just going to be trial and error as to whether she found items which ought to be together in any adjoining boxes. But it also struck her that if she got cornered in this room, she was going to have to have her bearings on the house in order to make the fastest escape. And with that in mind, she went back out and turned right to continue the few yards to the door across the far end of the hall, opening it expecting to find another room, and instead discovering that she had come out in the front hall she had crossed from the dining room.

"What a muddle!" she muttered, and made a point of walking the rectangular route the various corridors made around the ground floor until she was more thoroughly orientated, and knew where everything was. It would have been nice if Mrs Vance had been considerate enough to show her around; and Fleur could only presume that she would be using the loo she had discovered tucked away beside the cellar steps, which had no doubt only ever been used by the staff. Nothing like being made to know your place, she thought with a bitter sniff.

On the other hand, since Mrs Vance hadn't deigned to show her the place, she could hardly object if Fleur went exploring, and it occurred to Fleur that it might be no bad thing if she at least scouted out the upstairs. If discovered, she would have the valid excuse of wondering aloud whether there were any more boxes of books, since any quantity beyond what was already in the library would never have been fitted in, and Mrs Vance would only have herself to blame for not having given Fleur a proper introduction.

Also, if invited up there by Angelo Vance at any future point, it would be worth knowing in advance whether there was an upper lounge – as would not have been unusual in a house as big and prestigious as this – or if there were just bedrooms. Discovering just bedrooms would give her an advanced warning if he tried to lure her up there with tales of more boxes of stuff. And so Fleur went up the lovely old oak staircase, admiring the glass panel in the ceiling above it, which formed the floor of the room above and had to have a skylight above it in that room's ceiling. It let a lot of natural light flood down into the stairwell, and Fleur thought that was a good thing, since nobody could lurk in shadows at the stairs' bends.

Up on the landing, she realised that this flight did not continue on up to the second floor, and puzzled, she walked along looking into the various rooms which led off the landing, but also for that staircase leading upwards. The rooms above the dining room, the front sitting room, and above the library, were very much of the same dimensions as the rooms below, and were currently empty, but the huge lounge on the side of the house had both a bedroom and a generous en-suite in the space above it. Yet Fleur still hadn't found the stairs going upwards. Only as she returned to the stairs to go back down did she realise that beyond them, and over the kitchen below was another, larger bathroom, and what looked like it might have been a linens store. And there, beside the door to the linens store was another door, right above where the cellar steps went downwards from the ground floor.

"Now why on earth wouldn't you just have had

a servants' stair running right the way up?" Fleur wondered aloud, and then was even more surprised to see a very large and sturdy modern padlock on the door. As she looked harder at it, she also realised that the door itself had to be a replacement, because it was far more solid than any internal door had any need to be.

"Curious and curiouser," she muttered to herself, glad that she had come to look, if only to confirm that there were no extra boxes lurking up here. But it was as she began to descend that a sudden darkness flitted across the stairs, just as if someone had walked across the glass floor of the room above, blocking the sunlight from the skylight. Freezing, Fleur looked up, and though she saw nothing, she could have sworn she heard soft footsteps, as if of someone in slippers moving over a thickly carpeted floor. A someone who had to be locked in behind that stout door and padlock!

God Almighty, Mrs Vance was surely not keeping Angelo locked up, was she? No, that was ridiculous, and why would you keep someone imprisoned like that these days anyway? That belonged back in Gothic Victorian novels, not the twenty-first century. She must have imagined it, or a large bird must have briefly landed on the skylight.

As a shiver ran down her spine even so, Fleur took to her heels and shot down the stairs, suddenly not wanting to know if someone else was in this seemingly deserted house with her, and there and then she decided that she would take the books, box at a time, over to the cottage to catalogue. Only when she absolutely had to would she spend any amount of time here in this house in the library.

Once she got back into the library, she felt her heart rate return to something more like normal, and was chiding herself for jumping at nothing. *It's the menace of Angelo Vance looming over you, that's what it is*, she told herself sternly. *You felt vulnerable even before you got here, and then finding that the supposed 'cottage on the estate' is nothing like as detached as you'd hoped, just sent your imagination into overdrive. Come on, get started on the job. The sooner you start, the sooner you'll finish and can get out of here!*

And it was once she had opened the first box and tried to empty out its contents that she knew she had the perfect excuse to work back in the cottage, because there really wasn't any room to work in here. She could certainly unpack the boxes onto the desk, but there wasn't a chair to be found, and even standing, she had to squeeze between boxes just to get to the desk. Working in here was going to be impractical until she was something like halfway through the boxes and could clear some space. So she emptied the top three boxes she could reach out onto the top of the desk, sighed in resigned disgust at the higgledy-piggledy packing, and then carried the first armful over to the cottage.

She had got her laptop up and running and the program she used for cataloguing running, and was well into the first pile when Mrs Vance came to find her.

"Why are you in here?" she demanded imperiously, as she took in Fleur sitting at the kitchen table.

"Because the way the boxes have been stacked in the library has left me no room to get to the desk," Fleur said politely. "Once I've got through a few of them, I'll be able to work over there, but for now this was the most practical solution."

"Couldn't you have just moved the boxes out of the way?"

Fleur felt her irritation rising and struggled to keep it out of her voice. "Have you felt the weight of them?" she asked. "I'd have put my back out by the time I'd moved all of the ones I needed out of the way."

Mrs Vance sniffed. "The men who brought them in managed well enough."

"I'm sure they did," Fleur said through gritted teeth. "But for a start off, I'm not a man. I'm a woman who barely tops five feet two, and I don't do weights at the gym. And secondly, if they were professional removers, I bet they used a sack-truck to bring the boxes in several at a time. All they did was slide them off the truck base …am I right?"

The way Mrs Vance's expression soured told her that she was, even though the other woman didn't deign to answer that. Instead, with a "*Hmph*!" of disgust, she turned on her kitten heels and clicked out again, the metal caps on the tiny heels audibly fading as she stormed back across the cobbles of the courtyard to the Dower House. Clearly once crossed,

Mrs Vance could be an even bigger pain in the neck than her son, and Fleur was already wishing she had never agreed to come here alone. Right now, she could have done with Lucy backing her up over the impracticality of working in the library, if nothing else.

"Bloody hell!" growled Fleur, blessing the fact that she'd thought to bring her small travelling kettle with her, and a supply of tea bags and coffee, expecting to be more remote than this. Certainly, nobody had thought to provision the cottage, and she realised that if she was going to eat tonight, she was going to have to go down to the pub anyway. So much for keeping her out of harm's way that way! On the other hand, that was a good thing, because it would give her a chance to chat with the landlord and landlady, and find out what the chances were of getting a room down there in case of emergencies.

Therefore she happily worked on into the afternoon, making do with a few digestive biscuits instead of lunch, but looking forward to a decent meal later on. And she was engrossed in what she was doing when she heard Mrs Vance coming back to the cottage. Or rather, she heard Mrs Vance speaking angrily to someone on her mobile.

"I'm on my way over there now!" Fleur heard her say. "And I'm putting this on speaker phone, so you can hear what I say to her and she won't be able to distort it later on for you, the treacherous minx! I'm going to give her a piece of my mind for going behind my back to you like that!"

And since she was right at the door by that point, Fleur heard Mr Harris tinny voice amplified via the speaker saying with great annoyance,

"There was nothing remotely treacherous about what Fleur did, Mrs Vance! She was perfectly right to call us. And in the light of what she reported back, I have checked our records, and I can tell you that the *only* bank account we have the details for to bill for this job is your son's, and your son's alone. Therefore, we absolutely *cannot* add on additional fees for work done at your request without written permission for him. It simply wouldn't be ethical."

"Ethical!" screeched Mrs Vance, and Fleur could see her arm waving in full-blown Italian temper. "How many times do I have to tell you that Angelo has left me in charge of this job?"

As Fleur opened the door, Mrs Vance having turned her back to it to pace across the courtyard, she heard Mr Harris saying, "But that's the problem, Mrs Vance. *You* may have told us that, but Mr Vance himself has *not*, and we have to abide by our client's instructions. If he does want you to oversee the project, then it is simple enough for him to email us his permission on the email address he gave us. It could be done tonight if that's what he wishes."

However, at that Mrs Vance had turned to storm back towards the cottage and saw Fleur in the doorway, and snarled,

"So, you're spying on me now! Listening in on my conversations!"

"I'm hardly doing that," Fleur said evenly. "Not when you're yelling loud enough for half the neighbourhood to hear, anyway. And I thought I heard you saying that you *wanted* Mr Harris to hear what you had to say to me?"

"I do, you impudent girl!" Mrs Vance snapped back. "What did you mean by going behind my back like that?"

Before Fleur could answer, Mr Harris was interrupting her with, "Mrs Vance! …Mrs Vance! I would kindly ask you not to speak to my member of staff in that way. She has done nothing wrong, and it is not for you to reprimand her over your misconceptions! If you continue to speak to her like that, I shall have no choice but to tell Ms Constantine to leave immediately, and inform Mr Vance that we will undertake the cataloguing here at our own facility. Since the books are still in the boxes they were shipped to you in, it would be a simple matter to have a carrier collect them and bring them here. But let me make this perfectly clear: you will not abuse our staff while they are working for you!"

If looks could kill, Fleur would have dropped on the spot with the one Mrs Vance gave her, but at least she turned on her heels and stalked off back to the dower House, berating Mr Harris all the way. Within the hour, Mr Harris was ringing Fleur, telling her,

"If you get any more aggravation from her, you leave and come home. *She*," and Fleur was rather shocked at the venom Mr Harris put into 'she', "has had the audacity to threaten me with the directors! I am *not* standing for that! I was straight on the phone and informed them of the situation, so much good *that* will do her!"

"Oh dear, I'm so sorry," Fleur apologised, knowing just what it meant to disturb the directors with the everyday running of the company. "I didn't mean to cause this much trouble. I just didn't want us to hand on a bigger bill than agreed and then have Mr Vance refusing to pay."

"It's not you who's the trouble!" Mr Harris said firmly. "No, Fleur, you did absolutely the right thing. It's Mrs Vance who is being unreasonable. But what I was ringing you to tell you, is that it's now been agreed at the top level that if you feel in any way uncomfortable, or that you are being subjected to verbal abuse, we would expect you to pack your things and come straight back."

He lowered his tone to a more confidential level, making Fleur think that he was in his office with only a paper-thin wall between it and the open office the others shared. "Between you and me, Angelo Vance needs us every bit as much as we need his money. We're probably the only reputable company left whom he hasn't irredeemably pissed off! So if he wants this work done, he's got to keep on our right side too."

"That's reassuring to know, and thank you for telling me," and Fleur told him about Mrs Vance wondering why she wasn't working in the library, and of her expectation that Fleur would lug all the heavy boxes around just so that she could continue in there. "There isn't even a chair to sit at," Fleur finished. "I don't think she has a clue as to how much detail I need to record for each book for the insurance purposes. I swear the woman thinks I'm just going to unpack them, scribble down the title and author, and then arrange them prettily on the shelves!"

"God help us," Mr Harris groaned. "Look, can you face carrying on there for another day or so? It's too late to do much now – although I'll try – but I'm going to do my best to speak to Angelo Vance in person, and find out just what sort of job he wants done."

"I'm sure I can manage that," Fleur conceded, but when she came to finish for the night, and went to go and find something to eat, to her horror she found that she hadn't been left a key for the cottage. There was certainly a substantial Yale lock on the door, but search though she did, Fleur could not find a key for it. That would mean leaving the cottage open, with her laptop and everything in it, if she was to get back in, while the person who had that key could walk in any time unannounced, and that decided it for her. She would go to the *Fox & Hounds,* and if they had a spare room for the night, that was where she would stay.

Chapter 5

It was as she was driving back out of the yard, all of her belongings back in the car, that she saw Mrs Vance come out and stare at her in fury. However, Fleur had no intention of stopping and winding the window down, and drove on. At the *Fox & Hounds* she was greeted warmly by the landlady and assured that there was a room available, and that she even remembered Fleur from when they had all stayed there before.

In fact, the warmth of the welcome was such a relief that Fleur found herself unburdening herself to Debbie, the landlady.

"I just didn't feel safe there," she confided, since she was the only one in the dining room side of the pub on this quiet Monday evening. "I mean, who has the keys to that cottage and yet I didn't?"

"I don't blame you at all," Debbie said with a sniff of disgust. "What on earth was she thinking, expecting you to stop in the place like that? And I tell you something else. There have been some nasty rumours going around of someone up there. One or two of the girls in the village have reported feeling spied upon from the grounds.

"I don't mean they were trespassing," she added hurriedly. "It's just that the estate fence comes up to the road for quite a way, and people have said they've seen someone lurking in the undergrowth up there, as if waiting for some unsuspecting soul to walk past. One of our barmaids used to walk home that way, but now she gets her mum or dad to come and pick her up, and they're only too glad to as well."

"That's not good," Fleur agreed, "but thank you for telling me. It makes me feel less of a wimp for not wanting to stay there. I'd rather take my chances with the drunks here." Then saw Debbie's startled look and told her of Mrs Vance's reason for Fleur not booking in right from the start.

"Bloody cheek!" Debbie fumed. "We've *never* had trouble like that here! And anyway, how would she know? She never comes down here! No mixing with the hoi polloi for her! You wait until I tell Danny what she's said, he'll be spitting blood over that." She reached over and patted Fleur's hand. "You stay here with us. Much safer. Much, much safer!"

And once she was tucked up in the comfortable bed, and knowing that she was secure behind the pub's full alarm system, Fleur couldn't have agreed more. She'd never have got a wink's sleep up at the cottage, of that she was sure. But the last thing she did before crawling into bed with one of her favourite books was to ring Lucy and tell her what had happened, but also about Mrs Vance lying about the state of things at the *Fox & Hounds*.

"God in heaven, this just gets worse and worse," Lucy said angrily. "Don't go back up there first thing, Fleur. I'll ring Harry at home and bring him up to speed. I'm sure in the light of this he'll want you to come straight back."

"Oh no, please, Lucy don't do that! I feel like I'm causing all this trouble for everyone."

"Trouble be buggered!" Lucy declared firmly. "It's not you! Why in God's name did the woman feel the need to lie about the situation at the pub? It's nothing to do with her!"

"Maybe she took umbrage at something which she thought they'd said about her?"

However, Lucy wasn't having that. "No, no. There's something going on far beyond that. If that was all it was, why wouldn't she have wanted a whole team of us on the job? Do you see what I mean? We could have all headed out to *The Rookery*, maybe taking it in turns to drive each day even if we weren't staying locally at the pub – Hell's teeth, it's not that far! And we'd have got the job done in a fraction of the time.

"In fact, I don't know why she wanted you to stay at all. The only reason we did it the last time was because Angelo Vance was paying us the overtime to start early and finish late! This is sounding more and more as if she has some reason for wanting to isolate *you*."

"But I've done nothing to her!" Fleur protested.

"Well maybe it's not you personally," Lucy conceded. "Perhaps she just wanted one of our staff up there on their own so that she could bully them into doing whatever she wanted. Maybe she picked on you precisely because she'd learned somehow that Carrie-Ann couldn't have gone, and recalling you, thought you'd be easier to get than me? After all, all of our professional details are up on the company's website, including that Carrie-Ann is only part-time, and that I'm the team leader.

"You don't know, she might think that as team leader I'm supervising several jobs, which would prevent me from giving her my full focus. From what you've said, she seems to want your undivided attention. A psychiatrist would probably have a field day with her given what we're learning – dear God, a woman of her age having temper tantrums like that! She needs to bloody grow up and realise that the world doesn't revolve around her!"

"Actually, that's all rather reassuring," Fleur said with some relief. "Yes, I can see how I would seem the clear choice if she's just gone by our profiles, and the vague memory of me being into all things pagan. But it also makes it less of a personal thing. If I'd been the part-timer, she might have gone after having Carrie-Ann here instead. *Phew*! That's actually quite a relief!"

And it was. Feeling that it was more about who'd been available stripped a lot of the stress away from the situation for now, and once she had got to bed, Fleur had a remarkably dream free and refreshing night.

Going down to breakfast the next morning, she was chatting happily with Debbie when her phone rang, the screen announcing that it was Mr Harris calling her again.

"I'm so sorry to call you this early," he apologised when she picked up, "but I wanted to keep you informed of what's gone on."

"Oh?" Fleur wasn't sure she liked that sound of that, and Mr Harris' apologetic tone told her that he wasn't that happy about it either.

"I managed to get Angelo Vance by email late on yesterday, and the next thing I know, I'm getting a phone call from him at eight o'clock last night at home."

"How on earth did he get your home number?"

"*Humph*! Via one of the directors. I won't say which one, but suffice it to say that I rang *him* at home and told him exactly what I thought about him doing that! You do *not* hand out private numbers to clients, no matter who they are. …Anyway, Vance was nothing if not apologetic."

"Really?"

"Yes. It surprised me, actually. He was far nicer to speak to in person than he's sometimes been in the past. Enough that I'm starting to wonder whether Mr Bronson has been rather disparaging with him in his previous dealings with him. You know that Mr Bronson has aristocratic connections, and tends to play on them heavily with our similarly inclined clients, but he can be very derisive of people who he sees as 'new money', i.e., men like Vance who've made it in e-commerce and the like. He wouldn't come out and say to Vance's face that he thinks him a jumped up pleb, but my goodness, he can put an awful lot of attitude and insinuation into polite words!"

"Good grief! I can see that he might have ruffled Vance's feathers considerably in that case. So yes, maybe that's why Vance has been such a pain to deal with previously."

Fleur heard Mr Harris' sigh of relief. "I'm so glad that you can see that. So, you'll appreciate that after having Mr Vance apologising repeatedly both for the confusion and for his mother, I really was a bit on the back foot when it came to negotiating."

"Oh dear."

"Indeed. And the first thing, is that Angelo Vance has not put his mother in charge of the job at all, but doesn't want to upset her by publicly seeming to call her a liar." He sighed heavily again. "You can't fault the man for caring about his mum, can you? At least he's perfectly normal in that."

"No, you can't," but Fleur was getting a very unpleasant feeling about where this was going.

"He's agreed that he'll put it in writing to us that he's happy for you to do the research on his mum's boxes of stuff as well as his own." Harris gave a short bark of a laugh. "Said he'd never hear the last of it until she got it done, but at the same time really respected the fact that we'd deferred the matter back to him. And I think he was genuine in that. It's like we've gone up in his estimation for not just slapping your extra time onto the bill, and then arguing the toss with him after all the work's been done.

"The thing is, Fleur, he's asked if you wouldn't mind carrying on with the work, since you're the one person who might pick it up if his mum really does have some undiscovered gem, not just a collection of rather dated New Age rubbish. He's also deeply apologetic about the fact that the boxes were unlabelled and just dumped in the library. That wasn't what he'd asked to be done at all. He said that they should have all been stacked neatly over to the one side so that you had somewhere to work, and be able to put some of the books up onto shelves at least temporarily. It sounded to me as though he's going to read the riot act to the movers for leaving them as they did."

"Well, that's something."

"It is indeed. And he's going to speak to Mrs Vance and tell her that if you think the easiest way to work in that muddle is to take the books across to the cottage, she's to leave you be to get on with the job. Oh, and he *does* want a full cataloguing, not just a simple indexing. He was surprised that you weren't given an envelope with his requests inside when you got there."

"I got nothing! Just whisked into the Dower House, and Mrs Vance going on the charm offensive to get me to work on her stuff first!"

"I said that was what had happened, and I don't think he was any too pleased about that, even though he wouldn't say so. He told me that he'd like you to also use your judgement on what you find, and if there are volumes in there which really don't have any value or significance, then to put them on one side so that he can decide if he wants to keep them or not."

"Oh! I wasn't expecting that. Okay, then, I'll go back up there today and see what happens."

"Please do," Harris said gratefully, "but if you are made to feel in any way uncomfortable, or Mrs Vance starts having another go at you, you have my full permission to pack up your stuff and leave. It'll be no reflection on you. Mr Vance will then have to arrange for the books to be brought up to us, and we'll do the work in our own facility."

It was therefore feeling considerably better about the whole situation that Fleur drove back to *The Rookery*, making sure that she got there nicely before nine o'clock so that she would be set up and ready to start work at the beginning of the working day. What she wasn't expecting was to see Angelo Vance himself coming out of the door of the Dower House to greet her.

"Sod, damn, and blast!" she muttered under her breath, trying to paste a smile on nonetheless.

She was even more taken aback when he very politely said, "Ms Constantine, I'm so sorry about all of the confusion yesterday. I really do appreciate you coming back to continue this work. Please, let's go into the cottage and I'll explain things more fully."

Okay, so that wasn't what she'd been expecting, and at least the cottage was a rather less intimidating space than, say, the cavernous room with the French windows, or worse, her having to sit in the Dower House's lounge with Claudia Vance looking daggers at her at the same time. Even more of a shock was to see that someone had brought supplies into the cottage. A very smart coffee maker was now sitting on the side, with some top brands of coffee lined up beside it, and a clear pack of rather delicious Danish pastries were beside them.

"I didn't want to make the coffee until you got here," Angelo began, turning with a smile to add, "Didn't know if you'd prefer tea."

"Oh! Err …no. Coffee is fine, especially in the morning. I don't drink it later in the day because it keeps me awake, although I do love it."

"This Italian blend okay for you, then?"

Given that it was one which Fleur could never afford for herself, she nodded enthusiastically, taking the time to look more closely at Angelo as he busied himself with the machine. In the past, she'd only seen him the once and from some distance, leaving Lucy to do any confronting over the collection of the papers, and so this was the first time she'd been within arm's reach of the man.

Probably an inch or so shy of six feet tall, he had a mop of thick and glossy near-black hair, which fell in waves down around his collar. His skin had an olive tint to it, and Fleur guessed that he'd only have to have a glimmer of sunshine for him to tan perfectly. But although he was also very trim, and clearly kept himself fit, what she now saw for the first time was that he was equally no bulked-up man. A runner, maybe, but not someone who worked-out to build a lot of extraneous muscle up; and that had Fleur wondering, because although she herself was only around five-feet-two when drawn up to her full height, she reckoned she could fight back against him with some degree of success.

That bothered her, because from Lucy's description, and having seen a photograph of the unfortunate Claire standing next to Lucy, Fleur was fairly sure that Claire was a much bigger woman than herself. So how had she been so overwhelmed by Angelo? Granted, the poor woman had been taken totally unawares, but every account said that she had fought back hard, and therefore the business of Angelo turning up at the train station the next day with not a mark on him now confused Fleur considerably. Someone of Claire's build would not have had to reach as far as herself to claw at Angelo's face, for instance. Nor would it have been as easy for Angelo to reach over Claire's shoulders and pin her down – which was what had been said in the online news report Fleur had found of the incident. It just didn't make sense.

And then Angelo turned around, and just for an unguarded instant, Fleur caught a glimpse of a terrible sadness in his eyes. Not arrogance, nor the kind of smugness she'd half expected from him after having got her trapped back here. Nothing even close to anything like that, just pain of a depth that almost had her catching her breath.

"Ooh, that smells so good!" she said to cover her slight gasp.

"I'm glad you like it." And he seemed to mean that.

Bringing the two lovely white china mugs with a gold trim over to the table, and the cello tray of Danishes, he sat down opposite her and began,

"I'm so sorry for all the confusion, and I want you to know that I totally understand why you would have wanted clarification over what was expected of you."

"Thank you. I hope Mrs Vance understands that I wasn't trying to be difficult. It's just that I need this job, and I certainly can't afford to antagonise my employers."

Angelo gave a smile, and for a second Fleur was complete under the spell of both it and those deep-brown, puppy-dog eyes. "I promise you that by the end of today she will," he said ruefully. "When I told her that she was to consider the Dower House as her own, I didn't expect her to …to…"

"Get the bit between her teeth quite so much?" Fleur suggested, and was rewarded with a genuine hoot of laughter from him.

"That's it! You've got it in one!" He rolled his eyes. "When I had some complaints from the stores who've delivered things here, I just thought that they'd misunderstood her. Mum can be so very Italian sometimes. You know, fiery! And people tend to think she's being aggressive when she's just passionate about something." His expression clouded. "But having spoken early this morning to the company who brought the boxes of books here, it's clear that something rather more than that has been going on."

"Oh dear."

Angelo seemed to be wrestling with something as he twice began to speak and then stopped, finally saying, "Look, can I tell you something in confidence? You've played fair with me, so I want to be the same with you, but this mustn't become public knowledge, alright?"

"As long as it doesn't compromise my position with my bosses, I think I can promise that."

"Oh, it's nothing like that," he instantly reassured her. "You see, my mum had a terrible relationship with her father. He was very much the old-school type of father. Spare the rod and spoil the child – all that kind of thing."

"Ouch! That wouldn't have worked out well with a wife and daughter with all the Mediterranean fire in them."

His relief at her understanding was instantly clear. "You have it. It led to some spectacular showdowns, and at times with him being quite brutal with her. As a result, she never really had anywhere she thought of as her actual *home* while she was growing up. And that's why having the Dower

House as her own was so important to her, and why I was happy to tell her she should treat it as such.

"Oh, she adored Italy, still does, but at the end of the day the *castello* was always going to go to her uncle – my great-uncle Antonio – and so as her grandparents got older, he automatically took over the running of it and the estate that went with it. And he may have loved his older sister – that's my Grandmother Angelina – but I don't think he anticipated his offer of somewhere to stay translating to having them living with him for years on end."

"No, I can imagine that would wear thin in most families."

"It did, especially once he married and his wife wanted to make changes to the décor and stuff, and at every turn my mum and her mother were contradicting her. When I was little, I didn't get it. I thought he must be a right miserable sod. But as I've got older, I've found myself a lot more sympathetic to him, and why he eventually told them that if they wanted to carry on living there, then they'd have to move into one of the cottages in the grounds.

"Mum has never forgiven her Uncle Antonio for that. She thought it the most degrading thing to do to his own sister and niece. But the thing is, it may be a *castello*, but it isn't that big, and hasn't got that many bedrooms. So once his own children started coming along, there genuinely wasn't enough room for all of them under that one roof."

"Was that when your mum had to come over here to school?"

"God, you are quick on the uptake! Yes, mum came back over here permanently for a while, and if I'm honest, she had probably been her own worst enemy back in Italy. Since I've been old enough to have those sorts of conversations with her, she's always proudly declared that right from an early age she had boys wanting to be with her, meaning I suspect that Great-uncle Antonio had no desire to have a string of lovelorn lads hanging around his gates when he had small daughters of his own. But, of course, that threw her back into contact with her father – my grandfather who I inherited this place from, I mean."

"Do you think his perceived brutality was actually him in a clumsy way trying to rein in some of her worst behaviour?" Fleur speculated. "I don't mean to criticise your mum, but teenage girls have a very skewed view of the world, and what she saw as just having fun, he might have seen as her not only inviting trouble, but doing something potentially dangerous?"

Angelo blinked. "Do you know, I hadn't thought of it in quite that way, but even just going back to some of the wild things I did in my late teens, I have a very different perspective on them nowadays. In fact, I can't believe that my mum let me get away with as much as I did."

That, Fleur thought, was a confession she would never have expected to come from this reputed wild playboy. And she was even more surprised when he continued thoughtfully,

"What you've just said does make a lot more sense of some of the things she said he did. Like locking her in her room. For heaven's sake, by her own admission she used to wait until he – or more often his housekeeper at the Cheltenham house – was in bed, and then sneak out to nightclubs, and that was when she was fourteen!" He shivered. "If I ever have kids, I pray that no daughter of mine goes into some of the clubs I've been into at that kind of age. Bloody hell! These days it gives me the shivers just thinking about it!"

Angelo Vance, you are nothing at all like I expected, Fleur thought in amazement. *Where is the demon attacker you're supposed to be? Were you really totally innocent of the crime you've been accused of?*

Chapter 6

Mentally struggling with this likeable and intelligent version of Angelo Vance, Fleur was rather glad when he concluded that strand of their conversation with,

"I hope you can now understand why my mum might have gone a bit over the top with her asserting her right to say what was going to be done here. It wasn't wholly correct, but this is probably the first time in her life that she's had a place where she feels she can dictate what goes on in it. She shouldn't have been like that with you, and I can only apologise again."

Feeling that to say anything less than, "It's okay, no harm done," would be churlish, Fleur was relieved to move onto what Angelo wanted done with the books. He, it transpired, wanted them to be fully catalogued so that they were both itemised for insurance purposes, and so that those he didn't want to keep could be sent straight to auction without further inspection.

"Take whatever time you need to do the job," he said affably. "I'm in no hurry to start buying and selling, not least because I need to see how much space I've got here once all of the books are up and on the shelves."

"Do you have any preferences for what's to be kept?" Fleur wondered.

"I do love history," Angelo admitted, "but I'm not enthusiastic about ploughing through those dusty old Victorian versions of the Great British Empire. For me this library is more about having a sensible balance between those books that are a good investment, and should therefore be kept, and those which I'd actually want to keep myself. If you sort the boxes out, and then put all of those I'll definitely be keeping in some meaningful order on successive shelves, then if someone comes here for a photo shoot, I can always pose in front of them and keep my paperback thrillers out of sight on the opposite wall," and he had the good humour to give a self-deprecating and rather sheepish grin over the thrillers. This was Angelo Vance the shrewd business man in action, but acknowledging that he wasn't necessarily buying into his own PR at every step, which was quite endearing.

"So you won't want to be keeping the *Transactions of the House of Commons* in multiple volumes then?" Fleur dared to tease him with.

Angelo's face was a picture. "Jeez! Really? I have those?"

Fleur couldn't help but laugh. "Yes, you do. But so does every stately home in England and few large houses that aren't even that. It's similar to the four-volume set of the life of Disraeli. He may have been a prominent Victorian prime minister, and they are prettily bound, but because of that they're as common as muck and worth nothing. So, I'm guessing that they can go on the 'for sale' pile?"

"Absolutely! I don't think I'll be ploughing my way through those, not even on the deadest of evenings out here."

Fleur laughed along with him. "Thank you for being so clear about all of that. It makes my job a lot easier. I'll definitely sort the books into different groups: the ones you ought to keep because they're worth it in terms of money; the ones you might want to keep even if they're not that great an investment; and the ones you can safely send to an auction room or even a charity shop."

"That would be great." Then Angelo mentally threw Fleur by adding with a frown, "I just don't understand why Mum didn't give you the letter I left for you which explained all that."

Feeling that any comment she made would only come across as critical of Claudia Vance, Fleur just smiled faintly and dipped into the Danishes, which Angelo had opened and pushed her way. Personally, she thought that Mrs Vance's attitude wasn't just about getting to have a place of her own at last, despite what Angelo believed. It was far too controlling for that, and it made Fleur wonder just how much of a trial having his mother right here on the premises was turning out to be for Angelo. What he'd said about the removal men rather hinted that they had been on the receiving end of a tongue-lashing from Mrs Vance, and in response had dumped the book boxes as fast as possible in order to get away at speed.

She was even more confused as she walked across the yard with the first armful of books for the day, to hear Angelo and his mother arguing. The day was fine and the Dower House's side door was open along with most of the windows, and so Fleur heard him saying,

"But Mum, I *gave* you the envelope! What did you do with it?"

"I told you!" Fleur heard Mrs Vance snap back. "I put it on the library desk for the damned girl! It's not my fault if she's lost it!"

"Mum, she hasn't merely lost it. She never got it! What I was telling her about what I wanted done with the cataloguing was news to her, I swear. There wasn't a hint of guile about her, and it would be stupid of her to have gone to all the trouble of getting her bosses involved if it was nothing more than her own carelessness. Surely you can see that?"

"Well, I'm telling you that I put it on the desk for her! It would have hardly got up and walked away by itself, would it?"

There was a pregnant pause and then Fleur heard Angelo saying in a very dismayed voice as if calling after his mother. "Mum? …Mum? …Please tell me you haven't? …Oh no, please, not *again*!"

Whatever else was said was lost, because they must have moved through into the kitchen at the front of the house, and Fleur was hardly going to go creeping around there to eavesdrop further. It did make her wonder, though, if only because of the tone of Angelo's voice. He sounded downright desperate and despairing, so what on earth had his mother done before that would have him so worried? Was Mrs Vance a recovering alcoholic, perhaps? Or had she been enough of a wild child that she'd been into drugs and struggled to stay away from them even now? Whatever it was, Fleur was sure it truly was serious and she resolved to keep her eyes peeled for any clues while she was here. If nothing else, she didn't want to become entangled if the drugs' squad turned up here on a raid!

However, the family argument didn't spill over her way, and she found herself getting pleasantly absorbed in the work, vaguely registering the sound of something sporty pulling out of the courtyard and roaring off down the drive. No doubt Angelo had other places to be was her presumption, and so she was more than a bit surprised when he walked back into the cottage kitchen in the late afternoon.

"I can only apologise again that you weren't given any keys to this place," he said as he came in, and Fleur looked up to briefly see that same awful pain in his eyes before he took a deep breath and seemed to be able to guard himself once more. He brandished a set of keys which looked to have been freshly cut, and then placed them on the table beside Fleur.

"I've just been into Worcester to get these done," he declared. "I have no idea what happened to the set I left for you," and for the first time Fleur thought he was lying through his teeth. Wherever those keys were, Angelo knew. So why lie about them?

"I really wasn't happy about not being able to lock up my work," Fleur replied, giving the acceptable excuse, not that she straight up felt in danger here even now, but then was shocked at Angelo's response of,

"I quite understand, and in the light of that, I've been in touch with Mr Harris and told him that I'm quite happy to pick up the bill for you continuing to stay at the *Fox & Hounds*. I wouldn't expect you to stay here, knowing that a set of keys to this cottage have gone missing, and who knows who might have access to them now."

There it was again, that feeling that the last sentence was an outright lie. But more troubling was the feeling she got that he was actively encouraging her to stay at the pub. That was directly opposite to what Claudia Vance wanted. What on earth was going on here that he would do that? Was he worried that she might see his mother doing something which, if made public would ruin his golden boy reputation? Or was it something worse? That was the trouble with knowing about the Anglo Vance of old – she couldn't quite trust the face he was currently presenting to her. Part of her wanted to believe that he was worried sick about his mum, but the other part of her kept prodding her to keep in mind his self-centred persona, which was very well documented in the public sphere and there for all to see.

"That very understanding of you," Fleur said, trying to be gracious about it. "This laptop isn't mine, it's the company's, and I wouldn't be happy leaving it somewhere unsecured."

"Quite," Angelo said with a watery smile, which tugged at Fleur's better nature and her inclination to be sympathetic.

God, you really are worried about something, Fleur thought, *and I don't think it's something as trifling as the replacement cost of a new laptop – which you could probably pay for out of your spare change and not notice, even for one as good as this*. And that turned her mind again to the rape of Claire. Was she misreading him and he was scared that something might happen so that he was faced with a similar accusation? And if so, was he dreading Claire's case being brought once again into public scrutiny, or maybe even a fresh examination of that evidence which might lead to a retrial and a different verdict? Whatever it was, right now Angelo Vance was definitely not the cocky, arrogant, arse she had seen from a distance in the past, let alone the version of him that Lucy had had to deal with, so something severe enough had happened to stick a big pin in that bubble of ego.

"It's quite nice to get some separation from work," was what Fleur actually said. "I don't mind working on until six-ish if I can then have the evening free, so the pub suits me fine. Would you believe, Debbie, the landlady actually remembered us from the last time we were here – though I personally didn't stay overnight that time – so it's all very convivial down there."

"I'm glad," Angelo said almost wistfully, as if a convivial night down the pub was something he could only dream of these days.

"Do you end up having to buy a round for the whole village if you go down there?" Fleur asked sympathetically, having visions of the canny farmer's lads thinking it was fair game to touch the rich bloke from up at the manor for a few beers, should he dare to show his face on their turf. Even in the twenty-first century, some of these small farming communities could be very insular when it came to rich outsiders coming in, and doing what they saw as trying to lord it over them. Yet strangely her words had the effect of fractionally relaxing Angelo, who gave a half laugh and said,

"If it was as simple as buying a few rounds, I'd be only too glad to run up a tab that would make the landlord's month, never mind his day."

"Oh?" Fleur hadn't meant it to come out with quite such curiosity, but to her surprise, Angelo made the few steps to the chair on the other side of the table and slumped into it, plonking his elbows on the table and burying his head in his hands for a moment. When he looked up, he gave an exasperated shake of his head and then began,

"It wasn't just Mum whom her father rubbed up the wrong way."

"Oh dear! It goes back that far, does it?"

"I'm afraid so. Grandfather's family have owned this manor house for hundreds of years – or so I've been told. The trouble was, he expected the people in the village to treat him like the lord of the manor still."

"Ouch, that was never going to go down well at any point since the Second World War."

"No, it didn't. He didn't do himself any favours when the village was trying to raise money to save the village shop, that's for sure. They wanted to buy it off the bloke who owns the property, you see. Not that that was Grandfather, I hasten to add. A predecessor – whichever one it was …might even have been his father – had sold off huge chunks of the land long ago, so someone else was the owner, but it was Grandfather's refusal to contribute to the fund-raising which blackened his own reputation around here. Especially as the man who was running the main house here as a hotel had just at that point negotiated his new lease on very favourable terms, and was daft enough to brag about it in the village. So the perception was that Grandfather was flush enough with cash to give the hotelier a big financial break, but wouldn't help the community."

"I thought the hotel's lease wasn't renewed?"

"Oh, it wasn't this last time. This is the previous time, around fifteen years ago when they asked for a twelve-year lease, not twenty-five. They got the renewal for a shorter time because they weren't sure how long they'd be able to keep on going. Something to do with a downturn in English tourists at the time, apparently. By the time Grandfather died some ten years after that, it was clear that the hotel wouldn't be carrying on, which was why I allowed them to just let it run to the end and then leave."

Fleur thought for a moment, then said, "I'm guessing, then, that if there were fewer guests at the hotel, then there were fewer people spending their money down in the village? Which would mean – from their point of view – that it was harder to raise the money for a shop they probably needed far more than any visitor would?"

Angelo's smile this time was completely genuine. "That's pretty much the whole argument in a nutshell, Ms Constantine."

And though she had never meant the words to come out, Fleur found herself saying, "Oh, please, call me Fleur," and then wondered why she would give him that opening to be more personal with her. *Bloody hell, girl,* she chastised herself. *There you were, determined to keep him at arms' length, and then you give him permission to call you by your first name – like that isn't inviting trouble!* Yet there was also a part of her that was starting to feel really sorry for Angelo. As yet she couldn't put her finger on quite why, but all of her senses were screaming at her that this man wasn't the villain he'd been made out to be; which was troubling if it meant that at some crucial point in the future, she would let her guard down just when she shouldn't.

"What a lovely name," Angelo was saying – which ought to have been creepy and yet wasn't, because again Fleur had the sense that he genuinely meant it.

"Blame my romantic Greek grandmother," she said with a laugh.

"Ah, so you know what it's like to have that link to the Mediterranean!" he exclaimed.

"Yes, but my lot were mostly very laid back," Fleur laughed. "Not much Latin fire in any of them, although Grandma could have won medals for being stubborn. They were easy to be around, if a bit infuriating if you wanted them to get het up over something." She wasn't about to go into her family's internal strife right now – that would be opening up too much.

"I'd give a lot for a bit of 'laid back' in my family," he said with feeling. "So many arguments in mine, and so many times when one part of the family wasn't talking to the other over something which they'd never tell anyone else why," and he rolled his eyes in disgust.

Unable to stop herself, in part because that thing of one half not talking to the other rang a lot of bells with her as well, Fleur's curiosity again got the better of her, and she asked, "Were you close to your grandfather? I know you've said that things were strained between him and your mum, but was it better for you?" She saw his surprise, and hurriedly qualified with, "Only you seem very determined to save this house. If you have no happy memories of it, wouldn't it have been easier to simply sell it? Out here on the Worcestershire-Herefordshire border, with all the relatively easy connections to the various motorway networks, you wouldn't be short of buyers wealthy enough to afford a place like this."

Angelo paused, and Fleur wondered if she had overstepped the mark. After all, he had no reason to justify his actions to her. He could buy half a dozen houses and live in none of them for all the difference it would make to her, and he certainly had no reason to humour someone who could easily be replaced on this job.

"It was primarily Mum," he said, and now Fleur had the feeling that he was being very careful about what he said to her. "What her motives are she's never said, but it was very important to her that this place stayed in the family." He gave a shrug and that strange half smile again. "She's my mum. What could I say? It's not as though I couldn't afford it."

And though Fleur wanted to ask him whether he ever intended to live here himself, she felt it was politic to shut up now. This far he'd been all helpfulness and kindness, so it wouldn't do to rock the boat and make him regret helping her. It was bad enough that she'd had no choice but to ruffle Claudia Vance's feathers over the billing, so she had no reason or desire to repeat that with Angelo, even though once more she had that weird sense that he hadn't been wholly truthful with that last statement.

"Your mum's very lucky to have you taking such good care of her," was the compliment Fleur paid him, and yet the words weren't out of her mouth before she saw that inner flinch of pain in his eyes.

What complicated kind of relationship did Claudia and Angelo Vance have to cause that? And he seemed to have no words to answer her with either, making her say brightly,

"I've only got another armful of books to go to end this crate, so I'll do those and then call it a day. Thanks for the keys. I'm a lot happier leaving piles of books here on the table now that I can lock them up." She wasn't going to say that there was no way that she was leaving the laptop here overnight, though. There was too much personal information on it for that, including the phone numbers of other members of staff at the firm. And if Angelo knew that there was definitely another set of keys somewhere on the estate, Fleur wasn't going to give that person a chance to come in at night and hunt through the records.

As long as the door is properly locked, your books are your concern, she thought as Angelo left. *But I'm not risking getting stalked or trapped like Claire was – not me or anyone else. You could be a veritable Jekyll and Hyde, Angelo Vance, smiling to my face now, but turning into someone much darker once you think I'm trusting you.* Yet the other internal voice argued back, *if anyone's doing the stalking and trapping, I don't think it's Angelo, though I think he knows full well who that person is. And for that alone, he's not to be trusted, because he's knowingly protecting that person as a priority ahead of the safety of everyone else.*

Chapter 7

After another restful night at the *Fox & Hounds*, Fleur drove up to the house the following morning, fully expecting to be carrying on where she had left off with the library books. So it was something of a shock to find the cottage door unlocked. At first, she thought she was just using the wrong key when it didn't turn, but then common sense told her that a wrong key wouldn't have gone all the way in like this one did. And so it was with a feeling of dread that she tried the handle and then found the door swinging open.

"Bloody hell!" she muttered, both angry that the mystery person had clearly been in here last night, and at herself for being sucked in by Angelo's puppy-dog eyes. *He's trouble!* she told herself sternly, as she nudged her way in, balancing in one hand the sandwich she'd asked Debbie to make for her during breakfast along with the small container of milk she'd also bought off her, while lugging her large laptop case in the other. *Stop being so damned gullible!* Then stopped in shock as she took in the kitchen.

When she had left last night, everything had been clean and tidy, but now there were cardboard boxes dumped on the table, the books which had been on the table had been carelessly dumped over on a work-surface, and the coffee maker looked as if it had been used. Carefully putting her stuff down on the chair, she walked over to the coffee maker and inspected it. For a start off the power switch was on, and she knew beyond a doubt that she'd made sure everything was turned off before she left. Moreover, there were dried dribbles of coffee on the bottom which hadn't been there before, and the packet of espresso blend was open. That hadn't been the one Angelo had used yesterday when he'd made coffee for them both, and Fleur would never drink anything that strong, being somewhat sensitive to too much caffeine.

"Who the hell has been in here?" she wondered, turning around to look about the place, and shiver ran down her spine as she realised that somebody could be upstairs right now, because the door to the twisting stairs was closed and latched, so she wouldn't hear them as long as they didn't move about.

Feeling a bit foolish, she nonetheless moved the spare kitchen chair and wedged it right in front of the stair door, which opened outwards into the kitchen. There, if anyone came downstairs in a hurry, they'd be both slowed down and falling over the chair, and that would give her time to run outside. And in the spirit of that, she also made sure that her car keys were in her pocket, not in her case where she normally put them. It would be a bit uncomfortable sitting down with them digging into her, but better to suffer that if it made a quick escape possible.

But then she turned back to the table and gave a groan. There was no way that she could start work until she had moved all of these, because they took up the whole table top. It was also bloody irritating, because she had been trying to work methodically through the library boxes, whereas now she would have no idea which heaps these had come from. Was somebody – like Angelo or Mrs Vance – mistakenly thinking they were helping her by doing this? Because they most definitely weren't!

"Tea!" she fumed, going to find the kettle. Luckily on the way to the pub last night she had called into the local community store, which was open until the early evening, and had picked up both ordinary teabags and some herb tea. *I'm not touching that coffee*, she thought with a shudder. *God knows who's had their fingers in that!* And with the same thought she took the kettle's lid off and poured out what was inside it out into the sink. What she didn't like the look of was a whitish substance in the bottom, because somehow it didn't look quite right to be lime-scale such as she had in her kettle at home. Tentatively she sniffed at it, but that told her nothing, so all she could do was rinse the kettle out well, put a small amount in and boil that, then throw that away too, before putting the kettle on properly for her tea. On the one hand she felt a bit foolish and acting all paranoid, but the sensible part of her said that it only had to be some kind of laxative powder to give her a very unpleasant day, and was Mrs Vance spiteful enough to do that?

The thought that it was Claudia Vance who had been in here was only strengthened by what she found when she opened the first box. This wasn't a box from the library, this was Mrs Vance's stuff!

Carefully lifting the first item out, it was immediately clear that somebody had looked at it recently and rather clumsily rewrapped it. The folds in the old cloth which it was wrapped in had yellowed and permanently creased with age, but weren't where it was folded now. In fact, it looked like it was an old pillowcase, and as Fleur opened it out she found a quaint bit of embroidery on the one edge. This was no antique but something just old and very homemade, which only intrigued Fleur all the more, since it spoke of someone caring very much about whatever this was, regardless of its monetary value.

"What have we here?" she mused, pulling a heavily leather-bound book out of the pillowcase, and setting it gently down on the table. The leather of the front cover had a tooled design on it, but there was no title or author on it, nor on the spine. Getting the two foam book supports out of her bag, she positioned them so that they would support the old spine and then with her cotton gloves on, eased the book open.

"Wow!" she gulped as the first pages appeared. This was no printed book, but something which had been handwritten, and with great care. The handwriting was very neat and tidy, but in a very spiky script that wasn't quite Victorian clerk's copperplate but equally as villainous to decipher. What she didn't need to be able to read the hand to understand were the astrological charts and diagrams, equally carefully drawn onto what must have been blank pages. Whatever this was, it certainly wasn't merely one of several diaries, kept to record day-to-day minutia.

It took all of her willpower to not sit down and start reading it straightaway, but her professionalism took over, and she knew she needed to unpack the rest of the box to discover if there was any context to what was in each box. Had they all just been packed up randomly when someone had wanted them out of the way? Or had they been packed away one or two at a time, over many years, each one being put aside as the star charts had changed during the years? The phases of the moon, in particular, would change every year, so charting them would take many pages over the course of the life of one grimoire, she thought.

By the time she had got the first box unpacked she had to sit down and have a strong tea just to stop the butterflies in her stomach. There were collectors, especially in America, who would pay a fortune for a collection like this, and for all that she had warned Mrs Vance not to expect her bits and pieces to be worth much, Fleur had the distinct and wobbly feeling that she was looking at the find of her career. And eight big boxes in all? Even if one of them held just the tarot cards – and there'd have to be an awful lot of those to fill a packing-box of that size – then even so there were a huge number of grimoires here! Was this the Vance family's secret inheritance, and if so, how far back did this go?

Taking a deep breath, Fleur knew that she would have to unpack the rest of the boxes to get some idea of continuity. The paper these grimoires were written on would give her one set of clues, but also the changing handwriting might give a vital indication of which writers followed one another. And thank heavens Angelo Vance had been amenable to her working on these boxes of heirlooms, because she would hate to have to put this on hold having seen what she had already.

As the day progressed, she carefully unwrapped book after book, making sure to keep each one with its pillowcase or piece of cloth, checking it and making detailed notes about it, and then carefully rewrapping it. Already she was getting the feeling that she might need to speak to Sue at work, who was the expert in needlework styles, because the random bits of embroidery could prove to be very useful additional clues as to dates. But then as the day wore on, she found herself with another dilemma. Should she leave these books just open here in the kitchen? If her initial hunch was right, then they were as valuable as anything she had come across this far in the library, and potentially even more. So did she want someone carelessly rummaging around in them, wrapping and unwrapping the books, but then sticking them back in the wrong coverings?

That was a genuine concern, because quite aside from whoever the possible stranger was who had brought them here, already she had found two books which she was sure had exchanged wrappings, going by where the old folds lay. What if there was something in with one of these old books? It might only be a handwritten letter, but if taken out of all context, it could potentially take that book from being very significant to utterly meaningless.

"Oh hell!" she swore angrily, realising that the only way around this was to go and speak to Claudia Vance and ask her to please be patient. Perhaps if she hinted that the grimoires would be all the more valuable if kept with the right wrappings? Would that make any difference to the woman? Given the way the packing boxes had been dumped in the kitchen, and then somebody – whether Mrs Vance herself or an unknown person – had then gone sloshing coffee around near them, Fleur had the nasty feeling that impatience ran in the family, along with an inability to work out what was valuable and what not.

Just the thought of someone plucking book after book out of their coverings, dumping them on the table, and then knocking a mug of coffee over and drenching the bottom ones, was enough to give her the shivers. No, somehow she had to protect these books. And so bracing herself for another round of arguments, she got everything as packed up as she could for now, and then having put her laptop and bag into her car, walked across the courtyard.

Yet she was barely halfway across when she got the uncomfortable feeling that she was being watched. Stopping in her tracks she looked around. Not a soul was in sight. But for a moment she could have sworn she heard a nasty laugh. It was faint and muffled, as if from behind a closed window, and that made her look harder again at the main house. However, on the ground floor there was only the kitchen door along with the tiny windows of the downstairs loo and the pantry facing this way, and she was instantly certain that it wasn't from either of those that the sound had come. On the first floor it was a similar story, with just the window of the main stairs – and a small window at that – plus the ones to the laundry store and the rearmost bathroom facing onto the courtyard.

Shaking herself, she was almost convinced that she'd imagined it when she heard it again, and this time she was more prepared.

It was to her right – so definitely the main house not the Dower House.

Not the ground floor.

Not the first floor.

The creepy second floor! The one with the padlocked door to it! And her eyes shot up to what she guessed was the landing window of those locked stairs.

For one brief second, she knew she saw

someone at that window. A someone who looked uncannily like Angelo Vance! A someone who had his head thrown back in evil laughter!

And yet that made Fleur angry, not frightened. Who the hell did he think he was to play mind games with her like that? Did he really think her such a fool as to not be able to work out his perverted little tricks? To be all nice to her face, and to try and gaslight her when she was off balance?

Pulling herself up to her full height, what little there was of it, she marched smartly around to the side door of the Dower House and rapped on it hard. It was all she could do to keep her temper in check, not least because this was raking up all sorts of unpleasant memories of what it had been like to live with her ex's idiot friends trying to put the frighteners on her. They hadn't succeeded, but it hadn't made it any the less of a trial to live with, particularly the enforced absence from her mum and sister, and so she was running out of patience fast with the Vances and their cat and mouse tactics.

When Claudia Vance answered the door, she seemed taken aback by Fleur's angry countenance.

"Is something wrong?" Mrs Vance asked rather coolly.

"I sincerely hope not," Fleur declared brusquely, "but I thought I should tell you that somebody came into the cottage between when I left last night and when I arrived this morning."

"Oh, don't be ridiculous!" Mrs Vance huffed.

"Really? Then it wasn't you who brought all the

boxes of your notebooks and tarot cards over and dumped them on the kitchen table?"

Claudia Vance recovered herself fast, but Fleur was sure that she wasn't mistaken in seeing genuine shock in her eyes. Nor did she quite manage to conceal the anxious glance over her shoulder to the sitting room, making Fleur wonder where she could have been all day if she hadn't noticed that the boxes were gone? So no, it hadn't been Mrs Vance herself who had done that. But if not her, then who?

However, Mrs Vance was bluffing well, saying, "Oh, Angelo! He's such a considerate son. He knows how much those things mean to me. He must have taken the boxes over before he left for London last night."

"Last night?" Fleur couldn't help herself snorting incredulously.

"Yes, last night!" Mrs Vance riposted, obviously not pleased at having her son's movements questioned by what she no doubt thought of as the hired help.

But then Fleur realised that the sleek sports car which she had seen when Angelo was also around had been absent all day, which was no doubt why she had subconsciously assumed that he mustn't be here. That didn't mean he couldn't have driven it around to where it couldn't be seen from any part of the houses, of course, but if so, then it might also mean that Mrs Vance wasn't aware of him sneaking back and hiding up on the top floor. What to do, what to say?

"Erm… I thought I should let you know that I've had a preliminary look at three of your boxes," she said in more conciliatory tones, "and I wanted to tell you that you have quite an extraordinary collection there." She didn't have to fake her enthusiasm for that, at least. "Indeed, I can say in all truth and honesty that I have never come across a collection like it – but that means that right now I can't begin to put a price on it for you. A lot will depend on being able to date the individual items, and it's about that that I wanted to speak to you.

"Can I beg you please to not unwrap anymore of the grimoires? I know it must be so tempting to get them all out and look at them, but I really need you to be patient and let me unpack them carefully. Those pillowcases, and old pieces of what might be table cloths or curtains, which each one is wrapped in might give us vital clues as to their ages. In fact, I'm seriously thinking that I need to get another part of our team to look at the fabrics, because if there's any doubt about dating the books, then the embroidery might narrow dates down considerably."

She stopped, looking hard at Mrs Vance to see whether she had been taking any notice of what she'd said. And there it was again, that look of surprise, as if she hadn't been the one to go rummaging through the boxes.

"At least two of the books had been put back in each other's wrappings, you see," Fleur added, but this time watching Mrs Vance even more closely.

She was good, Fleur had to give Mrs Vance that, but not quite good enough. This woman was no professional actress, and there was only so much she could fake. So Fleur was sudden sure that she hadn't been the one to go through the box opening the parcels up.

"Oh… Oh dear," Mrs Vance blustered. "Oh… Angelo and I thought we had been so careful to put everything back the way we found it, even making sure that the folds were in the same place."

Fleur was struggling to not exclaim, "Really?" or roll her eyes at what was obviously a lie, but then wondered if Angelo had gone back after they had looked at the books together, and that was when the books had been inadvertently swopped over? Was Angelo schizophrenic? Or bipolar? Or, heaven help him, presenting a multiple personality disorder? Fleur knew very little about the way any would present itself, especially to a complete lay person like herself with not a scrap of medical knowledge of psychological disorders. All she did know was that someone – and it could just as easily be Mrs Vance herself – was showing one personality to her in open meetings, and quite another behind her back.

"I'm going to get going now," Fleur said resignedly, "but I just wanted you to understand that far from helping things along by unpacking the books, you could actually seriously hinder me in doing a proper job on your heirlooms, and might even reduce their value." And then just in case Angelo was having some psychotic episode upstairs which Mrs Vance was trying to cover for, added, "I'm going to securely lock up the cottage because those books are potentially so valuable, and ask you to make sure that *nobody* goes in and disturbs them while I'm gone. It's for your sake, Mrs Vance, not mine."

There was a firm nod of the perfect coiffure. "Yes. …Yes, I'll make sure of that."

"Lovely. Then I'll see you in the morning." And feeling that she had best go before her curiosity and irritation got the better of her, and she started cross-questioning Mrs Vance, Fleur went back to the cottage, ostentatiously locked up – rattling the door to make absolutely sure it was secure – and then got into her car.

Mrs Vance had come out into the courtyard to watch her leave, for some reason looking far from pleased, and it was because Fleur was looking back in the car's mirror at her that when she glanced back for a final look, just as she was about to round the bend in the drive, that she saw it again. Up on the top floor in one of the two main front bedrooms, someone had thrown the window wide open. The lower sash had been shoved up so that it fully overlapped the top one, and a man was leaning out on the window sill – a man who looked uncannily like Angelo Vance!

Chapter 8

"I simply don't get it." Fleur was sitting in her bedroom at the *Fox & Hounds* having just told Lucy everything over the phone. "I'm beginning to think that both of them are as mad as a box of frogs! Those books didn't just get up and walk over to the cottage by themselves. *Somebody* took them there! But unless Mrs Vance can't remember what she did from one day to the next, I would swear that it wasn't her. And in fairness, those boxes were bloody heavy. I wouldn't have wanted to lug one of them all the way across the yard, and certainly not all eight of them. So given that Mrs Vance is a bit taller than me, but a lot more slender in build, the sheer practicality of carrying those weights makes me think it wasn't her.

"I mean, for all I know, they could have a handyman or gardener who comes around – I haven't been there long enough to spot someone like that, but it doesn't mean they don't exist. But why be coy about it if it's that? Or potentially she nabbed some poor delivery guy who came before I got there, and strong-armed him into doing the moving? Given the experience of the mover's guys, she can be damned belligerent when she wants. Or just say that

Angelo was doing his usual impatient trick of wanting everything done as the immediate priority? It's not like we haven't had experience of that before!"

Lucy snort of irritation echoed down the phone. "We sure did! None of us could wait to get away from him. But you know, Fleur, what you've just said about him possibly being schizophrenic in the very real and medical sense – not just being sarcastic about him – does make some sense."

"Really?"

"Hmm. …Thinking back to the first time we went there in particular – which of course was before you joined us – it was so weird. One day he'd be all suave and neatly turned out, and you could see the business brain which made him earn all that money in the way he acted and the decisions he made. But then you'd come across him on another day, and his hair would be all over the place and he'd look as if he'd just rolled out of bed at two in the afternoon. …Of course, given his reputation with women, that's exactly what we thought he had been doing! And on those occasions, you could practically feel him undressing you with those eyes. *Yuk*!" and Fleur could visualise Lucy's shudder which went with that.

"Creepy guy?"

"Oh yes! Definitely 'creepy guy' when he was like that! And that was when he'd make his most random and ridiculous demands, sometimes going right back on what he'd said the previous day. But then you'd meet him the day after and he'd be asking us why we were doing something, and he'd be so surprised when we told him that he'd bloody-well asked us to!"

"That's exactly it! Honestly, Lucy, it's like there are two people we're meeting."

Lucy snorted again. "Except that he was wearing the same clothes. I mean, come on, Fleur, who the hell would put somebody else's shirt on that they'd been wearing the previous day? And on a few really gross occasions, the shirt he'd worn the days before, too!"

Fleur was stunned. That was her fledgling theory shot down in flames. "The same shirt? Not just one you'd seen him in a few days beforehand so it could have been washed and re-worn?"

"Naah! And without wanting to gross you out just after your dinner, but you could *smell* that it was the same shirt, if you get my meaning. *Phwar!* On those days you wanted to tell him to go and take a bloody shower and use some deodorant! God, you could even see the old sweat marks under the arms! It sure wasn't pleasant to be near him. Vile though it sounds, I even think he was wearing the same underwear and socks, and I don't need to tell you how I'd know that, do I? And on two singular nauseating days he then wore them all for a third time! What had been neat and business-like on day one was pretty vile by day three. So no, no other person would want to have been wearing those clothes by then."

Fleur was stunned. "That's just freaky. The man I met was so nice to be around precisely because, amongst other things, he smelled nice. Like he'd used some really high-quality soaps, but not smothered in aftershave or colognes, I mean." She didn't want to add that there had been something equally pleasant lingering under the faint hint of lemon soap, which was undoubtedly male pheromones, but very clean and healthy ones. To say something like that to Lucy would only make her fret even more that Fleur was being taken in by Angelo, especially as the man she had described sounded disgustingly dirty in his personal habits.

Instead, she said, "How terrible if it is a mental disorder, though, especially if on his sane days he knows that he's lost it previously. It might account for why his mum is so keen to cover for him. After all, the media getting hold of its favourite naughty boy going slowly insane would kill his career quicker than anything. Maybe that's why he wants to come and live at *The Rookery*? It's private, and he can have his mum on hand to make sure he's looked after, while he has proper carers in the big house?"

"That's a thought," Lucy conceded, though not sounding wholly convinced, "And it makes as much sense as anything about him."

"Okay, then in the light of that, do either you or Carrie-Ann fancy going into Worcester library and seeing what you can dig up on Mrs Vance? If she was as much of a wild child as Angelo implied, I can't imagine that she got away without so much as a single mention in the local papers when she got into trouble."

"Why do you want that?" Lucy was intrigued.

"Well, if whatever this is runs in the family, and Mrs Vance has a touch of it too, it might explain why Angelo in his turn seemed so worried about her. And if she was into drugs in her youth, I don't want to suddenly find myself surrounded by burly police officers, and them discovering packets of cocaine casually littered about the place! Let's not forget that she'd have had her wild teenage years in the seventies, and there was still something of the sixties' drugs culture hanging on. Not the chemical pills of the nineties' raves, but the old-fashioned weed and coke would have been accessible enough to a young girl who could get her hands on plenty of money – and I reckon Claudia Vance wouldn't have had any scruples about pilfering a few tenners or twenties from her daddy's wallet."

"Blimey!" Lucy gasped. "I see where you're going with this now. Yes, it would make a lot of sense if Mrs Vance had the odd nasty habit, and even more so if she carried on with it when she was pregnant with Angelo. God knows there must have been enough of it about with Jacko Vance and his crew! You can't believe that she never as much as smoked a spliff when she lived with him. Sex, drugs, and rock 'n' roll! Holy-moly, what a life she could have led!"

"…And what might be lingering of it now!"

"Yes, I can see why that might worry you. Okay, I suspect Carrie-Ann will be itching to have a go at that, and she has to walk past the library to go and pick her kids up, so she could kill the odd hour in there quite easily."

Fleur laughed, because Carrie-Ann was always regaling them with the latest celebrity gossip and with great relish, so having the chance to do a bit of sleuthing of her own would be right up her street. *Miller, Bronson & Carter's* premises took up all of a once grand house in one of the side streets off The Tything in Worcester, which was the main street leading out of the city centre past the railway station. The workshops took up the ground floor, and also out in what had been the stables and the odd brick-built garden store, with the offices being upstairs, and what had been the garden acted as much-needed parking space for the company's large vans, but gave access out onto a quiet back street which ran parallel to the racecourse. So it was easy enough to walk from there into the riverside area where the library lay, by cutting down the back ways. Therefore she would hardly be imposing on Carrie-Ann since she cut through that way anyway.

On that happier note she rang off, leaving Lucy relieved that she was back and safe in the pub. But for herself the nagging thought that she was missing something wouldn't leave her alone. She had been halfway towards believing that there was another member of the Vance family living in the big house whom she had yet to meet, but what Lucy had said about the soiled clothes had convinced her otherwise of that. And so she sat on her bed and began an internet trawl for Angelo Vance.

Various YouTube videos came up, and she sat and watched several of them. The first few she hit upon had her wondering whatever there could have been about Angelo to make him such a viral sensation, because to be frank, although he was very easy on the eye, and he actually talked a lot of sense, Fleur couldn't help but think that most of the late-teen/early twenties fans would find him just plain boring. And then one came up which had her sitting bolt upright in bed and gawping at her laptop screen. This was a whole other Angelo Vance! Dishevelled and wild, he made inflammatory statements, peeled off his shirt to sit in just a vest top displaying perfectly honed muscles and a lot of a very manly chest, and had that sexy bad-boy look about him which made sensible women lose control.

"Bloody hell!" Fleur gasped as it came to an end, but then looked at the responses to the video – or vlog, as she supposed it would properly be called. This was the stuff that had fans raving about Angelo! Hundreds of posts commented on this one, some people getting into quite heated online arguments about what he had said.

Too engrossed by now to switch off the bedside light and go to sleep, she opened up a new tab and did a Google search for Angelo's name plus the date of the vlog. To her amazement there were news articles about Angelo's fight with the tech giants trying to get extracts of the infamous vlog taken down, and his protests that it wasn't him who had made it. Quite who else it could have been Fleur couldn't imagine, because aside from the slight slurring in the voice, which rather implied that he'd been more than a tad drunk at the time, the voice was the same, and so were a lot of the mannerisms.

On she searched, feeling a bit as if she was watching for a train wreck, voyeuristically knowing it was about to happen and yet unable to look away. The one she had initially found by sheer good luck happened to be the first of the dodgy vlogs, and the one which had catapulted Angelo from minor online celeb' to compulsive watching. Nine times more over the course of a few years the regular vlogs got interrupted with the explosive and inflammatory ones, and as Fleur skipped forward and watched each one, she could begin to see why they had become such addictive viewing. Even stranger, in the next couple after each of the 'bad boy' ones, Angelo appeared looking pale and – as time went on – often haggard in the aftermath, and these aftermath vlogs were often short and apologetic.

Speculation ran rife as to whether he had gone on drug binges, ex-girlfriends came out of the woodwork to announce sudden break-ups with Angelo after those wild vlogs had been aired, and every time, Angelo's private life went under the microscope of public inspection. There was even some nasty rat-bag of a drug dealer who spoke to one of the tabloids in an 'exclusive', where he gave times and dates of when he had supplied Angelo with some pretty hard-core drugs, though he then went suddenly silent and vanished when the police got a warrant to force the newspaper to give up the man's name.

And what attracted almost as much attention was Angelo's seemingly frantic attempts to get the vlogs removed altogether. Yet time and again he wasn't taken seriously because the videos were uploaded to his own online sites, with the presumption being that he must therefore have done it himself – because who else would have had a secure login to them? His own websites soon had them down, but he couldn't begin to control the rampant 'sharing' which had already gone on, and hundreds of versions and samples were still out there, still being viewed and haunting the online shadows like malevolent ghosts out to taunt him.

In the midst of all of this very public mud-slinging, Fleur found herself feeling increasingly sorry for Angelo, and so, it seemed, had some of his fans who sadly only inflamed the gossip by getting into vitriolic exchanges with his critics. It couldn't have been pleasant for him to have his sex life aired in public, along with all of his private business, and however much he had initially courted fame, the reality must have been grim and potentially frightening. What must it have felt like for him to have girlfriends whom he thought he could trust, then turn on him for a pay-out by a tabloid and their own brief moment of fame, with the attendant encouragement to make their time together into the most salacious of news?

Horrible, thought Fleur, *just horrible. And if the poor man is genuinely unwell, then this is even more unfair. Nobody deserves this amount of invasion of their private life.*

Yet it also explained some of why Claudia Vance was so aggressive if the family had had their trust betrayed so many times. It couldn't have been pleasant for her as a mother to watch her son being dragged through the muck so publicly and so often. *And if she has her own mental health problems, is it any wonder that all the stress might have made her worse?* Fleur sympathised. It made her vow to be more understanding towards both of the Vances where possible. At the end of the day, amazing and potentially valuable though the boxes full of grimoires and tarot cards were, they were still only inanimate objects, whereas the Vances were people who could be hurt and could psychologically bleed if not physically. Did it really matter if something got damaged by them when they owned the damned things? As long as they didn't blame her, she should try to avoid getting into any further confrontations with them.

Those good resolutions got tested badly, however, the moment she arrived back at the house the next morning. Going into the cottage's kitchen, she was relieved to see that all of the grimoires were exactly where she had left them the previous evening. It was only when she turned around to face where she had neatly stacked the other books from the library that she got a surprise. The books were gone!

"Oh hell, no!" she groaned. "What have you done now?"

Dumping her bag on the chair, she didn't even take her jacket off before hurrying across the courtyard. The kitchen door was unlocked, which was suspicious given that Angelo's car was nowhere to be seen, and surely Mrs Vance had no reason to be using the big house's kitchen when she had one so well-appointed in the Dower House?

Muttering under her breath, Fleur strode through to the library and flung the door open, what she saw there making her let rip a string of very unladylike swear words. Somebody had just opened box after box, totally disregarding her own methodical approach. Worse, they had put a substantial number of those books onto the shelves, but in no sane order other than the colour of their binding! Where were the ones she had already catalogued? Which ones were they?

"*Aaaagh!*" she screamed in fury and frustration. Now she would have to start all over again! It was enough to make her swear vigorously for a second time, and what brought her to an abrupt halt was hearing that laugh again, that malevolent and nasty laugh echoing around upstairs.

Stamping out into the hallway, she yelled, "Mr Vance! Mr Vance, this isn't funny! I know you are paying for my time, but I am *not* going to keep doing this work twice over!"

Behind her Mrs Vance's voice said. "Who the hell do you think you are talking to like that?"

Spinning around, Fleur jabbed an angry finger at the library. "Your son, Mrs Vance! The one who did all of *that*!" And seeing that Claudia Vance was about to shout back, Fleur raised her own voice further to say, "Your son – the one who is upstairs laughing at me! The one who thinks it's so bloody funny to totally wreck all the work I've already done on these books!"

Claudia Vance's anger vanished like the air out of a popped balloon, and Fleur saw her struggling to retain her control when she said, "I can assure you that Angelo is not here."

"Well *somebody* is," Fleur insisted. "There's nothing wrong with my hearing, and I definitely heard someone laughing at me when I yelled at finding this."

"I …We …We have someone in working upstairs," Mrs Vance lied. "You must have heard them."

"Well can I speak to them?" Fleur asked angrily. "Because I want to tell them straight that this is no bloody joke!"

"I really don't understand what you are getting so irrationally angry about," Mrs Vance said, obviously trying to deflect Fleur. "No, you cannot go and speak to them. It's none of your business what we do in our own house …or who we employ." That last was so clearly an afterthought that Fleur knew that there was no tradesman up there.

Dragging in a deep breath, and remembering her decision the night before to be more tolerant of these two if they actually were both delusional or something, she forced herself to answer the first part of Mrs Vance's comment.

"I am not getting irrationally angry, Mrs Vance. Nor am I going to get into an argument with you about who did this, since you seem determined not to be honest with me on that matter. But whoever took the books out of the cottage and the boxes, and then put them on the shelves in such hopeless and random order with others from in here has just eliminated all the work I've already done. I do not have an encyclopaedic memory which can just recall which books I've catalogued and which not. I will have to go back through every one of these books and check them against my records. And with the way those ones are mixed in with ten times their number, just getting that done will take me all day."

In truth she could probably do it faster, but she was trying to impress upon Mrs Vance the level of chaos this had wrought. It didn't work.

"But they look so pretty all colour matched like that," Mrs Vance riposted. "Can't you just leave them where they are and work along the shelves? Just do the ones you haven't done so far, and then skip the ones you have?"

Fleur stared at her in disbelief. Had this woman never entered a library in her life? Did she have no concept of how impossible it would be to ever find anything in such mayhem? And then the reply came to her.

"Mrs Vance, how do you think I am going to do what Mr Vance asked me to do in that case, hmm?" Claudia Vance looked at her blankly, forcing Fleur to elaborate, "He wants me to sort out what's worth keeping and what he can safely send to auction. Well I can't do that if I don't separate the books out. Because with no rhyme or reason as to how these books are, I can hardly put on the record, 'the sixth book from the left, on the third shelf down, on the fourth bookcase from the door,' can I? Not if I come back in tomorrow morning and find that *whoever* it is who is doing this, has had another unpacking session in the night, and even these books aren't where they are today."

Mrs Vance tried to brush it off. "Oh, keep all of them! They're only here for decoration, anyway."

Fleur could feel a scream building up inside of her again. They were back to this again – Mrs Vance trying to take over what was done, and going directly against what Angelo Vance himself had specified. "That's not what your son wants doing, Mrs Vance. He specifically told me that he also wants room for his own books in here."

"His books? He doesn't have any books!"

Oh dear God! Who was lying now? Did Mrs Vance really not know her son that well at all? Or was it Angelo who had concocted a fabric of lies just to lure her in? There was no point in arguing further with Mrs Vance whichever it was.

"Very well," Fleur sighed, feeling she had to get out of here and away from Mrs Vance before she said something which would end up getting her fired. "In that case I am going back over to the cottage to continue working over there."

The sly smile that she got from Mrs Vance had Fleur wondering whether this had just been another ploy to get her to focus on the grimoires and tarot decks, but if so, it was about to backfire on her spectacularly. With Mrs Vance still over in the big house doing God-alone-knew-what, Fleur made sure that the cottage door was firmly shut and then rang into work.

"I'm sorry, Mr Harris," she told him, "but this working situation is simply impossible. It's not just me. I don't think any of us could work under these conditions. Can we do as you suggested and have the whole lot taken to the workshops?"

"Absolutely we can," he agreed, "and I shall ring Mr Vance and let him know too. I'll get the lads with the vans down to you straightaway. It's hardly going to matter how they pack things up now, what with the mess that's been made of everything. As long as none of the books get damaged in transit, that's all we need to bother about for now."

"And do you think we can take the grimoires as well?" Fleur pleaded. "Honestly, Mr Harris, I think we may have a collection of almost international importance here, and I'm very loath to leave it so exposed with someone as unstable as Mrs Vance around the place. If Mr Vance is now paying for them to be catalogued too, can we deal with them on the premises as well?"

"We most definitely can!" Harris agreed. "Get them all packed up again and ready to go. I may even come down myself, because I think you're going to need back-up when Mrs Vance finds out what's happening!"

Chapter 9

Feeling that the situation could become very explosive and very fast, Fleur worked at speed to pack up the grimoires, making sure that the boxes were taped shut securely. Then sat praying that the vans would turn up soon, and not daring even to make so much as a cup of tea in case they came as soon as she had made it. The quicker she could get out of here the better!

So it was with enormous relief that she heard the familiar sound of the big diesel engines rumbling into the courtyard. Alec and Tyler were in the first van that made a neat turn in the courtyard and reversed up to by the kitchen door, and she was relieved to see Rob and Joe in the second one pulling just far enough into the courtyard to allow the other one to drive straight out.

"God, am I glad to see you guys!" she almost sobbed. "You're my knights in shining armour today."

Tyler gave his cheeky grin. "Blimey! That's the first time I've been called that!"

It made her laugh and at least that broke some of the tension for her, but she hurriedly warned them, "Watch out for fireworks, because Mrs Vance is somewhere about and she's in full Italian temper mode. Please, can we get the stuff loaded up as fast as possible? I just want to get away from here."

Alec, the team leader, stopped in his tracks and looked at her hard. "Good grief, she really has got you spooked. This isn't like you, Fleur."

"I know, but there's something going on here, Alec, that's really giving me the creeps. Come on inside and I'll show you, but could you others get the boxes that are packed up in the cottage first? If they're already on the van and behind the others, it's the perfect excuse not to unpack them again – and there's a good reason why I want that to happen, but I haven't the time to tell you that now."

"Come on Rob, we'll go and get those," said Tyler, as Joe followed Fleur and Alec into the house.

She took them first into the library. "Look at it!" she almost wept. "What a bloody mess!"

"I'll get the sack-truck," Joe told her, giving her arm a reassuring squeeze as he went past her. "If we get all the sealed boxes straight out and onto the van, Rob can drive that off while the rest of us pack up the remainder. At least we'll have more room to work then."

"Thank you," Fleur said gratefully, already feeling better for having reasonable and sensible people around her. "But come and have a look at this, Alec – that is if we can get upstairs without Mrs Vance having a screaming match!" She led the way straight across the hall to the main stairs and up them, then leading Alec around past the laundry room to the other stairs. Then she froze.

"Oh my God!" she gulped softly, for the padlock was looped over the hasp on the frame and the door was unlocked. Putting her finger to her lips to shush Alec, she leaned in close to him and whispered, "This door was firmly locked the first time I came up here. I only came upstairs looking to make sure that there weren't any other boxes of books abandoned up here."

Suddenly from above them there came a stream of very irate and fluent Italian in Mrs Vance's voice, and Fleur gestured to Alec for them to make a fast retreat. When they got back to the ground floor, she told him,

"I don't know what the hell is going on, but there's someone else up there and it's a man; someone I think Mrs Vance sometimes locks in. If it's not Angelo Vance, then it's his bloody doppelganger, because he's the spitting image of him from a distance. But he's the one who's been playing games with me. When I came in this morning and got so upset at finding all the books messed up, I could hear him laughing at me from up there. And it was a really nasty, evil laugh, like he's not quite sane. You know I'm not easily intimidated, but the thought of crossing a madman puts the frighteners even on me. I mean, what the hell is he like that Mrs Vance feels the need to padlock him in up there? If she feels she can't even trust her own son not to be a danger to her? ...If it really is Angelo, that is."

Alec's eyebrows had gone up and up as she was telling him this, but just as Fleur had the awful feeling he might be thinking that she was making all of this up, there it came again, that nasty, creepy laugh echoing down the stairwell. It stopped Joe in his tracks as he wheeled the sack-truck out with the first of four boxes piled on it, and it made Alec jump in surprise.

"Okay," he said, visibly shaken. "Point taken. That's creepy – definitely creepy! Come on, let's you and me get packing in here."

"Don't worry about what goes in where," she told him, Tyler, and Rob, who had already got the eight boxes secured in the back of the van. "As long as you aren't over-filling the boxes, and not bending the books in any way, it's more important to get them sealed up and away."

The four of them began working at speed, the men taking it in turns to wheel the heavily laden sack-truck out to the van and use its hoist to lift it up to the van's floor. Mercifully, Mrs Vance remained unseen, though they did sporadically hear further burst of irate Italian drifting down from upstairs. Within the hour, Mr Harris had also arrived, for which Fleur was very grateful. Dressed in his inevitable tweed suit, and cream shirt, he could have passed as a well-to-do farmer or country gentleman, and with his touch of grey hair at the temples, carried an air of distinguished authority with an ease that Fleur envied.

As he walked into the library and saw what they

were packing up his jaw dropped. "Good heavens, Fleur! When you told me what was going on I didn't imagine chaos on quite this level! What on earth were they thinking?"

And as if on cue, Mrs Vance's voice came from the midway landing on the stairs,

"What was who thinking?"

"Mrs Vance…" Mr Harris turned and assumed his most business-like posture.

Before he could say anything else, though, Rob went past with the sack-truck, and Mrs Vance let out a shriek that would have done a harpy proud. "What are you doing?" she all but screamed.

"We are doing what we agreed with Mr Vance," Harris said calmly. "We agreed that if it proved impossible to do the job here on site, that we would take the books back to our workshops and do it there."

"No!" Mrs Vance wailed. "You can't do that! You *mustn't* do that!"

"Mrs Vance, there is no 'mustn't' about this," Harris told her, though his tone had got a touch frostier. "This is what I agreed face to face with Mr Vance. And as I told you before, since he is the one paying our bill, what he says goes."

"But he didn't mean it!" Claudia Vance was getting more frantic by the minute. "They have to stay here! *She* has to stay here!"

Mr Harris' voice had reached polar temperature. "*She*? Do you mean Ms Constantine? Because if so, firstly, I would remind you that I will not tolerate our staff being verbally abused or denigrated, and she is most certainly not yours to make arrangements for at will. And secondly, what possible reason do you have for making such a demand? Ms Constantine is professional and trustworthy, and she will do no less of a perfect job working in our facility than she would here."

God bless you, Mr Harris, Fleur thought with relief, feeling a bit of a coward for hiding behind the door of the library so that Mrs Vance couldn't see her right now, but fearing that putting in an appearance would only make matters worse.

"*He* won't like it!" Mrs Vance wailed, and for the first time Fleur thought that there was a tinge of fear in her voice. Who was it that she was so bothered by?

Obviously Mr Harris' thoughts were running along the same lines, because he riposted with, "Who won't? Mr Vance? Why would he not like it when we are doing precisely as instructed by him?"

"My *son* won't!" Mrs Vance snarled back, but then as Mr Harris said,

"Is Mr Vance here, then? Why didn't you say so? Shall we go and ask him?" Claudia Vance went white, and Fleur – who had been covertly watching through the gap by the door's hinges – was worried enough that she was going to faint to hurry out into the hallway to join Mr Harris.

"Mrs Vance, are you alright?" she asked anxiously. "Would you like me to go and get you a glass of water?"

"I don't want water, you silly girl," Mrs Vance snapped, even though she was having to hang onto the stair-rail to support herself. "Why couldn't you do as you were told, and come here and just do the job? Why have you had to make all this trouble?"

"Fleur isn't the one making the trouble," Mr Harris tried to point out, but was taken aback himself as Mrs Vance's torrent of words continued with,

"I don't know why he's so fascinated with you, really I don't! You're not the prettiest girl who's ever come here, and from what I've seen of you, you aren't the nicest either. But who knows why men want what they want? There's no reasoning with them sometimes, especially not when it comes to their obsessions. He thinks you'll be a kindred spirit, but I don't. I think you'll hurt him, just like the others. But you're the one he's taken a shine to, and if he wants you to stay, then stay you must! I'm not going to play the demanding mother keeping him from the woman he wants."

"Who?" roared Mr Harris furiously. "Who are you talking about, woman? Because this is intolerable! I shall be having a very strongly worded conversation with Mr Vance about this, because it is wholly unacceptable for Ms Constantine to be spoken about …to be *used* in such a manner! And depending upon his response, we shall be terminating this contract forthwith, and your boxes can come back here for you to do with as you wish, but *Miller, Bronson & Carter* take the safety of their staff very seriously…"

"*Aaagh*! *Nooo*!" Mrs Vance's wail cut across the remainder of Harris' words. "No! Not Angelo! No don't tell *him* I said that that!" Her slender frame was now shaking with sobs, and Fleur was genuinely worried that she was having some sort of complete mental breakdown. But as she stepped forward to go and try to reach Mrs Vance, the woman turned on her heels and fled back upstairs shouting back at them, "*No*! Don't you *dare* tell Angelo *I* said that! I'll tell him you lied! You're all liars and thieves! He doesn't understand either. Oh mio caro ragazzo. Mio povero dolce ragazzo. Non la meriti. Perché la ami più di me?"

For a moment all of them stood in stunned silence, hearing the door to the stairs above – or so they presumed – being slammed shut, and the weeping fading away as Mrs Vance retreated to the top floor.

"What the hell did she say at the end?" Alec asked of nobody in particular, but Fleur was able to answer,

"My Italian is a bit rusty, but I think she said something like, 'my darling boy', and, 'she doesn't deserve you'. But what was really weird was that last sentence. I'm pretty sure she said, 'why do you love her more than me?'"

"That's strange, even for a devoted Italian mamma," Joe said with a shake of his head. "Reeks a bit of Oedipus, doesn't it?"

"Who was he?" Rob asked.

"Greek bloke who got a tad obseessed with his mum, is the short answer," Alec supplied, "But there really is something wrong with this family if Angelo Vance is jumping his mum's bones, however hidden they think they're keeping it."

"That's just gross," Rob said with a shudder. "For God's sake, let's get this lot loaded up and get out of here." As he went past Fleur he gave her a sympathetic glance and said, "No wonder you wanted out. I don't think I could manage a day here without wanting to smack someone or run like mad to get away."

Even Mr Harris rolled his sleeves up to help with the last of the packing, and in what was possibly a record time even for professionals like them, he was soon leading the convoy of two vans and two cars off down the drive, insisting that Fleur follow directly behind him so that she wasn't the last one to leave.

"Let's put the two vans behind you," he said firmly as they all got ready to go, and the other men had agreed, reversing the vans further up the tarmaced track which ran past the cottage so that Fleur could go ahead of them. It might have sounded melodramatic, but as Fleur's car went out from between the Dower House and the main house, she was sure she heard an angry scream, and it wasn't Mrs Vance!

Chapter 10

On the drive back to Worcester, Fleur was glad that it was a fairly warm day, because she needed the window open and a good stream of fresh air blowing in to stop her from feeling lightheaded. This much stress was doing her no good at all. Whether Claudia Vance was barking mad, and had made Angelo's obsession with Fleur up in her head, or whether he really was fixated with her, it was still disturbing. In fact, the more she thought about it, the more bothered Fleur became. It was one thing to know that somebody fancied you, even if you didn't fancy them back. It was quite another to feel that you were being actively hunted down by someone whose grasp on sanity was tenuous at best.

Luckily Mr Harris must have guessed how unsettling the whole confrontation had been, and wouldn't hear of her going to help unpack, instead making her come into his office, where he plied her with strong tea and a plentiful supply of chocolate biscuits.

"I can't apologise enough," he said sincerely. "We knew that something was strange about the whole request for you to go alone, but please believe me, Fleur, when I say that I had no idea that it would be like that."

He seemed to be struggling to find adequate words to describe the situation, and it occurred to Fleur that in a strange way she was coping better with this than he was. She might never want to repeat the unpleasant experiences which had gone with her divorce, but at least they now gave her some kind of reference point to anchor her emotions with. That had been personally targeted at her, and for far longer than what had gone on at *The Rookery*, and with a lot more at stake for her. Therefore, once she had calmed down from the initial shock, it was easier to put this into context as an unpleasant incident, but not one which was going to be life-changing. This time around she wouldn't have to avoid visiting her mum and sister, for instance, and that helped her.

As the tea did its trick of bringing her firmly back to earth, she felt able to say,

"Please, Mr Harris, don't go in on the attack with Angelo Vance."

He looked at her in astonishment.

"That's very charitable, Fleur, but I really think…"

"…No, I'm not being charitable. I'm serious. What if Angelo genuinely knows nothing of this? I mean, were Mrs Vance's actions those of a woman fully in control of herself? I don't think so, do you? So, if the poor woman is coming apart at the seams, it's a bit unfair to go beating her son up about it, and assuming that it's his fault, or that he could in some way have predicted it."

That brought Harris up sharp as he took on what Fleur meant, and she continued,

"That bit about 'why does he love her more than me…,' well the guys might not be so far adrift talking about Oedipus, because what if Mrs Vance has some bloke hidden away out there who is her lover, and she's chosen him because he's so like her son, at least in looks? I know that sounds a bit fantastical, but it makes a lot more sense of why Angelo Vance comes across all reasonable when we meet him face to face, and then the messages we get relayed through his mother are all over the place." She wasn't going to bring up the strange anomalies with the YouTube videos right now, since she doubted Mr Harris even knew what YouTube was – they were a whole other can of worms, and for all she knew, Angelo might have since had therapy for whatever had ailed him back then, and dragging it back up would only reopen old wounds.

"Oh dear. …Oh, goodness me. Yes, it would hardly be appropriate to cast blame before we are sure where it ought to go," Harris admitted. "I have to say that it does you a lot of credit, Fleur, that you can think so clearly about this. I would quite have understood if you had wanted to make a formal complaint on the matter, especially given your reservations at the start."

Fleur gave him a watery smile, "Well I must admit that the words 'I told you so' have been lurking in the back of my mind. But the truth is that once I began to wonder whether this was a case of one or both of them actually being mentally ill, it changed things for me. Maybe it's because of having a sister who has her own problems, and knowing how some people can be so unsympathetic and cruel, but I try to see whether there might be some genuine reason why someone is behaving as they do, rather than just getting angry with them."

She watched as that sunk in with her boss, and was glad to see that even if he wasn't happy right now, that some of his anger had dissipated.

"I think I'd better go and ring Mr Vance," Harris said, but with little enthusiasm.

"And I'll go and join the others," Fleur said, by now rather glad to get out of the office before the fur started to fly again.

After she'd told Lucy what had happened, though, Lucy's verdict was,

"Harry's just bloody relieved that you aren't going to sue the pants off the company like Claire did hers! Let's face it, with a precedent like that already having gone through a court, you'd be in with a good chance of winning compensation, even in just an industrial tribunal."

"Oh Lucy, no, I wouldn't do that. For a start off, what Claire went through was life-changing and really bloody serious. I'm just a bit shaken and bothered by this, and I meant what I said to Mr Harris – I seriously wonder whether Mrs Vance isn't having a breakdown, and has some bloke hidden away who's the double of her son. For pity's sake, it might be some absolute rogue who is totally taking advantage of her because of that! And she may not have told Angelo about him because the other one has some kind of hold over her. She could be more of the victim in this than ever I am."

"*Hmph*!" Lucy sniffed disbelievingly, but then the door flew open to their tiny office space and a breathless and excited Carrie-Ann burst through.

"Guess what I've found out!" she exclaimed, waving a handful of photocopied pages at them. "I've got the dirt on Claudia Vance! ...Ooh! Fleur! ...What are you doing here?"

"Long story, let's just say that I'm not going back there on my own. But never mind that, what did you find out?" Fleur saw Lucy looking at her askance. "Well, it might have a serious bearing on things, mightn't it? And if Mr H is about to go and rip Angelo Vance a new one, we might need to go and stop him."

Carrie-Ann's eyes swivelled back and forth between them. "Eh? What? What did I miss?"

"I'll tell you later and in gory detail if you want," Fleur promised, "but come on, what did you find out?"

Carrie-Ann flopped down in her chair but with a broad grin on her face. "Well, you were right, Fleur, she didn't escape some notoriety in the local rags! Granted it only ever made it as far as the very local papers, but she certainly raised an eyebrow or two there. Listen to this…" and she picked up the top one of the photocopies and began reading,

"'Yesterday evening police were called to a disturbance in a house in the centre of Cheltenham. At the scene they found a dozen teenagers, all drunk and under the influence of drugs. The house belongs to the stockbroker, Mr Aleister Kingsford, son of the renowned local wartime hero, Major Ignatius Kingsford, and it has been reported that the instigator of the party was none other than the Kingsford daughter, Claudia. A former attendee at the college," …I presume they mean the private college? "…young Miss Kingsford has now been expelled from there, and with no other school in the area willing to accept her, has ended her school days early since she only had four more months to go before turning sixteen." Carrie-Ann looked over the paper. "Sixteen? Fancy getting chucked out at sixteen!"

"Ah, but don't forget, the school leaving age *was* sixteen back then," Lucy reminded her. "It's only comparatively recently that everyone's had to stay in education until they are eighteen unless they have something like an apprenticeship to go to. All of *us* stayed on because we did A-levels, but others in our schools left at that age."

"I know that," Carrie-Ann protested. "It's the bit about no other school wanting her that shocked me. Not one, even at that age and for such a short time!"

Fleur nodded. "She has a point, Lucy. I know you didn't grow up around here, but back in the seventies, there were still loads of private schools in this and the neighbouring counties in what had once been big old private houses. We are still talking about the seventies, aren't we, Carrie?"

"Oh yes! This report is from late 1973."

"So aside from the Malvern colleges which are still going, there were a lot of others around back then. Which means Carrie is right – it was almost unheard of for someone as rich as their family not to be able to bribe *somebody* to take Claudia on, and all the more so precisely because she would leave in only a handful of months' time. She must have been perceived as truly bad for money not to talk like that."

"Fleur's right," Carrie-Ann said with glee. "Claudia Kingsford, as she was back then, was lucky to get away with not being sent to a remand school. There was a fair bit of circumstantial evidence, but nothing concrete, you see. It was only because the police couldn't absolutely prove that she had *supplied* the drugs that she got off with a hefty fine. Or rather her father did, since he was deemed to have been responsible for her because of her age."

She brandished the page and the next one. "You can read all the details for yourselves, but the police were convinced that even if she hadn't bought the drugs herself, that she had quite knowingly invited the drug dealer to the house who did. And that was taken more seriously than it might have been in those days, because one of the boys there had to be rushed to hospital by the police, who raided the place only just in time. He had a really bad reaction to something – possibly LSD? – and was never quite the same again. It was the Kingsfords' misfortune, if you care to think of it like that, that he happened to be the son of a local magistrate."

"Jeepers!" Lucy muttered. "Talk about bad luck! And poor lad. But then again, LSD is nasty stuff, and back then he wasn't the only kid who ended up permanently mentally damaged by it."

"I know Angelo said that her father was almost brutal to her," Fleur added thoughtfully, "but thinking about that incident from an adult perspective, you can't help but have a bit of sympathy for him. She sounds as though she was a right handful in those days, and if he had spent a lot of time apart from the family – as Angelo also said – then the reality of what Claudia was like must have come as a horrible shock to him. And men of that generation were wholly unprepared for dealing with the first generation of truly liberated young women.

"In the sixties, women were still struggling to get a lot of their freedom, but by the seventies it was becoming more of the norm for girls to do many of the things that lads had got away with for generations. But that doesn't mean that their fathers had a clue as to how to cope with them. And with Claudia's mother staying in Italy with the mentally handicapped younger daughter, he was to all intents and purposes thrown into being a single dad, yet without any model as to how to cope with that."

Carrie-Ann had been increasingly nodding along with what Fleur had said. "I think you're right," she now added. "It says in the follow-up article that Mr Kingsford apologised profusely to his neighbours for the disturbance and distress his daughter had caused, and assured them that she would be spending the summer away from Cheltenham. Presumably he locked her up at *The Rookery*?" and she looked to Fleur for confirmation, who said,

"I think he might have intended that, but the way Mrs Vance tells it, she was home alone down there, and had a group of her 'friends' come and stay with her in the Dower House. Again, the way she tells it, she was popular because by that time the main house was a hotel, and there was a swimming pool, and presumably a bar.

"Well, if all of those 'friends' came from the kind of wealthy families who just handed their kids money, and told them to stay out of their way over the summer break, you can imagine that a financially struggling hotel, out in the sticks, wouldn't have been too worried about serving alcohol to underage teens as long as they paid. They were hardly likely to get into cars and drive away to draw attention to what was going on, so what went on at the hotel presumably stayed at the hotel. I also got from Angelo that if Claudia was at *The Rookery*, then her dad was at the Cheltenham house, and if she was sent to the Cheltenham house, then he went to *The*

Rookery as often as possible. So maybe he went away damned near every weekend, which was why she was able to have the party without him knowing it was happening?

"Admittedly, it doesn't make him much of a father, and they sound like they couldn't stand the sight of one another, but then perhaps he was horribly ignorant of just how much trouble Claudia could get herself into? Apparently there was a housekeeper left to keep an eye on her, but again, was this some nice middle-aged lady who'd had a fairly conventional youth herself, and it was beyond her to cope with a wild-child such as Claudia?

"At the end of the day, she would only have been an employee, and Claudia might have threatened to have her dismissed if she told on her? You know how spiteful some teenage girls can be, and Claudia sounds as though she was a right little madam. Let's face it, the tantrums she's thrown now kind of indicate that."

"That does all sound plausible," Lucy agreed. "But that isn't all you've got, surely? What are all of those other pieces of paper?"

Carrie-Ann flashed them another grin. "Oh, there's more alright! I got to wondering how naughty posh girl Claudia Kingsford met up with one of the bad boys of rock, and why on earth her father let her marry him? So I decided to go and look for the marriage record. I was wondering if her father was even there, you see, or whether they eloped and he found out too late to stop it." She paused dramatically, and Lucy suddenly gasped,

"*Nooo*! Shotgun wedding?"

Carrie-Ann high-fived her. "Got it in one! Sweet little Angelo appeared just three months after the wedding, and both of Claudia's parents were there, because her mum acted as one of the witnesses. So clearly, they were both there to make sure that he made an honest woman of her."

"Hang on a moment, though," Lucy protested. "By then it was the mid-nineteen-eighties. It was hardly the end of the world to get married 'just in time' by then, and she was hardly a kid anymore."

But Fleur wagged a finger at her. "If you moved in the Kingsfords' social circle it was. They would have been expecting to be able to put an announcement in the county magazines of their daughter's engagement to some respectable chap, and then a decent year or two later to announce the wedding – preferably at some suitably old church, with the reception at the local country club at the very least. Remember, Aleister Kingsford was some kind of stockbroker, and in those circles a wedding is as much a corporate entertaining event as a family shindig. Bad enough that his wife refused to leave Italy most of the time, so he had nobody to play hostess for him at nice dinner parties where he could schmooze other players like himself. But to have his daughter get knocked up by some scruffy Brummie rock-star must have been the absolute pits by his standards."

Then she thought of something else, because Carrie-Ann had been pronouncing the father's name 'Al-eester', rather than 'Al-ister' or 'Al-as-tair' as most people would have. "How did Aleister spell his name, Carrie?"

Carrie-Ann spelled it out for them.

"That's not the usual spelling of Alastair," Lucy immediately said.

"No, it's not," Fleur agreed, "And the one person I've ever come across who spelled it that way was the infamous Aleister Crowley, and even you two must have heard of him. He was one of a handful of influential men – alongside W. B. Yeats, the poet, and Arthur Edward Waite, who created the most well-known tarot deck – who were responsible for the revival of mysticism in England around the start of the twentieth century. So why would you call one of your children after him if you weren't into all of that? Because that spelling would certainly arouse some comments – albeit not many in later times."

She waved a finger again. "And remember, to the outside world the Kingsfords had presented themselves as a good Catholic family, so they were already living something of a double life. Being nominally Catholic gave them a good excuse to not get involved on things like the local parish councils. That wouldn't have seemed too odd to those around them, and it must have given them the chance to keep themselves at a bit of a social distance without causing comment. After all, as you said, Lucy, by then we're into the modern age. It wasn't like it was the sixteenth or seventeenth century, when being a Catholic could put your life at risk. They could be quite open about it without censure. But if any of their neighbours had known about their pagan inclinations, well, that would have been a very different kettle of fish."

"But how can you be so sure that they were into Aleister Crowley, and …oh, what was that society of his?" Lucy wondered.

"You mean the Golden Dawn?" Fleur supplied, and got a nod. "Crowley didn't actual found it, but he was heavily influential and a pretty unsavoury character, and by the 1920s he was living in Sicily where he had set up a fake abbey. There were stories of bestiality, drug abuse, and neglected children from various random couplings at the place, with nobody taking responsibility for the kids; and there was a big exposé on him when somebody died there because of the awful conditions. In fact, Crowley himself didn't die until 1947, which means that potentially this Aleister's parents – or even Aleister himself – could have known him personally. So yes, in modern times and in polite county society, you wouldn't want to be broadcasting it about that you were buddies with the druggie occultist who regularly scandalised people.

"As for how I can be sure that they were still active pagans, Lucy, well I can't. But somebody very carefully locked all those grimoires and tarot decks away for safe keeping. If they hadn't meant anything to any of the family anymore, why not just get rid of them? That's what most people did, which is why it's so rare to find a big family collection like this still surviving. Most folks would look at those and simply see just handwritten notebooks that dotty old Aunt Agatha was always muttering over, and recall that she was the one who always had too many cats. So why not bin the lot?"

As an ardent cat lover, Lucy laughingly protested, "No such thing as too many cats! …But I take your point. Without the grimoires, you would accept their cover story of being normal Catholics, and never wonder why they weren't part of the establishment country set that goes hand in glove with the Church of England. And even if they weren't actively contributing to those grimoires by then, they certainly cared enough about them to hide them away. Didn't you say to me that Mrs Vance said that they were up under the eaves in the Dower House, and behind a locked door?"

"She did. So even when the family had to let the whole place out to pay off the death duties, they still made sure that those boxes were safe." And now she hammered her point home. "Which makes me wonder just how furious they would have been at Claudia for rolling up with a rock-star? Talk about drawing attention to the family – there's nothing quiet about that, is there?"

Carrie-Ann waved another photocopy. "Coverage of the wedding! Not exactly the society papers, but the music press was out in force. …And here you have it, the photo that says it all. Claudia

Kingsford in her flowing dress, with full bump on display, and dear old Jacko Vance looking stoned out of his mind, while a man who I think we can guess must be her dad, Aleister, standing behind her and looking fit to spit nails through the church door. Not much of the 'respectable' about any of that, is there?"

"Nothing remotely," Fleur agreed, "but almost worse would have been the unwanted publicity. This wasn't a family who would have just laughed off antics like Ozzy Osborne was pulling off on stage in that era, and while I know that Jacko Vance wasn't anything like that, not even in his stage persona, there was still an awful lot of black leather and inverted crosses on display. If Aleister himself had been brought up to believe that the family's dark secrets should never come to light, he must have been frantic.

"…Ooh, and on that train of thought, did you by any chance find out when his own father died, Carrie? I know I saw that huge family bible of theirs, but at the time I wasn't really taking note of who had been alive and when."

Carrie-Ann tapped the side of her nose and winked at her. "Super-sleuth Carrie-Ann is on the case! I got Mum to take the kids to school and got digging in the library as soon as it opened. And yes, you're on the right track if you were wondering whether Aleister's own parents were still alive and so would have known Claudia. I did some digging into the house, because I wondered whether Claudia

Vance had always been in line to inherit it, or whether some male cousin nearly got his paws on the place."

She paused dramatically. "*The Rookery* has been inherited more times by the daughter of the family than not! Now isn't that a turn up for the books?"

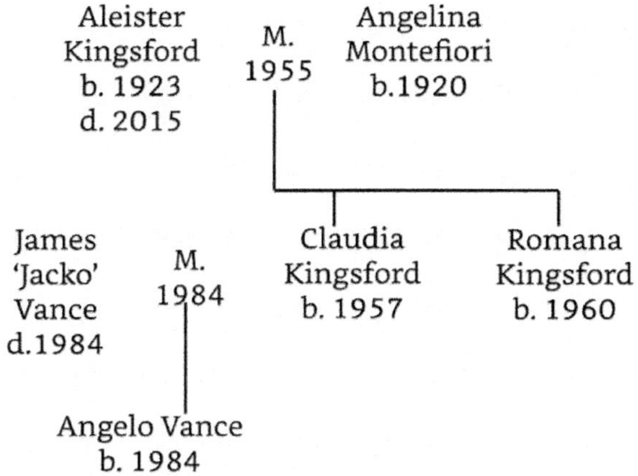

Chapter 11

Carrie-Ann continued, "Claudia was born in November '57, but her father Aleister was born way back in 1923 – so by the time she came to stay with him, he was quite old to have a child of her age."

"That sort of fits with what Mrs Vance told me," Fleur said thoughtfully. "She said her parents met at the end of the war but didn't marry until …I think she said 1955. Aleister Kingsford would have been thirty-four when Claudia was born and her mum could have been the same age or a year or two older. So if you allow for her mother to have been a little old to have her first children, that would potentially explain why her younger sister had problems. Their mum could have been nearer forty by the time the sister arrived, and we all know these days how rapidly the problems escalate for older mums."

Carrie-Ann carried on. "So Aleister inherited *The Rookery* in 1954 when his own father died, and that was when the death duties forced him to let the house out as a hotel for the first time. That all makes sense, too, doesn't it, because if his father wasn't keen on having an Italian daughter-in-law, then they might have had to wait until the old man died before they could get wed?"

"What was his name?" Lucy asked. "The father's, I mean."

"That was the Major Ignatius Kingsford I mentioned before, who was decorated for some act of bravery in World War One. Aleister seems to have been something of a last attempt for a son by his parents, because once I'd got Ignatius' name, I went digging on him, and found that he was born way back in 1895. He was also one of the men who married an heiress to the estate, one Annora Fitzpatrick, who was three years older than him."

"That doesn't sound very Italian," Lucy protested with a frown.

"Ah! You're a generation adrift," Carrie-Ann informed her. "*Aleister*, Claudia Vance's dad, did indeed married someone called Angelina Montefiore. It's his *mum* who was the Annora Fitzpatrick who married Ignatius Kingsford. There's something to the effect that he signed up at the beginning of the war, and being nineteen when it broke out, was amongst the first wave of volunteer soldiers – as opposed to the regular army – who got across to France just in time for the Battle of the Somme in 1916. But of course, that might just be what got put around later on, because that only gets mentioned after World War Two, and as archivists, we all know how skewed tales can get in just one generation!

"What is curious, is that he and Annora married in 1914, and within the year she had their first daughter, Dulcibelle, so the marriage was certainly fertile enough at that stage. Now whether Ignatius didn't make it home often, or didn't want to come home much, but they had to wait until December 1919 for the next daughter to appear, and the third arrived in 1921. But of course, by the time Aleister came along even later, his oldest sister was ten years old, and I found on a voters register that Dulcibelle Kingsford married someone called Harold Westcott when she was just twenty-one in 1935. Now of itself, that's not much, you'd think, but that Westcott chap got killed early on in World War Two and Dulcibelle died of complications in birth around the same time – or that's what I infer from the fact that her date of death coincides with that of a baby girl also called Annora after her grandmother."

She looked up from her notes and grinned at them. "But this is where it gets a bit juicy, because the youngest daughter of the original Annora and Ignatius also dies, but as a kid of about three in 1924 – so just after Aleister was born. However, the middle one then got removed from the household by the courts of the day in 1937 because of what were reported as 'unhealthy attachments' to her by an uncle, who was living in one of the cottages in the house grounds. He got sent to an asylum, and all went quiet at *The Rookery*. I hasten to add that this is all tabloid press stuff, not proper records, but that's not the kind of memory you'd want dredged up if you were Aleister, is it?"

"Hell, no!" Lucy agreed, but Fleur was staring off into space, her brow furrowed in concentration.

"I'm sure I'm not wrong in thinking that there was someone called Westcott who was also involved with the Golden Dawn," she said pensively. "It wouldn't be that man himself, I don't think, but it could well be a brother, a son, or even a cousin."

"*Oooh*! Spooky!" Carrie-Ann giggled. "Well one other thing I can tell you about that time is that Aleister's mother – that's Annora Fitzpatrick, as was – went from being mentioned in the social pages a lot all through the between-wars years, despite having kids at home, to her being a virtual recluse. She went straight from being the mistress of the whole of *The Rookery*, to taking over the cottage in the grounds which the brother had lived in, which I discovered because she wasn't on the voters' roll at *The Rookery*. And that has to mean Annora's brother, surely, because of him already living on the estate. Her husband William Fitzpatrick's family were presumably somewhere else entirely.

"And what's more, I don't think the move was because of death duties, because this is way before Ignatius died! It sounds like he went to live somewhere else and she and the kids stayed over here, so it looks very like they were separated for a while, if not actually divorced. The brother only lingered in the asylum for six months, and then he died under mysterious circumstances, but the newspaper reported on it – because he was still newsworthy after only such a short interval – saying that he'd been claiming that he'd been hexed by his mother and sisters!"

"Hang on a moment," Fleur interrupted. "Mother? Who was his mother?"

"Annora," Lucy said impatiently, but Fleur shook her head.

"No, no! Annora was Ignatius' *wife*, not his mum! So wasn't she therefore the molester's *sister*? What was his name, Carrie?"

"Oh..." she squinted at a printout. "Erm... Wantelo Fitzpatrick! What a name!" She flipped a page then returned to it. "I've just got the names Loretta and William Fitzpatrick as the parents of Annora, so presumably his parents too."

Fleur frowned. "And you said sisters, as in more than one? But I thought at least one of them died?"

Carrie-Ann was almost bouncing on her seat in excitement. "No, no! Now *you're* getting the generations mixed up! It was Annora and Ignatius' *daughter*, Ismena, who died! So she would have been Wantelo's niece. Therefore, if Wantelo was accusing his mother and his sisters of hexing him, then that mother has to have been Loretta – his and Annora's mum – and the sister either Annora herself or some other sisters.

"Anyhow, as nice young ladies of a certain class, Wantelo's nieces would never have been allowed inside a prison to visit back in those days. It was Morwenna, the middle one of Annora and Ignatius' girls who got molested, and who was allowed to come home once nasty uncle Wantelo was locked up after the trial. She went to live with her mother at the cottage. Gosh, those women really did control what was going on at *The Rookery*! I wonder how Annora and her mother did it? How did they get to a man in prison?"

Okay," Fleur said in some exasperation, "but in those notes does it say who the other sister was? Because if what's-his-name…"

"Wantelo," Lucy supplied.

"…If Wantelo was saying his sisters – plural – helped his mother hex him, then there had to be another girl in that generation besides Annora."

"Oh gosh, I see what you mean," Lucy breathed, staring off into space and clearly thinking hard.

Carrie-Ann was going through her notes like a terrier after a rabbit. "Got it!" she cried triumphantly. "A sister called Kadilia! There was Annora, then Wantelo, then another boy called Muldobrai, and then Kadilia."

"Hell's teeth!" Lucy hooted. "Where on earth did they dig those names up from?"

As Carrie-Ann only shrugged, Fleur said cautiously, "I think they might be Romany names, you know. I recall seeing some old newspaper reports where such names were mentioned.

"Romany?" Lucy gasped. "How the heck would Romanies get their hands on an English country estate?"

"Beats me," Fleur admitted. "I'm just saying that that's the context in which I've come across names like that before."

"How bizarre," Lucy murmured, and Carrie-Ann agreed.

Meanwhile Fleur held her hand out for the photocopies, because in her excitement Carrie-Ann was letting them get all mixed up. While Carrie-Ann continued to speculate wildly to Lucy about romantic gypsy lovers, Fleur got the photocopies into something more like date order, which was why she spotted something which Carrie-Ann had missed.

"Hold on a moment, folks, the first lot of death duties which cripple the estate come long before Ignatius dies. It's the death of *Annora's* father – that's Ignatius' father-in-law and Claudia Vance's great-grandfather, William Fitzpatrick – back in 1930 at the good age for that generation of seventy-one, that caused them to have to move out of *The Rookery* for the first time. Annora may certainly have inherited the place from him, and was therefore the owner as named on the documents you found, Carrie, but the scandal with the 'uncle' didn't happen until 1937. In 1930 they only went as far as the Dower House, and leasing the main house out for the first time. And if this electoral role is right, Carrie, they all went to live at a house in Hereford in '37 – which they just rented as an expediency rather than buying by the look of it – not to any cottage in the grounds.

"Hmm, I wonder what went on that this brother of Annora's – him with the glorious name of Wantelo – even had access to his sister's children? Was he living at the Dower House with them, or at least in the grounds, still? And why didn't *he* inherit instead? Because if he'd contested the will, back then, as a man he'd have been in a strong position to receive at least half of everything, and that would have meant the estate being sold unless Annora and Ignatius could have bought him out.

"Or was the offending 'uncle' even a blood relative, such as Wantelo, or just someone they called 'uncle', as would have been normal for a friend of the family back then? That report you found in the newspaper of the day only calls him an uncle, Carrie. They don't actually give his name. We've just assumed it was him because he's the one we know of. Had Wantelo and the other boy died by then? …Because if they had, that makes far more sense of Annora inheriting over them."

Carrie-Ann scrunched up her nose in distaste. "Well, whoever he was, maybe the creepy 'uncle' did his fumbling when they went on visits to the old house? If it had become a hotel by then, presumably there wouldn't have been any problem with the whole family getting rooms for the weekend? If they were in that well-to-do social set, maybe they went there for parties?"

"That could be it," Fleur admitted, "but I suspect that what they call a cottage, where the 'uncle' was possibly living, was something a lot larger than what we think of by the name. If we're not seeing it on the estate now, it's probably because it got sold off in the second round of death duties, being marketable as a decent rural family home. More to the point, surely it's more likely that Annora wanted to return to her family home often and took her kids with her, even if Ignatius didn't? Perhaps she, more than her husband, wanted to return to living there, but couldn't until they were financially more secure again? And let's not forget that in the 1930s, England wasn't even close to coming out of the Great Depression, so cash was pretty short, even for well-off people like this family. Whoever they were, they'd have been struggling to make that death duty payment to the government."

"Sorry, but who was it who died 1930, again?" Lucy asked.

Fleur looked up from the pages. "That's the great-grandfather, William Fitzpatrick, who Mrs Vance showed me in the family bible – Annora's father and therefore Claudia Vance's great-grandfather, and the chap who had a brother who was a monsignor in the Catholic Church, if I remember rightly. So that generation were really trying to keep the illusion of devout Catholicism going, but after all, William was born in 1859, so very much the Victorian gent.

"Hmm… If this family tree that you found online and printed out is correct, Carrie, William Fitzpatrick looks very much as though he was picked out as a suitable husband for a Loretta Boswell –

Annora's mum – whose family already owned *The Rookery*. I reckon it was in order to maintain that appearance of decency if they were hiding their pagan lights from view behind their Catholicism, because they married in 1870, and that's still five years before the Theosophical Society was founded."

Lucy looked bemused. "The *what* society?"

"Sorry," Fleur laughed, "I tend to forget that you didn't get into this in your studies like I did. Okay, so long-story-made-short, the Theosophical Society was founded in 1875 in New York, and its intention was to reconcile Eastern and Western philosophies, especially in the light of the fashionable fascination with places like Egypt. Members went as far afield as India to study Buddhism, and they were positively modern in wanting to found a universal brotherhood without discrimination on the basis of race, creed, or colour."

"Wow! How 1960s! That's pretty forward thinking for 1875!" Lucy exclaimed.

"It was, and in amongst its investigations were those into the occult, but its real significance in our case is that it was the first time you get that veneer of respectability put on pagan practises – which is why I said that William and Loretta's marriage five years before then could have been to keep up appearances. Sadly, it wasn't long before the Society split into two because of internal disagreements, one half of which became known as the Hermetic Lodge, and that's where I've come across the surname Westcott before."

"*Oooh*, as in Dulcibelle's husband?" Carrie-Ann suddenly connected.

Fleur nodded. "Yes, but remember that Dulcibelle was William and Loretta Fitzpatrick's granddaughter, so a fair way on in time from when the famous Westcott was lecturing at the Hermetic Lodge and them trying to keep all things pagan hidden. It still makes it a damned interesting connection, though, as if these families kept in touch with one another – or at least some branches of them did, even if the main ones didn't so much. But what you need to know is that the Hermetic Lodge spawned the Hermetic Order of the Golden Dawn – yes, *the* famous Golden Dawn – along with a hefty dose of rituals taken straight from the Freemasons."

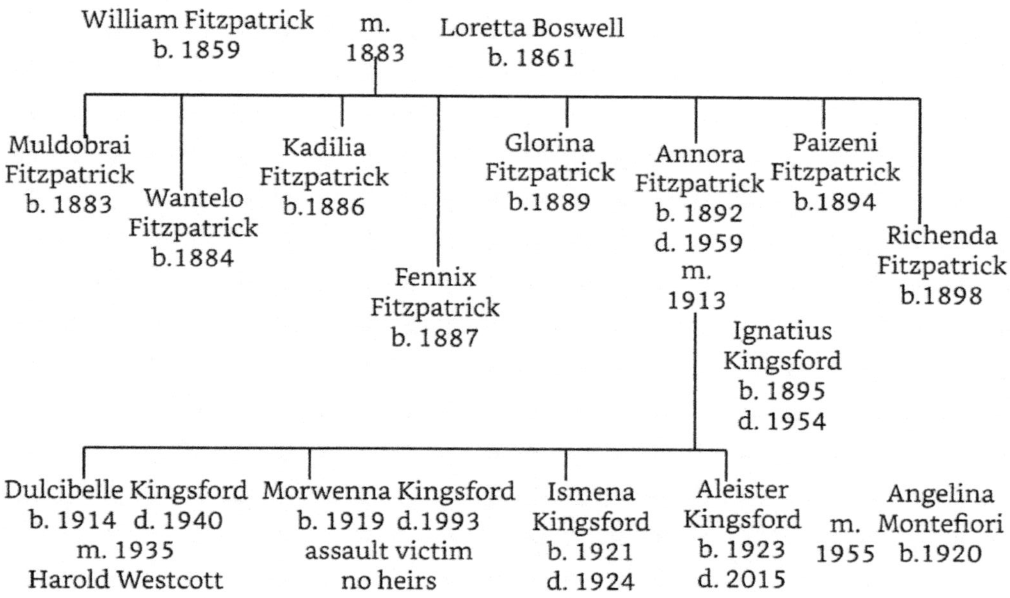

William Fitzpatrick b. 1859
m. 1883
Loretta Boswell b. 1861
Muldobrai Fitzpatrick b. 1883
Wantelo Fitzpatrick b.1884
Kadilia Fitzpatrick b.1886
Fennix Fitzpatrick b. 1887
Glorina Fitzpatrick b.1889
Annora Fitzpatrick b. 1892 d. 1959
m. 1913
Ignatius Kingsford b. 1895 d. 1954
Paizeni Fitzpatrick b.1894
Richenda Fitzpatrick b.1898
Dulcibelle Kingsford b. 1914 d. 1940 m. 1935 Harold Westcott
Morwenna Kingsford b. 1919 d.1993 assault victim no heirs
Ismena Kingsford b. 1921 d. 1924
Aleister Kingsford b. 1923 d. 2015
m. 1955
Angelina Montefiori b.1920

Chapter 12

"Bloody hell!" Lucy gasped. "The funny handshake brigade? But then that makes sense when they were so incredibly secretive that they could place men at the top of institutions like the police even in modern times."

"You're catching on," Fleur said with a smile. "These are people who practically suck up secrecy with their mother's milk. Now, if I'm recalling my reading back at uni right, if William was a Freemason, he couldn't have been a Catholic, and vice versa. They were mutually exclusive. So I think we can rule out any Masonic connections specifically for him. But then when you remember that the Spanish Inquisition wasn't disbanded until 1834 – a mere twenty years before William was born – then the Catholic Church wasn't exactly short of secretive institutions within its ranks even as late as his own father's days."

"As late as that?" Carrie-Ann gasped. "I thought the Inquisition died out long before then!"

"It did in other countries," Fleur confirmed. "But in Spain you could almost say that they were there by royal appointment, and so they continued to be very powerful there for much longer than anywhere else other than Italy – although don't forget that even by then you aren't talking about a unified Italy as yet, but lots of fractured independent states, which is possibly why the Inquisition managed to hang on for as long as it did. …But to get back to Claudia's great-grandfather William, where do you think that brother of his who is Monsignor Alberto Fitzpatrick was?"

"Not Spain, surely?" Lucy said incredulously.

"Spain," Fleur confirmed. "So what better cover for our pagan lot here on the outer reaches of Worcestershire, and a spit and a whistle away from the Welsh border at a time when there was a huge resurgence in Celtic mythology, but to have a daughter marry the brother of a monsignor in the Catholic Church? Because you can bet your boots that back in the mid-nineteenth century the disbandment of the infamous Inquisition had made the news over here!"

"Good grief, they were covering their tracks," Lucy agreed. "I wonder why?"

"I think so," Fleur agreed. "So, we were talking about circumstances surrounding Morwenna, daughter of Ignatius and Annora, who was the lass who got molested by *somebody*, weren't we? And about who amongst the family died when. Well William, Morwenna's grandfather, died in 1930 having outlived his wife, who was originally Loretta Boswell, born in 1861 and who died in 1913. And I'm thinking now that had she lived for long enough, that Loretta would have insisted that her daughter Annora inherit the house – just as she had – and if not her, then her granddaughters Dulcibelle or Morwenna should be the one to have *The Rookery*, because in her eyes that would have been the direct mother to daughter line of inheritance, and quite disregarding her son-in-law Ignatius! Of course, we still need to find a date of death for William and Loretta's sons – that's Annora's brothers who could have contested the inheritance – to confirm this idea. However, despite Annora outliving her father William, for the first time in several generations, the house got passed down to a man, i.e., to Ignatius, the son-in-law.

"Now doesn't that make you wonder whether once Loretta died, and in light of this very liberated and un-Victorian female attitude to succession, if William told his son-in-law Ignatius that he was to make damned sure that the house passed to his own son, Aleister? After all, for William, Aleister was still his grandson by direct descent, so he was very much keeping it within the family even if the inheritance had to go via son-in-law Ignatius first. Admittedly, by the time the First World War and the influenza epidemic of 1919 seem to have done their worst to William and Loretta's brood, there was only Annora left to have kids and keep the line going.

"Which, by the way, kind of confirms that whoever the molester was, he was unlikely to be Annora's brother, Wantelo. Because if the molester died within the same year he got sent down for his sins, then that has to be 1937 or maybe '38 by the time it came to trial, and his father had died back in 1930. So there would have been no good reason at the time of William's death in 1930 that Wantelo couldn't have inherited. That in turn means that if he didn't inherit, then he's unlikely to have been alive in 1930, let alone 1937.

"And you have to see that inheritance matter in the light of William then pushing for his son-in-law Ignatius to take over the estate. If he felt that strongly about it, why wouldn't he have prioritised his actual son Wantelo over the man his daughter had married? And this copy of the census, Carrie..." and she brandished the offending sheet in the air, "shows that up to the 1901 census there had been *three* sons plus two more daughters besides Annora and Kadilia.

"In fact, Loretta was having a child about every eighteen months to two years, and Annora wasn't even the oldest. So when Loretta died on 1913, she couldn't have known that her heritage would run so short in the female line as to make it hard to pass on that way. Moreover, her husband was still alive, as well, and so were her sons! So there's no way she could have overridden all of them in her daughter's favour when she wouldn't have been seen as the owner anyway in those days – William would.

"...And what I was saying a moment ago now really comes to the fore, because I think that Loretta herself was possibly the daughter of a Romany gypsy on her mother's side..."

"Good grief, how can you tell that?" Carrie-Ann cut in to demand.

"Because on the marriage certificates that you've got the info on here, Loretta's mother's maiden name is Annie Petulengro, and her father is Harold Boswell, farrier."

"But how the heck do you know that signifies a Romany?" Carrie-Ann wondered.

Fleur laughed. "Ah well, that's because of my own family history. You all know about the Greek side, but on the other I had a granny who was herself the daughter of a full-bloodied Romany. She taught me how to read the tea-leaves," then saw Lucy looking at her tea mug and laughed again. "Sorry, Lucy, but if you want me to do a reading, you'll need to have a cup of proper china tea with the big tea-leaves. I can't do a thing with the leavings from a Typhoo teabag!"

Lucy, who preferred her tea as black as night and thought green tea was for hippies, pulled a face. "Damn! I thought you might be able to give me the numbers for the lottery on Saturday night."

"Sadly not," Fleur laughed back. "If I could do that, I wouldn't be working here! …But looking at this print-out of the online family tree again, it looks very much as though whoever did it knew their stuff, because they've linked Annie Petulengro through the documents with the birth of Anselina Petulengro in 1839. It's lucky that Annie's father was working as the farrier on *The Rookery's* then substantial estate, because if they'd been fully itinerant gypsies her birth probably wouldn't have been recorded at all in the 1841 census."

Then she stopped and gasped, not quite able to believe her eyes. "Oh my God!"

"What!" Lucy demanded. "Don't keep us in suspense."

Fleur gave a little giggle. "Well, I don't know where that family bible came from that Mrs Vance showed me. I'm guessing that it arrived at *The Rookery* with William Fitzpatrick, but the Fitzpatricks weren't the owners of *The Rookery* in the previous generations, not by a mile."

Carrie-Ann, always the one to scent a scandal, sat up with wide eyes. "Ooh! Do tell!"

Fleur laughed. "See here? William Fitzpatrick, born in County Clare, *Ireland.* Well, that's one heck of a long way from western Worcestershire, isn't it? William marries Loretta in 1881, so he's old enough not to need parental consent, and of course back then as Catholics, they'd still have had to legally get married at a registry office too, which is the record we've got here. He's shown as the son of Joseph Fitzpatrick, also from County Clare, so I think we can safely say that the Fitzpatricks only get their hands on *The Rookery* with this late-nineteenth-century generation. That long line of relatives in the 'family' bible has nothing to do with *The Rookery* before William! So much for Mrs Vance thinking that her father's lot were the hereditary lords of the manor. Or if they really were, then it wasn't *this* manor!"

"But who did own *The Rookery* back then?" Lucy wondered.

"Hang on a tick, I'm just searching! …Ooh! The 1841 census has someone called Henry Kyrle-Quain as the owner of the house, with his mother, Lady Felicia Kyrle-Quain living in the Dower House with her manservant Henrik Bitanyi."

Lucy's jaw dropped further. "Henrik Bitanyi? That doesn't sound very English! Doesn't sound Irish, either!"

Fleur grinned back at her. "My best guess would be Hungarian, and he was probably some wealthy Hungarian nobleman's servant when he travelled over here, and then Henrik made a run for it. But what's got my imagination running wild is that Henry Kyrle-Quain is a young man of twenty-four, and his widowed mum is only forty-two – gosh, she married young, didn't she, wonder why there were no other kids – yet she's living in a house with a manservant who is just twenty, and with no other servants."

Carrie-Ann gave a giggle. "Do you think Henrik was serving the dowager between the sheets as well?"

"It seems pretty likely, given that by the 1851 census Lady Felicia is back as the owner of *The Rookery*, and living with her is Henrik Boswell, her butler, though now there are other servants there."

"*Sheesh*! It's one damned scandal after another with that lot!" Lucy exclaimed. "So what happened to the son?"

"Let's see if we can find out," said Fleur, grabbing her laptop and heading into a Google search. It didn't take long. "Sir Henry Kyrle-Quain, extinct barony of Quain of Foxwood, lost his family's fortune at cards and ended his days in a debtors' prison in 1846." She looked up at her friends. "So what's the betting that Henrik Bitanyi was a card sharp? A few sleights of hand, and before he knows it, poor Henry K-Q has lost his home to his mum's bit on the side, and he's having to pack his bags?"

Outside of the room, the long-case clock in the hall struck two o'clock.

Lucy groaned. "Damn, that's my lunch-hour over with. I can't really sit around doing this anymore."

However, Fleur waved her back down. "No, this is all relevant, Lucy. Don't you see? If we're going to establish the ownership of all of those books, we've got to know who owned the house and when. Selling a set of family grimoires with this kind of full back-story is only going to increase the interest in them, and if the potential sale price increases, then even if Angelo Vance doesn't want to sell right now, then at least the insurance value we give him will be valid."

"You have a point," Lucy conceded. "Okay then, just a few minutes longer. So, we're back at least a hundred and fifty years now, right?"

Fleur nodded. "More or less. And going back to those censuses of 1841 and 1851, we've got Henrik Bitanyi presumably getting his leg over Lady Felicia in the big house, and Anselina's – a.k.a. Annie's – father, Josef Petulengro, along with the rest of their family, working as the farrier and horse man on the estate. Now given how many Romanies at that point in history came to western Europe from Hungary, what would you bet that they knew one another?

"Josef carried on working with the horses, but presumably young Henrik catches Lady Felicia's eye and ends up in the house? And by 1851, young Anselina/Annie is now Lady Felicia's lady's maid, and Josef is now head coachman. And his wife, Mezelly Petulengro, is now the cook! Two other daughters, Loverin and Lamentina, are working in the house, and two boys, Teiso and Shadrach, are general handymen about the place, looking after the garden with another gypsy – going by his surname – Harodain Boswell, as head gardener, but who strangely is living alone in the coach house and not with the rest of the family. That rather confirms that Josef by now has moved into the main house. And I'm more than a bit curious about the fact that it's this gardener who has the English gypsy surname of Boswell. Who is the Boswell who's Loretta's father? Is it him or Henrik? Did one of them anglicise a gypsy surname to fit it?"

"When does Lady Felicia die?" Carrie-Ann wondered.

Another quick search revealed that Lady Felicia's death in 1856 was reported in the newspapers of the day, primarily because she was the youngest daughter of someone who had made a name for himself during the Napoleonic Wars.

"She was sixty-three, so not young but not that old, either," Fleur told the others. "No surviving children, but then that's not so surprising, because if she was already in her late forties when she started enjoying herself with Henrik, she was unlikely to get pregnant again by him."

She flipped another of the photocopies over. "But by 1861 Henry Boswell, as Henrik now appears to be calling himself, is married to Annie, and they have baby Loretta – gosh that family had a thing about girls' names beginning with 'L'! – and a three-year-old boy called Elias. So it sounds as if Henrik/Henry was also enjoying himself with Annie before they married! And although Boswell is well known as a gypsy surname, it's a lot more English – and therefore sort of respectable – than Bitanyi. Hmm, wonder what happened to Harodain Boswell, the gardener? He seems to vanish. What a lot of curious name changes!"

"So remind me, when did William Fitzpatrick marry into the family?" Carrie-Ann asked.

"Err… 1880," Fleur supplied, "and I'm guessing that 'Henry Boswell' – whichever man he turns out to have been – was dead by then if he was born around 1821. I know he'd only be about fifty-nine, but equally, in the Victorian era people did die younger. That name is not on the 1881 census print-out, anyway, and if he had been, surely he would have been named as the owner, not William, Henry's son-in-law? What I do find interesting is that Mezelly and Josef Petulengro are still living there, along with the rest of the family. Whatever arrangement they came to with William Fitzpatrick, in that 1881 census when he first appears, it's very much a case of him living with them, and not the other way around, despite him being listed as head of the household. He moved in with his wife's grandparents and his mother-in-law!"

She turned and high-fived Lucy and Carrie-Ann. "I think we've found our witches whom the grimoires belong to!"

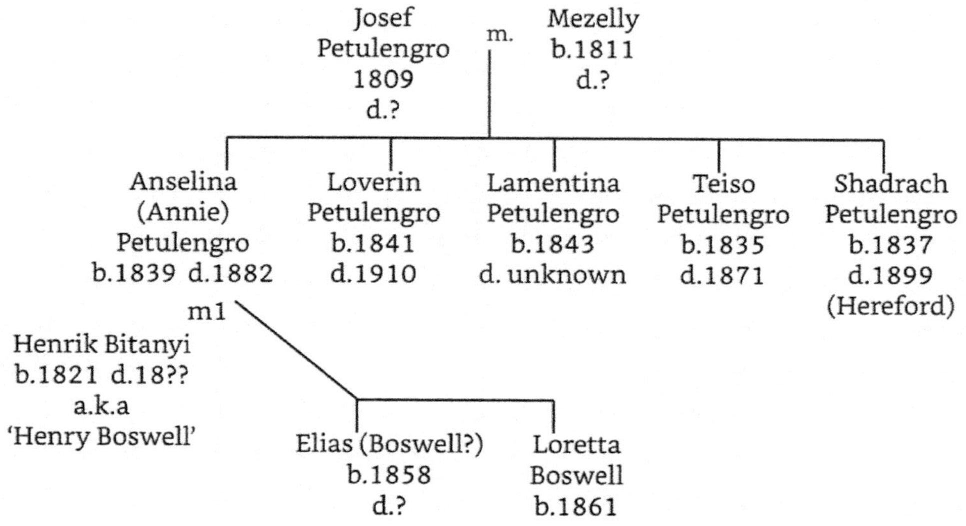
Josef
Petulengro
1809
d.?
m.
Mezelly
b.1811
d.?
Anselina
(Annie)
Petulengro
b.1839 d.1882
Loverin
Petulengro
b.1841
d.1910
Lamentina
Petulengro
b.1843
d. unknown
Teiso
Petulengro
b.1835
d.1871
Shadrach
Petulengro
b.1837
d.1899
(Hereford)
m1
Henrik Bitanyi
b.1821 d.18??
a.k.a
'Henry Boswell'
Elias (Boswell?)
b.1858
d.?
Loretta
Boswell
b.1861

Chapter 13

"Hang on a tick," Lucy protested, "would they have been literate as travelling folk? No disparagement to the Roma, but even in this day and age, the low level of literacy in those communities is a cause for concern, so would it have been any different back in an age when there were only charitable schools for a few kids?"

Fleur smiled. "I think you're underestimating the incentives they would have had to get literate. Come on, they've moved up in the world and with nothing to stop them from staying there except their own limitations. In their shoes, wouldn't you want to make sure that all of your kids could read and write? I bet Mezelly couldn't when she started working as the cook, but I'd equally bet that it didn't take her long to grasp that she'd need to, if only because people like the local butcher would have presented her with written bills. She might never have sat down and read a newspaper, for instance, but within her world she'd have soon learned that skill. And the same goes for Annie once she started working as Lady Felicia's maid."

"That tracks," Carrie-Ann agreed. "So what I found out has helped?"

"Helped?" Fleur said with a huge smile. "It's thrown the doors to understanding what's going on wide open! Now if I find a name, it's going to make a lot more sense to me of who is being talked about, or who might be signing their name." She stood up and took a deep breath. "Right then, time to get down to the nitty-gritty, and get those grimoires unpacked!"

Fleur's first challenge was where to work. Lucy and Carrie-Anne were going to use their main workshop area to do the cataloguing in, but Fleur felt the need to spread the grimoires out in order to see just what she was working with, and there was one place where she could do that without disturbing anyone else. Up in the attic space, where the Georgian and Victorian servants had once had their bedrooms, there was now a large open loft area. The decision to create it had come about when the company had needed to deal with the restoration of some antique and very long curtains, and, not wanting them to get damp by using the cellars or former outbuildings, Sue and her team had created the workspace in the attic. Along one side there was a workbench which ran the full thirty feet of the attic, but there were also trestle tables which could be set up down the centre of the long thin room, the whole area being lit by north-facing skylights as well as the original small end windows, so as to not bleach anything delicate with direct sunlight.

So now Fleur went in search of Sue, and asked if she could take over the space for a while.

"I'd also like you to come and inspect the fabrics when I've got them all out," she told Sue. "It's not remotely high-status stuff, but I think you might find it interesting. And if you can give me a clue as to dates of any of the fabric, that would be really helpful."

"Sounds interesting," Sue agreed. "Give me a call when you need me and I'll come and take a look."

However, the next challenge was getting the boxes up there. With the company being in such an old and listed property, there was no lift up to the attic space, and Fleur knew it would take her ages – not to mention it being exhausting – if she had to go up and down the four flights of stairs with just an armful of them at a time. It was time to butter up the men!

Finding them doing nothing more urgent than cleaning the vans, Fleur bribed them with promises of packets of biscuits for tomorrow, and soon the men were carrying up a box at a time between two of them. Paper in such quantity was extremely heavy, and Fleur was under no illusion that getting up all those stairs carrying one box might do some real damage to a back, so she fully understood why they wanted to share the loads. Even so, they were pausing at the offices on the first floor to flex cramped muscles, and Fleur was effusive in her thanks for their help.

As soon as the first boxes were up there, Fleur began unpacking, at first just keeping the grimoires in their cloth coverings. She started with the ones she'd already looked at, but keeping them still wrapped at this stage. What bothered her was that as she was working, some of the parcels she picked out felt like old friends, comfortable and familiar, but there were some that had what she could only describe as a nasty vibe coming off them. And as best she was able to tell at this stage, she had the feeling that it was some of the more modern ones that she was getting that sensation of revulsion from.

It took her most of what was left of the afternoon to get the boxes unpacked even to that stage, because she wanted to be careful with them. At least the tarot decks were easily identified simply by virtue of them being much smaller, and there weren't that many of them packed alongside the books, not all in one crate. It certainly made her wonder how Mrs Vance could have known she had a collection of cards if she hadn't gone through that many boxes. Did Mrs Vance know more about these than she was letting on? Had someone, such as her father, told her about them, albeit with a warning never to dabble with them?

Once she had them all neatly spread out along the workbench it was time to call Sue up. Clutching her notebook in her hands and primed to start making notes, she said to Sue,

"I'd like your reaction to these and any clues you can give me about dates. Apart from a few, I don't think they've been disturbed at all – although that raises a lot of questions about how Mrs Vance knew or presumed that they are all grimoires! But that's a question for another day when I've got them all unpacked.

"There could be nothing more than diaries in some of these wrappings, and that's why I'm being cautious, because things like handwriting might not overlap between volumes. So what they're wrapped in might be the best clue we have as to dates for some of them. I've had to put number tags on each one just so that I know which one I'm referring to in my notes, but the dating sequence is likely to be all over the place in their current order."

Luckily Sue was as intrigued as her, and looked along the workbench at the long, double line of packages. "Good grief, you've potentially got quite the collection here, haven't you? Like you said to me downstairs, these aren't going to be in the price range of first edition novels or anything, but with the current high interest in the arts and artefacts of ordinary people, the market value of these could be a lot higher than if they'd been discovered fifty years ago.

"Right then, let's start with your number one. …I'd say that this is really good quality cotton, so not the kind of thing you'd expect to find in a working-class house. But if this was discarded as too worn in a better household – and looking at that faded and thin patch where someone's head once rested on this pillowcase, that's not an unreasonable assumption – then I think that this one might date from the end of the nineteenth century. The embroidery is fine work of the style that was fashionable then, if not particularly fancy, so more country house than stately home."

And so they worked their way along the line, Sue carefully unfolding the pillowcases or pieces of cloth so that she could see them, but not taking the contents out as yet. That was for Fleur to deal with. However, by the end of the day Fleur had a long list of details for each of the items, and some idea of where they might go in terms of dates. With Sue's help, she resorted the books into something like date order, although that was very much to within two or three decades at a time.

What she did notice was that it confirmed that the earliest parcels were the ones with which she felt most comfortable. There was something very homely and grounded about those, with even Sue saying how endearing some of the simple embroidered flowers were.

"These are more like I would expect to see coming from a normal family," she said, as with a smile she carefully smoothed the fabric on one of the oldest items. "Look at that poppy. Just lovely! And cornflowers, ragged robin, and ox-eye daisies. These are very much meadow flowers, not plants you'd find in a manor garden – or at least not by this time. But so well executed that you can tell exactly what they're meant to be. I tell you, Fleur, these could fetch quite a good price just as a collection of antique folk embroidery."

Fleur placed her hand on the old cloth and felt a warm tingling sensation which Sue was obviously oblivious to. It was something which she associated with handling Grandma Rose's tarot deck, or rather the one she kept for general readings. There were a couple of special decks which she had kept for doing finer work with which Fleur had had less experience of, but which were still carefully packed away at her mum's house. Until now Fleur hadn't thought much about ever using those decks. They were just precious memories of her grandma. But now she was hoping she could remember enough of what Grandma Rose had taught her, because she had a feeling she was going to need it.

Leaving the attic, she went downstairs to where Lucy was just locking up the workshop for the night.

"Well, the good news is that once we got past the packing cases where the Vances had done their worst, the other stuff has been packed up in some sort of logical order," she told Fleur as they walked out together. "Carrie-Ann and I can crack on with those tomorrow without any problems, so you can focus on the grimoires."

"Thank you for that," Fleur said with a smile, "because I think they might prove more interesting than we suspected."

By the time she got home there was that heavy feeling in the air that said that there was a good storm brewing, but for once Fleur wasn't wholly convinced that it was just the weather. The weather forecast said that there was heavy raining coming in during the evening, but nothing about thunder or lightning, and yet Fleur had the kind of prickly feeling on her skin that normally she associated with a good summer thunderstorm. *Trouble's brewing*, she thought as she unpacked her bit of shopping she'd brought in with her – including the promised biscuits for Alec's team – and try as she might, that evening she just couldn't settle to anything.

At first, she put it down to her strange experience at *The Rookery* still haunting her which, her common sense told her, would not be so unreasonable. To learn that someone was obsessed with you ought to be unsettling when it was somebody you hardly knew. And yet in her heart of hearts, Fleur knew that that wasn't it – or at least not the main part of it. The one good thing was that she knew it wasn't anything lurking in her own flat.

The very reason she had bought this place once her divorce settlement had come through, and she'd returned to Worcester from university, was because this had been a new-build. It stood on the site of one of the oldest inhabited parts of Worcester and within easy walking distance of work, but her flat was right up on the second floor of the low-rise block, albeit not exactly a penthouse, and so a very long way up from anything which might have got raked over during the excavations to put in the foundations. It had been a quite deliberate choice to have a top floor flat at the back of the complex, despite its proximity to the elevated section of railway line which ran close by. Few trains ran at night in this era of reduced services, and she was on the other side of the buildings to one of the few nightclubs Worcester possessed, so she never got disturbed by late-night revellers. All of which meant that she felt totally safe having her windows open on warm nights, and tonight she opened the French window onto her bedroom's tiny Juliet-balcony.

As the rain began lashing down, luckily being driven away from her side of the complex, she stood and let herself be taken over by the elements. Connecting herself back to nature had always been her way of calming down when life got stressful, and she found it easy to slip into a meditative state as the city went quiet. It was a Thursday evening which meant student night at the clubs, and therefore much later on when the nightclub threw out, there would be some distant sounds of the students from the university rolling back to their halls of residence which lay on the other side of the railway arches; but for now, nobody was venturing out into the deluge and she could meditate in peace.

Normally when she did this, she found herself drifting to somewhere like the countryside of Northumberland and the Scottish Borders, which she had explored on weekends while at university. The unspoilt countryside had helped her recover after the ordeal of her divorce, and one of the things she missed having returned to Worcester was access to truly empty spaces, the countryside in the Midlands rarely being wholly empty of people because of the large built-up areas within it. Walks down by the River Severn were pleasant, but as with any city, there were often out-of-work men loitering down there, and as a woman walking on her own Fleur never quite let her guard down to the degree needed to meditate. So she had been longing to let her mind just drift over the Eildon Hills or the Cheviots as she closed her eyes, but it wasn't to be.

As soon as she fully relaxed, she mentally found herself not in the countryside, but back in her Grandma Rose's living room. The front door of the little old Edwardian terraced house had come straight into the front room, and so it was rather drafty and rarely used, everyone congregating in the middle room which she was now seeing again. This had been the home of her gypsy grandmother, her mother's mum, and yet her father's Greek mother was there tonight too, which was odd because in life they hadn't liked one another at all. Yet something had brought them together, and Fleur got a sense of urgency from both of them.

"Fleur, you need to be careful!" Grandma Rose told her. "Those books you're handling …some of them have a bad residue."

"She's right," Grandma Luisa agreed, and that all by itself convinced Fleur, because it had to be something bad if she would agree with Rose. "Those books were handled by powerful witches. Some of them were good people, but not all of them. There's blood on their hands. They did evil things."

With her mind's eye, Fleur saw Grandma Rose roll her eyes at Grandma Luisa. "Yes, there's blood on <u>some</u> of them," she said emphatically, "but some of what was done was done out of dire necessity. Trust your instincts, Fleur. I taught you well, and you're a natural. But make sure that when you go back that you have your protection up. Wear your pendant that I gave you and put on my crystal bracelets. I know you have them, and they'll help ward off some of what's leaking out of those books."

Now it was Grandma Luisa's turn to look sideways at Rose. "Wear your crucifix, my love and trust in God."

"Much good that will do!" Rose scoffed. "These were women who were outside of your Church for generations. They won't recognise any potency in a silver cross. If anything, it'll bring their anger down on Fleur, because they and those like them weren't just shunned by the Church, they were actively persecuted by them. And I don't just mean burning at the stake – there are other ways to persecute someone, and do it for years, without leaving a visible scar! Blessed be that I didn't live in such times, because I would have been an outcast for being what they would have derided as a kitchen witch, a wise woman, and with no more justification than because I know my herbs and medicines and could deliver a child safely."

Seeing Grandma Luisa's spirit taking a deep breath to launch into a retort, Fleur quickly got in with, "Then thank you both for coming to warn me! And yes, I will wear both lots, because any protection will be welcome. I felt the bad vibes coming off some of those books even through their coverings, but I hadn't thought it as bad as that."

"Well it is!" Grandma Luisa said very firmly. "So be careful!"

"Yes, the bad is potent stuff," Rose again qualified, "but there is good there too. If you'll take my advice, trust your instincts as to which is which, and store them well apart from one another. …Don't look at me like that Luisa. There's much Fleur can learn from the good books. A lot of old herb lore that one day might stand her in good stead.

"But listen carefully, there's one tarot deck that you should only handle with thick gloves on. It belonged to someone very bad, and was never used for good. You'll probably feel it before you open it, but if you need any confirmation, it's a Tarot of Marseilles – you know, like that reproduction of the old deck I showed you. I don't sense any of the others being quite so fully that design, though there are others that are probably based on it. If you can find leather gloves to handle it with, then all the better, but at a push your thickest cotton ones will do, just don't let it touch your skin – don't let it make that connection to you."

"You can use my best leather gloves," Luisa said gruffly, struggling to unbend enough to acknowledge that Rose had made a good suggestion. "I know you have them."

"Oh Grandma Luisa, that's lovely of you, but you were a much tinier lady than me. I can't even get my hand inside one of them. Thank you all the same, though, because I know Grandpa Nik bought you those and you loved them." Even as she was saying that, though, Fleur was struggling not to laugh, because Rose's expression was priceless as she looked from Fleur to Luisa and back again as if to say, 'you stupid woman, she's half as big again as you!'

"I've missed you both so much," was what she said aloud to them in her meditative state. "I wish I could sit down and just talk with you again like I used to. I miss Dad loads too. Isn't he here?" She thought that if it merited her grandmothers making their peace, however temporarily, then the danger must be very real and that had her wondering why her father wouldn't have come to warn her as well.

"Your papa watches over your sister constantly," Grandma Luisa said affectionately, "especially since that husband of yours caused so much trouble," yet making Fleur inwardly groan that somehow Carl would rear his ugly head in times of trouble, even if it was only in the form of an unwanted reminder.

There was another roll of the eyes by Grandma Rose. "Your son has <u>two</u> daughters," she reminded Luisa pointedly.

"Yes, but Bettina is so fragile," Luisa swiftly defended her son, and there it was, the reason why the two grandmothers had fallen out so badly by the end of their lives.

Rose loved Bettina too, but in a massive family argument had warned her daughter and son-in-law that they were ignoring Fleur, and that one day that might come back to haunt them. Luisa had been the kind of woman who doted on her son, yet all but ignored her daughter, resulting in Fleur hardly knowing her aunt on that side. It hadn't helped that, despite Bettina being three years younger than Fleur, she herself had grown up strangely in Bettina's shadow where her father's family were concerned. The only reason she was as close as she was to Grandma Luisa was because it had been her and Grandpa Nik who had taken them in when her father, Tony, had died. If they hadn't been on top of one another in the modest-sized house, Fleur knew that they wouldn't have had anything like as much contact.

With Rose it had been very different. She had tried to ensure that Bettina – or Betty, as she was known as to her and her side – hadn't spent her life wrapped in cotton-wool, and that Fleur got her fair share of attention, but it had only been after Fleur's marriage had fallen apart that her mother had tearfully confessed that Grandma Rose had warned them long ago that Fleur's ex, Carl, had a nasty streak, and that they shouldn't have been so quick to make heavy hints that Fleur move in with him. Three adults and two teenagers living under one roof had become rather congested, and it had only been afterwards that Fleur had realised just how much she had been encouraged to leave. Yet oddly that made her take Grandma Luisa's current warning all the more seriously. If it was bad enough for her to notice that Fleur was once again heading into danger, it must be bad.

Equally typically, it was Grandma Luisa who faded first, and Fleur couldn't help but smile at the way that Rose seemed to breathe a sigh of relief once she was gone. Turning to Fleur with a smile of her own, Rose's spirit said,

"Dear me, she doesn't get any better for being dead, does she?" making Fleur laugh. "But whatever she was or is, like me she's very worried about what we sense around you, Fleur. The other thing I must tell you is to be careful of a man who is coming and going around you. He is not what he seems! There are two of them, very alike, and you must make sure to find a way of telling which one is which! One is a poor soul who is entrapped by wickedness and deserves your help. The other is pure evil. An evil which has come through his father's line, and that father is not the man you think he might be. I am

constrained as to how much I can tell you, because you know that you have to be able to act upon your own free will. But we can warn, and I am warning you now – look beyond the physical! Look beyond the outer face in front of you and watch for signs of the man inside. That's the only way you will tell them apart."

And with that Rose faded, and Fleur realised that the wind had shifted and the rain was starting to blown into her face as she leaned on the balcony.

Chapter 14

When her alarm clock went off the next morning, Fleur wondered whether the warnings had just been imagined, because for the rest of the night both grandmothers had figured vividly in a succession of dreams. Yet when she got out of bed and saw her best leather gloves out on the chest of drawers, she knew that she had to have dug them out before she went to bed. It was probably no bad thing that they had hardly ever been used. Bought years ago for the winter funeral of Grandma Rose, they were somehow such a poignant reminder of her that normally Fleur found it hard to wear them. Now, though, that link to Rose made them all the more important.

Her jewellery box was open and waiting too, and now Fleur took out several items. Grandma Luisa's heavy silver cross was easy to slip on and tuck under her shirt, being on a fairly long chain, but Grandma Rose's triskele of three hares conjoined by their ears was on a shorter chain, and would be visible at her throat unless she did the top button up. Given that Fleur almost never wore jewellery of any kind, that might incite comment from the others, especially as she added her own black tourmaline pendant given by Grandma Rose, too. That always drew comments because it was a crystal wand tipped top and bottom with amethyst, and caught the light beautifully.

Rose's most powerful pieces, though were a pair of beautiful bracelets, which Fleur would only put on once she could tuck them inside her gloves. That was partly to keep them close to her skin, but also to make sure she didn't snag and break them. Many of the stones were old and hard to find, starting with two lovely rare pink fluorites, two soft creamy tinted chlorites, a couple of pale fire agates shot through with richer bands of flame, a rich coloured carnelian in each, two true green jade pearls, two exquisite small pieces of ocean jasper, two exceptional blue tourmalines, and then making up the rest of the stones were amethysts, smoky quartz, and tiny beads of jet acting as the spacers. Consequently, there was about as much psychic protection contained in these as it was possible to get.

Where Grandma Rose had got the stones from, Fleur had never found out. Indeed, she wasn't even sure whether her grandmother hadn't so much created them as inherited them, and just restrung the bracelets when the original wire became worn. What she did know was that the one time when Grandma Rose had put them onto her, she had felt the charge of psychic energy coming off them like a superhero's wrist bands. Whatever today threw at her, she felt better for knowing she had these with her.

She also breakfasted carefully, taking the time to be mindful of what she was eating and drinking – nothing processed but keeping it all wholesome – and also packed some special herb teas to take in with her, as well as an insulated bottle of herb tea which she could sip from as she worked. Sometimes you just couldn't be too careful.

At work she took the packets of biscuits across to the garage to Alec and the others, where they were pounced upon, especially as the four were heading out to a house clearance today, which would mean lots of heavy lifting for which they would need sustenance. She briefly popped her head around the door of the workshop, but Lucy wasn't there and it was too early for Carrie-Ann to be in for her shift, and so taking a deep breath, she headed up to the attic. The moment she opened the door she could feel the energy in the room, which was almost crackling like static.

"Alright, alright, I'm coming," she found herself saying, picking up on a sense of impatience, though it was of somebody or somebodies wanting to get down to work again, not in any threatening way.

Once she had put her things down, well away from everything else, the first thing she decided to do was to check over the tarot bundles. Sure enough, the aura rising from the one was enough for her to know that this had to be the one Grandma Rose had warned her about, but somebody else must also have had concerns about it, because she now remembered thinking that this one was in an awful lot of packaging when she'd been moving them yesterday. Someone in the past had been taking no chances with that one, either!

Pulling on the bracelets and then her leather gloves, Fleur took a couple of deep steadying breaths and then grasped the offending bundle firmly with both hands and took it over to the far corner of the room.

"Come on, you! Let's have you out of the way!" she said to it firmly, but making sure to put it in a corner where it would get light, not shadows. There was no way she was giving it anything dark it might feed on.

With that one removed from the work area, she took the leather gloves off and put a pair of her normal cotton work gloves on. Carefully rearranging the seven other bundled decks into something resembling a circle, she went back to her bag and dug out the three small jam jars she'd brought with her, put in them her three disk incense holders, then lit three small cones of incense, and once they were fully smouldering, wafted the smoke over the top of the decks. Incense smoke was a good way to quickly cleanse an area, and she wanted the taint of the bad deck gone as fast as possible.

She was taking a bit of a chance, because if Sue came up here and saw that she had something burning – even though it was fully contained, only as small as the cones, and only smouldering without any actual flame – she would still be horrified. With that in mind, Fleur opened a skylight at each end of the room to let the smoke drift out, but was surprised to feel a sense of relief pervading the area of the side table where the decks lay. It was almost as if they were glad to have the miasma of the other deck being lifted away from them in the smoke, making Fleur glad that she had thought to bring the Frankincense with her.

Stranger and stranger, thought Fleur. *I'm glad the grandmas came to warn me. I wouldn't have liked to walk in on this unprepared.* And now that she came to think about it, the different decks had each been packed in amongst the grimoires, not all together, so maybe this was the first time in many a long year that they had all sat side by side? Was that why they now reacted to the presence of the toxic one? However, this wasn't something she could talk through with Lucy or any of the others. They'd all thought her choice of academic research project odd enough as it was, and she'd never quite summoned the courage to tell them that it had been because of Grandma Rose's own notebooks that she'd become fascinated, let alone that she occasionally used them. Someone who practised pagan rituals in their midst might be more than most of them felt comfortable with.

But that meant that she needed to get stuck into dealing with the grimoires so that she could report back with something Lucy could grasp, and so for the morning she got on with carefully unpacking each one out of its cloth bundle, making notes all the time. Some of them had what she thought had once been crushed dried herbs packed away with them, and even though almost all scent was long gone, by the time she paused for lunch there was a faint but definite aroma in the room of lavender, lemon balm, rosemary, and something which she thought might be juniper.

Upon her initial brief inspection, some of the grimoires were little more than notebooks of the sort that Grandma Rose had kept, filled with recipes and notes on what 'spells' had been most effective, though Fleur knew that these days they would be classed more as mild invocations, or incantations made in hope rather than a full-on belief that they would work straightaway. None of them felt in the slightest way offensive, and it was all Fleur could do not to sit down and get engrossed in reading. However, to her surprise, there were also a handful of old printed books in there too, evidently bought as reference works and yet being kept very carefully away from whatever the original library at *The Rookery* had contained. None were anything like valuable, though, and could probably be discarded unless they had been seriously annotated in such a way that would tie them to the grimoires.

"Now you all behave yourselves while I'm gone," she found herself telling them as she left to go and join Lucy for lunch, and for one brief instant she could have sworn she 'heard' a woman's merry laugh, as if saying 'what us?' mischievously.

Downstairs she was greeted by Lucy and Sue who had already arrived in the tiny staffroom and had the kettle going.

"How's it going?" Lucy asked as Fleur dunked a teabag in her mug.

"Absolutely fascinating!" Fleur answered with enthusiasm. "Just as a social history it's an amazing find." She grinned at Sue. "You were bang on with which ones were the oldest. But what's got me really gripped with these ones is that they're a mixture of handwritings. It's as if the women in one family were trying to make sure that all of the old chants and charms that they had learned at their mothers' knees got written down at last. I think I can tell which is the first one, too, because the letters are very wobbly, as if that person has only just learned how to write."

"Do you think it's the mother?" Lucy wondered, turning to Sue and telling her about Carrie-Ann's digging.

"So it could be her?" Sue asked enthusiastically.

"Mezelly Petulengro?" Fleur said. "Yes, I think it might well be her who started these. She does her best for the first part of the book and then the other hands start to appear. But what's interesting is that you can see those other hands growing in confidence as you get into the next couple of books. They get more fluent, and if they're not the neatest of writers, you can tell that they are writing more naturally, whereas that first hand always seems to be doing it very carefully and having to concentrate," and she giggled.

"What?" Lucy demanded with a smile.

"Oh, it's just that I have this vision of an older lady in a mop cap sitting at the kitchen table, really concentrating, and with her tongue poking out the way kids' sometimes do when they're that focused." What Fleur couldn't say was that that image had come to her most forcefully, but with great affection, as if she was picking up on one of Mezelly's daughters coming in and seeing her mother trying to write something down. It had come as she had rubbed some of the 'dust' between her fingers, deciding that it must be rosemary. But then rosemary was for remembrance, wasn't it? So maybe someone had held that rosemary and said words over it to enhance its recalling properties?

Mentally shaking herself and reminding herself that Sue and Lucy would think her barmy if she started talking about visions of the past, she hurried on with,

"We've also got a copy of Ebenezer Sibly's *New and Complete Illustration of the Celestial Science of Astrology* from 1784, which is in near perfect condition; John Middleton's *Practical Astrology* from 1679; and George Wilde's *Treatise on Natal Astrology* from 1894. So it looks as though the women of the family were trying to keep up to date with their craft."

"Hardly a craft," Sue snorted with a derisory laugh, making Fleur cringe internally. This was exactly the attitude she'd fear she'd encounter.

"To them it was," she countered, but keeping her tone light. "It mattered a lot to them. Let's face it, Macaulay's *History of England* is hardly accurate by modern standards, but it was a respected text in its day."

"And that's why I leave the books up to you lot," Sue said airily, and returned to eating her sandwich.

However, Lucy was more professionally interested. "Any other books?"

Fleur sighed. "Well, there's an old copy of the *Grand Grimoire* which isn't really surprising – that was so well known, and to be frank, despite some of the illustrations, it's not hard-core demonology by modern standards. There's one called *Egyptian Magic* by an author called A. E. W. Budge, which has hardly been used, so I'm thinking that they realised pretty soon that the practices of ancient Egypt weren't terribly relevant to them. Both of those could go for resale, because they're nothing special book-wise."

Lucy scrutinised Fleur's face. "But? I sense there's a 'but' coming? What's got you looking worried?"

Luckily Sue had got up and walked out by now, and so Fleur took a deep breath and decided to take a chance. "Look, you know I had a pretty alternative upbringing, right? You know about my Greek grandma who we lived with, but as I told you, my mum's mum was a proper gypsy – that's how I came to get interested in grimoires and tarot decks. So will you just take my word for it that another other book is really bad news?"

"In what way?" Lucy could see that Fleur was serious and didn't want to dismiss her worries out of hand.

"Okay, …it's a book called *The Book of Black Magic* by Arthur Edward Waite, printed in 1910."

"This is the same Waite who you told us designed the tarot deck?"

"Yes. I've actually read a copy of it in the past, and Waite himself makes some very clear distinctions between white and black magic, and of the fact that white isn't automatically good, nor black evil. But this particular copy…" and Fleur shuddered. "This one someone has annotated, and they've made a concerted effort to try out and refine rituals for summoning. And there's also an old *Goetia* – no publisher and no date, but probably late nineteenth-century – which essentially contains rituals based on what they thought Solomon would have used to summon demon lords or spirits or whatever, and again it's been heavily annotated." She gave another shudder. "I honestly don't want to send these to some charity bookshop where a kid might get their hands on them, but equally, I don't want them going back to Mrs Vance either when she's in such an unstable state."

Lucy looked at her askance. "You seriously think they're *dangerous*?"

Fleur sighed. This was the trouble with trying to explain things to someone who couldn't feel a thing. "Do I think that some teenage Goth is going to summon a terrible legendary demon king like Balam in their bedroom just by chanting what's in this book? No, of course I don't! But there are nonetheless energies in this world that a lot of people are oblivious to, and not all of them are good. I know you don't 'believe', Lucy, but I went with my gran the one time to help her calm things down in a house. The people who lived there were bloody terrified by this time, and they weren't fanciful folk by any means. Their teenage son and a couple of mates had been fooling around with a Ouija board, which is never a good idea, but then he'd gone on and set up his own little dark altar, lit up the incense, and tried to summon a demon who would help him cheat on his coming exams."

Lucy guffawed, but then saw Fleur shaking her head solemnly and said, "Are you seriously telling me that he succeeded?"

"In what he thought he was doing? No. But you don't have to open the gates of Hell in the full biblical sense to tap into some very dark energies. I would say that he was in a pretty fragile mental state to start off with, because he'd been quite badly bullied at school. But then when his rituals all went wrong and he found that something was lurking around him all of the time, he really went to pieces – and I mean he was under full hospital psychiatric care for a long time afterwards!"

"Jeez! That's not funny!"

"No, it's not. And something was throwing things around in the house at night. It wasn't the lad, because it happened when his dad was sitting beside him on the bed trying to stop him from having hysterics. I tell you, Lucy, something very primal and dark had been allowed into that place, and I've never forgotten seeing my gran actually sweating with the effort of sending it back where it had come from. And I could feel it too. It was like some nasty oil-slick in the air that you couldn't see but could definitely feel. And I'm getting a whiff of that same nastiness off these two books. So, unless Mrs Vance specifically asks for them back – i.e., she already knows they are there – I'm going to keep them here for a while and then send them to be pulped. Neither is worth anything moneywise, and it'll be safer all round if they never get opened again. I'm not asking you to believe in what they contain, just in the damage they could do to some unwitting and vulnerable person."

She didn't say to Lucy that she wouldn't even risk sending them to be pulped, just in case someone spotted them and pulled them out of the pile before they went it. One night she would take them away with her and in a quiet place she'd burn them to ashes. If there was some passing mention of them in any of the grimoires, then if the collection ended up in a museum somewhere, it would just be assumed that they'd been lost along the way. After all, there was at least a century for them to have gone astray in.

"Well, if you feel they're that potentially hazardous, and they're worth nothing, then I'll back you in doing that," Lucy said cautiously.

"Thank you! You know I wouldn't normally ever suggest such a thing, but I really think both could be seriously injurious to Mrs Vance's mental health, honestly, I do." But Fleur thought that if there was anything else that ought never to return to *The Rookery*, then she would smuggle it out without mentioning it.

If she got caught, she would get seriously disciplined, because destroying items on one employee's whim just wasn't company policy, but in this instance, Fleur felt that her moral compass had to be her guide, and if it was going to be this hard to convince even Lucy, who knew her well, then she'd have no chance with someone like Mr Harris. Left over pieces of material could be covered by saying that some items had been double or triple wrapped, she hoped, because the fabrics were too good to burn as well. Some serious 'cleansing' ought to do the trick with them and make them safe, and the wrappings from the two books were already tucked safely away on the attic's big bookshelf, waiting for her to decide how best to do that.

Chapter 15

Returning to the attic after lunch, Fleur stood and studied the books for a while. It was time to start rearranging them again into a refined chronological order, not least because she wanted to be able to record a definite progression in the contents, which would confirm their value if she could see one hand going directly from one grimoire into the next. Yet the tarot cards were also calling to her. What was bothering her regarding them was that it was now Friday, and so if she didn't do something with them now, they were going to be locked away up here all over the weekend, with nobody to spot it if things started getting spooky. Sue might scoff at her beliefs, but Fleur knew that she would be scared witless if anything kicked off up here when Sue was alone. Therefore it was down to Fleur to make sure that the place stayed safe.

"It's always the way," she remembered Grandma Rose once saying to her. "It's all a load of baloney until it's you sitting wetting your knickers in some dark corner, too scared to come out because of the thing you can't quite see that's howling and wailing, and throwing the crockery about. Then it's 'how soon can you come and help me.' *Tsk*! People!"

It's no good, I'm going to have to take those two books and the tarot deck and put them somewhere else, she thought resignedly. *But at least if I stick them in a corner of the outside workroom it hardly matters if they get damp.* Even so, she dug through the drawers in the workbench until she found some waterproof bags, partly because when she came to burn the dangerous books she wanted them to really burn, not be smoking damply, and partly reasoning also that what successfully kept the damp out ought to keep other things in.

She was just trotting down the stairs past the first-floor offices with the offending bundle in a carrier bag so that she wasn't in full contact with it, when Mr Harris' door swung open and who should walk out but Angelo Vance.

He stopped dead in his tracks looking horrified. "Ms Constantine," he said weakly, but then couldn't seem to continue.

Carefully putting the bag down on the floor out of the way by a side table which held the firm's brochures, and hopefully where Mr Harris wouldn't spot it, Fleur walked towards him.

"Hello, Mr Vance," she said pleasantly. "How are you?" That wasn't a bland question because he looked dreadful. There were dark circles under his eyes as if he hadn't slept a wink last night, and he had a haunted look about him.

He seemed nonplussed by her question, instead stumbling over his words as he in turn asked, "Are you okay? …I mean, after… After what…"

"After what your mother said?" Fleur prompted kindly. "I may have no medical qualifications, but even I can tell that she's not well, and I don't judge people who are ill. I just hope you can get her the help she needs."

She could see Mr Harris lurking in the doorway behind Angelo and so was careful to keep her words calm. What she really wanted to do, though, was to give this poor man a hug, because he seemed to be at his wits' end. Why were all her senses screaming at her that he needed her help so badly?

"God, that's really kind of you," he gulped, unable to believe that she was being so reasonable.

Fleur smiled to remove any offence as she said, "I have to admit that I'm not keen to return to the house on my own, as you can imagine, but if you are worrying that I'm about to make your mum's life hell, or go running to the press, please don't. I'm not that sort of person."

She seemed to have put him a little more at ease, because he gave a huff of relief before saying, "I don't know what got into her, I really don't. When Mr Harris phoned me and told me what she'd said, I was horrified. Please believe me when I say that though you are a very nice person – and you've proved that all over again just now by being so understanding – I have *never* obsessed over you! There is no way that you're going to find me stalking you or anything creepy like that. I wouldn't! I just wouldn't. Not you, not any woman …not anybody!"

"I didn't think you would," Fleur reassured him, "but it's good of you to tell me to my face. It saves a lot of misunderstanding."

"Is there anything I can do for you to make amends?"

Fleur had an inkling that he might be wondering whether she was going to jump at the chance of a fat cheque from him, but instead suddenly had a thought.

"No, I'm fine," she said with another smile. "But there's something *I'd* like to show *you*, if you have the time?" she saw Mr Harris' eyebrows going up, and said directly to him, "Is it okay if I take Mr Vance up to the attic and show him the things we've got up there?"

"Err, yes, I suppose so," Mr Harris said dubiously, but then realised that Fleur was miming leaving the doors open as she stepped aside and waved Angelo Vance towards the stairs going up. If he tried anything here, then one shriek from her and the entire office would be up there, and in her mind, this was a controlled way of discovering how Angelo would behave when alone with her. And so she grabbed the bag and hastily followed Angelo, taking the lead at the next turn in the stairs.

"Here you are," she said, opening the attic door with a flourish. "These are what were in those boxes you helped your mum get down from the attic in the Dower House."

"I didn't help her," Angelo responded, perplexed. "The first I knew of them was when she showed them to me down in the lounge. I presumed she must have asked one of the workmen to help her lift them down."

How curious, Fleur thought, *and yet Mrs Vance definitely told me that it was you and her who got them down and looked at them.* And on this occasion her instincts were telling her that he was being completely frank. Then was even more surprised when he added,

"It was she who told me what was in them. I have to admit that I never looked. I was still a bit too taken up with the technical side of getting the house restored at the time, I'm afraid. So it was enough for me that Mum wanted them looked at by whoever catalogued the books for me. I never really questioned what was *in* the boxes, beyond that it was old stuff to do with the family, I knew nothing."

"Oh wow! Well then come and take a look at these," Fleur said, leading him towards the oldest books. For half an hour she talked him through the books, the still bundled up cards, and the coverings that they'd all been found in. And as she talked, she could see him relaxing and starting to get really interested. Even better, there wasn't a hint of him leering at her, or watching her more than what she was pointing at.

"So you think you can identify who wrote these?" he asked with real enthusiasm.

"I think we can make a good attempt," Fleur replied. "I don't know how pleased your mum will be when she discovers that, far from being hereditary lords of the manor going back to who-know-when, that you actually have what might be described as a mixed pedigree. But thinking back to what you told me about your grandfather, doesn't it make rather more sense of the locals' antipathy if somewhere in the village folklore there's a memory of the big house being won by some gypsy scoundrel in a card game?

"William Fitzpatrick – the incomer from Ireland who married Loretta Boswell – only died in 1930, so if there are any folk in their nineties in the village, they might actually remember him. And his mother-in-law, Annie – who started life with the very Romany name of Anselina Petulengro – died only in 1900, so well within the living memory of the grandparents of people who are now middle-aged or older. We're talking about your Grandfather Aleister's own grandfather and great-grandmother here, and Aleister was about seven when his grandfather died, so people of his own generation in the village might well have known a lot more about the family than you do!"

Angelo stared at her in amazement. "Oh, my god! That makes so much more sense of it all! No wonder Grandfather playing lord of the manor got up peoples' noses!"

"It does put a very different spin on it, doesn't it?" Fleur admitted. Feeling daring, she ventured to ask, "Did your grandfather Ignatius dislike your own father, Jacko?"

"Bloody hated him as far as I know. Why?"

"Well taking it from Aleister's point of view, he may have spent his whole early life being told to keep the appearance of respectability going at all costs. After all, *his* grandmother – that's Loretta, who didn't die until 1900 – was a full Romany, so the veneer of nobility was pretty shallow. So how would he have felt to find his daughter rolling up with some rock singer from the backstreets of Birmingham? Not even one of the posher parts?"

Angelo looked at her with wide eyes. "Bloody hell! That does change things, doesn't it!" He groaned. "I do wish Mum wouldn't be so damned secretive about the family. It would have been so much easier if I'd known some of this years ago when I took over the house."

"It would have made a difference?"

"Definitely! For a start off I would have made much more of an effort with the folks in the village. I was working on the basis of them just being hacked off with what they saw as an age-old right still being pursued in the twenty-first century, even though I wasn't bothered about being lord of anything. But if they've regarded our family as unwanted interlopers in fairly recent generations, then that's a bit different, isn't it? I've sort of had an idea for a community project for part of the grounds, you see, but put it on the back burner as something to come to later on. But there was no reason why it couldn't have been set in motion a lot earlier if it would have healed that rift.

"I thought about creating a park with a picnic area on the village edge of the grounds, you see, because there's nowhere in the village for the young mums and the old folks to meet up and just have a chat. There's no park, not even a village green. They've either got to go to the pub and buy drinks, or the café and fork out for coffees and cakes, and I'm not so out of touch with the world that I don't realise that many people can't afford to do that very often. Mind you, Mum was dead against it..."

"Oh dear." What else could Fleur say? But clearly Mrs Vance was trying to keep up that distance with the village for whatever reasons of her own. Then something else occurred to Fleur. "Look, I don't want to sound presumptuous or like I'm sticking my nose in where it doesn't belong, but could I make a suggestion?"

Angelo smiled. "Given how reasonable you've been, and all the work you've already done for us, suggest away."

Taking a deep breath, Fleur plunged in. "I know your mum is thrilled with this find, but... for people with mental health issues, books like this aren't the healthiest things to have around." She hurriedly clarified that with, "I've seen this in my own family. My sister has Down's Syndrome, and our gypsy grandmother was always really careful to keep things like her tarot decks well away from Betty.

"Part of it is that they're too susceptible to imagining all sorts of things into what they read. And I know that isn't your mum's problem at all, but if she's stressed and feeling desperate about something, then there's a real danger that she might start experimenting with things from these grimoires, if only to try and get things going the way she wants, and that really isn't good. I've heard of cases where folks get het up when the 'spell' doesn't work, and then start trying more and more outlandish variations in the hope that one of them will work.

"So if you decide that you want to keep these, can I suggest that you store them in a house where your mum doesn't have ready access to them? Of course, if you decide to sell – and I have to tell you that there are collectors of this sort of thing out there who will pay handsomely for such a collection – then that doesn't apply. And there are even folk museums who would love to have something like this gifted to them, if you were feeling generously inclined. But I thought I had to say something because from what you've said, your mum will be dead against selling."

Angelo had already been nodding at what she was saying, and immediately said, "You're so right. Mum would have a fit if I sold these, but for myself I'd be glad to hand them on to a good museum. Sadly, I don't think I'll get the chance to do that, or at least not without upsetting her so much that she doesn't talk to me for months or even years. But I do have a large apartment in London where I could keep them, and I really appreciate what you're trying to tell me, because I've been getting more and more worried about Mum of late. I definitely don't want to have anything hanging around in *The Rookery* that will unbalance her even more."

Fleur was just thinking as they turned to the door to leave that there it was again, that unspoken thing that she suspected was also what was worrying Angelo to death, when he grabbed hold of her and swung her into his arms.

She screamed in shock, but then screamed again as the bookcase which had been behind the door, and only a foot or so away from where they had been standing, crashed down, effectively sealing them in. As she stood shaking in Angelo's grasp, and realising that if not for him the bookcase would have come down straight on top of her, she heard running feet and voices coming up the stairs.

"Fleur! Fleur! Are you alright?" Mr Harris called as he panted up to the landing.

"Err, yes… Yes, I am, thanks to Mr Vance. He pulled me out of the way just in time. The big bookcase has fallen over right across the doorway."

"Impossible!" Mr Harris gasped. "That was screwed to the wall!"

Looking up, both Fleur and Angelo saw the hole in the plaster where not only the screws but also the rawl-plugs in the wall had been pulled clean out.

"Well it's not now," Fleur called back, "Though we can see the holes where it was."

"Can you move it?" Mr Harris' secretary, Denise, called. "We can try pushing from this side if it would help?"

Angelo and Fleur bent down and tried tugging at the bookcase, but it was a huge brute of a thing and it had been full of Sue's departmental files. Some of the lever-arch files were strewn across the floor, but others were still on shelves, albeit at lopsided angles.

"We're going to have to empty it a bit first," Angelo called back. "Can you hang on a moment, please?"

Together they hurriedly started piling the files onto the nearest table, and it was only when Fleur put her hand on the bag she'd been carrying, that it dawned on her that the toxic bundle had been on a shelf, dumped there out of the way when she'd brought Angelo up here. That shook her in a whole other way, because now she knew that the bookcase sealing them in had been no accident. But who had it been directed at? Herself for knowing what it was, and trying to counter its influence? Or Angelo for wanting to sell the collection? Either was worrying, and suddenly Fleur couldn't wait to get out of the attic and get those items as far away from here as possible.

Chapter 16

Unfortunately, even with Mr Harris, Denise, and Megan the accounts clerk, all shoving from the outside, and Fleur and Angelo pulling on the inside, they couldn't move the bookcase, not even with all of the files taken out. The door opened enough for Fleur to be able to look through the small gap and speak directly to them, but that was all.

"I'm so sorry," Mr Harris apologised, "but you're both going to have to wait until Alec and his team get back from the house clearance. Four strong men pushing from this side might have more effect, but we're getting nowhere."

"I'll go and get you a cup of tea and some biscuits," Megan volunteered. "We should be able to get a mug through the gap."

Well now's the time when I find out for real what Angelo Vance is like, Fleur thought with some trepidation. Granted he'd pulled her out of danger, but that could just have been his good reflexes. What he'd be like when stuck on his own in her with her for a couple of hours might be a very different matter.

Once the tea had come and Denise had brought them a refill, Fleur decided that she might as well carry on working. What she wasn't expecting was for Angelo to come and join her. As she went through the next few books, making her notes, he asked intelligent questions, and Fleur found herself wondering more and more about him.

But something else she noticed was that he appeared to be getting increasingly worried about the confinement. She noticed him looking about the place worriedly, and that he was becoming rather pale, which made her wonder whether his continued questions were as much to try and distract himself. The attic was hardly a small enclosed space, but Fleur knew that claustrophobia came in different forms.

Therefore, after she'd answered a lot of his questions, including ones on her thesis, she plucked up the courage to try and get him talking, and asked him,

"What made you go into the blogging thing? Forgive me for saying this, but it just doesn't seem to be you. That desire to push your opinions out into the world." She could hardly say, 'you don't seem the self-obsessed, arrogant prick, type to me,' which was what she was thinking.

He laughed, albeit shakily. "No, it's not. In truth I wanted to be musician. I desperately wanted to have a dad I could talk to, and Jacko's music was the only way I got any hint of what sort of person he was. When I was little, Mum just got too upset to talk about him, though at least back then, she used to listen to his records sometimes.

"At boarding school, I had this beat-up old guitar, but I practised and practised on it until I drove the other kids mad. I started a band with a couple of mates and we were full of big dreams about going on the road. Whenever Mum wasn't around, I'd listen to my dad's records and wish I'd known him. Because, you see, something changed once I was older and at school in England, and suddenly she couldn't bear to listen to them at all. I even wondered whether she was scared that I'd be just like him and die young, because it was the only explanation I could think of, and she never said a thing."

He suddenly looked really sad. "When Mum found out, I've never known her be so angry. She absolutely lost the plot. Smashed up my guitar. Threw away all of dad's CDs, including the bootleg copies that I'd managed to collect. Grounded me for three months out in Italy initially, but then when I tried to run away, she locked me in my room – literally!"

He seemed haunted by that memory. "I think that was the first time I really began to wonder about Mum, because that room had certainly been made to keep somebody locked up away from the world in. It had its own wash basin and toilet, and there was a hatch in the door where she passed me my food through."

"Good God! That's awful!" Bloody hell, no wonder the poor man was having trouble coping with being trapped up here in the attic! It must be raking up heaven knows what in the way of bad memories, and once again Fleur had the feeling that she needed to help him.

"It was. I was only sixteen, for pity's sake. I honestly thought I was never going to see the outside ever again for a while. And what was worse, through the walls I kept hearing Mum talking to somebody as if she was talking to me. Mum as she was when she was being just 'mum', not this psycho who sometimes called me by other names."

"How did you get out?"

"I don't honestly know, because I swear she was putting something in my food. I'd lose whole days, and then when I'd come around, somebody had been in and put clean sheets on the bed and stuff. But then one day I woke up and I wasn't in her house but in my great-uncle's *castello* and he was there. He told me that he'd had my mum taken to a hospital for treatment, and that he and my great-aunt would be looking after me until I got better."

That's something that never made it to the papers! Heavens, I can see why you'd want that kept quiet! Fleur thought as Angelo carried on,

"Physically it didn't take too long to get back on my feet, Great-aunt Sophia was an amazing cook and she was so kind, making me all the things I loved to eat, and I felt safe with them. But one of the residual problems was that I couldn't face the idea of getting up on a stage in front of an audience anymore. In fact, it took me until I was into my late twenties before I could cope with being in any sort of crowd."

"Ah! So talking to people via a blog was safe for you!"

"It was. I could talk to them about the music and all the things that I loved, but without having to confront them face to face. So if someone disagreed with me, it wasn't the end of the world. It didn't linger with me the way it did if someone argued with me in person. Mum was in hospital on and off for years after that, and when she came out, she seemed so fragile. Even if I could have faced an audience, I just couldn't bring myself to do something that would upset her that much again."

Fleur placed a sympathetic hand on one of his where he was leaning on the workbench. "Did you think that it was you and your music that had tipped her over the edge? Too many memories of what she'd lost?"

He could only nod, and Fleur could see that he was still genuinely upset by the memory. "Have you ever had help yourself for what went on?" she asked gently.

With a sniff he straightened back up. "Oh yes. Booked myself into a good private clinic a couple of times once I'd got my own money. And yes, they've told me over and over that it wouldn't have been just me. She must have been teetering on a knife edge for a very long time, and it could just as easily have been something else which tipped her over."

He walked over to the box of tissues and helped himself to a couple, turning away from Fleur to furtively wipe his eyes. "It's just that when it's a parent it's different, isn't it?" But then he looked at Fleur and sighed. "But then you probably don't know. I expect you had lovely down-to-earth, sensible parents, who loved you and never made you feel inadequate."

"Oh, you don't know the half of it!" Fleur quickly responded. "My mum is great. Always has been. But from the moment my sister was born she sucked up all of my dad's attention – even away from Mum. I'm sure he did love us, but it was as if he felt that it was his fault that Bettina – or Betty as we always call her now – had Down's, and that he had to spend his every waking hour making up for that. There was one point when I was about eight when I began to truly believe that my mum must have been married before, and that that man had been my real dad. A dad who had died before I could remember him. Because Dad never seemed to even know I was there except to tell me off.

"It was only when the parents of one of my school pals saw them at some function, and said something to the effect that it was a shame that he couldn't find it in him to care more about his step-daughter that it all came out. But do you know what? He blamed me! He called me a naughty, jealous little girl who ought to think more about her poor sister."

"Jeez! That's awful!"

"It was. There was an almighty row, and it ended with mum threatening to get a divorce. As it was, she moved things around in the house. Although I was the oldest, I'd been shoved into the small bedroom because Betty had needed a lot of medical equipment to help her when she was little. Well Mum moved Betty into that room, and she and I shared what had been Betty's room. Mum bought another single bed and slept in there with me, and although after a year or so she went back in with Dad, I don't think they were a couple anymore.

"It was so sad, and all the more so because after he was killed in a car crash when I was fourteen, we had to go and live with his parents, who were just as bad. I ended up getting married stupidly young, and my mum only managed to move out when her own mother died and left her her little house. Now she and Betty have a small two-bedroom bungalow, and she's trying to undo all the harm Dad did, so that Betty doesn't go through life acting like a spoilt brat, and turning people against her. I love my sister and I feel sorry for her, but I don't always like her, if that makes sense."

"It makes perfect sense," Angelo said gently. "And it makes sense of why you've been so considerate towards me. Thank you, and thank you for telling me, too."

Fleur smiled back at him. "Well, it helps sometimes to know that you're not the only one who's been through a family meat-grinder. When they cut us, it cuts deeper than anything else does, and it doesn't heal as well, either."

But at that there came a creaking from the doorway and then a thump. Alec and his team had arrived and were trying to open the door. That proved to be a lot harder than anyone expected, though. One corner of the bookcase immediately dug into the wall at the hinge end as soon as they managed to move it a few more inches, and the gap was still too small for either anyone to get in and help them, or for Fleur and Angelo to squeeze their way out. Worse, Angelo was now starting to visibly shake, and there was sweat standing out on his brow.

"Don't worry," Fleur quietly reassured him. "You're not going to be in here much longer. If necessary, they'll call the fire brigade and the door will just get hacked down. You're not going to be stuck all night."

Realising that Fleur had guessed that this was reliving his worst nightmare, Angelo gave a tense nod, and then went across to the small end window, throwing it open and gulping in the fresh air. But then that gave Fleur an idea.

"Hey, guys!" she called out. "You know there's the parapet around the edge of the roof? And there's the stonework gutter behind before the roof-tiles start? Has one of you got a good enough head for heights that you'd be okay with getting out of the landing window and coming in through the one in here? Only I think with another man on this side we might just shift this."

Alec's voice came back through the gap, "Why didn't I think of that! Of course!" just as Tyler called through,

"I'm game for that. Hang on, Fleur!"

Only moments later, Tyler was wriggling his way in through the small window Angelo had been at.

"Piece of cake," he said cheerfully. "It's only a few feet, and the parapet is high enough that you don't feel right on the edge."

Joe was now also squeezing his way in through the window, although rather paler in the face than Tyler, and Fleur guessed that for him the eight feet journey along the stone gutter behind the parapet hadn't been anything like as easy. He landed on the floor and huffed a sigh of relief, clearly glad to be back inside.

"Thanks, Joe," Fleur said softly, Tyler having already gone to the bookcase, "I owe you all more biscuits!"

"No probs," Joe managed with a weak smile, but then he was with Tyler and Angelo, hauling at the base of the bookcase. With three fit men on this side, it now only took a few good tugs to get the bookcase further back into the room, and as soon as the door opened, Mr Harris and Alec hurried in. Surveying the damage where the plugs had been ripped out of the wall, Mr Harris was stunned.

"What on earth would have made that happen?" he asked rhetorically.

"I don't know," Fleur told him, "but I'd have been crushed like a bug if it hadn't been for Mr

Vance's quick reactions. He pulled me out of the way just in time."

Mr Harris looked even more distressed at that, no doubt imagining the health and safety reports that he would have to have written had that happened. If the possibility of Fleur suing the company over sexual harassment had been bad, that would have gone to a whole new level. Fleur herself, though, was more worried about Angelo. He was still pale and stressed, and although he politely declined yet more tea offered by the solicitous Megan, she still wasn't happy about him getting straight into his car and driving away. As Mr Harris was shooing everyone downstairs, and insisting that they call it a day now, Fleur managed to sidle up to Angelo and ask,

"Would you like to come for something to eat before you try to drive back? There's a burger place a short walk away over by the railway arches which does good food, or there are other places up on the Tything, which is only a step or two away as well."

"The burger bar sounds good if they do a veggie option," he said gratefully.

"They do a nice falafel burger, and even a vegan one, though I haven't tried that."

"Falafels sound great!" and his stomach growled appreciatively too. "Sorry about that," he managed to laugh. "I haven't really eaten today."

"Then you definitely need to eat before you drive," Fleur told him firmly. "All that stress has probably dropped your blood sugar levels to an all-time low. I would hate to have you crashing your car on my conscience if you went faint. If you wait outside, I'll just grab my stuff."

But what she immediately did after racing back up to the attic, and grabbing her own bag, was to also snatch up the bag of books. No way was she leaving that to fester up there now! If the bad energy could cause the bookcase to fall after just one night up there, the whole weekend was far too dangerous. She thought about grabbing the other tarot packs too, but then had second thoughts. Right now she didn't know who was good and who bad from amongst the women who had owned these cards, and the last thing she needed was to invite the wrong one amongst them into her home. Once there in her flat, a troubled spirit might prove hard to dislodge, and so she left them be. Without the toxic elements they ought to be safe enough just for a weekend.

Running back downstairs, she patted her bag as she shot past a startled Mr Harris,

"Just getting my stuff!" she called cheerily, but then once down at ground level, made a quick detour to the outside workshop. That was already locked up, but there was a small lean-to at the end which covered the extractor fan that sometimes needed to be used, and she tucked the waterproof bag into the side of the lean-to. It would be safe enough there, because the yard was well secured at night, and she didn't think any cat or fox would be pulling it out. Animals had more sense than to mess with anything which felt that wrong.

Only as she met Lucy by the yard gate was she challenged, and that was for a very different reason.

"Vance says you are taking him for something to eat?" Lucy hissed at her in horrified tones. "What are you thinking, Fleur?"

Aware that Angelo was standing only a few yards away, Fleur kept her response quiet as well. "For heaven's sake, he could have let me *die* up there! And he told me something in confidence, but let's just say he has good reason to be very distressed in confined spaces – a kind of claustrophobia. I know the attic isn't small, but getting trapped in there really freaked him out. I'm not inviting him back up to my flat, Lucy! It's a burger in a public place, and only a stone's throw from the main police station! How much trouble could I possibly get into?"

"Hmph!" Lucy sniffed, not impressed. "You just make sure he doesn't follow you home!"

"Oh Lucy, look at the state of him. He deserves some sympathy, not badgering or having accusations thrown at him. I'm not saying that Claire made stuff up," she added hurriedly as she saw Lucy starting to bristle, "but this man assaulting her? No. I don't think so. Not unless he was totally off his face on drugs, and does he look that way to you right now? He may have his demons, but I don't think he is one."

Chapter 17

At the burger shop they found a table outside, the weather throwing one of those unexpected warm spring late-afternoons at them, and though the patio heaters were on, it was still pleasant. Also, Fleur thought that after his fright in the attic, Angelo might recover a lot better with some space around him.

"Where are you parked?" Fleur asked, and was glad to hear him say,

"On the racecourse."

That meant that he would be going in the opposite direction to her when they left, even if she walked part of the way with him to point him in the right direction.

"What a great little spot," Angelo enthused, looking around at the collection of units created under the high arches of the railway, as it rose on its blue-bricked Victorian viaduct to head towards its river crossing. "Is that a pub down there?"

"Yes, *The Arch Rivals*. It's a great place, and very popular with the students. Just around the corner is the new central library – *The Hive* – which serves as the university library and also the city archives, and over behind the arches are some of the halls of residence, so there are always people around here, even quite late on in the evening."

She was keeping it sounding as if she was giving him the tour of this bit of Worcester, but was also hinting that this wasn't a place where it would be easy to get her alone. All her senses were telling her that Angelo wasn't a threat, but her brain kept reminding her that someone had badly beaten and raped Claire, and that that someone had looked very much like Angelo Vance. And after Lucy's prompting, despite what her instincts were telling her right now, that might yet turn out to have been him.

"I love places like this," Angelo enthused. "I love this mix of the old industrial architecture and the new uses. I had no idea that there was somewhere like this in Worcester. I usually think of Birmingham or London if I want to visit somewhere similar."

"Do you stay in London a lot?" Fleur asked casually, but now seriously wondering how much Mrs Vance was left on her own at *The Rookery*. For a woman with her problems, it might not be the best place to be, but then Fleur could also see that a big city might give Mrs Vance too much anonymity to do as she pleased as well. You could be anonymous in a big city in a way that was impossible in rural communities.

After what he'd told her, she could also see that while Angelo might care about his mother, too much contact might be very unsettling. For all that he was a fit and healthy man now, and therefore not in danger of her physically overwhelming him, if she had spiked his food in the past, Fleur could fully understand that the possibility of her doing it again could be a genuine worry.

"I've got a place right by the Botanical Gardens at Kew," he said, then grinned ruefully. "God, that sounds pretentious, doesn't it?"

Fleur laughed. "Just a tad! But then if you can afford it, why wouldn't you want to live somewhere nice?"

"It is nice," he admitted, and Fleur could see his expression softening just at the thought of it. "It's the first and attic floors of a detached house, so I've got neighbours downstairs – which Mum hates! She wanted me to buy a complete house …which I could have done for what I paid for it…"

"But I'm guessing that after what you told me she did, maybe you feel a bit safer knowing that there are other people in the building?"

"That's exactly it. Yes, the house is detached, but only in the normal kind of way. Not with acres of land around it like *The Rookery* has. And even out on the balcony, or if I go down the steps to my share of the garden, although it's not exactly overlooked because there are a few trees on either side, I'm far from isolated, either." He leaned back and took a drink of his Coke. "To be frank with you, I keep that place as just mine. I don't even entertain there. It's somewhere where I can be a relatively normal person, and I bought it after I'd made the mistake of taking a few casual girlfriends back to my previous place, and then found photos of it appearing in the glossy magazines."

"That's the trouble with everyone having a phone with a decent camera on it, I suppose," Fleur sympathised. "One excuse for a trip to the bathroom and a few clicks along the way, and that's your privacy invaded."

Angelo nodded mournfully. "So when the chance came up for me to take over *The Rookery*, I thought, 'what a great place to have parties at', or to do any business entertaining I might need to do. It's big enough that I can invite people to stay over, and to get caterers in to provide meals. I don't have to have them in my private space." And that, Fleur thought, was the first believable reason she'd had off him as to why he was investing so much in *The Rookery* from his own point of view, not just concern for his mother.

Yet his expression became bleak again. "I honestly thought that giving Mum the Dower House would be the solution to all our problems. She'd be somewhere nice and quiet, where hopefully she wouldn't get all stressed again, and I'd have someone living on site whom I could trust to keep an eye on the place. But somehow, it's not working out like that, and I don't understand why." And there it was again, that sudden feeling that Angelo actually had a fair idea of why it wasn't working out, but couldn't bring himself to tell her.

The burgers arrived at that point, putting a stop to the conversation as Angelo devoured his falafel burger and the portion of rosemary coated fries, and Fleur nibbled away at her fries and coleslaw. When he decided that the ice-creams had to be tried as well, she was easily tempted into joining him, and so it was only as they sat back to enjoy a coffee afterwards that much in the way of conversation started up again. While her colleagues had been around, Fleur had remained professional, calling him Mr Vance, but now it was so easy to revert to the easy conversation they'd had back at the cottage, before everything had turned so weird at *The Rookery*, and to call him by his first name, especially when he reverted to calling her Fleur.

"What do you think you're going to do now?" Fleur asked. "Do you think you can leave your mum out there alone? I know it's only about twenty miles from Worcester, and probably only fifteen at most from Kidderminster or Stourport, but in many ways the whole estate is very isolated."

"That's my worry," Angelo agreed. "I don't want to make things worse for her, but I'm utterly stuck. I think she'll go absolutely nuts if I even suggest selling up, but having seen the way she's become since living there, I really don't think it's the best place for her to be. This odd connection she's got with the place has got me baffled."

"Odd? In what way?"

"Well, before her father died – so back when I was a little kid – she never wanted to go near the place. I know this may sound strange to you, but I had never set foot in it until much later, and that was after the reading of the old man's will. The house in Cheltenham, yes. But while Grandfather was alive and living at *The Rookery* in the Dower House, Mum avoided the place like the plague. I put that down to her difficult relationship with him at the time. You know …her just wanting to avoid having family rows or something."

"That would be understandable."

"Yes, it would. So, when she suddenly became all enthusiastic about me taking the place over, I thought it was her way of spitting in the old man's eye, metaphorically speaking."

And suddenly you're lying to me again, Fleur thought. *Right up to this point, I've no doubt that you've spoken the honest truth, but something about that reason you took on the place isn't right. Or at least it's not the whole story, and by a very long way.*

"We sat in that solicitor's office hearing Grandfather's will being read," he was continuing, "and her whole attitude changed."

'And that's an even bigger lie!' Fleur heard Grandma Rose's voice in her head chipping in. *'He's hiding something to do with that will, and it's really important.'*

"Did your grandfather want your mother to inherit?" Fleur asked innocently "Because that sounds like him wanting to pull the strings even from beyond the grave if he did."

"Oh, he was pulling the strings, alright," Angelo said bleakly, and that was definitely straight from the heart, making Fleur think that something in the will had been addressed directly to Angelo himself.

"*Tsk!* Families, eh?" she sympathised, and got a watery smile. "So all of a sudden, you got saddled with the family's crumbling mansion? Did he always expect you to restore it?"

"Oh, the restoration? No, that was never stipulated. That was me not wanting to deal with ancient plumbing, and wiring that threatened to burst into flames if you plugged too much in. Like I said, it dawned on me that I could entertain there, so it had to be made safe. The builders took one look at it and declared that they wouldn't risk plugging in as much as a power drill until it had been rewired! So that was my decisions made. But Grandfather wanted it to stay in the family, though God knows why. We're hardly royally connected – and even more so after what you've discovered."

And again, Fleur felt that nudging from the beyond by Grandma Rose that the old man really had wanted the house to stay in the family, but for some sort of very dark reason.

"I think it might be to do with the scandal of the family's very common ancestry," Fleur suggested, hoping that she might prompt him to further revelations. "After all, the names will be on the deeds of the place, won't they? If it went up for sale, and then someone looked and went, 'Ooh! Who were all of these?' and started digging out of curiosity, you can imagine a local newspaper being interested, if hardly *The Times* – local human interest, and all that stuff."

Angelo blinked. "Oh hell! Yes, of course. I'd forgotten that in all of the stress over trying to get out of your place. Jeez, Grandfather would have shit bricks if people found out that his grandmother was a gypsy! What little I've heard of him, his own father was a real stuck-up sort, so something like that coming out would have mortified them both. Thanks for that, Fleur, that's made a lot more sense of things."

So that wasn't the reason the old man gave in his will then, Fleur thought, *if you are so surprised at the idea. And your surprise is genuine,* adding, "I'll keep digging if you like? I love getting into ancestry stuff, and given my own gypsy roots, I'd love to know more about Mezelly and Josef Petulengro."

"I don't know how you're keeping track of these people," Angelo sighed but with a grin. "So what connection are they to me, again?"

Fleur laughed. "Well, I can't remember all the side shoots without digging out my notes, but the gypsies interested me, so I remembered them. If I'm recalling it right, Josef – or Joe, as he becomes referred to later on – and his wife Mezelly arrive at *The Rookery* to work for the then owners, who were that Lady Felicia and her son, Henry Kyrle-Quain. As far as I've got, we don't know whether Henrik Bitanyi arrived with the Petulengros, or whether they just happened to meet up once he was working there too. But in the ten years between the 1841 census and the 1851 one, Henry Kyrle-Quain loses ownership of *The Rookery* and then dies, and his mum moves the dubious Henrik in with her into the main house. Henrik ends up marrying Joe and Mezelly's daughter Anselina, and she changes her name to Annie. Those two – Henrik and Anselina – are your direct ancestors through your mum's line."

"Sheesh! A gypsy girl and some kind of itinerant Hungarian card sharp! What a combination!" and Angelo laughed. "So who comes between them and Grandfather?"

"Oooh, hang on a tick," and Fleur dug into her capacious bag and pulled out her notepad, plus the sheaf of photocopies which Carrie-Ann had made. "Okay, so Henrik and Anselina, or Henry and Annie as they changed their names to later on, had several kids, but the oldest daughter is Loretta. I know it makes it complicated, because Henrik changes his name to Henry Boswell, no doubt to give himself some veneer of Englishness. So Loretta is always referred to as Loretta Boswell – she is *never* Loretta Bitanyi – so I think he must have been calling himself Boswell by the time of her birth, even if he hadn't legally changed it. Mind you, it sounds as though Henrik/Henry had a pretty lax attitude to all things legal anyway! But it's Loretta, his daughter, who's the one who marries William Fitzpatrick, and it's *his* family bible that your mum has squirreled away in the Dower House."

A thought occurred to her. "I don't get why she hasn't guessed that the earlier people in the family lists aren't the owners of *The Rookery,* though? In the censuses he appears in, William always gives his place of birth as County Clare in Ireland, and on the marriage certificate his father is from there as well, so I would presume that they have a lengthy history back over there."

Angelo rolled his eyes. "I suspect that one thing that Mum inherited was an ability to close her eyes to the things she didn't want to see. As far as she was concerned, just the having of a family bible would be enough. She probably never looked that hard at the people listed. The fact that there was the appearance of a whole line of them going back centuries, would have been all she bothered about."

"Fair enough, I suppose. I forget that not everyone is possessed of my insatiable curiosity. But from your point of view, William and Loretta are your great-great-grandparents. Incidentally, although Henrik/Henry and Annie only married in 1860, and Loretta was their first legitimate child, there was an older boy born illegitimately. What happens to him I haven't found out yet. For all I know he might have died as a child, and that's why he didn't inherit, but there were other sons, yet Loretta is the one who gets the house, and that's downright strange for the time.

"Now William and Loretta have a whole tribe of kids, but the influenza epidemic and World War One reduce them down to just one daughter, Annora Fitzpatrick, who is your great-grandmother, and it's she who marries Ignatius Kingsford and has your grandfather, Aleister. But William – your great-great-grandfather – is the man who lives on until 1930, and might well have been an influence on your grandfather. Their lives certainly overlap by a few years. I have a feeling that he might have been appalled at the way that the house had been handed on down through the female line. Despite the fact that in the end he presumably only had a daughter to inherit, he possibly made it clear to his son-in-law, Ignatius Kingsford, that his son – your grandfather – in turn *must* inherit."

"What a bloody tangle," Angelo sighed, and Fleur didn't have the heart to tell him about his grandfather's sister who had been molested by her maternal uncle. That was an unsavoury chunk of the past that could wait for another day. Instead, she asked,

"Knowing now that the boxes your mum wanted me to look at contained the grimoires, it puzzles me why she would want me to investigate them at all? After all, you've said that she would never want them sold – so the auction value doesn't matter. Was it insurance? Because after her rant at me when I was trying to sort the other books out, it came across as if she didn't fully grasp what would be needed for an insurance valuation, either."

Angelo gave a grunt of disgust. "Honestly? I have no bloody idea! Mum is so full of contradictions these days I couldn't begin to tell you why. Back in the long-distant past she would have wanted shot of them as soon as possible. But since she's come over here and heard Grandfather's will, it's as if all of her priorities keep rearranging themselves. She has me totally baffled at times."

And that, Fleur thought, was him being truthful again. It seemed unlikely that Claudia Vance had wanted money from the sale of the items now, but had she picked on Fleur in the hope that she could tell her whether some of the spells and concoctions would actually work? On the one hand that sounded far-fetched, but on the other, it came part way to explaining why she was so insistent on having someone with what she possibly saw as knowledge of the arcane working on them. However, that was something she didn't want to ask Angelo tonight when he'd had such a rough day.

"Are you driving back to *The Rookery* tonight?" she asked.

But Angelo shook his head. "No, I think I'll go to the Cheltenham house. I want to get my own head straight again before I tackle Mum. I'd like to think I'll be able to persuade her to sell up and make a fresh start somewhere else, but in truth I doubt that will happen, and it's the row that will ensue that I'm not up to facing tonight."

"I think that's very sensible," Fleur said supportively. "Decide what steps you might be able to get her to take for now. You don't have to win this battle all in one go. Would she accept a holiday back to Italy, for instance? I don't mean back to your family home over there, but maybe offer her a break at some all-inclusive resort on the Amalfi Coast, for instance? Somewhere where she can just relax."

"I think *I* might take up that suggestion," Angelo said with a wan smile. "Just the thought of it has me wanting to book it. But Mum? Who knows? She might, she might not. I don't know what to say to her anymore without making things even worse."

Fleur made sympathetic murmurings but understood exactly what he meant. When Grandma Luisa had been alive there had been many times when she wondered if there was anything she could say to her that wouldn't be taken the wrong way. Grandpa Nik had been a pussycat, never getting het up about anything, but although Grandma Luisa had rarely got into shouting matches, she could give the cold shoulder like nobody else.

They went their separate ways shortly afterwards, Fleur walking Angelo down to by *The Hive* so that she could point out where he was parked, and then once she was sure that he had walked out of sight, hurried around to the gate into her complex and inside. He would have to be very fast to turn around and come back in time to see exactly where she went to, and meaning Fleur felt perfectly secure that night. So for the rest of the evening she sat and just relaxed, with a good book and some of her favourite music playing.

Chapter 18

Her night was once again punctuated by vivid dreams of both grandmothers, but with it being a Saturday, Fleur was able to sleep on and get up feeling refreshed. At first, she just pottered around, doing all the usual domestic stuff like putting washing on, then went out to do her weekly shopping, and for once she found some comfort in the familiar routine. This was the settled rhythm her life had subsided into, and if there were times when it felt a touch empty, she also knew that it would be quite a leap of faith for her to move in with someone else again. And that was why she found it disconcerting that her thoughts kept returning to Angelo. Why, in light of her own experiences, did she find it so hard to believe that he was as bad as everyone thought?

You thought that Carl was a nice bloke, and look what he turned out to be like, she told herself sternly. *Grandma Rose tried to warn everyone he had a dark side, nobody listened, and look what happened! However sorry you feel for Angelo Vance, he's a troubled soul. You don't need that.* And that was what prompted her actions for the rest of the day. She felt she had to get her head clear.

So far she'd been running on instinct, reacting to incidents as they had happened, and she knew that that wasn't good.

There was racing on down the road at the racecourse, so she couldn't do her normal walk to relax today, but tomorrow would be a different matter, and she resolved that whatever the weather, she would get out in the fresh air and blow a few mental cobwebs away. Today, however, she thought she might do a bit of digging on the genealogy sites and see if she could unearth some more on the Romany side of Angelo's family. If she could get to grips with them, she had the feeling that she might be more comfortable with dealing with the grimoires. Moreover, if she went around the corner to *The Hive* to do it, she would be able to get access to things like old newspapers as well, and anything which kept her research away from her home had to be good.

Setting Angelo within the context of a disreputable family would do a lot to help keep her on her toes around him. And so mid-afternoon found her on the uppermost floor of the library where it was quieter, getting engrossed in what she repeatedly found herself thinking of as the Petulengro family history. She was able to swiftly confirm that what Carrie-Ann had unearthed was pretty much all there was to find on Claudia Vance, and aside from a society announcement of the marriage of Aleister Kingsford to Angelina Montefiore in January 1955, there was nothing else on her parents either. With Claudia Vance that was primarily because she was still living, and therefore certain records weren't accessible, yet that wasn't the case for Aleister even if Claudia's mother could potentially be alive over in Italy. But then that lack wasn't so surprising if Contessa Angelina had fled back to Italy as fast as she could, and Aleister had been splitting his time between there and London in the early days.

It's no good, I'm going to have to look at Aleister's siblings and parents, Fleur thought with a sigh, knowing from past experience that it was folly to dive straight back into the earliest known generations and presume that they would match up with the later ones. Yet something about even the thought of Ignatius Kingsford had shivers running down her spine, and although her brain was telling her that it was the unsavoury links to Aleister Crowley that was doing that, her psyche was saying that there was something more to it than that, and that Ignatius had been a truly wicked man. But there was only one way to confirm or deny that, and so Fleur went digging.

Several hours later she had answers, although they weren't necessarily ones she was happy about. Aleister's sisters weren't a problem. Ismena, the youngest, had died just as Carrie-Ann had said, while Dulcibelle, the oldest, had died with her infant child in 1940. The unfortunate Morwenna – victim of the child abuser – had emigrated to Canada after the death of her mother, Annora, in 1959, presumably not feeling safe without any other female member of the family around her, and so she was long out of the picture even by the time Claudia was a toddler, much less married and having children of her own.

And Fleur was able to find a newspaper obituary of her death in Canada in 1993, (perhaps placed by Aleister in the local press) and mentioning a will showing that there were no children, but what little she had going to her female partner. It was tactfully phrased, as if speaking of a business partner, but Fleur had no doubt that they'd been living together. *And who could blame you for being off men after what you went through in that family,* Fleur thought sympathetically. If Morwenna hadn't been that way inclined as a child, she'd surely had experiences which would have made her reluctant to ever trust another man again. But at least all of this confirmed that there was no trail to follow beyond Ignatius himself in that generation.

The late Ignatius Kingsford had certainly been quite the WW1 hero, singlehandedly storming a machine-gun nest and thereby saving many of his comrades. But something about the reports set Fleur's nerves on edge. With another man she would have been mentally applauding his bravery all the way. But with Ignatius there were hints that he was by nature something of a maniac, and it didn't sit quite right with the concept of yet another young lad signing up under-age to 'do his bit', either.

Luckily, he had been with a Midland regiment, and so although there was the usual dearth of records in the national archives, thanks to the incendiary bomb in World War Two which had obliterated much of the War Office's archives, there were local snippets in newspapers which implied that prior to that, Ignatius had been a wild child, and became one of those men who revelled in the destruction of war in the way no normal soldier did. Such a hero might have considered staying on in the army at the end of the war, but the army had seemed to want to get rid of him at speed – even faster than the normal demobbing process – and that couldn't be good, even if she couldn't find the details of why.

What really had Fleur's flesh creeping, though, was reading that Ignatius' family had come from Leamington Spa, and not that far away from the infamous Aleister Crowley's family, although by that time, Crowley had long since broken contact with them if what she recalled of reading about him in her studies was correct. There were no concrete links to Crowley, but Fleur had the increasing and uneasy feeling that Ignatius had had something of an unhealthy obsession with the man long before he had named his only son after Crowley in 1923. And with a start she recalled finding an old photograph alongside one of the notebooks she had unpacked, which although it was of nothing more than an old house, had set her skin creeping. Now, though, she did a swift internet search and found that her flash of insight was right – the house in question was Boleskine House near Loch Ness, and from 1899 up until 1913 that was where Aleister Crowley had lived on the rare occasions he wasn't abroad somewhere.

Ignatius – and Fleur was sure in her own mind that it would have been him who owned the photograph – as a late-teenager going to Crowley's retreat in the Highlands, and potentially taking part in one or more of Crowley's rituals was a grim thought. But even worse were her recollections of the nastier sexual practices which had gone on around Crowley. Bearing in mind that it had been Ignatius' unfortunate daughter Morwenna who had been assaulted, had it been some associated of Ignatius' from those days who had been the culprit, not his wife Annora's unfortunate brother Wantelo?

"Oh no!" Fleur gulped, then realising that someone was looking across at her, clamped her hand across her mouth as she wondered, *Were you a bit simple, as they would have put it back then, Wantelo? Were you as much a victim of this unknown man as Morwenna was? Crowley was bisexual, so is the reason why Ignatius and Annora didn't have any children in nearly six years because he, too, was bisexual, and at the time spending time with a male lover instead of his wife? Was his lover the man living at the cottage in the grounds?*

All of those were questions she felt it was really important to answer, but one thing was screaming at her loud and clear: the nastier grimoires were potentially Ignatius', and if he was a fully-fledged member of Crowley's set, if not the actual Golden Dawn, then it behoved her to treat them with extreme caution. Who knew what bizarre invocations and rituals the man had performed with them? According to a good many reports, Crowley had left something very nasty lurking at Boleskine House, and even people who weren't considered susceptible had nonetheless had some very unpleasant experiences around there, not to mention the two most recent fires which had all but gutted the house.

And long may it stay a ruin, Fleur found herself wishing, as she willingly shut the files on those members of the Kingsford family. *Is there something equally as dark and feral lurking at* The Rookery? *Is that why I thought there was someone upstairs? Please God it isn't just me who has seen that other person who looks like Angelo! Please let him at least be a real flesh and blood human being, and not something dark preying on my subconscious when I'm there; because of anyone, I'll be the one to pick up on something like that.* And there and then she vowed that if she ever had to go back there, she would go armed with Grandma Rose's bracelets and any other kind of arcane protection she could conjure up.

Looking out of the nearest window, Fleur realised that it was later than she had thought, having got engrossed in her research. The earlier Fitzpatricks would have to wait until tomorrow, after she'd been for her walk, and the good thing about *The Hive* serving the university was that it was open on Sundays when normal libraries would be closed, so there wouldn't be any problem with her coming back later on tomorrow. Packing up her stuff into the satchel-bag she used, she slung it across her shoulder and headed downstairs.

It was second nature to her to wear her bags slung crosswise across her body, leaving her hands free, it having begun when she had been pushed around by Carl's buddies and she'd once lost her bag with her house keys in. That had been a terrifying few days, with her worried to death that they might gain access to where she was living. Luckily some kind passer-by had taken the bag to the nearest police station, and the keys and all of her things had still been in it. But she'd never forgotten that close call, and had made sure that her bag could never be simply dropped ever again.

Outside the main doors she paused under the overhang, scrutinising the drizzle outside, and wondering whether it was really worth putting the hood on her coat up when it was just a short jog up the road to the gates of her complex.

That was when she heard it.

"There she is!" she heard coming from the darkness of the bike shelter across the broad walkway, and a chill ran down her spine.

Was she jumping at shadows just because of what she'd just been reading? Was it nothing more than a lad waiting for some other girl or woman to come out? Yet all of her instincts screamed 'no' at her. That voice, even only heard from a distance, and quietly at that, sounded uncomfortably like Angelo Vance, and she immediately turned around and went back into the foyer of the library, making as if she was going back into the light to check something in her bag.

Luckily, a group of students went past outside, obviously having been out in the town for the afternoon. They were going the other way to where she'd been heading, but now that was all to the good. The last thing she wanted was to lead her unwanted shadow straight back to the complex gates, because sooner or later someone would go in who could be conned into letting him in with them. And so she scampered out into the damp and hurried to catch up with the group, who were chatting and laughing together.

A quick glance over her shoulder told her that she hadn't been imagining things. Two shadows, one bigger than the other had detached themselves from the gloom of the bike racks and were heading her way.

Quickening her pace, Fleur hurried to catch up with the students, managing to never let them be out of sight of her until she caught them at the entrance to the halls of residence grounds beyond the railway arches. As she got right up behind them, two of the girls turned around and looked enquiringly at her.

"Would you mind if I walked with you?" Fleur asked a little breathlessly. "Only I seem to have a random man following me and it's freaking me out."

"Oh my God! That's horrible," the one girl immediately sympathised, while the other motioned her forwards into the group.

As she did so, from the dark of the railway arches there came a furious, "Fuck!"

The three rearmost students jumped as they heard it, and then closed ranks even tighter around Fleur.

"Do you want to go to the police?" the one lad asked, clearly knowing that they only had to make the short walk out onto Castle Street to get to the central Worcester police station.

"No, it's okay," Fleur said with a shaky smile. "Whoever he is, he'll probably be long gone by the time I could get anyone to come back here. It's Saturday evening, after all. The police have probably got their hands full with more serious stuff. …But I'd really appreciate it if a couple of you could walk the loop back with me to by *The Paul Pry*."

The Paul Pry was one of Worcester glorious old Victorian pubs, and lay no further in the other direction to Fleur's home than *The Hive* did. But from here it would be possible to come out on the narrow lane on the far side of the students' halls and double back under a different section of the railway viaduct. That would be the danger point for Fleur, because whoever it was who was hunting her clearly knew that that was where she had taken Angelo for the burger, and so might be lurking around there. Once across that narrow lane, and on to where the pub sat on the corner with the main through route of The Butts, Fleur would be fine, because The Butts was never free of traffic, and only a total madman would try grabbing a woman in front of everyone there.

"Tom and Sam can walk you," one of the girls volunteered, and the two biggest lads promptly nodded. Since they looked as though they were probably going to spend tomorrow on the rugby pitch, diving into scrums with relish, Fleur could see why their friend had volunteered them, and gratefully accepted.

In fact, she didn't see any sign of anyone suspicious at the railway arches or at any other point, so she was feeling considerably better by the time she got to her gates, Tom and Sam having insisted on walking her all the way once they knew she was only a few yards down the road from the pub. With profuse thanks to her saviours, Fleur thankfully shut the security gate and hurried inside. She did pause at the door to her section, and look back at the main gates, but there was no sign of anyone loitering there, nor peering in as if trying to spot where she had gone. So it was with relief that she got into her own flat and bolted the front door behind her.

Yet she didn't put on anything more than the hallway light. Going over to the French windows in the lounge, she carefully opened the one and leaned out onto the Juliet balcony. It didn't look onto the side where the lane was running between the railway line and *The Hive,* and on up to the pub and burger bar, but was virtually on the corner, ninety degrees from it. And so leaning out into the darkness, Fleur had a good view of the lower part of the lane and the steps around the library.

Nobody was there.

Or at least nobody she was bothered about.

"Oh, thank God for that!" she breathed in relief. And for a brief moment she wondered whether she had imagined it all. Was she so freaked out by what she'd read that she had started jumping at shadows that weren't a threat?

Leaning back against the glass she drank in the evening air, feeling her pulse rate returning to something more like normal. Another group of students went by, laughing and chatting. Just another ordinary Saturday night, she told herself, almost starting to feel embarrassed for having put Tom and Sam to so much trouble.

And then she saw them.

Hurrying out from further up the lane, she saw a man and a woman. Definitely the same man and woman she had seen behind her, because the woman was wearing a distinctive coat with a fur-edged hood, and the man had the same wild hair.

She shrank back into the room, leaning over and tugging the curtain across the closed half of the window so that it threw her into even deeper shadow. But even stood inside her living room now, she could see the pair casting about them down below. They were definitely looking for someone or something, and Fleur had no doubt that she was it.

She couldn't hear them over the sound of the students, but the man was clearly arguing with the woman, who was tugging at his sleeve and making gestures in another direction. Then the moment came when they stepped into the light of one of the streetlamps. As the glow of the light hit them, the man turned around, one hand dashing his damp hair back from his face.

Angelo Vance!

But this was Bad Angelo. The out-of-control man from the vlogs. The one who made such inflammatory statements. This wasn't the considerate man Fleur had chatted with. This was someone very angry and potentially dangerous to cross, and Fleur was under no illusions that he would consider her to have crossed him, though what she might actually have done – other than refuse to work at his house – she couldn't say. But then was this version of Angelo totally sane?

Remembering what Angelo had told her of his mother keeping him locked up and drugged for a long time, had that done some terrible damage to his mind? Was he suffering from some sort of split personality, where the one part had no recollection of what he'd done when the other took hold? If so, he was very much to be pitied, but Fleur was not going to be the one to try and bring him back from that abyss. That was a job for mental health professionals.

As Angelo and the woman, who Fleur was now sure was Claudia Vance, headed down towards the riverside car parks, Fleur closed her window and immediately drew the heavy drapes across. Quite often she didn't bother doing that except on cold nights, happy to be able to look out at the night sky. But tonight, she wanted the security of feeling cocooned in her den, of not being spied upon. No sane person would scramble up onto the railway lines at night, which was the only way anyone could get even a peek in at her windows, but the man she had seen down on the street was nothing like sane.

Chapter 19

Sunday morning came in bright but blustery. Perfect weather for a nice brisk walk, and although Fleur did consider not going out in light of what had happened the night before, her determination won. She had refused to be cowed by her ex-husband's bullying friends, and she was damned if she was going to become a prisoner in her own home just because of one crazy client from work. Fleur had never been the athletic sort, but she did have a stout pair of walking boots, which she put on to go out in. They would keep her feet dry while walking on the wet grass of the racecourse, but also, if anyone tried to grab her, they would be solid enough to do some damage with a good kick.

"Never take your feet off the ground unless you can't help it," she remembered her instructor telling her. "Once you're on one foot, you're off balance. Try kicking them in the groin and you're as likely to have your foot grabbed and find yourself being tipped onto your back. Don't let that happen!"

But at the same time, he'd also taught her that if trapped in someone's grasp, then a heel rasped smartly down your assailant's shin could be very painful. Certainly enough to be the distraction you might need. And so Fleur was counting on the hefty boots delivering a painful dissuasion to anyone daft enough to try grabbing her.

So she set out in the late morning, having given it time for people with families to be out and about enjoying their own Sunday pre-lunch walks. Determination was one thing, folly quite another, and Fleur had no intention of going out when it was still quiet and she was the only person around. And for almost all of her walk that proved to be the case. Families from the east side of Worcester were out and about at the Barbourne end of the racecourse, with small children taking their first wobbly rides on bikes, and other people enjoying the bright morning walking their dogs. Closer to the river she encountered a couple of groups of runners, all of whom exchanged cheery hellos with her.

Of all places, it was as she was walking back towards the main gates of the racecourse, across an area already filled with the cars of people coming into Worcester to enjoy the riverside, or to have a Sunday brunch at one of the many cafes and restaurants, that danger struck. She was just walking past a tatty old Ford Transit van when from behind it, and her, a hand snaked out and grabbed her arm, spinning her around.

Suddenly she was face to face with Bad Angelo, as she'd come to think of him, but recoiled as an almost suffocating wave of garlic and curry overwhelmed her. His grip tightened,

"Gotcha bitch!" he crowed. "You don't get to fuck *me* around!"

But even with her eyes almost watering with the stench, which seemed to be oozing out of every pore as well as his breath, Fleur wasn't cowed. As he pulled her closer, she lashed out with a boot, catching him squarely on the shin.

"*Aaagh*! You fucking cow!" he yelped, tightening his grip even more.

Yet as he snatched at her with his other hand, Fleur moved too. Far from tugging away, she reached out and got a grip on the little finger of the hand holding her, and without hesitation, snapped it back, breaking it at the joint above the knuckle and bending the knuckle joint painfully.

Bad Angelo let out a scream of pain, and just as her instructor had said would happen, his grip on her failed.

"*Aaagh!*" he screamed again. "You bitch! You fucking bitch!"

Not that Fleur was waiting to see what would happen. As he bent over, clutching his hand to him, she struck again, ramming her elbow backwards and hard into him. She'd hoped to hit his face, but she was too short to manage that. What she did achieve was a sharp poke to a spot just above his collarbone, and she heard his next scream cut off in a gasping cough. He must have doubled over further because spurred on, she pulled her arm back and jabbed sharply again, this time feeling her elbow connecting painfully with bone.

As she now turned to fully face him, she could see that he was wearing stout jeans, so that was a different manoeuvre she couldn't do, because it necessitated being able to get a grip on his testicles through whatever he was wearing.

'Don't worry about being a lady,' her instructor's words echoed in her head. 'Just grab hold of his family jewels and twist. I promise you he won't come back for seconds!' However, with Angelo now almost doubled over she could risk moving behind him, and with her fury spurring her on, she stepped back and booted him hard between the legs from behind.

With a coughing, snivelling, wail, Bad Angelo collapsed onto the sand the racecourse keepers had laid down yesterday for vehicles crossing the racetrack. Yet from behind her Fleur now registered a shriek of fury, and someone else barrelled into her. Without even thinking, Fleur instinctively bent over, so that the person's momentum carried them over the top of her, falling in a heap almost on top of Bad Angelo, and giving him a kick to the face with a heeled boot as she went. Claudia Vance was evidently not used to such rough contact and screamed hysterically. And though Fleur was braced for her to get up and start clawing at her, instead Mrs Vance registered her son on the ground and immediately focused her attention on him.

Needing no encouraging, Fleur took to her heels, vaguely hearing someone in the distance shouting, "Call the police! They've just tried to mug that lady!"

She didn't stop running until she was up by *The Hive*, then doubled over herself, as a stitch in her side suddenly had her gasping for breath. Damn! That had been close! Too close for comfort. But what to do about it? Should she call the police, or maybe just walk up to the main police station and report it at the desk? However, if she did, then she would have, in all conscience, to also report that she knew who the man and woman were, and somehow, even after the nasty fright she'd just had, there was the part of her that was thinking that there must be something terribly wrong with Angelo to bring on such a sudden and dreadful transformation.

Nobody who was that mentally ill deserved to be stuck in a police cell, and now that the initial fright was subsiding a little, Fleur was wondering whether they would be any threat at all to anyone else. Most probably they were focusing on her because they wanted her to dredge up something from the grimoires which would transform their lives somehow. Certainly, they had shown no signs of being in any way interested in anyone else from *Miller, Bronson & Carter* – not any of the men who had helped to cart the precious books away, and certainly not Mr Harris, who of any of them ought to have been next in the firing line, if only because he had backed Fleur up so vigorously, and had set the removal of the books in motion.

Suddenly feeling drained, Fleur made her way back home and got changed, then unable to face cooking for herself, decided that for once she would go up the road and take advantage of *The Paul Pry's* excellent Sunday lunch. By the time she had devoured the roast and had a couple of pints of real ale, she felt considerably better. Even more so, because once at the door of the pub, she had a clear view down the road to the gateway of her complex and beyond, and knew that she could get home without being stopped. Quite what she would have done if the Vances had been lingering she wasn't sure, but then realistically, that would be the point when she would have to suppress her compassion for their states of mind and call the police. Mercifully that didn't happen, and Fleur was able to go home and spend the rest of Sunday flaked out on her sofa watching old movies.

Getting up for work on Monday, her next big question was how much to tell her colleagues what had happened. Much as she hated the idea of lying to Lucy, she knew what Lucy's knee-jerk reaction would be, and that it would involve suing the behind off the Vances. Nor did she feel particularly comfortable confessing all to Mr Harris. He, too, was likely to see everything in a slightly skewed context.

She still wasn't sure how she felt about all of it by the time she'd walked in, left her coat in the staffroom, and gone up to the attic room. Mercifully the atmosphere up here was considerably better given that the toxic books and tarot deck were missing. But over at the end of the workbench where the most recent grimoires lay, there was still a very definite nasty atmosphere, confirming what she had found on Saturday, that the time of Ignatius Kingsford's rule at *The Rookery* had almost certainly been the time when some of the worst abuses of the arcane had taken place.

"I'm not dealing with you today," she told those books, "so you can sulk all you like over there. I'm off to the other end to look at the good stuff."

Not that she'd forgotten the bag that she'd hidden on Friday. That couldn't stay there forever, because sooner or later someone was going to come and check on the workshop's extractors. Where on earth she was going to hide the items more permanently, at least until she could destroy them, was a whole other problem she had yet to find the solution to.

Once the refuse collection for the week had been done for her block, she could potentially hide them down behind her own bins, at least for a few days, but for now Fleur knew she had to put that to the back of her mind and focus on something work related. She couldn't have Mr Harris coming upstairs and finding her idly staring off into space, not after the kerfuffle of Friday. He'd be signing her off for a week of rest at speed – not least because Claire's suing of her employers would still be in his mind, and he would want to demonstrate that he had shown due care for Fleur – but Fleur desperately wanted to get to grips with the notebooks right now.

And so focusing on the first half dozen, she got into the detail of examining handwriting, ink, and paper, until she felt that she had them in the right order of creation. When she went onto the next half dozen, she ended up revising her chronology, moving one of those back into sixth place and another up into seventh, but other than that she reached a point where she felt she had this first dozen correctly sorted. Now she could legitimately get into investigating the contents so that she could catalogue them properly.

Sitting down at what was normally Sue's desk by the east window, Fleur opened the oldest notebook. And a notebook this definitely was. The difficult handwriting scrawled across the pages, but seemed to be trying to keep it to one recipe per page.

Yarrow, she read, *eases coughs and the weak stomach. Makes a good beer flavour.* By which she presumed the writer meant it was one of those useful herbs often added to home brews to give it a bit more flavour, back in the days before different hop varieties were commercially used. *Take 30 heads of yarrow and steep in hot water in a covered pan, then leave to stand,* it continued. All very normal, and familiar from Grandma Rose's concoctions; indeed, Fleur could remember being given Grandma Rose's homemade yarrow cough mixture as a girl and could vouch for its efficacy.

Page after page went on like this, some recipes longstanding and proven, others a bit random, but then Fleur suspected that since some of the oddest ones weren't complete, that the writer was trying to recall what she'd been told long ago and was hoping that at some point she would rediscover the complete recipe. The second book saw the first attempts of the younger members of the family to contribute, and Fleur could see the childish writing gradually improving in the second hand which came in. Yet these were still very much recipes such as many a family must have had back in Victorian times, when doctors catered to the rich who could pay them, and ordinary folk had to take their chances with the local wise woman and hope she was up to the task.

Therefore all of them contained some form of healing for something, even if it was as random as what Fleur guessed were in-growing toenails, and it was with quite a start that she came across the third entry in the third book which was very different. It began,

Master is a weak man. He doth nothing to stop Henrik harm Mistress in the night and make her bleed.

"Jeez!" Fleur gasped aloud in her surprise.

I am afreared for our Ani. Henrik does look at her wrong. No grown man should look at a child like that. Joe does take her out with her as much as he can or I keeps her in the kitchen with me and the babies. Young master goes away often. I think he is afeared of Henrik. We are much frighted by what might happen if he dies and Henrik becomes master here, for Mistress is under his spell. She will not stand up for herself or her son, and Master Henry is no match for this

Hun demon. Henrik knows what he ought not. He has potions he hides in his room and wont let I take food to Master and Mistress but must serve them himself.

"Bloody hell!" Fleur sat back in her chair. By 'Hun demon' she guessed that Mezelly was referring to Henrik's Hungarian decent, which probably meant that the Petulengros hadn't come from Hungary, and could well have been from a Romany family who had already been in England for a few generations. Certainly Mezelly's speech patterns were very much local old rural, and she hadn't been educated enough to do anything other than write how she spoke. What was more, when she came to look back at the first two recipes, they were just neater copies of ones she had already seen in the previous books. Clearly Mezelly had copied them out, or had one of the girls do it, so that if anyone happened to pick this book up it would seem like the others on a casual opening.

Then she turned the page and gasped again.

I found Henrik collecting White Bryony in the meadow and asked him why for tis one to use sparingly and only by those with the wisdom for it be fatal if used wrongly.

Again, Fleur thought that 'wisdom' was Mezelly's way of say with the right education or knowledge, but couldn't spell those words. But Henrik gathering a herb which Grandma Rose had warned her was toxic except in the most minute of quantities, that didn't sound good at all.

He told me to mind my buzness. Who be he to tell I? He be nowt but another servant but a dangerous one.

I hurried home and while he were out I went hunting. I found dried Christmas Roses in his room. No doubt if I aks he will say tis but for to slay the rats with once ground into sommat. But I fears young Masters bad belly may come from some of this being sprinkled on his food. If Henrik doth as I fear and rapes Mistress regular he wont use it on her since it will rid her of any child of his.

Fleur vaguely recalled Grandma Rose saying something about powdered hellebore being used in the old days to stimulate a woman's period and thereby terminate an early pregnancy, that being one of the reasons why she had warned Fleur not to touch the tiny pot she too had kept to ward off mice from her garden shed. Mezelly's lack of punctuation meant that sometimes she had to read a sentence twice to get the full sense of what she meant, but there was no doubt that she was worried that young Henrik Bitanyi, as he undoubtedly was still called back then, was already trying to inveigle his way into the home of Lady Felicia Kyrle-Quain.

By the time Fleur had read of Mezelly discovering a mixture of hemlock, black henbane and opium poppy, just waiting to be ground up, there was little doubt in Mezelly's mind in the past, and Fleur's here in the present, that Henrik had got fed up with waiting and was going to put an end to young Master Henry as soon as he'd served his purpose. Socrates was probably the most famous victim of hemlock poisoning, but there were some who also thought that the strained juice of mashed up hemlock stems was what Shakespeare had been referring to in *Hamlet,* as the liquid poured into the old king's ear, thereby administering it close to the brain and speeding up its effect while remaining undetected. Both of those cases Fleur had heard debated by student friends in the past, and so she was not going to dismiss Mezelly's fears. But what had made Henrik subsequently wait to take *The Rookery* in a game of cards if he had already been planning murder?

The answer came on the next page. Mezelly had not been a woman to be easily intimidated, and had told not only her husband, Josef, but also the young gardener, Harodain Boswell. The three of them then confronted Henrik one evening, telling him that they had sent word to the wider Romany community of their suspicions, and where to attach blame should one or all of them fall ill and die. Since the threat of a whole tribe of gypsies coming after him with vengeance in mind was not something to be taken lightly out in a rural community, and in an age when such a thing as police were unknown, Henrik seemed to back down, and suddenly the notebook returned to more normal recipes.

Yet barely had the next notebook been started, and with the apparent intention of teaching young Annie, Loverin, and Lamentina the basics of folklore and medicine, than Henrik reared his ugly head again.

He have done it! was scratched into the paper so violently as to leave gouge marks. *Poor Master have been cheated out of the house by Henrik! And twas done in front of many of the local gentry so there is no going back on it. My Joe and Teiso witnessed it as they waited on the gentlemen at their game, it not being fitting for women to be present, or so they said. I thinks it be more to do with us having the sense to stop things if they gets out of hand. Men do be so foolish when the thrill of the chase be on them, even if it be at cards not with hounds and a fox.*

So that was how it had been done! Fleur had to admit that Henrik had been cunning, but also wondered how he had got the money to enter into such a game in the first place? Had he blackmailed gullible young Henry Kyrle-Quain, and had such a hold over him already that the young master had had no choice but to invite the servant to the game? Fleur thought possibly not, if only because it would have to have been a powerful grip for anyone to have on a young man who seemed to have led a fairly blameless life. Moreover, in that case the other gentry might have objected to Henrik's presence. Men like that did not sit idly by and let some lowlife crush one of their own. No, rogue Henrik must have been gradually worming his way into these games from lower down the ladder, probably cheating his way into accumulating enough money so that he could buy his way into the game. If Henry Kyrle-Quain hadn't been the sort to frequent illicit gambling dens, it didn't mean that some of the others at that ill-fated game hadn't, and it was quite possible that one or two of them had lost heavily to him already in the past, their payment being written off against Henrik's introduction into this high-stakes game.

Absolutely fascinated by now, Fleur turned the page and saw the name Lady Felicia, but also some sort of stain on the page.

"What's that?" she murmured, bending in closer to look at something which she thought wasn't just a dirt or grease mark, and as she gently rubbed over it with a finger, the world went black.

Chapter 20

Oblivious to the real world of the attic, Fleur was swept into another place and time. It was the large kitchen of a substantial house, and she knew instantly that this was the kitchen in *The Rookery* as it had been in Mezelly's time. Much darker than the room she had walked through only days ago, the place was full of steam and the smells of cooking, despite a window being open out of sight but felt by the draft. She was looking through the eyes of Mezelly, or so she assumed in those first moments, and was proven right when a delicate woman in a fine dress appeared in front of her and spoke, calling her Mrs Petulengro.

"Mistress," Mezelly said, dropping a respectful curtsy. Most cooks in big houses would have been sure enough of their status not to be quite so subservient, but Mezelly was obviously painfully aware that she was not of the same order as the other cooks in the surrounding area.

"Mrs Petulengro, I need your help," the fine lady said, and almost dropped onto one of the simple chairs pushed back against the wall.

"Mistress! Are you unwell?" Mezelly's genuine

concern rippled through to Fleur.

"I fear I may be," the other woman said faintly. "Or rather, I am missing my monthly courses, and… and…"

"Oh, no!"

Like Mezelly, Fleur knew what that meant. Lady Felicia was pregnant! But Mezelly added,

"Forgive me for asking, milady, but could it just be your age? Tiz normal for these things to stop. I don't mean to be impertinent, but have you been more irregular of late? If so, you may be worrying needlessly."

Lady Felicia smiled faintly but shook her head. "I wish it was so, truly I do, but for the last few mornings I have been nauseous," then seeing that Mezelly didn't understand the word, clarified, "very sick, very sick indeed."

"Oh Lordy!"

"Indeed. And now I must trust you to help me get rid of it, for that man must not have an heir through me – even illegitimately – to whom he could hand on an estate. My poor Henry may have lost this estate, but my late husband recognised that Henry might be a foolish owner of *The Rookery*, and made sure that the estate which came to me on my brother's death was entailed away back to a younger male cousin of mine, should Henry fail to hold on to here. It's is currently let out, and I get the income, and should that man throw me out of here, that is where I could go to. Only when I die is when my cousin will inherit, but not if I should have a child not excluded in the document, do you see?

"He never dreamt I would have another child, let alone a male one after his death, who might inherit my old home instead of Henry. Dear Roderick tried his best, making Henry wait until he was twenty-five before he could take on this estate without legal help, but he couldn't fully disinherit his own son. But he hoped that if the worst happened that my cousin would care for me in my extremis."

"And Henrik thinks he can get his hands on that place too if he has a child by you?" Mezelly guessed, and Lady Felicia nodded, a tear trickling down her paper white cheek.

Mezelly walked over and patted her mistress gently on the hand. "Don't you worry, milady, 'tis early days and that babe is barely with us yet. It won't take much to start your courses flowing again." But Fleur felt Mezelly's worry that a pregnancy at Lady Felicia's age might prove fatal, and also her making the sign to ward off evil once she turned away.

In the vision Fleur watched as Mezelly carefully prepared a herbal tea, and then sat with Lady Felicia as she drank it.

"When you leave Henrik to his smokes after dinner, I'll bring you another," Mezelly promised. "One ought to be enough, but this time let's not take any chances, eh?"

"No, no chances," begged Lady Felicia, and still needing to lean a hand against the wall for support, left the kitchen.

In an instant Fleur was back in the present, but knew that that hadn't been her daydreaming, or even briefly nodding off. That had been very real, and though she couldn't account for how it had happened, she didn't doubt for one second that she had had a glimpse directly back into the past. Checking that she hadn't been out for hours, and relieved to find that it had only been minutes, she rubbed her finger over the same patch on the paper again, but this time nothing happened. Did it only work one time, or had the strange stain on the paper had nothing to do with it? There was only one way to find out, and Fleur skimmed through the pages until she found a similar stain.

At this point she got up and went out onto the landing, because after the clout from the falling bookcase on Friday, the door no longer shut properly. It was probably nothing more than the hinges getting warped, because it was a stout enough piece of wood in itself, but it still meant that Fleur couldn't get quite the privacy she would have liked right now. Mr Harris walking in and seeing her in a trancelike state would not be good, and she certainly dared not shove a chair against the door, because what plausible reason could she have for doing that? It certainly wasn't that cold that she could use the excuse of a draft, and anyway, as soon as you got out onto the landing you could feel the warmth from the offices below percolating upwards. So Fleur needed to be very sure that she would remain undisturbed.

Luckily it sounded as though all the office doors were shut, and their occupants behind them, so unless Lucy came looking for her, the chances were that she would be okay. And so taking a deep breath, and making sure she was sat squarely on her chair and not likely to fall off, Fleur rubbed her finger over the next mark.

Immediately she was back in that other time, though this time she was sure it wasn't Mezelly's eyes she was seeing things through. Looking down she saw much younger hands, ones not yet roughened by years of scrubbing out pots and pans and daily chores. Annie, then, and going by what she was doing folding fine silk underwear, at a time when she had become Lady Felicia's maid. But her hesitancy said she hadn't been doing it for long, either, and then the girl turned and just for an instant Fleur saw her face in a mirror.

Good grief! Annie couldn't be more than twelve or fourteen! But then, of course, in those days it was normal for girls to go into service very young. The only thing that was off about this situation was that Annie wasn't being introduced to service with the menial tasks, but had gone straight into being a maid – something she shouldn't have expected to do until she was maybe ten years older and had worked her way up. But then Fleur thought that this was another indicator that this was no ordinary household. Henrik must have been close to paranoid about others finding out what was going on at *The Rookery*, and would rather use the servants' families who were already there, rather than risk bringing in an outsider who might leave after a few short months, and then go around the neighbourhood spreading gossip about what they had seen.

Trying to keep a hold of her sense of self, Fleur tried to recall what she knew of the family. Ah, yes! In that 1851 census Annie, or Anselina as she had still been recorded as back then, was Lady Felicia's maid, so if she'd been born in 1839 then she would indeed have only been thirteen at the time. Yet if this was 1851, it was only five years before Lady Felicia's death in 1856, and seven years before that illegitimate child of Annie's was born in 1858.

But in this trying to sort out who was who and when, Fleur had stopped concentrating on the past vision, and so it came as a real jolt to hear an oily voice saying in a heavy foreign accent,

"Make sure you are doing that properly, little bird," and seeing through Annie's eyes a tall man, who was probably barely thirty, leaning against the door frame watching her in a way that made both Annie and Fleur's flesh creep. He was good-looking, if you liked that sort. The word which came instantly to Fleur's mind was 'louche'. A word which for some reason she always associated with between-the-wars debutants and the kind of oily, sordid, and disreputable young men of the Roaring Twenties who tried to prey upon them, and were good-looking enough to get away with it. 'Rakish' was another word she'd have used to describe him.

A rough, infinitely less desirable, and almost-but-not-quite Clark Gable conveyed the general impression, though the famous film star wouldn't be known for a century yet. The thin moustache; the dark, smouldering eyes; the tangle of thick dark hair that framed his face which wasn't fashionable at the time; all of which may have seemed so alluring to a lonely Lady Felicia. If she hadn't had much male attention in years – and given that she'd had a son old enough to inherit once his father died, she evidently couldn't have appeared to have much in the way of obvious financial advantages to those local widowers who might have wanted to increase their lands by taking another wife – she could well have been easy pickings for a man like Henrik, especially if he'd been practicing his charms in the times he'd been travelling before coming to England. Had this rogue started with the ladies' maids and worked his way up?

And yet to Fleur's more discerning eyes he was already starting to lose those charms. What had no doubt once been beautiful, clear olive skin was now roughening and looking dull with the lack of Mediterranean sun. There was the start of a small paunch, and around the chin a loosening of skin which could develop into jowls. And that very Greek or Italian look about him had Fleur thinking that despite his name, Henrik probably wasn't native Hungarian at all, or at least if born there then not to Hungarian parents. This was the era of the Austro-Hungarian Empire, which had also swallowed up

Slovenia and chunks of what was modern-day Croatia, and so it was far more likely that Henrik's parents had been poor Italians or Croatians, who'd had to go and find work with their conquering neighbour's country.

Yet as Fleur watched on, if she'd expected young Annie to be cowed by this man, she was about to be surprised.

"Ain't you got your own work to do, Henrik Bitanyi?" Annie challenged him back. "I thought you was supposed to be lookin' at the orchard with Harodain today? You was so fast to want this place, but it ain't all about wanderin' about in your nightclothes 'til midday, y'know! Master Henry might'a done that, but he paid a man to do the work for him. You'm too tight-fisted to carry on payin' the factor, so you'd better roll your sleeves up and do somethin' yerself, or it'll all go to wrack and ruin, and you'll be back out on your arse in the streets where you come from!"

"You surly minx!" Henrik hissed, and moved towards her as if to strike her.

But in a flash Annie had grabbed Lady Felicia's powder puff and blew the fine talc straight into his face. As the talc got in his eyes, Henrik swore vilely, but Annie wasn't cowed.

"You just remember there's my pa, my two big brothers, and Harodain all here, but there's only one o' you! Harm can come to a man out here on his own. We'd all swear to the magistrates that we seen footpads lurkin' about the place. Robbery gone wrong, y'see? They came in the night and went afore any of us saw 'em. A proper master would'a had a pistol or two, and knowed how to use 'em. But you ain't a proper master, are yer? Just a nasty, jumped-up card shark. Be off with yer!"

With a snarl, Henrik disappeared out onto the landing, but moments later an even frailer looking Lady Felicia appeared at the doorway.

"Be careful, Annie," she warned. "He is not a man to be crossed. He's dangerous, and he knows things. He has a hold on some powerful people in the area. People who have secrets they don't want to come out, and which he knows. He could make a lot of trouble for you and your family with the law if he was so minded."

Annie nodded, making Fleur's view of the room bob alongside hers. "Aye, milady, I knows that. But he knows that we ain't just the poor farmin' folk either. We might be settled, but our travellin' families are far and wide, and if he harms us he'll get hunted down. A gypsies' curse might not be the same as the law, but you can slip past the law, you can't avoid the curse!"

Again the room vanished, leaving Fleur sitting aghast. Had Mezelly and Annie cursed Henrik? Like them she knew that a true gypsy's curse was not to be taken lightly. She herself knew of a publican who had badly offended the true Roma – not just a bunch of travellers – and he had died of cancer within the year when he had been fit and healthy up until then.

Others had said it was just his misfortune, and that something like cancer could strike fast out of nowhere. But Grandma Rose had always believed it to be the curse and so did Fleur, who had witnessed the furious gypsy doing the deed, and knew the pure venom and vengeance behind it.

She desperately wanted to flip through to find the next stain, for she was sure now that these had been some concoction deliberately placed on the pages to give someone later on the insight into what had happened. But equally, she had to get some work done. What was really bugging her now was the question of whether Annie had really married Henrik Bitanyi? On the one hand, those good looks did remind her somewhat of Angelo, bearing in mind of course that six generations separated them, but on the other, his might truly be down purely to his mother's side. And if Annie had enough fire in her to stand up to Henrik as a young lass barely in her mid-teens, why had the grown woman gone on to have seven children in all by him later on in life?

That spoke of her doing more than just her wifely duty. So had Henrik later on got more of a grip on the Petulengro family? And if so, what on earth could it have been that would force them to leave Annie wed to such a man? Because this wasn't simply a case of Henrik getting an heir and a spare out of Annie, and then her doing nothing more than living at the big house with him.

The family tree Carrie-Ann had dug up had shown that after illegitimate Elias, Annie and Henry

Boswell – whoever he now turned out to be – had had Loretta, from whom Angelo descended, but then the third child had been a son who had been fully legitimate. As long as that son had lived, Annie would have had her get-out from having more children by Henrik/Henry, and yet those other kids had appeared at regular intervals, not just with a late child suddenly appearing after a first heir had died – not that Carrie-Ann had found death dates for any of those other children.

And did any of this have any bearing on the strange situation regarding Angelo's inheritance of *The Rookery*? Because the stranger things in the past got, it increased Fleur's conviction that Angelo's great-grandfather – the unpleasant Ignatius – had known something of it. Worse, the more Fleur found out, the more she was wondering whether Ignatius Kingsford had been trying to ensure it never came to light? Or whether he had discovered that someone had actually got away with murder, and had been hoping to replicate it?

But if that was the case, who had murdered whom? Was Henrik the murderer or the victim?

"The clues are in these bloody books, I know they are," she fumed in exasperation, not least because since yesterday and the Vances' attack on her, this had become very personal.

She hurried through the rest of the third journal, putting slips of paper into the pages where there were more of the strange marks, and then moved on to the fourth and fifth books. For a while there were all four hands contributing, but gradually one younger one took over. That someone, and Fleur suspected either Annie or Loverin or Lamentina, was now starting to date entries, which made her life a lot easier in some ways. It made it easier to see that life had remained on something like an even keel for the Petulengros through the early 1850s. The books remained filled with cures and treatment, and advice on growing certain herbs to give the best potency. Therefore it was only when they began recording attempts to find a cure for whatever was now ailing Lady Felicia, that entries began to take a more sinister turn.

Mother does not know what ails Lady Felicia, the young, bold hand recorded, and obviously referring to Mezelly. *Milady is suffering terrible stomach pains, yet none of our cures for women's complaints are easing them at all. Nor do cures for digestive problems, not that milady eats enough to keep a bird alive, so she does not over-indulge.*

Fleur immediately wondered whether it might be something like cervical or uterine cancer that was the problem, and of course back then there would have been no way of knowing until after her death, and then only if a proper doctor could be persuaded to do an investigation and open her up. Post-mortems were far from being as common as nowadays when an unexpected death occurred, and the local doctor might have been willing to sign a death certificate just on the strength of Lady Felicia having been declining for so long.

Then came the entry,

Henrik is becoming desperate! He changed his name in law last week to Henry Boswell to seem more English, and has spent days at Lady Felicia's bedside badgering the poor soul to make him her sole heir in her will. Yet she is not well enough to leave her bed, and her man of law is declining to change anything, saying that milady was in her right mind when she made the will, but is now so dependent upon opium for the pain that she can no longer be regarded as so.

Mother and Father fear that in his greed Henrik will do something dreadful. He fears them and our family connections, but not as much as he fears losing this house. We now eat nothing other than what Mother or Lamentina have made and never left unattended, for Father and Shadrach had a terrible belly last week. Teiso and Harodain escaped it, for they were away at market, and only came back late that night. But Father and Shadrach had eaten pies Lamentina had made and left out for them, knowing that they would be out at dawn to harvest the upper field, for rain was coming in and we need that wheat. We fear Henrik came in the night and poured something into the pies, for such a purging as my father and brother had almost as soon as they had eaten them was not natural.

A curse upon Henrik, for we have now had that field of wheat spoiled. For though all four of us women went out and did our best, we got less than half in before the storm by the time Father and Shadrach had staggered back, and were able to tell us. That monster will go hungry alongside us, for the estate is now in near ruin thanks to Henrik, and we cannot buy in more. May his innards rot and his brain canker! His evil infects all he touches. It is time he went!

Chapter 21

'Time he went'? The words took Fleur's breath away. Had the Petulengros murdered Henrik?

She looked up at the clock. Nearly lunchtime, but she couldn't stop yet, nor could she move on until she had found out more of what had happened. And so tucking another slip of paper in, with the note on it of, 'suspicion of Henrik's murder', she read on. The next entry came straight afterwards and was only a week later.

Henrik, for we shall never call him Henry, has struck again! This time he caught Annie alone sorting the linen. Curse the man, he came from behind and hit her over the head before she could fight back. When she came around he had her on the bed and was having his evil way with her. She says he was muttering about having an heir to follow him come what may. She was too dizzy to fight and was still lying there weeping when Lamentina and I went to find her, for she was late for dinner. Mother has given her the herbs to make sure that any child of his does not take, but this is another sign of Henrik's madness. How does he think he could pass the child of a maid off as Lady Felicia's?

There were a few more recipes, then came another entry, dated July 1856.

Lady Felicia is in her last days. Her pain is dreadful and mother has made a terrible decision out of love for her. Lady Felicia has always been so kind to us. Now we must be kind to her. We cannot use the opium the doctor left, for he would surely notice the bottle suddenly being empty, but far from the house, Harodain has been growing a special herb patch for us. Henrik knows nothing of it, and must never, for it contains only dangerous plants. We need the hellebores to keep the rats and mice at bay, but he thinks we buy the powder at market ever since he saw Harodain burning the original plants in the garden. But in the ruins of the old sheep pens, Harodain has made some sheltered gardens where he grows what we hoped we would never need.

We shall use henbane, a little white bryony root, and some belladonna, along with some of our own precious small supply of opium poppy seeds, for we have dared not risk growing too many of those in case they self-seed and Henrik spots them. All of us are most anxious about doing this, but we cannot sit by and watch our beloved mistress suffer like this, and all the more so because Henrik has control of her medicines, and we suspect he does not give milady the full dose, still hoping to get her to sign something. He is the very Devil's man! How can he watch her suffer like that and not give her the means to ease her pain?

A day later came the note,

She is gone. A blessing upon her soul, for she deserved none of this. Her fool of a son brought Henrik into the house, fancying himself grand enough to have a foreign manservant, yet within weeks discovered he harboured a viper. Master Henry paid dearly for that, for Henrik ruined him and he died a debtor, but Lady Felicia was the innocent in all of it, and for that we shall pray for her soul, and curse Henrik's to eternity.

"Bloody hell!" Fleur breathed, only to realise that there were footsteps on the stairway and then Lucy was in the room asking,

"What's wrong? That sounded a bit dramatic. Are you okay?"

Fleur huffed. "I'm fine, but you won't believe what I've just read in here …and yes, Lucy, I know I'm supposed to be cataloguing these, not getting engrossed in them, but this is important!" Keeping it to the point, she told her about Henrik and Lady Felicia, concluding, "I think we have to go back to the Vances once I've done and see what Mr Vance wants done with these, because if we sell them for him, it has to be with him knowing that there's as good as a confession to murder in here."

"Good grief!" Lucy exclaimed. "Yes, that does complicate things, doesn't it? On the one hand, the potential price for the notebooks would rocket up with contents like that. The infamous Angelo Vance having that kind of history could really bring in the bidders! On the other, does Angelo Vance want it public that one of his ancestors was a murderer?"

"Exactly! And not just one, either. The whole Petulengro family seem to have decided upon this course of action, not just one on their own. They really weighed up the dangers of what they were going to do. In Lady Felicia's case, these days a good barrister might be able to argue for a plea of manslaughter rather than murder, because it sounds as though she was terminal and with only days left to live anyway. And however misguided it might sound, they were acting out of compassion for her, not malice."

Lucy scruffed her fingers through her hair. "That's a very fine line, though. Jeez, I wouldn't want to be on a jury that had to make a decision on that one. …Anyway, I came to tell you the kettle's on and Carrie-Ann and I are going for lunch. Come on, time for a break from all this weirdness."

Yet as Fleur followed her downstairs, the big question that kept niggling at her was, what happened to Henrik afterwards? Having done it once, did the Petulengros go on and murder him? And if so, who on earth was Annie married to? Because that man, whoever he was, was the ancestor of Angelo, and it wasn't good if he was a murderer, even if he wasn't the evil Henrik. How to tell a pair as unstable as Angelo and his mother a piece of news like that, and what on earth would their reaction be?

Lunch passed in a haze of general chatter, with Fleur just about managing to keep focused on it enough not to arouse suspicion. And if she scuttled back upstairs to the attic sooner than she might, she was able to cover it with a burst of enthusing about handmade inks and fascinating drawings of plants – which was entirely true, since the Petulengro women had done their best to draw a likeness of some of the rarer plants. Moreover, she would love to get a chemical analysis done of those odd stains on the books, because that was really intriguing her now. What had they used, and also, what had they done to enhance it? The latter was something she wished she could talk over with Grandma Rose, because no lab in the world was going to give her that answer.

Back at her desk, Fleur did her best to move on with the job at hand, but it was no good, only a few pages on she came to another mark and the cryptic note of,

Curse him! He is the lawful owner of the house. Lady Felicia's death changes nothing for us.

Unable to stop herself, Fleur immediately rubbed the spot on the page.

She was in the kitchen of the house again, and this time she was seeing things through Loverin, the middle daughter and writer's eyes. A mature couple were sat at the table, probably in their late forties, but looking older than that as ordinary folk would do back then. Three younger men were sitting with the family, who were eating an evening meal, two of them so like the older man that Fleur knew that they had to be his sons, and Loverin's side of the link recognised the older but more slightly built one as her brother Teiso, making the other Shadrach. The family resemblance was strong in the girls too, with the older one who had to be Annie sitting very close to the other young man, while the youngest sat beside her mother, looking for all the world like a ghost through time to what Mezelly must have looked like at that age.

The kitchen door burst open and in swaggered Henrik, red-faced, now portly, and clearly drunk.

"You will lay out my finest coat again tomorrow!" he belched. "I *will* have a wife to give me sons! And it won't be any of you whores!" And he slammed back out again.

Joe gave a snort. "Looks like Sir William gave him short shrift with his proposal to Lady Caroline, then."

Mezelly rolled her eyes. "What did the fool expect? She's a proper high-born lady. Why would Sir William marry his youngest daughter to a rogue none of the gentry will invite to their houses? None of them are going to let him within a mile of any daughter of theirs. He'd be lucky to get a merchant's girl, and then only if they aren't from around here and have never heard of him."

"He's probably poxed to the eyeballs, anyway," Shadrach said with a sniff of disgust. "I heard in Hereford that he was rolling in the stables of the *Black Swan* with Dirty Molly at Easter, and no man with any sense would touch her, not even drunk! Thank heavens he hasn't had at you since then, Annie! You'll be fine, but Dirty Molly isn't."

"No, she's not long for this earth the last I heard," Mezelly said with a sad shake of her head. "So sad that a lass like her should lose her mind after seeing her man die. And shame on her family for not taking her in, and leaving her no choice but to lie with whoever would pay, just to survive."

Through the link Fleur felt Loverin's agreement that family was everything. To be without that was to be poor indeed.

"What are we going to do about *him*, though?" Teiso asked.

"What can we do?" Joe replied. "May he rot for eternity, but we're tainted by having worked for him for so long. Old Sir Roderick might have been the one who took us on and gave us a chance, but who remembers that now? Who remembers that we were here years before *he* arrived? We wouldn't get work with anyone around here.

"Anyway, who would take all of us on together? We'd be lucky if two of you girls could get a place in the same house, and one of you lads in the stables at the same. The family would be broken up, and we might not see one another beyond once a year." And the chorus of dismay which rippled around the table told Fleur just how tightly knit this family was.

Then with a sudden lurch which made Fleur reel, the scene shifted again. In the previous scene it must have been winter, or at least some time when it was cold, for she had felt the heat of the range on Loverin's back. Now it was at least spring time, possibly even early summer, for the scent of flowers wafted in, and the kitchen door stood open allowing a shaft of bright sunlight in. There was nothing sunny about the mood in the kitchen, though. Annie was sobbing in the arms of the man who wasn't her brother, and who Fleur realised must be Harodain, who was saying vehemently,

"I won't let this happen again! Not to my Annie, not to any girl!"

"I daren't risk giving you the herbs again so soon," a very choked up Mezelly said, and Fleur saw how Joe had his arm protectively around her shoulders, trying to give what comfort he could in what was looking to be an impossible situation.

"He trapped me in the laundry," Annie sobbed. "He rushed in and shoved me so hard I fell over, then he was on me and pouring the poppy down my throat before I had a chance to fight him off."

"She was still drowsy when we found her, Harry," Loverin told the man, confirming him as Harodain, but also giving Fleur a flash of memory of 'seeing' a staggering Annie, with her bodice ripped open and her skirts all torn.

Henrik must have gone at her like a savage animal for her to be in that state, Fleur realised, and the anger felt by her family was totally justified.

"For all his fine talk," Teiso was saying, "he's realised that the only heir he'll ever get is by raping one of our girls, because they're the only ones he has access to nowadays. Now that he never gets invited to any other house, he has nobody to take advantage of."

"And that's why I won't let either of you two swop places with me in the house," Annie bravely said to her sisters, though the tears were still flowing. "It's not me he particularly wants. It wouldn't matter to him whether it was me or Loverin or Lamentina who actually had the child. The having of it is all he cares about. And I wouldn't give much for the chances of a girl child living long, either. It's a son he needs, and that's all he'll accept. He wouldn't give a damn if he ruined us all, and turned us out on the streets with babes in our arms if they were girls."

Lamentina asked, "Could we not appeal to Justice Markham for help? After all, it was Henrik being found with his hand down Lady Lucy's dress at the hunt ball that finished his chances with the gentry, and everyone knows how furious Justice Markham was that it should happen to his daughter. We only suspect Henrik tried it on with other ladies, but her we know of for sure."

"But ask him to do *what*?" Shadrach asked. "Lammi, Henrik's the rightful owner of this place. Even Justice Markham can't throw him out. And the same goes for what Pa said. Yes, Justice Markham might help us to get other places, but we'd still be split up. And I want to be able to ask Paradise Lee to stay and be my wife when her family come through in the summer. I can't do that if I'm not here. And who around here would take on a man with a known gypsy wife? Paradise has the Sight like her mother and grandmother, and has told too many fortunes at the summer fairs not to be known as one. They think our kin are all rogues and thieves."

"Aye," Joe agreed. "I was beyond grateful to Sir Roderick, because your mother couldn't have stood another bad winter on the road with yet another babe on the way. Nobody else cared if we lived or died."

Straightening her shoulders, and brushing her apron smooth again, Mezelly looked around at them. "Then we have no choice. It's us or him. He has to go."

"Ma!" exclaimed Lamentina and Loverin together, appalled.

Teiso grimaced. "And how does that help? Once he's gone, a new owner might throw us out anyway."

"Not if we're clever," Mezelly said firmly. "Harry, you're the nearest one to him in height if not build. For the next couple of months, you don't go to market, you don't go anywhere where anyone other than us will see you. When my cousins, the Lees, come through with the Bucklands and the Smiths, that's when we do it. Before they arrive, we start dosing that monster with whatever we can. Anything to keep him stuck here. If he dies from purging, that's too bad, but die he must and slowly. We have to put it about that he is sick, sick enough not to be out and about as he normally is, but still have him here and living should the doctor choose to call."

Joe grunted. "I doubt he will. He had a fair idea of what Henrik was doing to the mistress, he just couldn't prove it. He'll leave Henrik to stew, I'd bet money on that."

Mezelly nodded. "It'll have to go in something only he has, so it'll have to be the wine. But the good thing is, that rough stuff he swills down his throat every night by the tankard-full is strongly flavoured enough to mask anything, as long as I don't make it too potent."

"But what then, Ma?" Teiso fretted.

"Then, my son, we put it about that Harry has gone off with our kin to wed one of their girls, and Harry takes the place of Henrik. We'll colour his hair to match Henrik's – a bit darker around the back, and shaved off at the temples to match his receding. If anyone looks like coming here, we'll have to powder his hair at the sides to match the grey, but I doubt anyone will be coming for a long social call."

"But Harry's broader shouldered than Henrik!" protested Teiso, who seemed to be the family worrier.

"Yes, he is, brother," Shadrach agreed, but with a grin. "Henrik's fatter in the belly by far, though!"

"Oh!" gasped Loverin. "And he's made me pad up the shoulders on his coats so that he looks more the fine gentleman, and not like a rotten apple stuffed in velvet! It don't hide his paunch, mind. Nobody be fooled by that! Only last week, when I took my lace to market, the miller's wife was saying as how she saw Henrik riding by, and how he had to have the bottom buttons of his coat undone, and how she could see his belly bouncing up and down!"

"Exactly," Mezelly said with a satisfied smirk. "So when Harry appears nearer to Christmas, why, all that fat have gone in the purging! Would you believe that!" And she gave a broad wink. "The parson preaches that the Lord moves in mysterious ways, don't he? Well, who'd 'a' thought it? That brush with nearly meeting his Maker done what everything else couldn't, and made dreadful Mr 'Henry Boswell' into a more God-fearing man. Praise the Lord, the parson'll say, and hopefully so will others."

"And after that?" Loverin asked cautiously.

Mezelly looked her straight in the eye. "After that, I reckon if we live quietly and respectable here, nobody's going to bother us. And by the time we need to get someone to draw up a will for the new Henry Boswell, he'll be someone everyone accepts. We ain't going to be in a rush to throw parties for the fancy folk, are we? That'd be where we'd fall down.

"That evil swine upstairs had been to enough fancy places to know how to behave, and how to carry it off, long afore he came here. None of *us* do. So we don't even try to. We make out that after his illness, 'Mr Boswell' accepts that he's not wanted by the gentry. He've had a change of heart. Seen the error of his ways. Don't want to be out and about so drunk it's only his horse knowin' the way back that gets him here some nights. It'll fit with his change of heart in other ways. We keep it simple, we keep it to what we know, but this is the last year we live under that monster's shadow."

The room faded, leaving Fleur once more in shock. She had considerable sympathy with the family's predicament, remembering Grandma Rose telling her about her own father, and how despite having a regular job in the local factory, and being respected by his workmates, he'd always been the first under suspicion if anything went missing. And if either of her great-grandparents had wanted to meet with their wider family, then they'd virtually had to sneak out of town and meet them away from the general population out at the camp. There was never any question of them inviting their travelling kin to the house, not if they didn't want the landlord to throw them out, anyway. And like Josef Petulengro, Grandma Rose's father had been forced into the settled life when a difficult pregnancy had made it impossible for her mother to stay on the road.

So Fleur fully understood what had been at stake for them. What she wasn't so comfortable with was their solution. And yet the more she thought about it, the more she realised that Mezelly had been right, it had come down to a stark choice for survival – the whole Petulengro family, or Henrik. But if that was the case, where was Henrik's body? Was he buried somewhere at *The Rookery*? And was that the reason why Angelo's grandfather had been adamant that the house stayed in the family?

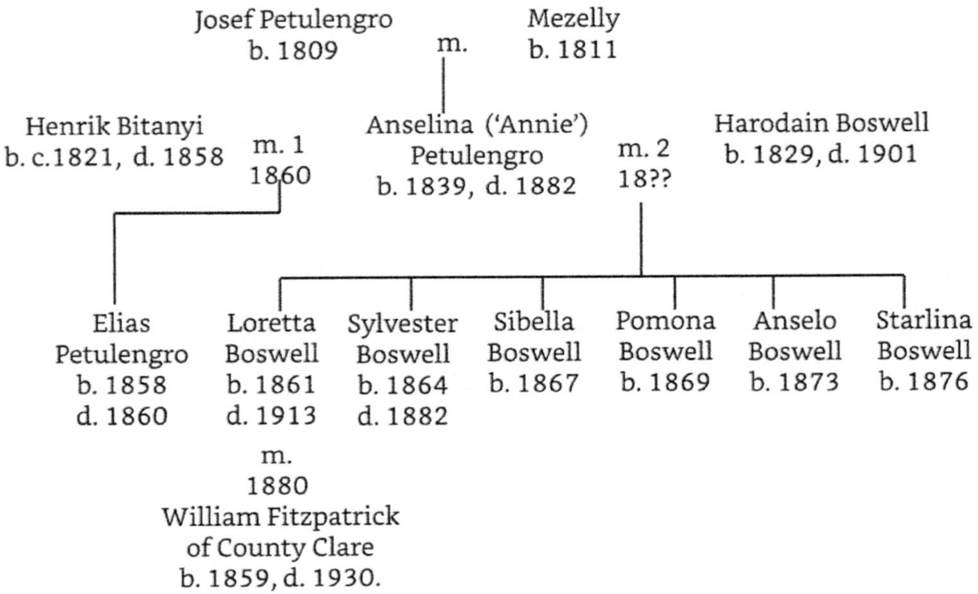

Josef Petulengro
b. 1809
m.
Mezelly
b. 1811
Henrik Bitanyi
b. c.1821, d. 1858
m. 1
1860
Anselina ('Annie')
Petulengro
b. 1839, d. 1882
m. 2
18??
Harodain Boswell
b. 1829, d. 1901
Elias
Petulengro
b. 1858
d. 1860
Loretta
Boswell
b. 1861
d. 1913
Sylvester
Boswell
b. 1864
d. 1882
Sibella
Boswell
b. 1867
Pomona
Boswell
b. 1869
Anselo
Boswell
b. 1873
Starlina
Boswell
b. 1876
m.
1880
William Fitzpatrick
of County Clare
b. 1859, d. 1930.

Chapter 22

Urgently flipping through the pages, Fleur was desperate to find the entry which told her what the Petulengros had actually done. It didn't take long.

Saints be praised, he is confined to bed, Loverin wrote. *Mother began with a simple and light purging. Nothing that would arouse suspicion, and she began the morning after he had rolled back in the worse for drink. So he put his bad belly down to that. But she has made sure that he has never been able to fully rise since then. May God forgive me for thinking this, but he is at last learning what it is like to be at the mercy of someone else. He gets good food. He is not starved. And he gets plenty to drink of both nourishing broth and wine. Heaven be praised for Ma's quick thinking on that, because he sent Shadrach to summon the doctor, who reluctantly came after Shadrach had given him the money, which in truth was more than he would normally charge – even the good doctor is not above greed, it seems. Yet he tasted the broth Ma had prepared, and the milk pudding, and declared that if 'Mr Boswell' did not get well on such nourishing fare, then maybe he would do well to lay off the wine for a while!*

Oh how we laughed down in the kitchen after that, for Henrik refused outright to be deprived of his nightly tankard of wine, saying that it was the only thing keeping him going. How little he knew! So much so that two weeks on, Ma has had to cut back what she is putting in it, because we need him to last until later in the summer. For now, we just need to make sure that he cannot leave the house.

"Good grief!" Fleur murmured, hurriedly turning the page. The date on that one showed that the family had been too busy keeping Henrik confined to bed to write much in the following weeks, or at least the women had. However there came one bad bit of news dated June 1857, which when Fleur looked back was three months on from when they'd decided Henrik must die.

My poor sister is with child. There is no doubt, and she is beside herself. She has no desire to carry the child of that monster, and yet one quickens inside her, and there is nothing Ma can do without risking her life too. A child's life is precious to us, no matter what, and yet we all feel that it will be a trial to keep this one. Pa has said it may be best to keep it until it can leave Annie's side, and then when our folk come around again, let them take it away with them. We know it will be cared for, but at least Annie and Harry will not have to look upon its face every day, and the wicked reminders that will come with it.

I always wondered what would make village folk leave their children for our kin to take. How could they not love a child, I always asked Ma? But now I know. The girl Aunt Vashti had with her last year, and who she called Naomi, was got on a serving girl by her master, and the family had to let her go or risk being thrown out of their cottage for having a loose woman for a daughter. Already I was seeing that in a different light to when I was a young girl.

Back then, I thought a servant would be flattered to get such attentions. Now I know they would be repugnant, and thank the Lord that we do not have to face such a hypocrite of a master who would rape and then evict to hide his crime – it is a small mercy, given what we have been through, but one I am grateful for. But it is only with seeing the dread on Annie's face every time she puts her hand on her belly that I truly understand.

Worse, if we are to carry off this glamour, and substitute Harry for the monster, then Harry cannot marry Annie right now. It would not ring true that he would leave with our kin in August with a new bride already beside him, and we could not hide Annie away forever. But that means that Annie must bear the slur of being unwed at the time of the child's birth, which poor Harry feels most keenly. It is little consolation that Ma and Pa say that they will find a way for them to wed and have children of their own. The gossip in the village will have already condemned Annie for her loose morals.

"Poor Annie," Fleur sighed. She of all of them seemed to have suffered most from living alongside Henrik.

She glanced up at the clock. With luck she could squeeze another hour and a half's research in before anyone started wondering why she was so reluctant to go home. And so pressing on, she found a brief entry right at the end of July, recording that the dreadful Henrik had passed much blood and then finally died. But there was a relieved entry after it telling of the early arrival of the travelling folk, and not Mezelly's cousins but her actual family, the Smiths. 'Harodain' could disappear soon and 'Henry' remain in his place.

The crucial entry, though, told of two of Mezelly's brothers and a strapping son of each, who helped Joe and Shadrach carry Henrik's corpse away and bury him. To Fleur's amazement, the family had kept a cider barrel empty for the purpose, and when Henrik expired, had folded him up like a piece of Salt Cod and stuffed him into the barrel. Many bottles of his rough red wine – which none of the family could stand – had then been emptied in on top of him, thereby effectively pickling him in vinegar, and preventing any awful stench from leaking out.

Harodain had shown himself to be a willing participant, for he and Shadrach had cleared a substantial tract of rough land. And now, with the help of the rest of the family, a whole orchard of cider apple saplings were going in in one weekend. With the whole field so dug over and trampled, the barrel going into the ground in one much deeper hole beneath a tree would not be noticeable.

Loverin wasn't so foolish as to leave a map of where they had buried Henrik, but she did say that it was in the land beyond what she called 'the rise', which was presumably fairly evident from the house back then. Whether it would be so now, when many of the trees would be that much more mature, was another matter, and Fleur had noticed a fair few oaks and a splendid row of horse chestnuts while she was there. Had they been there back then? The oaks, maybe; but the horse chestnuts, possibly not. That could all make the detecting of where Henrik lay a good deal harder, and that gave Fleur another conundrum – should she tell Angelo about this?

The Angelo she had talked to face to face she had no qualms about telling. But the man who had grabbed her in the car park? He was a different kettle of fish altogether. What kind of random accusations might he throw at her? If no physical body could be found, would he accuse her of trying to blacken his family's name? Of threatening to go to the press, or spill the beans online, and thereby drag him through another round of dirt slinging? She wouldn't, of course, but might he in his delusional state think that, and heaven forbid, decide to go on the offensive and sue her before anything could happen? Damn it, she was going to have to tell Mr Harris about this, if only for her own and the firm's protection.

But not tonight. Tonight, she would go home and rest. Yet as she passed the doorway to go downstairs, she felt herself being pulled towards one of the tarot decks, and for reasons she couldn't have explained, found herself pocketing the one deck.

Back safely in her flat, Fleur first made sure she sat down and had a proper meal, securely grounding herself, but also lighting some candles and a white sage smudge stick, and cleansing the dining room end of the lounge where she was going to work. When she was done, she would go around with the smudge stick again, and was glad that the dining end was furthest away from the bedroom she used. With the lounge end window open a crack to let in fresh air as well, that was as best she could do to ensure that nothing unwanted lingered.

And so having got everything as ready as she could, and putting on Grandma Rose's bracelets – because you couldn't be too careful about these things – Fleur spread out the cloth she used to do her readings on across one end of her table. It was a lovely piece of printed Indian cotton, and Fleur loved it because she could wash it should it become 'contaminated' by something unwanted. So if she got the jitters from anything at all tonight, it would go straight into the washing machine on a good hot wash.

As for the spread, she had already decided to do a Celtic Cross – a sound, tried-and-tested spread which she was very familiar with, because tonight wasn't the time to get creative. And so she opened up the packet of cards, and gently teased them out across the cloth. Before doing anything, she wanted to get the measure of the cards themselves.

To her surprise they were a design she recognised as having come from Bologna back in the mid eighteenth century. She hadn't expected the Petulengros to have anything quite this good or old, because the cards were of a lovely quality, and despite having obviously been extensively used, they weren't in bad condition. Someone had most likely brought these with them from the Continent, because Fleur was sure that gypsies over here in England wouldn't have had access to cards like this unless they had found someone selling them in London. And a purveyor of arcane items like that would have charged way over what a gypsy family could afford, even if they effectively were going to be the tools of their trade.

The images were also ones she felt comfortable using. She knew of decks created later in Florence around 1806 and in Milan in the 1830s, which although very beautiful nonetheless made her uncomfortable. There was something a lot cleaner about the lines of this deck, less revelling in the dark side of things such as in the Death card or the Devil.

Drawing Death in a reading often freaked people out, but its meaning was a lot more subtle than just the death of a person. It could represent change, transformation, and transition, and even when drawn reversed – i.e., upside down and with a more negative connotation – it was just as likely to mean resistance to a change or transformation. Therefore although it was hard to symbolise death without imagery showing either a skeleton or the grim reaper, Fleur preferred the less morbid representations, and was relieved to see those here.

She was also going to use a signifier – a card to represent the heart of the matter – and had decided upon The Fool. To her it had elements of both sides of Angelo. Upright, The Fool was innocence, spontaneity, and a free spirit, all of which embodied Good Angelo. Reversed, it meant recklessness and risk-taking, which to her was Bad Angelo without going for the full embodiment of evil, thereby holding true to her own determination not to condemn him if he was genuinely mentally ill. Certainly jumping on her in a public place as he'd done yesterday had been reckless, for there had been no knowing whether a passer-by might have come to her rescue, or even a policeman from nearby. And so The Fool seemed to be a good starting place, without jumping to conclusions about Angelo from the outset.

Picking up the rest of the cards, Fleur now gave them a very good shuffle. Had anyone been watching, she would have looked more like a croupier at a casino than someone about to do a card reading, for she used several techniques of shuffling and cutting the cards to really mix them and ensure that no residue from a previous reading lurked in them.

Then setting them down, she took several deep, steadying breaths, and began. Cards were selected viewed from the reverse side, and so all that Fleur had before her were the sepia tinted line drawings on the backs of the cards. The revelations would begin once all of the cards were selected, and she began turning them over in order.

With the cross itself placed, along with its four attendant cards in line on the right, Fleur sat back and took another few breaths and a sip of the wine she had poured beforehand. This was where it got interesting, and potentially scary! And right away Fleur became aware of other women in the room with her. The one she felt most strongly was the familiar essence of Grandma Rose, which was reassuring, because if anything started going wrong, Grandma would be sure to warn her. Yet she didn't feel threatened by the others, either, and suddenly she got a whiff of home baked bread, but also of lavender and rosewater.

"Mezelly?" she said softly, and the scent of that bread got stronger. But who was the other one?

"Lamentina?" she called, thinking that since the youngest girl had seemed to be working in the kitchen alongside her mother, that it would be her. Yet the fragrance didn't shift, almost getting overwhelmed by that whiff of home cooking.

"Loverin?" And suddenly the lavender got stronger. "Ah! So you were the one strong in the Craft like your mother!" Fleur realised aloud, and could have sworn she heard a soft but friendly laugh.

"Okay then, ladies, let's see what I'm dealing with," she said, and turned over the first of the centrally placed cards, and the one which lay directly on top of The Fool.

The Wheel of Fortune. Now that was interesting, because in this position it signified what was happening in the present, and this card meant a turning point, or life cycles changing. It certain confirmed that there was at least one major shift happening in Angelo's life, or maybe even taking place right now. Was it even his mental state? Perhaps not. *Don't jump to conclusions until you've got all of the cards*, Fleur reprimanded herself, and turned over the second card.

This one was positioned crosswise over the first, and in the interpretation Fleur used, represented the challenge in a situation, but could also mean something actively working against the first. So it was quite a surprise to see another of the major arcane – those being the twenty-one primary cards which differentiated a tarot deck from a normal pack of playing cards. But Justice, in this position? Did that mean the challenge was to see justice done in the sense of the law and truth, or was it more about cause and effect?

Putting the card back down, Fleur turned to the first of the four cards which sat at the compass points around the central cards. The third in the sequence lay to their left and represented the past, and again Fleur was slightly shocked to see the Nine of Swords. Compared to modern playing card suits, in tarot decks, Cups equalled Hearts; Coins equalled Diamonds; Batons or Wands equalled Spades (but with the imagery actually originating in ancient Arabic cards where they were polo sticks); and Swords equalled Clubs. She always thought of the suit of Swords as the most difficult of the four suits, because they all had that cutting edge of a sword element about them, where even the good stuff didn't come easily. But the Nine was one of the tougher ones even in that set, representing anxiety, fear, depression, and even nightmares.

"Bloody hell, Angelo! You really have been through the mill," was Fleur's instinctive response, and from her three disembodied watchers she immediately got a sympathetic murmur of agreement. And that in itself was interesting, because from their perspective they seemed to view him as the victim, not as Fleur's persecutor.

Moving across to the fourth card, representing the future, this time Fleur gasped, "Oh my God!" when another major arcane card appeared, because this was The Tower. Always depicted as a fortification crumbling, or even violently exploding apart, The Tower warned of sudden change at the very least, and in the extreme, the querant's world crumbling around them. Upheaval, revelations, and/or awakenings were also meanings which could be read into this card, and whatever the finer nuances, this card meant that huge changes were afoot for Angelo in the not-so-distant future.

But would they be for good? That was something Fleur found very disturbing. She had no wish to be the cause of further misery being heaped upon him, but equally this could be coming from a source which she had no control over.

So it was with some relief that she turned over the fifth card for goals and aspirations and saw The Lovers. That, at least, was something heading towards normal. It didn't have to be romantic love, but could mean harmonious relationships with those close to you, and having heard about Angelo's odd and strained relationship with his mother, Fleur could well believe that he would long for that to settle into something more normal. Having had a difficult relationship with her own dad, and feeling that he never saw beyond her sister, Fleur knew what it was like to listen to other people talking about comfortable and relaxed contact with parents, and wishing that she could have the same. Yet, alongside possibly wishing for a romantic partner, Angelo must have often wondered why he should have been completely deprived of his father, *and* have a mother whose affections didn't just fluctuate, but positively ricocheted from one extreme to the other.

"*Phew*," she breathed, "what a reading this is turning out to be! I wasn't expecting anything like this."

The sixth card revealed underlying feelings and/or situations, and to Fleur's dismay another difficult card came up. The Seven of Wands stood for feelings of exhaustion and being overwhelmed, of being ready to give up. And thinking of how Angelo had appeared so tired and drained, Fleur was ready to believe that, underneath the brave face he was putting on things, he might actually be at the end of his tether with whatever was going on. But again, this spoke of someone trying to cope with something, not of someone almost wholly reactive, as Bad Angelo was.

Indeed, nowhere in any of this could Fleur see any strong indicators of Bad Angelo. He might be the cause of some of these feelings and situations, yet he didn't seem to be the one that they were happening to.

"How odd. How very odd," she muttered, turning to the last four cards which lay in line to the side of the cross.

The next card symbolised advice and also something of the self of the querant, and another major arcane card appeared – The Chariot. Usually depicted as something like a Roman chariot being driven at full tilt, it was another card of action.

"Control, willpower, determination, and action," Fleur murmured. "Somebody up there wants you to act, Angelo. Wants you to be decisive about something. I wonder what?"

By now if her three ghosts had had breath, she would have felt it on the back of her neck, because there was the distinct sensation of them waiting right behind her with bated breath as much as she was. They definitely weren't influencing anything about this, and as The Chariot had appeared there had been a ghostly '*Ooh!*' from Loverin.

Nor were the shocks over. The eighth card represented external factors, but could also mean those that were quite close, such as within the home.

"The Devil?" Fleur squeaked. "Holy-moly! Where does that fit in?" She knew full well that it didn't mean the Devil in the biblical sense. Angelo wasn't being possessed. But it did mean that there was something attaching itself to him and restricting him, yet the one meaning which Fleur's senses positively screamed at her was of a 'shadow self'.

Everyone had a dark side. The part of themselves that they tried to keep hidden, in whatever form it took. But suddenly Fleur was sure that what the cards were trying to tell her was about an actual other person.

"Gran? I'm getting really strong vibes of a shadow self here. You said that I needed to be alert for *two* people, and that I needed to learn to distinguish between them? Is this telling me that my first thoughts that there was someone pretending to be Angelo were actually right? That whatever Lucy at work said, somehow or other we've all been encountering two totally separate people, and yet thinking that they're the same?"

The sensation of, '*yes!*' swept over her, and from all three spirits.

"Bloody hell!"

Hurrying to turn over the next card showing hopes or fears, for the first time a reversed card came out, and oddly it was The Hanged Man. In his normal aspect, dangling from one foot with his arms folded as if accepting his fate, he meant letting go and new perspectives, which wouldn't have been out of place in this reading. Angelo letting go of his past would be completely understandable. Yet reverse it indicated stalling, but also an actual need to pause, but with the potential for movement still there.

"Are you holding yourself back, Angelo?" Fleur wondered, and again got that positive feedback from her watchers.

"Okay then, last card – the outcome. Heavens, I'm almost frightened to turn this over. …Ooh! The Two of Cups reversed! …I don't know whether this is good or bad."

The suit of Cups dealt with emotional situations, and presented reversed like this, the Two meant break-ups and disharmony. But who was breaking up with whom? Did it mean that Angelo needed to make a clean break, or was someone going to break away from him?

'*Look at the whole spread, Fleur*' Grandma Rose's spirit told her. '*Look for the cross-links.*'

"It's no good, I'm going to have to refer to my book," Fleur said with a sigh. Grandma Rose had done enough readings to be able to automatically go to this extra level, but Fleur hadn't the experience. And so going over to her bookshelf she pulled out a large book, which gave a much more detailed explanation of each card and their connections with one another.

Turning to Justice as the first of the major arcane in the spread, it gave Fleur a jolt to see that if it came up in the same spread as the Nine of Swords, then there was an implication of feelings of guilt over the past, and mistakes which needed to be acknowledged. And with the Nine in this spread sitting right there in the position of the past, there was no getting away from it – something in Angelo's past needed to be reckoned with, and his feelings about it sorted.

The Lovers with The Devil actually indicated some sort of abusive relationship, and thinking about what Angelo had said about Claudia locking him up, Fleur was sure it was her this was talking about. And sitting where they did in the spread only emphasised that. Angelo might want both a romantic liaison and a happier family life, but his mother and whoever this other person was, were definitely abusing their relationship with him.

"At least that confirms that someone else is involved, I suppose," Fleur mused, but then came a triple link. The Chariot with the Seven of Wands spoke of an ongoing battle, but one which was soon to be won.

"Okay, so that underlying situation is going to get resolved, is it? That has to be good." But then she saw that the Seven of Wands with the Hanged Man, when reversed, meant standing up to opposition.

"Flaming hell! Are you going to stand up to your mum and this other bloke, then?"

'*Yes, but he needs help to do it*,' Grandma Rose's spirit said. '*That's what he's waiting for. That's what he needs.*'

But the final crunch came with discovering that The Tower with the Two of Cups reversed meant the end of relationships. A major relationship around Angelo was about to crumble permanently.

Sitting back in her chair and looking at the spread, Fleur went over the meanings several times in her head, and all the while there was the sensation as of the three women almost holding their breaths, waiting for her to come to the right conclusion. They couldn't push her. She had to do this of her own free will, but there was nothing to stop them showing her that she'd got it right once she'd decided.

"Bugger it," Fleur sighed, rubbing her hands over her face and giving a huff of resignation. "I'm going to have to draw Bad Angelo out into the open, aren't I? I'm going to have to get him out somewhere where other people see him alongside Good Angelo. It's going to have to be public, so that once and for all, everyone knows that the real Angelo isn't the monster. And worse, I'm going to have to do it without telling Good Angelo what I'm doing, because somehow or other, his mother and this monster have got him trapped."

Chapter 23

The surge of affirmation which washed over her told Fleur that she'd come to the right conclusion. How to do it was quite another matter, though. And then she had an idea.

"Can I ask you something – particularly Mezelly and Loverin? …This grandfather of Angelo's – is he the source of whatever it is that has Angelo tied in such knots?" That got a definite 'yes' from all three. "So if I carry on working through the notebooks, will I find out what was going on with Ignatius and Aleister?" Again, that got a very positive 'yes' from all three ghosts.

Then suddenly the penny dropped for Fleur. Of course! Mere hours ago, she'd been reading about how Mezelly and her daughters had got rid of a man who had been preying upon them. Had one or both of these men got their hands on those lethal recipes and tried to do something similar? Or rather the reverse, and get rid of a wife who offended them by being the only reason they had the owning of *The Rookery*, not in their own right.

Yet when she asked, Loverin managed to make herself heard enough to say, *'Yes, but it's more complicated than that. You have to look at what comes between. Look to Loretta and Annora. I am constrained not to tell you more. But remember what happened to Annie when you do.'*

And with that she and Mezelly were gone.

"Well, Gran, that was a turn up for the books!" Fleur declared, carefully taking a photograph of the spread for future reference, and afterwards, putting the cards back into the pack. Then recalling Claudia Vance's snooping habits, decided that she would give the cards another really good shuffle. She had no idea whether Mrs Vance had a clue about doing a proper reading, but just in case she did, Fleur didn't want to leave her any hints which might prompt her to wonder whether Fleur was onto her. And Fleur did now think that whatever twisted game Mrs Vance was playing with her son, she would see Fleur's involvement as acting against her.

That brought something else to mind.

"Gran," she asked tentatively. "You know when I was at *The Rookery*, and Mrs Vance had that meltdown? Well, she spoke of someone who at the time we all thought was Angelo being the one who wanted me to stay at the house. But I'm thinking now, that Angelo was telling the truth when he said it wasn't him. So is it this *other* person, this *other* man, who for some weird reason wanted me to stay?"

'It is.'

"And thinking about the cards we've just seen, he isn't just some random stranger Mrs Vance has hooked up with, is he? Not some bloke she took a wild fancy to because he reminded her so much of Angelo – though it would be pretty sick to want to make love to your son's double. He's closer to them both than that, isn't he, because he's got some kind of hold over Angelo too, and it's not just threatening his mum. If it was just that, Angelo has enough money that he could whisk her away to somewhere well out of reach, so he himself has to be having his own hands tied in some way or other."

'*You are absolutely right.*'

"Hmm. So a blood relative, almost certainly."

Grandma Rose didn't comment on that, but suddenly vanished as though she'd been pulled back before she could say any more and influence Fleur. That didn't stop Fleur going to her laptop once she'd smudged the room again, and going onto the family ancestry sites to search for more relatives. Yet hunt though she would, Fleur could find nobody who'd been missed off Carrie-Ann's family tree who fitted the bill. The person who'd created the tree had been a cousin of Jacko Vance's, clearly intrigued by the family Jacko had married into. And whoever they were, they'd certainly been thorough, backing every entry up with links to things like birth, death, or marriage certificates, or censuses or voters' registers.

Moreover, following that family tree on Angelo's paternal side, everyone else seemed to be living perfectly normal lives up in the West Midlands with their spouses and children. Not one of them leapt off the page as a potential blackmailer, and who else was there left aside from Claudia's sister,

Romana, back in Italy – who given her mental disabilities was an unlikely plotter and schemer to this extent. Fleur didn't have access to international records, so she couldn't check the Italian side, but again, a family who already had a castle was unlikely to be hankering after a moderately nice English country manor.

"Who the heck are you?" Fleur fumed, as she closed things down for the night, and tried to switch off enough to be able to get to sleep.

Her alarm clock went off all too soon on the Tuesday morning, for Fleur had still been awake at two in the morning, unable to switch off her busy brain. Falling asleep at what had to have been coming up three o'clock, and then getting up at seven, was not a recipe for being bright-eyed and bushy-tailed. Nonetheless, the prospect of getting on the trail once more was sufficient to get her up, and out early enough to be able to go and treat herself to an almond croissant from one of the bakeries, and a packet of jam doughnuts for the staffroom. She was also careful about how she left her complex, even more alert for someone lurking around the main gates now than she had been before.

However, at the office she knew she had to do the deed of informing Mr Harris. It simply wouldn't be fair not to tell him of the deaths, and also, she reckoned that having discovered this, he would be more lenient towards her scrutinising the contents of the other journals as a precaution against other dirty deeds coming to light. And so as soon as he was in, she went downstairs and tapped on his door.

By the time she had gone through what she'd found, she felt obliged to go and fetch him one of the doughnuts and a fresh mug of coffee.

"Bloody hell, Fleur!" he groaned – and it was unknown for Mr Harris to swear in front of the staff, so Fleur knew he was properly distressed by this. "What the hell do I tell Vance?"

Suddenly having an idea, Fleur suggested, "Why don't you email him and ask him for a video conference call? If I tell him and can show him the pages of the books as I go, that ought to convince him that we're not just making this up." *And I can see his face without being in the same room as him! If he's all battered and bruised, then I really don't know what I'm going to do, because after a couple of days the bruises ought to be coming out nicely.*

"That's a very good idea," Harris agreed. "You go and carry on digging through those damned things, and when I've got it set up, I'll call you down."

However, if Fleur had been expecting to get called before lunch she was mistaken. For whatever reason, it was taking Mr Harris longer than expected to get in touch with Angelo, and so Fleur carried on with her work. Yet to her relief there were no more terrible confessions. Annie's son Elias was born, but turned out to be a sickly child, too much so for him to be given to the wider travelling family. However, he did not live for more than three years, which seemed to have been a blessing all round – for him for not suffering anymore, and for Annie and the others for no longer having a constant reminder of Henrik's abuse.

Despite Fleur's scepticism, the family actually managed to pull off the substitution of Harodain for Henrik, and their quiet life at the manor ensured that with no scandals to remind them, the neighbourhood gradually seemed to forget Henrik's sins and accept this new, quieter version. Annie and Harodain married by license in Hereford only months after Elias' death, tactfully avoiding a ceremony at the local church, and Loretta appeared a mere six months later. She was baptised in the parish church another three years on, along with a newborn son called Sylvester who was the legitimate son of 'Mr & Mrs Henry Boswell', in 1864.

Daughters Sibella and Pomona followed at two-year intervals, to be followed by another son, Anselo, and a final daughter Starlina in 1876. Otherwise, the books were filled with more recipes – often becoming more like the family cookbooks than witches' grimoires – and including yet more cures as they learned of them.

Meanwhile, Shadrach and his family took over the home farm when the original farmer got too old and nobody to succeed him, and Teiso died before his parents, meaning neither of Joe and Mezelly's sons contested Harodain's right to pass on the house to his and Annie's children. Lamentina married one of the Bucklands and chose to return to the travelling life, Loverin recording that she declared she never wanted any child of her own to be born in the accursed house. Loverin herself never married, and Fleur thought she detected more than once a longing that Harodain/Henry might have chosen her, not Annie.

Other odd snippets hinted that Annie later on rather played on having been the victim of Henrik, to her sister and husband's growing annoyance, especially after Mezelly and Joe had passed on, and there was nobody left living to contradict Annie but those two. It seemed that they also had to warn her more than once about nearly letting something slip about what had gone on, and that Annie's fondness for a tipple of gin and then talking unguardedly, had more to do with 'Mr Boswell' not entertaining than any lingering need to hide Harodain/Henry from the neighbours.

By the time the next generation were of an age for inheritance to start being talked about, Sylvester had died in an accident in 1882, falling from a barn roof while repairing it, and like Lamentina, Anselo had proved to have itchy feet and had joined his aunt and her family on the road. Neither son had shown the slightest interest in what their father and Loverin tried to teach them about the estate, although luckily the farm side of *The Rookery* was thriving under Shadrach and his sons' care. 'Henry' had managed to get new tenants for the other, smaller farm on the estate from out of the immediate area, and so they had accepted working with him

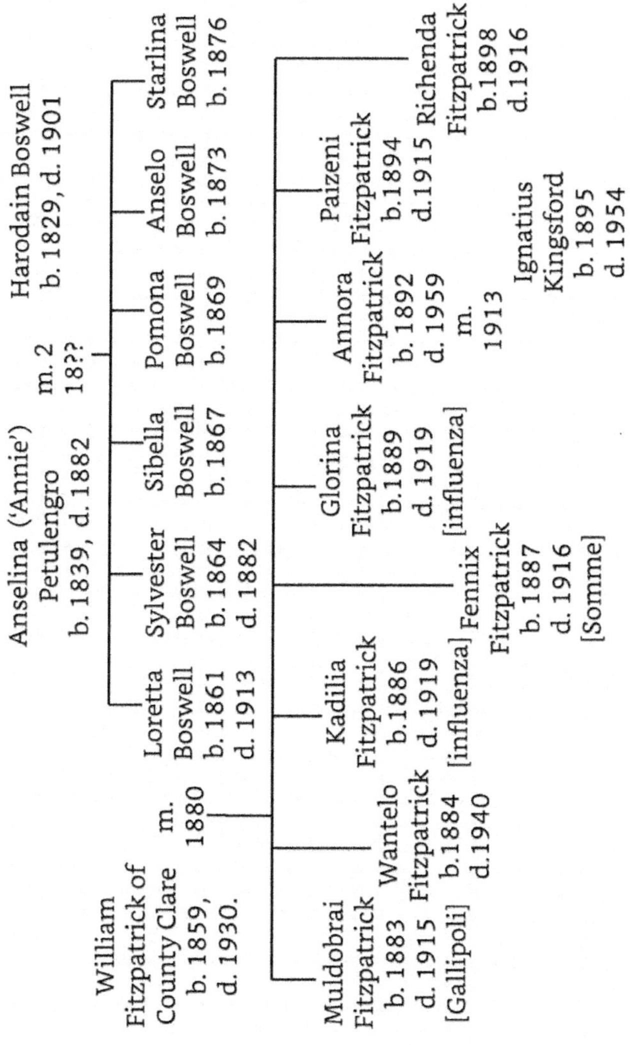

without question. That had left him to concentrate of the growing of cider apples, which were bringing in a tidy income by now.

Annie died while only in her forties, but from the rather unsympathetic note by her sister, it seemed that Annie had fallen down the stairs 'while taken with the drink', and had never recovered consciousness. This was also in 1882, and at that stage Loverin and 'Henry' seemed to work in much more convivial cooperation towards securing the estate for the family. Annie's daughters were more interested in saving *The Rookery* than her sons – perhaps because they knew that their potential choices of husbands would be limited, since no man of quality would risk marrying one of them even now – and Fleur was fascinated to read small notes in amongst the recipes starting later the same year about finding the right husband for one of the girls.

Luckily Loretta appeared to have fallen under her Aunt Loverin's influence, Annie being too involved with the younger children to bother much about her, and so when young Mr William Fitzpatrick came visiting the district, she flirted with him for all she was worth. William, it seemed was a charming but easily led young man, possessed of grand ideas above his station, and only too willing to marry into a family which had both the house and lands, but also a rather tarnished reputation, and who couldn't afford to be too picky.

From Loverin and Loretta's point of view, William was an affable young man, not overly blessed with brains, and therefore easily mouldable to fit their plans. If 'Henry' had any objections, then Loverin hadn't recorded them. But then after what his later married life must have been like with Annie, Fleur wasn't that surprised that he wasn't that concerned about the details of the marriage plans. As long as William looked after the women of the household, it seemed that 'Henry' was satisfied.

"But then you were older than Annie and Loverin, weren't you, Harodain," Fleur said with a sigh and leaning back in her seat. "Even if you weren't as old as Henrik, by 1883 you were almost certainly in your late fifties. And in that era, that made you coming into old age. If you'd been holding this family together since Josef Petulengro got old, I bet you were worn out – especially with a wife like Annie! Blimey, you really picked the wrong sister there, didn't you?

"Loverin was far more your soul-mate… but then when you first met Annie I bet you were a decent, normal enough bloke, not to notice the kid sister – which actually makes me like you more. You weren't the pervert, were you? And if their brothers didn't both about the wider estate, it must have been back-breaking work being the only man about the place."

She felt very sorry for Harodain. He'd been the quiet one, always there for the family, and yet never quite being able to impose his own wants and needs onto them. In that she was beginning to think that Angelo was a lot like him, and after all, since Angelo was Loretta's descendant, it was Harodain who was Angelo's great-great-great-grandfather, not the evil Henrik. So the mucky morals hadn't come down to

Angelo through his line, and that was strangely consoling, since it pushed that darkness much more towards the warped and twisted Ignatius again.

It would also be a lot easier to break the news to Angelo if she could now say that the death of Lady Felicia was a mercy killing and that of Henrik done to all intents and purposes in self-defence. This wasn't a family who had gone on a wanton killing spree. But this characterisation of William Fitzpatrick as slightly useless also bemused her. If he was like that, then it surely hadn't been him who had pushed Ignatius towards something extreme in order to make sure that *The Rookery* passed down through the male line. Indeed, it sounded far more as though William, who by the time Ignatius came on the scene would equally have been an older man in his fifties, had simply not been up to the task of standing up to him.

She broke for a late lunch, finding that Lucy was off work with a dreadful cold, and that was why she hadn't come and found Fleur for lunch. However, with it being a day when Carrie-Ann was not in either, she was sitting with the others when she realised that Tim from the furniture restoring side was making covert signals for her to come outside.

"Whatever is the matter, Tim?" she asked, as she joined him across the yard under the awning which the smokers amongst them used for cigarette breaks.

As he lit up, he said warily, "Look, I'm not trying to bad-mouth Lucy, but there's something you ought to know. Her attitude towards Angelo Vance isn't without its own motives."

"Eh?"

Tim wafted the smoke away from her. "We all love Lucy loads, okay? But… when it comes to what happened to Claire, she was more involved than she would like you to know nowadays."

Fleur looked at him askance, but it was so unlike Tim to be gossipy like this that her curiosity was piqued. "Fair enough. I'm listening."

Tim did a quick scan of the yard to make sure that nobody else was around. "So… These days Lucy and Bryony are a really tight couple, but back when we're talking about, they'd had a massive falling out."

"Good God!"

"I know. Hard to imagine, isn't it? But they did, and for a while they even split up."

"I've never heard a hint of this!"

"No, and you won't," Tim said with a warning wave of his cigarette. "But Lucy left, and the person whose sofa she was crashing on was Claire."

"Oh shit!"

"Oh, it gets worse. You see Lucy developed this real crush on Claire. It was nothing but a reaction to breaking up with Bryony, but at the time she fancied herself completely in love with Claire. The only problem was and is, Claire isn't gay. In fact, Claire became very uncomfortable with the way that Lucy was starting to behave around her. Enough that she asked her to leave."

"Oh Lord, I'm not going to like where this is going, am I?"

Tim shook his head sadly. "Lucy left only the morning before Claire got assaulted, and she's always blamed herself in part for that."

"Why? Claire was raped by a man!"

"Yes, she was. But you see, she was so off balance by what had been going on at her home – with Lucy even wandering into her bedroom in sexy nightgowns…"

"…Holy crap! No…!"

"…Oh yes! And Lucy had been quite snide about Claire complaining about a man chasing after her, because she thought Claire was trying to make her jealous – because that's what Bryony had been doing."

"Oh, no!"

Tim nodded, looking grim. "So poor Claire was all over the place, and it was partly because of that that her employers didn't take her complaints seriously. They'd heard via someone else about what a pest Lucy was making of herself, and so they thought it was all part and parcel of one bigger problem – Claire getting pressured sexually both at home and elsewhere, though not necessarily at that particular job."

"Bloody hell! That's awful! Poor Claire!"

"Poor Claire, indeed. Well then the worst happened, and to be frank, Lucy has never forgiven herself. Bryony instantly came around when it became known what had happened to Claire, and promptly marched Lucy back to their flat, not least because there was some doubt as to whether the assailant might not try to break into Claire's flat and do it again.

"Claire was in a women's refuge under protection, initially, and then the case floundered for want of evidence. Nobody doubted for a second that Claire had been raped. You couldn't see the bruising on her face and arms without accepting that – and I saw her, because I went down to pick up some of Lucy's stuff from Claire's flat while her sister was there with her, so that she didn't have to see Lucy.

"But Lucy has parcelled up a lot of her own guilt and shoved it onto Angelo Vance. He must be guilty, she thinks, because who else could have done it? And it's easier to blame him than to remember that if she hadn't been behaving so badly herself, then Claire wouldn't have been working late rather than going back to her flat."

"Shit! That really does put things in a different light. So do all of you lot who were here back then still think Angelo is guilty?"

Tim gave a knowing grin. "Oh, it's Angelo, is it? Fallen for the bad boy charms?"

Yet Fleur immediately shook her head. "No, Tim, stop that. It's more that I'm very worried about what's going on in that house. For a start off, when I was stuck up in the attic with him, Angelo told me something very worrying about his mother. Enough that I think she is genuinely not mentally stable and might even be dangerous.

"And the second thing is: I'm starting to wonder whether there are two people involved. One of them is the genuine Angelo Vance, who is a nice guy and absolutely tearing his hair out trying to do the best for his mum. And the other is a dead ringer for him, who for some reason his mum is hiding, and who has some kind of hold over both of them, but is in fact the one who assaulted Claire, and who needs bloody locking up before he hurts someone else. And that someone who gets harmed might just be Angelo!"

Chapter 24

Tim's revelation about Lucy ought to have really thrown Fleur, and yet oddly it only confirmed her suspicions. If Lucy had already been blinded by her own feelings when she first met Angelo, then she would have been looking for the worst in him before he'd even opened his mouth. And as she climbed back up the stairs to the attic, trying to get timings sorted out in her own mind, Fleur recalled that the very reason why the firm had been hauled in to assess *The Rookery's* contents that first time, was precisely because the Cheltenham firm had been in the midst of the court case concerning Claire, and had refused point blank to continue with the contract.

Freezing in mid-step on the top flight, Fleur gulped, "Jeez!" as it sunk in that Lucy would have been in something of a mess herself when she'd had those altercations with 'Angelo'. Had she even fully made it up with Bryony at that point? If not, then she would have been more than a little emotionally volatile right then – and Lucy had a full quota of the stereotypical redhead's volatility, that Fleur knew from personal encounters with it. All she would have seen was the man who had assaulted the woman she had a terrible crush on, and fond though she was of Lucy, Fleur knew that at the best of times Lucy had a tendency to jump to conclusions about people, and then be very hard to convince otherwise.

"Holy shit! Did you come face to face with Bad Angelo and Good Angelo, and not see the difference?" Fleur wondered aloud. Well yes, she must have, remembering what Lucy had said about the unwashed state of his clothes. And that triggered a recollection of her own. Down on the racecourse the smell of Bad Angelo had been overwhelming, and some of it had been body odour, she now realised. Well Good Angelo always smelled of nice soap or shower gel, and whatever there was of the man beneath it was of someone clean and just naturally male. So that was potentially a clue right there. If her nose wasn't revolted, the chances were she was talking to Angelo himself. If she could practically smell him coming, she'd best be on high alert!

Pausing, she wondered whether it would be worth going and talking to Marie, who had been in charge of sorting out the china and glass, because like Lucy and the other team leader, Mat, she would have come face to face with the man they thought was Angelo Vance. Mat wasn't in at the moment because he was out on another job, but she'd seen Marie's car in the staff parking area. And so hurrying back down to the ground floor, she went through into what had once been the old kitchens, and tracked down Marie in her office which had once been one of the pantries.

Tapping on the door, she waited for Marie to look up from her computer screen, then asked, "Am I interrupting, or could I have a quick word?"

"Pull up a chair," Marie said with a smile, pushing her specs up onto her head, and leaning back rolling her shoulders. "God, I hate the bloody paperwork side, even if it is all electronic these days."

Fleur smiled back. "I know what you mean. ...what I wanted to ask you about goes back to the first time you went to *The Rookery* to do the assessments. Can I ask, did you meet Angelo Vance face to face?"

"Why on earth do you ask that?"

Fleur took a deep breath. "Look, you've undoubtedly heard that I had a nasty experience there." Marie's expression said that she had, and so Fleur said very carefully. "Well, I'm starting to have some questions about the whole experience everyone here has had at that house. You see, I was sure that there was someone there who was a dead ringer for Mr Vance." She saw Marie's eyebrows go up in surprise and deflected her with, "Yes, I know, I thought I was being daft later on once I'd had chance to think about it.

"But the thing is, how do you explain the contradictory messages everyone kept getting? You presumably got them on that job initially *and* then later when you went back again to deal with the discovered Chinese collection. Lucy said she had them, and now I've had them. So either poor Mr Vance has a terrible case of dual personalities – in which case why ever hasn't someone got him into treatment?

"Or… I wasn't imagining things, and there's someone lurking around him and his mother who can do a very good impersonation of him, and is taking a perverse delight in dragging Mr Vance through the muck at regular intervals. I'll freely admit that I haven't a clue who that might be, but the extremes between the two sides of the man everyone thinks is Angelo Vance has me seriously concerned. So did you ever wonder what the heck was going on there?"

Marie's expression of disbelief had gradually changed into one of deep concentration. "Heavens, Fleur, you've got me wondering now. I have to say that where I was involved, most of the contradictory stuff was left in notes and via the phone, so it wasn't possible to say who had done what. But thinking back, I remember how Mr Vance would be so shocked when we presented him with one of those notes on the few times we saw him in person.

"And the more you make me think about it, the more I'm not sure anymore. You see, we all thought he was tearing across from London in the evenings, leaving the notes after we'd gone, and driving back the same night. Because whenever Mr Harris rang to speak to him, he always picked up at his London number – he wasn't even at the Cheltenham house.

Mrs Vance was, but he wasn't. But now I'm going back over it, and honestly… I can't imagine anyone doing that drive night after night. And it went on for weeks on end."

"Who thought he was driving? Why not take the train at least part of the way?" *Please don't say it was Lucy*, Fleur prayed, *because if so she's blinded everyone.*

Marie sighed. "Now you come to ask, it was Lucy who said he must have driven," and Fleur had to suppress the desire to groan. "It was all because of what was coming out in the court case over Claire, you see. The police were saying that they'd looked at the mileage on Mr Vance's car – which had only been serviced a few weeks beforehand *in* Cheltenham, and therefore they had that mileage – and it had hardly moved in weeks.

"There certainly weren't enough miles on the clock for him to have driven between London and Cheltenham once – let alone on to *The Rookery* multiple times – and so they focused on the trains, which was where Mr Vance's alibi was so strong. But Lucy was convinced that he must have had access to another car kept hidden in London. She was so angry about Claire getting attacked, and you know what she's like when she gets really riled about something. So she was fuming about Vance having the money to buy a car on the black-market or hiring one under a false name, and that the police weren't doing enough to catch Claire's attacker."

"Oh gawd," Fleur groaned, making Marie look at her in surprise. "Sorry… It's just that I'm beginning to realise just how much Lucy's knee-jerk reaction over Claire has muddied the waters. Everyone has been expecting Angelo Vance to be this duplicitous monster, not least because Lucy has insisted that he is, because she was so involved with Claire."

Hopefully that was tactfully put enough that if Marie hadn't known about Lucy's crush, then it still made sense. "But that means that whoever this other person is, he may have been extorting money out of the Vances, or at least leeching off them for years, and none of us noticed because we were all too programmed to see what he wanted us to see – just one man who is more than a little crazy!"

Clearly Marie hadn't been party to Tim's knowledge, because she didn't react beyond nodding over Lucy, and then the Vances. "Good grief, Fleur, that's a worrying thought, isn't it? But you know what? I think you might be on to something with this. It makes a whole lot more sense of what I remember happening.

"If there was someone staying much more locally and being hidden by the family, then of course it would have been a simple matter to slip into the big house at night and leave those notes. For heaven's sake, back then the front door barely had a decent lock on it, let alone the back door! We all thought that it was only because of the constant flow of visitors in and out of the hotel that thieves hadn't come in the night and cleaned out all the best pieces, because I can tell you that there wasn't anything like an alarm system to stop them!"

"Thanks, Marie. Look, if I need you to, would you tell Mr Harris that to back me up? Only I've found something very odd in those notebooks I've been working on, and Mr Harris is fretting about breaking the news to Mr Vance. But it's because of what he thinks the slightly bonkers version of Mr Vance will say.

"If I can convince him that the Angelo Vance who came here is the real man, and that aside from being stressed to breaking point, he's perfectly sane, we may be able to start separating these two men out. And it's not just lurid fascination on my part that's doing this. The company has to know who it's dealing with, and who is signing these contracts and then breaking them."

Leaving Marie slightly worried, and thinking very hard over her past encounters with the Vances, Fleur started to go back up to the attic, only to be collared on the stairs by Mr Harris.

"Ah, Fleur! I was just coming to look for you. We have a Zoom meeting with Mr Vance at four-thirty. Apparently, he's back in London, which is why it's taken me some time to trace him, but can you be down in my office for then?"

"Absolutely. In fact, I'll come a little early if I may, because I think I've discovered something else which is relevant."

"It's not more bad news, is it?"

"If you mean like bodies turning up, no it isn't. But it does affect Mr Vance. I'll give you the details later on, though."

Leaving him standing on the landing looking puzzled, Fleur hurried back to the attic. This only gave her a couple of hours to try and find out more, and if nothing else, she wanted to get through the journals up to the arrival of Ignatius in the family.

Her scrutiny of the next few volumes didn't reveal much. William and Loretta seemed to have settled into a perfectly normal life. Of Loretta's sisters, Sibella married a farmer from the other side of Hereford and vanished from the family personal records, and Pomona married a merchant from Worcester and also seemed to live quite distantly from the family at this point. Only the dramatically named Starlina continued to live with her sister and aunt, and it was she who gradually took over the writing of the grimoires as Loverin got older and her eyesight began to fail.

Of all of the women, Starlina was the one who truly got back into the magical side of things, making Fleur wonder whether she had been swept up in the resurgence of interest in the arcane which had arrived in the late Victorian era. Born in 1876, Starlina would have been a young woman in her twenties when men like Arthur Waite, Samuel Liddell Mather, and William Wynn Westcott were involved with the *Golden Dawn*, and it had Fleur wondering whether she been avidly reading newspapers, and had been a bit swept up in the romance of it all. Her notebooks now became filled with astrological charts, timetables of moon cycles, and a particular fascination with ancient goddesses. And Starlina had been prolific! She filled as many notebooks with her charts, incantations, and spells as the rest of the family had altogether hitherto.

And then Fleur found one book which didn't fit into this rambling sequence. Loretta hadn't given up and left her sister to do the writing at all, she had just been far more taken up with raising her family, but when she did write it was in the manner of her aunt and grandmother. A particular cough mixture which had helped ease whooping cough, a lotion which had eased the itching with chicken pox, and an herbal tea which had been particularly effective in helping William's gastric pain, were all written down in a neat but slightly spidery hand which contrasted vividly with Starlina's bold, sweeping handwriting. But in amongst these were again commentaries on the family.

I do wish Starlina would not fill my Annora's head with her nonsense, came an entry dated 1908. *With my Kadilia being only ten years younger than her, she dislikes her aunt seeming to lord it over her, just as Starlina used to resent me as the bossy, older sister. I get weary of the hissing fits between those two, but at least Kadilia takes Glorina and Paizeni with her when she goes out, and her scepticism over Starlina's magic has rubbed off on them. Oh how I wish Paizeni and Annora would be friends since there is only two years between them, but Annora finds Paizeni too dull and Kadilia too bossy, which has made her ripe for Starlina's foolishness. At sixteen she needs to be learning a skill which will see her through life, not dreaming of magicians who will conjure up riches out of nothing and allow her to live a life of luxury! Aunt Loverin and I have tried time and again to make her see sense, but to a young girl it is too alluring.*

Then two years later came an entry around which Loretta had drawn a thick black box. *My dearest aunt has gone. She died peacefully in her sleep and now joins Father, whom she loved far better than Mother ever did. To me she was a mother, the one who cared for and guided me through life. I feel as if half of me has gone with her. I am lost.*

She continued, *William is a dear man, but absolutely hopeless at dealing with the realities of life. Thank heavens we can now afford to have an estate manager, because if left to him we would be bankrupt in no time. And with the influence of their grandfather gone these nine years, Muldobrai, Wantelo and Fennix have been swayed by William's romantic and impractical notions. They found my uncle Shadrach's solid dependability over at the farm too boring to bother with, and since his death and despite his sons' best efforts, they have had no influence over them. I love my sons dearly, but I must find some way to ensure that none of them becomes the next lord of this manor, for that would spell disaster.*

Mercifully, though I was distraught to see the boy go, Muldobrai rushed off to join the army as soon as he could, thinking only of medals and glory, and although he is now a grown man of 27 and more than capable of finding his way back here when on leave, we have hardly seen him since, though I do not think that the fighting in the very last of the Boer War, and then elsewhere, has been as romantic as he thought it would be. Wantelo has never been right since he fell from his pony when a child, and I fear he will need looking after for the rest of his life. It would be a brave woman indeed who took him for a husband, for on bad days he wanders around scarcely knowing where he is.

Therefore I must trust to Kadilia and my other girls to see that he does not want for care. And as for Fennix, who is now coming into his teens, what will become of him? At least now he is still mostly away at school, but in the holidays, William takes him with him nowadays when goes weekly into Worcester, and the pair of them always return tipsy. This is not what I want my son to learn, yet I am powerless to stop it, for William is his father and in the eyes of society, the one who says what will and will not happen with his son.

"Poor Loretta," Fleur sighed. "You really were trapped by the conventions of the time, weren't you? And with your family past, you must have been warned by your Aunt Loverin not to rock the boat because of what had happened with Henrik. You sound like a reasonable woman, so I'd bet she had a quiet word with you and told you all."

However, this information enabled her to fill in some of the information she still needed on the family. If two of Loretta's three sons had gone away, and poor Wantelo wasn't right in the head, then it made it a lot easier to understand how the estate had been handed on to a daughter. However, there were three girls older than Annora, so how come it had been her of all of them who had got *The Rookery*?

"Yet another bloody puzzle," Fleur muttered, then looked at the time and realised that she would have to stop there, because it was time to go down and speak to Mr Harris.

Arriving down in his office, she very carefully told him of her suspicions. She never said a word about her own encounter with Bad Angelo – which was what she was still calling this other man for want of anything else – not least because she knew Mr Harris would never understand why she wouldn't have called the police. Finishing with,

"And Marie is now rethinking her encounters with both versions of Mr Vance, but thinks that I may have spotted something she and the others didn't. So you see, we have to sort this out, because the real Mr Vance is the one we have the contracts with, and this other person is causing trouble for all of us."

Mr Harris was looking horrified, but at least he hadn't dismissed her idea out of hand, though for a few minutes he didn't say anything at all. Finally he sighed,

"This is all highly irregular."

"Well the good news is that I haven't found any hint of any other bodies turning up," Fleur said, trying to brighten his mood, but only got a gloomy,

"I should hope not!"

Then a timer pinged, and with a groan Mr Harris turned to his computer and brought up the Zoom meeting screen. Moments later, Angelo Vance appeared on screen.

Chapter 25

To Fleur's intense relief there wasn't as much as a mark on his face. Not a cut, not a bruise, nothing. Yet her relief was tempered by concern, for Angelo looked awful. White as a sheet, and with dark smudges under his eyes, it was the haunted look in those eyes which worried her the most.

"An… Mr Vance, are you alright?" she asked urgently, just about managing to not give his first name with Mr Harris sitting beside her.

"No, not really," he answered shakily.

"Oh my goodness, what's happened?"

He looked balefully back at them, and Fleur knew he'd chosen his words carefully when he said, "She did it again. My mum spiked my food."

"No!" Fleur gasped in horror, knowing that he didn't just mean slipping some weed into his food, but fully knocking him out. "Are you okay?"

"I've completely lost Saturday and Sunday. I came around late on on Monday morning, and the first thing I did was call for a taxi to the station, and get on a train back here to London."

So he'd run for his refuge. Fleur couldn't blame him for that. The place his mother didn't have a key for, and which she didn't like, was probably the safest place for him right now. Meanwhile Mr Harris' gaze was going back and forth between them like a Wimbledon umpire, realising that there was something going on beyond what was being said, but totally in the dark. And seeing him, Angelo said guardedly,

"I mentioned to Fleur that my mother has been treated for psychoses in the past, and when I was young would put sedatives in my food sometimes to give herself an easier life. I would really appreciate it if this didn't become common knowledge, Mr Harris."

"No, of course not!" Mr Harris gasped. "Dear me. No, we would never divulge something like that." And slightly embarrassed, pushed his chair away and got up. "I think I'd better leave Fleur to bring you up to date with what she's found, then. I'll just go and… and…" with which he hurried out, closing the door firmly behind him.

Fleur smiled at Angelo. "Bless him, Mr Harris is a great boss, but he doesn't do well with emotional stuff. Don't worry, he really won't say a thing. But you… what on earth happened? How did she get it into you? And where the hell did she get such a thing?"

Angelo groaned and leaned his head into his hands. "I left you and went to the Cheltenham house like I said I would. I rang Mum and told her I'd be over around midday on Saturday, and that seemed fine. But then about eleven o'clock I had her on the phone in floods of tears. She was frightened, she thought she'd heard somebody outside, would I go over right away."

He sighed deeply. "I didn't for one moment think that there was an intruder, but she was in a state, so I thought I couldn't *not* go. After all, she is still my mum."

"I hear you," Fleur sympathised. "She played on your better feelings, and it's no shame on you for being taken in by her."

Angelo gave a wan smile. "Thank you for the sympathy, though it doesn't make me feel any less of a fool."

"No, don't do that to yourself. You weren't a fool. It hits all of us who've had parents who don't behave like parents ought to. We get all these social expectations thrust at us from all sides, and if you don't conform, people tend to think *we* are the spoilt brats who aren't grateful for what our parents did for us. Society doesn't have a norm for parents who just don't play the game like everyone else, so we get pulled every which way, while at the same time just trying to survive."

Angelo's smile was a little less faint this time. "When did you get so wise?" he asked wistfully.

"Oh, I can't take the credit. My mum's mum – that's Grandma Rose, the gypsy – she was the one who would take me on one side and talk sense to me whenever Dad and his side threatened to overwhelm me, and make me feel guilty for not being my kid sister's unpaid servant."

"Then I wish I'd had a Grandma Rose. My Great-aunt Sophia was lovely, but she never sat me down and talked to me quite like that."

"What a shame. …So come on, then, how did she do it? How did she dope you?"

"Bloody drinking chocolate, I think. I got there, and she was already calmer. Now I'm thinking that she just put on a bit of an act for me when I got there. Just enough to not make me suspicious. And to be frank, I was sodding knackered. It's not the easiest drive to make at coming up midnight, when there's no direct route and you have to take the minor roads for a lot of the time.

"So when she then offered to make me a mug of chocolate because she was having one, I honestly didn't see it coming. The fact that I pretty much flaked out straight away on the sofa in the Dower House didn't faze me at the time… I mean when I felt myself suddenly drifting off …because I just put it down to being exhausted. It was only when I woke up on Monday with a thumping headache, and realised I had…" he suddenly blushed.

"Ah, you didn't even wake up to go to the loo?" Fleur guessed, and got an embarrassed nod. "Yes, being out of it for that long would raise your suspicions."

"It did. So I got up to go and have a shower and clean up. But the moment I tried to stand the whole room was going round. I'm not kidding when I say I had to crawl up the stairs on all fours and into the bathroom. I stripped off and just sat in the shower for ages. After a bit I started to feel a bit better, and I managed to stand up without wanting to puke or faint. It took a bit of doing, but I got downstairs and fixed myself a couple of scrambled eggs on toast and started to feel a bit better. But it was when I put the radio on for the news and realised that not only wasn't it later on on Saturday, it wasn't even Sunday but Monday, that's when I panicked."

"I'm not surprised. That must have been a horrible shock."

"It was. Once I'd had something to eat I realised that half my problem was that I'd had nothing for days, and I was both dehydrated and my blood sugar levels must have been subterranean. So I drank a couple of pints of water, and then did a slow hobble across the yard just wrapped in a bath towel, found some clean clothes and called the taxi." He shuddered. "All I could think of was getting back here to safety."

"That was probably the best thing you could have done," Fleur agreed, then took a deep breath before saying, "Look, I think I know why your mum wanted you out of the way, but I'm not sure you're up for hearing that right now."

However Angelo's eyes had flown wide open and he cried, "Oh no! They came after you? Oh God, I wondered where Mum had got to, and why her car wasn't there, but I was in no state to do much of anything."

And there it was. That, 'they'. He knew who it was.

Part of Fleur was annoyed, but the other part understood that he must have had years of being bullied by whoever it was, perhaps even from childhood, and that kind of conditioning was dreadfully hard to break free of, even if you desperately wanted to.

"Who is 'they'?" she asked gently. "I think you owe me that, Angelo. And let me tell you that I've worked out that there's someone out there who is a dead ringer for you, and who impersonates you at times. I don't know who that is. But that's the man who raped Claire Marshall, isn't it? That was never you."

To her horror, Angelo dissolved into sobs, but then he managed to get out. "Oh, thank God! At last someone sees it! You don't know what a relief it is to finally be able to say this out loud."

"Jeez, Angelo, who is this guy?"

"He's my brother. My kid brother, Gabriele."

Fleur was lost for words. A brother? That explained so much.

"But where was he born?" she wondered. "There's no record of your mum having another child."

"Over in Italy," Angelo sniffed. "Although he was conceived over here."

"But who was his father? Jacko Vance couldn't have been, because he was dead by the time your mum could have conceived again."

"I don't know for sure, but I have a dreadful suspicion."

Suddenly Fleur was aware of voices in the outer office. "Look, this isn't the way for us to talk about this. If I can get a train to London, are you okay with me coming to see you?"

Angelo looked up into her face. "I have no idea why I trust you, but I do. There's a train from Worcester at five twenty-five that gets you in to Paddington at eight o'clock. If you text me when you're nearly there, I'll have a taxi waiting for you. There's one particular company I use who I really trust. I don't drive in London, you see, just keep a car at Cheltenham, so even if I was feeling fit enough to drive – which I'm certainly not – I don't have anything to pick you up in."

"No, that's fine! I'll do that! I'll be bringing some things with me to show you which I think will be quite a revelation about the past."

"Be gentle with me," Angelo said and only half-jokingly, "I'm still a bit fragile at the moment."

"See you later," Fleur said cheerily and ended the call.

Dashing out of the office, she shot past Mr Harris calling, "Gotta go! I've got to catch a train! Mr Vance wants to see the notebooks in person!"

"Fleur, no!" Harris' voice echoed after her. "No! Don't go! It's not safe!"

"It is," Fleur insisted as she raced back past him with her coat and her bag stuffed with some of the grimoires, both of them now out on the landing. "This is the real Angelo Vance. The good guy. And he deserves to know what's been going on in his past."

It was barely five o'clock yet, but Fleur wanted to get back to her flat and grab a few things on the way, and so she raced out of the firm's gateway and jogged up the road. At her flat she grabbed her small overnight bag and threw in a couple of tops and sets of underwear plus her wash-bag, which had all of the essentials in even if it wouldn't do for anything longer. But she also put in the tarot cards, which she hadn't taken back yet, and Grandma Rose's bracelets. She didn't feel the need to wear them yet, but definitely wanted them with her. And on a last impulse, she put on her pendant for protection. It wasn't Angelo she was worried about, but it felt as if she was being given a nudge in that direction which she ought not to ignore.

Trotting out of the door, she reckoned she just had time to make it to Foregate Street Station with time to buy her ticket, but if not, she'd just have to pay on the train. And so she was just coming onto Foregate Street when her phone rang, showing it was Mr Harris. Since he was her boss, she could hardly ignore him, but she struggled to keep the irritation out of her voice as she had to stop in her tracks to answer it. And she was just starting walking again when his words made her halt abruptly.

"Fleur!" he said urgently. "You don't need to go to London. Mr Vance is here! He says it was all a mistake, and that the call got routed through his

London home."

"That's not possible," Fleur said, gritting her teeth. "Mr Harris, you just can't do that – or at least not without a lot more technology than we or the Vances possess. That's not Angelo Vance! That's the imposter!"

"Of course it's Mr Vance," Mr Harris said with some irritation. "Who else would it be? Really, Fleur, this is getting silly. Just come back here. Mr Vance wants you to show him the grimoires."

"No! For the love of God, no, Mr Harris! Don't show him the books! There are recipes for poisons in there! He's the last person you should show those to!"

"Don't be ridiculous! The damned things belong to him!"

"No, they don't, sir! The man in front of you may look like Angelo Vance, but he's a very mentally disturbed relative. Whatever you do, do not let him inside the offices!"

"Excuse me?" Mr Harris sounded deeply affronted that Fleur should tell him who he should and should not allow in.

"Sir, I'm not being ridiculous or awkward. That man is very dangerous! I'm warning you for your own safety, please don't let him inside."

"Oh, for heaven's sake!" and Fleur hear him starting to punch the number code into the door lock, then the door catch and Mr Harris say, "Please come in Mr Vance …Oh thank you, Denise. …Goodnight, Megan," and then a scream.

"Mr Harris? …Mr Harris?" Fleur shouted into the phone, then heard a woman crying. "Anybody? …Are you alright!"

It took a moment, then a badly shaken Mr Harris came on the line. "He hit me! Angelo Vance hit me! And he's dragged Megan back inside and slammed the door."

The somewhat more muffled voice of Denise could be heard saying, "Mr Harris, I think you need to come and sit down. That's a nasty cut on your head." Then there was an even more distant scream, the sound of running feet getting closer, and then a snarling voice demanding,

"Where is she? Where is that bitch with my books?"

Even as she heard a shaky Mr Harris saying, "You know where she is. I told you. She's catching the train to London to see you," Fleur started to run.

Cutting off the call, she knew that the others would have to look after themselves. At least there were three of them, maybe more if others hadn't already left work, whereas she was on her own now. To hell with buying the ticket at the kiosk, she needed to get on that train as fast as possible.

Luckily the announcement that the train was arriving came on just as she was tearing in through the entrance, and without pausing, Fleur hurtled up the steps to the platform. As the long train pulled in, she ran further along the platform, finally pulling herself up into a carriage where she could look back along the platform but without obviously being in the nearest carriages to the steps. If necessary, she would wait until Angelo's evil brother had got on the train, and then at the last minute would get off again. With luck that would leave him rushing on towards London, and she would just have to catch a later train after she'd warned Angelo.

Yet her luck held. For five long minutes the train waited at the station, every one of them feeling like half an hour to Fleur. Then the whistle blew, the doors were locked, and the train began pulling away, rapidly picking up speed. In the last moments, as her carriage finally pulled level with the stairs, Fleur saw Bad Angelo, or Gabriele as she must get used to calling him, come pounding up onto the platform. His scream of rage was audible even from inside the train, and the poor station man who got in his way was practically lifted off his feet and shaken.

In an instant that was all behind her, though, and Fleur sank gratefully into her seat. Once the ticket collector had come past, and Fleur had paid her fare, she felt obliged to ring through to the office to make sure everyone was okay. Part of her was really annoyed that Mr Harris hadn't believed her. If he had, he would have gone back inside and made sure nobody opened the outer door.

But he hadn't, had he? It had been easier to dismiss her fears as just female fancies, rather than open his eyes and see that this man before him was not Angelo Vance. And though Mr Harris was a veritable walking encyclopaedia on everything antique, he was a complete Luddite when it came to technology. Without the ever-loyal Denise sorting things out for him, he was completely lost, which was why he had so easily believed that load of old nonsense about routing a call via London.

After she'd tried three or four extensions and still got no answer, Fleur didn't know whether to be even more worried or relieved. Either everyone had simply gone home to have a few stiff G&Ts after the fright they'd had, or something was seriously wrong. And with that in mind, Fleur thought she had no choice but to warn Angelo, and not just about his lunatic brother potentially trying to come up to London to find him, either.

After she'd passed on the worrying news, she had to drop the real bombshell. "Look, Angelo, I'm afraid the time for pussyfooting around this has passed. Mr Harris won't let this one go. He'll tell the police, and for your own sake, you have to tell them that it was your brother. If you do, and the Met send an officer around to confirm that you are where you said you were, you'll be in the clear."

"My mother will never forgive me," Angelo said dejectedly. "That will be the end of our relationship, I just know it."

"Your mother came bloody close to poisoning you!" Fleur riposted, her mind flashing back to the tarot cards and that warning of The Tower with the Two of Cups. This was the relationship which was crashing down! "What would have happened if you'd had an adverse reaction to whatever god-awful concoction they dosed you with? What if you'd done nothing more than vomited in your sleep? You could have still choked to death – because I'm guessing that you didn't wake up in the recover position, did you? You could have *died* on Friday!"

"I hear you," Angelo said, his voice already thick with tears. "I guess I knew that at some point this time would come. I just… I just hoped that it wouldn't."

Fleur's heart went out to him. It was a dreadful choice to have to make, and it dawned on her that what was making it worse was that it was now blindingly obvious that Claudia had chosen Gabriele over Angelo at every turn. Up until now, Angelo had been able to make excuses to himself for her, but the balance on those scales had finally tipped away from him this time, and he had run out of options.

"I'll be with you as soon as I can," she told him soothingly, already envisaging a long night sitting up making lots of mugs of tea while Angelo unburdened himself to her. Not that she minded. There'd been many a time when she'd wished she'd had a friend who would sit with her while she wept over her father's indifference, so there was no way she was turning her back on Angelo now.

"I'll definitely send a driver for you now," Angelo finished. "You'll know it's the right man because he'll be carrying a battered copy of *A Shropshire Lad*."

"Houseman? Nice choice!"

There was a wobbly laugh. "Don't get too impressed. It's just that I've never bothered about poetry, so it was random enough that neither Mum nor Gabriele was ever likely to think of it as a signal. It ensured that when I felt my most threatened, I'd always know who was my real cabbie, and who was possibly sent by my mother or grandfather."

"Oka*aay*," Fleur drawled. "That's going to be something else I think you need to tell me about when I get there. In the meantime, I'll watch out for literary-looking taxi drivers!"

Yet no sooner had she got off the phone to Angelo when it rang again, and this time it was the West Mercia Police. Once again Fleur found herself explaining how she had come to realise that there were two men who looked identical, and that yes, she was absolutely sure that the real Angelo Vance was at home in London. Luckily, she'd got Angelo to give her his address once she was on the train, just in case the cabbie didn't turn up, and so she was able to pass that on with the suggestion that the Met send someone round to the house immediately.

"I'm not even at Reading yet," she told the officer on the phone, "and Gabriele Vance was on the station back at Worcester the last I saw of him as the train pulled away. Even if he's caught a later train, he can't possibly be ahead of me. So if someone is at home at Mr Vance's flat in London, it has to be him."

And if you then find his double back in Worcester, I hope to God you arrest the monster and lock him up for the night! she thought, as she settled back and watched the darkening countryside flash by and the moon start to rise.

Chapter 26

Arriving at the gloriously Victorian edifice of Paddington Station, it suddenly occurred to Fleur that finding this taxi driver might not be that easy. There were multiple exits from the station, including the Underground, so where would he be? Out at a taxi rank or in here somewhere? Luckily Angelo was more used to this than her, and as she got to the ticket barrier at the end of the platform, there was a cheerful young Asian man clutching a book and scrutinising every passenger.

"Ms Constantine?" he said, before she could speak.

"Err, yes, that's me."

"Mr Vance sent me."

"Oh."

Her stunned expression must have told him she didn't know what to make of this, continuing, "He gave me a very good description of you, and said you would probably only have small bags, not a proper suitcase." He waved a hand at the thinning crowd. "There were not many people who fitted everything."

So Angelo was with it enough to do that, or more worryingly, had had sufficient bad experiences to know what to do. However, right now the cabbie was ushering her out through one of the side exits and then over to a top-of-the-range Lexus, proclaiming 'Luxury Transport Services' on the side, forcing Fleur to suppress a giggle. Clearly Angelo's idea of a taxi and hers were very different!

Not being used to visiting London very often, Fleur was horrified at the volume of traffic even at this late hour, and was relieved when they finally pulled onto a leafy street, and then onto the drive of what had previously been a large detached house, dating probably from somewhere just pre-WW1. What had once been a good-sized front garden had become the parking area for the residents, and Fleur saw several family cars pulled over to the one side. Those must belong to the downstairs neighbours, and looking at the house, Fleur realised that there was not only a ground floor but also a basement, meaning that both Angelo and the others had two floors to their homes in this building. And right now, the thought of a whole family in the same building – not just some elderly couple in a single-floor flat – was very reassuring.

The driver had only just handed her her overnight bag when the front door opened, and Angelo stood silhouetted in the hall light.

"Fleur! Thank God you've arrived safely!" He waved at the driver. "Thank you Raz! Bill me as usual."

"Right you are, Mr Vance. Have a good night," and Raz and his Lexus swept out of the drive into the night.

"Come on in," Angelo said with a smile, and waved her towards a second door part way down the hall, which was as substantial as the actual front door. Once through it, Fleur was immediately confronted with the stairs within Angelo's home, which once upon a time would have made an imposing statement when still visible from the hallway. A small pied-à-terre this was not! Still-pristine plasterwork formed the ornate coving and ceiling rose, and when Fleur reached the equally impressive landing, gave a gasp of surprise as cunningly created tall 'window' spaces made in the wall allowed her to see through to a dining room area, which seemed to have a huge row of patio doors giving out onto some kind of balcony.

A few steps further, and Angelo ushered her through into the room, which turned out to run the whole of the length of the back of the building in one sophisticated, long combined kitchen and dining room. The original coving of the former three rooms had been kept, elegantly separating the different parts without forming any sort of barrier, and with the whole being decorated in a soft almost-white, it was tasteful and spacious.

"Wow! What a lovely space!" Fleur said admiringly. "In my tiny flat I can never get this sense of space because it's a squash just to get the essential furniture in."

"Come on through to the lounge," Angelo said, going back into the hall and opening the door into yet another lovely room, which this time opened onto the front. The paint scheme was the same, with a lovely old Edwardian cast iron-and-tile fireplace, parquet flooring, a cream leather three-seater sofa occupying the bay window space, while a couple of matching leather armchairs sat on the other side of the fireplace. Minimalist white, floating, bookcases on the wall opposite the fireplace held a collection of paperbacks, while on the chimney breast was a huge oil painting of foaming waves and a turbulent sky in pale shades of blues and greys.

"Well it's easy to see that you don't have any kids coming around," Fleur said with a grin. "I shudder to think what chocolaty fingers would do to this room in less time than it takes to sneeze!"

For a second Angelo looked startled, then gave a guffaw of laughter, almost as if the pressure building up inside him had been release with that laugh.

"I suppose it does rather reek of 'professional single'," he admitted sheepishly, "but in my defence, this is the decorative scheme I inherited with the place. Only the painting and the books are mine. The previous owner was going to work abroad for a long time, and so wasn't keen to put all of this into storage, but preferred to sell and start over when he gets back. I just wanted a fresh start, so it suited us both."

Fleur grinned back at him. "Nice recovery, Mr Vance! I'll let you off with that one, then," and was gratified to see some of the haunted look leaving his eyes.

"The master bedroom is on this floor, but the others are upstairs, so you won't have to be on the same floor as me. I've put you in the guest room with the bay window. The only people who can see in are the squirrels and the pigeons, so I don't think you'll be disturbed."

"I'll keep an eye on those spying squirrels," Fleur quipped, then forgot everything else as Angelo showed her into a lovely room up under the eaves, big enough to fit both of her bedrooms in.

"This is your en-suite," he said opening another door, and without realising she'd said it out aloud, Fleur gasped,

"En-suite? This is double the size of my whole bathroom! And is that a walk-in shower? Oh my God! I've always wanted to try one of those!" Then she realised that she was rather embarrassing Angelo, and hurriedly said, "And why wouldn't you have all this gorgeous stuff? I would if I had the chance. Angelo, this is a lovely, lovely place you have here. I can see why you wanted to get back here as fast as possible. This is yours, and without a whole tribe of ancestors jostling for their memories to be seen."

He looked slightly startled, but then nodded. "You know I'd never thought of it in quite that way – of my ancestors crowding in on me at *The Rookery*. But now you've said it, that's exactly how it's made me feel. Maybe because of how my mum spoke of her father, I was always scared stiff of him, and yet in truth, given how little I saw of him, and never alone, it was more the thought of him than anything he ever did to me personally, or at least as far as I have any recollections. Yet it was more than just him. It felt like there was some kind of battle going on in the place."

Fleur had put her overnight bag on the floor, already thinking that she would have to be very careful with the pristine oyster-white sheets and duvet cover – which she couldn't imagine he laundered himself, and which was another question she needed to ask him, since that was a possible way for Gabriele to get to him – and now turned around to him in surprise.

"If you felt that, then I know Grandma Rose would be saying that you are a sensitive – someone who has latent psychic abilities, even if you've never tapped into them."

"Me? Good grief! I've never thought of myself like that," and Fleur could tell that he was slightly disbelieving.

"And yet you've said to me about feeling the need to have this… well for want of a better word, 'uncontaminated' space – which I think is more than just about privacy in the physical sense. With the various fairly radical changes that have been made to this house, coupled with the fact that it's probably only around a century old, it means that it doesn't have much in the way of vibes hanging around it. That makes it a very neutral space for you, which is why you can relax here."

Angelo looked dubious but didn't argue, instead asking, "So what is it that you wanted to show me?"

"I think we'd better go downstairs, and get at least a cup of tea or coffee going before I get into that. I would've suggested a stiff drink, but given that we've no idea what your mum doped you up with, that probably isn't such a great idea in case there's still enough in your system to react with alcohol. I really don't want to be calling for an ambulance for you tonight."

Smiling wanly, Angelo agreed, "I'd been thinking much the same. I got in and went straight for the malt whisky, then thought maybe that wasn't my brightest idea. I've been brewing up a lot of coffee since then. It's real coffee and supposed to be decaf, but I don't think it's that decaf when drunk by the pint! I'll probably be awake through the night now, but after being out for the count for so long, I'm almost worried to close my eyes."

"Don't worry. I'll sit up with you if you like," Fleur tried to reassure him. "But I'd love one of those decafs myself right now. Railway coffee is just revolting, and there's not much of it given how much you pay."

That made Angelo grin. "One Moka of decaf coming right up!" and indeed just the smell wafting through from the bubbling pot on the hob was enough to have Fleur almost drooling.

When they were settled in the lounge, both of them on the sofa and a large coffee table pulled up so that Fleur could spread the books out on it, she began. Starting gently with the basic details of the family, she gradually worked up to the deaths of Lady Felicia and Henrik Bitanyi, and how by then he'd become known as Henry Boswell.

"They weren't a bunch of murderers," she hurriedly reassured Angelo, as he sat open-mouthed at the revelation. "It really was a matter of them or him. What Mezelly did for Lady Felicia was done out of love, and I'm sure that right now there are lots of families with members in hospices who wish that they could spare them the similar suffering right at the end, in spite of our modern drugs.

"If bloody Henrik was withholding her morphine, then he was a right sadistic bastard, and her agony must have been intolerable. But you can then see why the family began to be worried about what he'd do to them. If he believed that they knew what he'd been doing, they were in effect witnesses, and I think he was wicked enough not to want to leave those kinds of loose ends lying around.

"The bit about Joe and his son suffering a terrible purging must have scared the living daylights out of them all, and by then, Mezelly and Loverin were experienced enough herbalists to have been capable of hazarding a reasonable guess as to what had been used on them. I've read on for many years' worth of entries since that point, and there's never as much as a whisper of them ever even thinking of doing anything like that again. You'd probably struggle to make the case in a court of law, but in my mind, it came down to self-defence."

"Hell's teeth!" Angelo said softly. "But that means that there are bodies on my land somewhere, doesn't it?"

"Not bod*ies*. Only one. Remember, Lady Felicia was deemed to have died naturally, and was buried accordingly next to her husband. The only skeleton waiting to be found is Henrik's, and that's probably under the roots of a big old tree. If that still stands it's going to make it virtually impossible to find, because I don't know if something like ground radar would work in an orchard.

"After all, he was in a wooden barrel, so the wood has probably rotted, and even the iron bands must be so much rust by now. If the tree roots have done their worst, even the bones might have been shifted apart. I only know what I've picked up from watching *Time Team* and stuff, but I think the way that they find graves normally is by the pockets of air where things like the coffin collapses, but if a tree's main roots have gone through it, the soil might have resettled much more firmly – or at least that's my theory. You're not going to be walking over the fields and suddenly find yourself coming face to face with a skull."

"Thank Christ for that!" Angelo said from the heart.

Fleur smiled at him. "I'm not just saying all this to stop you from fretting. Seriously! These weren't people with murder eternally in mind. They only came to that as the absolute last resort, and when they thought that if they didn't finish Henrik off, that he would do for them in twos and threes. But he's not your ancestor, Angelo. That man was Annie's second 'husband', who was Harodain. And he was a thoroughly decent man who did his best to keep a roof over the heads of the rest of the Petulengro family. In fact, I think the very reason why Mezelly suggested he take Henrik's place was precisely because she knew that he was at heart a genuinely good man."

"That's actually reassuring to know." Then Angelo thought for a moment and added. "In fact, if what you've told me is the correct chronology of events, he wasn't even party to the giving of the poison to Henrik, was he?"

"No, I don't think he was. The full extent of Harodain's involvement – and I'm going to carry on calling him that so that we don't get confused – is in the preparation of the new cider orchard into which they planted Henrik in his barrel."

Angelo sat and thought for a moment, then asked, "You said that you had a candidate for the bad stuff coming into the family. So if it isn't via Henrik, who is it?"

"Ah, well I haven't got as far as that man's own entries in the books, but I'm seriously looking at your great-grandfather, Ignatius. I've got a bit more digging to do on him, and like I say, I haven't yet reached the 'grimoires' I suspect he might have written, but already I'm starting to think that he wasn't just a distant admirer of Aleister Crowley's – I think at some point he actually met the man! And that really isn't good."

"It isn't?"

"No! Crowley was one of those charismatic people who seem to manage to sweep others along with even the daftest of schemes. And thinking back to the research I did for my thesis on twentieth-century pagan rituals and practises, Crowley's were pretty extreme even by the *Golden Dawn's* standards. In fact, they parted company with him because of some of his views.

"More to the point, Crowley was thought to be responsible for the death of more than one person, though not outright murder. But these days he'd be prosecuted in the same way any cult leader who brought their followers into danger would be, because he had no thought for others, and no conscience over using people. And it's that callousness about using others for his own ends that I think rubbed off on your great-grandfather when he was a young man, as well as some of Crowley's mucky sexual practises."

Angelo's eyes went wide again. "What do you mean, 'mucky'?"

Fleur wrinkled her nose. "Oh, I'm no prude. But Crowley had multiple partners, male and female and concurrently, for a start off. And I don't just mean he was bisexual. He was into stuff which was hardly more than free-love orgies at the commune he had at Cefalù in Sicily – conned his followers into believing he was working 'sex magic'," and she rolled her eyes.

"It was just an excuse to shag as many people as he wanted without taking any responsibility for the kids that resulted, some of whom died because of the insanitary conditions there, and because nobody was actively taking care of them."

"No! That's just wicked! Kids died?"

"Yes, they did. And this is the man who had a strong influence on your great-grandfather Ignatius. I've found a photograph amongst Ignatius' notes of a place called Boleskine House, which is up near Loch Ness and which belonged to Crowley. It seems very much as if pre-WW1 Ignatius went up there. He'd only have been a teenager, because he was just eighteen when he married Annora in 1913, so God only knows what his parents were thinking to be letting him do that. But then we don't know anything about them, because of course they aren't the ones whose journals I'm looking at.

"What I do suspect, and ought to be able to confirm, is that Annora's maternal aunt – the glamorously named Starlina – was obsessed with the occult. Your great-great-grandmother Loretta – Starlina's oldest sister – was despairing of the influence she gained over her own youngest daughter, Richenda, and also Annora, your great-grandmother. It seems that Loretta's husband, who was the Irish chap, William Fitzpatrick, was a bit of a weak reed. He didn't help her much in trying to instil some discipline into their kids, and I've got a sneaky feeling that it's going to turn out to be Starlina who introduces Annora to Ignatius.

"Annora was three years older than Ignatius, so she'd have been twenty-one and not needing parental consent when they married, which would mean that Loretta couldn't object in law, however much she disapproved. Richenda was younger and by six years, so Loretta could, and possibly did, put her foot down regarding any travelling from home that was done for her. But Annora was a young woman, so if she wanted to go to Boleskine with her aunt, then there wouldn't have been much anyone could do to stop her."

"Blimey! You don't think of stuff like that happening until the sixties."

"Ah, but the twenties weren't called the Roaring Twenties for nothing – lots of post-war need to live life to the full, and all that. And the Belle Époque which came before WW1, was all a bit larger than life, too. It's when the Eifel Tower was built, for instance, and when you had famous artists congregating in Paris. It's not all free love and drug taking, but it is liberated compared to the Victorian restrictions of previous decades."

"And where on earth did they get these names from?" wondered Angelo with a shake of his head. "There isn't a Bill or a Sam amongst them!"

"Ah, well that's a whole different thing. You might find it hard to believe, but names like Paizeni, Fennix, Anselo, and Starlina, crop up quite often in records of Romany families of the time – they weren't just plucking them out of their imaginations. I've got a great-great-something called Paizeni myself. There are some Old Testament names, such as Shadrach, but far less of the New Testament biblical names. If we could whisk back through time and listen in, I suspect that we'd find that many of these children in your past were named after favourite aunts and uncles of their parents. But of course, they would have been names no regular, settled family would use, even back then, and so just by names alone, the Petulengro and Fitzpatrick kids would have stood out amongst their contemporaries in the village as a bit exotic."

"I'm surprised a good Catholic lad like William Fitzpatrick didn't name his kids after a whole list of saints," Angelo said thoughtfully. "I presume he was a Catholic? And that's where the faith comes into our family?"

Fleur rocked a hand. "Hard to tell, strangely enough. If they'd been Catholics through and through, I'd have expected them to potentially have a bible written in Latin, given how far back the one I saw went. But that one was just a hefty version of the standard King James Bible. So I would rather suggest to you that William was Protestant."

"Really? I thought we'd been Catholic for generations! In fact, I was given to understand that that was one of the reasons why the Italian family tolerated Grandma Angelina marrying an Englishman like Grandfather Aleister Kingsford. He wasn't going to object to their children being brought up to go to mass and stuff."

Fleur gave him a sideways look. "Then I think it's fair to say that Aleister lied through his teeth!" She thought for a second, then added, "In fact I'd say it's far more likely that your grandfather was as embarrassed as hell about his father's wilder exploits, and was trying to cover them up. He must have found the Fitzpatrick family bible and thought it was manna from heaven. There it was, a readymade excuse for why the Fitzpatrick-Kingsfords of *The Rookery* weren't embroiled up to their aristocratic eyeballs in the local social scene.

"Why didn't they go to the parish church on Sunday? Oh, they're Catholic. Why wasn't Mrs Kingsford, or earlier, Mrs Fitzpatrick a leading light in the oh-so-Church-of-England W.I.? Oh, because she's a Catholic! Nothing to do with the fact that the family comes from a proud line of true Romanies, who back then would've been about as welcome in the W.I. as the plague in town! And an even better cover for the fact that his mum and dad were at one point completely taken in by one of the most notorious scoundrels of the first half of the twentieth century!"

"Good Lord, I hadn't even got that far!" Angelo exclaimed. "But it fits, doesn't it? All the excuses, all the lies."

"Yes, it does."

Suddenly from down below the doorbell rang most insistently.

"Who the hell is that at this time of night?"

Angelo wondered, getting to his feet. "For God's sake, it's bloody eleven o'clock!"

"Be careful, Angelo!" Fleur cautioned, hurrying to follow him down to his front door, and dreading finding Gabriele and/or Mrs Vance on the doorstep.

Instead, it was a uniformed police officer standing there.

"Mr Angelo Vance?" he asked, and beyond him Fleur could see the police patrol car pulled up onto the drive.

"Yes?" said Angelo, perplexed.

"I need you to come to the station to answer question with regard to the grievous assault upon Mr Mycroft Harris at the premises of *Miller, Bronson & Carter* in Worcester earlier this evening, for which you stand accused."

Chapter 27

Fleur yelped, "*Nooo*!" turning frantically to Angelo. "Did you not get a visit from them earlier?"

"No, I didn't, but I didn't think it that important," Angelo said, still looking utterly stunned, while the officer asked,

"What visit?"

Fleur thumped her head against the doorframe. "*Aaagh*! This is exactly why I asked for it to be done! …I'm sorry, Officer, but you see, I was on the phone to Mr Harris – who is actually my boss – at the time when Mr Vance, here, supposedly hit him! I was just about to leave Worcester to come here and heard it all on the phone. Then not ten minutes later, I was on the train which was just pulling away from Foregate Street Station, when the man who actually did the assault came running up the stairs and grabbed hold of one of the railway staff.

"I'm not joking! Get West Mercia Police to look at the security footage for the five-thirty train! You'll see a man, who looks like a very rough version of Mr Vance, grabbing a guard by the collar of his uniform and lifting him off his feet by it.

"But when I got to London, *this* Mr Vance – the *real* Mr Vance – had arranged for a car to come and meet me, and he was standing right here in this doorway when the driver left. In fact, the driver knows who he is, and spoke to him about adding the fare onto his normal account. And given that I was on the *only* train which could have possibly have got him here in time to even as much as get in at the same time as me, the other man couldn't have possibly have got here before me. Not on the train, and given the traffic I got caught up in coming from Paddington to here, absolutely definitely not by road! *This* Mr Vance has a brother, and it's that man – Gabriele Vance – who you need to be arresting, not my client."

The officer shifted uncomfortably. "I hear what you are saying, Miss, but I still have to bring Mr Vance in for questioning."

"Then I'm coming with you!" Fleur said assertively. "I'll get my coat!"

It took a couple of hours at the station of Fleur being absolutely adamant about what she had heard and seen, and Angelo's solicitor turning up and backing her up, but in the small hours an exhausted Fleur and Angelo finally got back to his flat. She didn't think for one moment that the police were convinced that Angelo had a double, but with the lack of evidence and her conflicting testimony, there weren't any grounds to hold Angelo on.

What was a surprise was that the solicitor seemed to know something of the brother, and backed her up. Given that she wasn't allowed in the room when Angelo and the solicitor were being questioned, she had no idea what had been said, but as they were leaving one of the policemen let it slip that Mr Oliver Walker, the solicitor, had confirmed what she'd said in that respect. However, he promptly vanished off as soon as a cab had been called for Fleur and Angelo, and Angelo was so wrung out that Fleur didn't have the heart to question him further.

With both of them heading gratefully for their beds, it was only when they both surfaced mid-morning that they talked again. Fleur had been up longer, not least because she'd had to ring into work and explain why she wouldn't be in. To her horror, Denise said that Mr Harris had taken the rest of the week off to recover, and that the directors were seriously considering cancelling the contract with Mr Vance and packing everything back up.

"No! Please, put me through to one of them," Fleur pleaded to Denise. However, Denise only relented once Fleur had recounted her own experiences.

"Yes, he did have his one hand in a bandage," Denise said, rather taken aback. "In fact, that was part of the problem. The evil sod had bound something hard and sharp into the back of his hand with it. So he hit Mr Harris with more of a backhander than a punch. I saw him flinch when he did it, but he was so off his face on whatever he was taking, that I don't think he felt as much pain as he should have. And that bandage was more like a boxing glove!

"But the worst of it was that when he'd been through into the workshop, and realised that his mother's books weren't there, he came out and punched Mr Harris again. Several times! And with his good hand!"

"Oh, Jeez!" Fleur groaned. "Poor Mr Harris." But was silently thankful that she'd taken all the grimoires up to the attic. Clearly Gabriele had seen the ordinary books and jumped to wholly the wrong conclusion as to why his mother's weren't with them.

"Poor all of us," Denise said, now sounding shaken. "He really hurt Megan. She's got some nasty bruises on her arms where he grabbed hold of her and shook her. He slapped me, and he's torn my coat where he tried to pull me about."

"Denise! This is really important! Have you done anything with that coat since?"

"No. No, I haven't. I can't bear to look at it just yet."

"Then for the love of God, put it into a large plastic bag – a clean bin liner will do – and take it to the police. They probably didn't ask for it at the time, because you were all saying that it was Angelo Vance who did the deed. But I'll bet that there's some of the attacker's DNA on that coat where he tore it. Ask them to get it looked at by an expert, because Angelo's.

"...Aagh, no! No, it'll be the man who raped Claire's whose DNA will be on record. But it will be easy enough to get Angelo to give a sample too. This might be a way of proving once and for all that Angelo didn't rape Claire, and he didn't attack Mr Harris."

"God, you're really sure about this, aren't you," Denise said, but with her doubt sounding in every word.

"I am!" said Fleur emphatically. "This man came after me, Denise, and the way I whacked him, he has to be bruised. Did the man you saw have bruises?"

"I'll say! That's what made him seem even scarier. He was black and purple all over one cheek bone, and with a big purple bruise just below his jaw on the other side. And his lip was split, puffy, and bruised!"

So Mrs Vance's heeled boot had cut his mouth. Fleur wasn't sorry about that. And she was rather gratified that her two jabs had done some damage, but right now she responded with,

"That's how I know they aren't the same man! *I* put those two big bruises on the man you saw. Walloped him damned hard with my elbow! But the Angelo Vance I met here in London doesn't have a mark on him. Not a scratch! And both of his hands are fine. I told the Met police this, Denise. Said I'd swear to it in court if necessary. So now we *have* to make sure that the right man gets arrested and prosecuted before he hurts anyone else. You don't want that brute to get away with hurting Mr Harris, do you?"

Fleur knew that was a bit low, because she and everyone else knew that Denise was besotted with Mr Harris, even if he never noticed it himself. She wouldn't do this for herself, but she would to protect the man she adored.

It worked. "No way am I letting him get away with that!" Denise declared, suddenly decisive. "Okay, I'll do that. The coat's only been hung up on the back of the door in my spare room. Even the cat hasn't been in there."

"That's great! So you get that bagged up when you get home – because your DNA will already be all over the coat, so you won't be contaminating anything – and then take it down to the police."

By the time she got off the phone, having had to go through all of her arguments again with Mr Miller, Fleur felt as if she had already run at least a half-marathon since getting up, and decided that she could be excused going and seeing if she could at least make a cup of tea. Mercifully Angelo's tea making equipment was more of the old-fashioned teapot variety, compared to the high-tech chrome monster of a machine for every sort of coffee known to Italians, and so Fleur soon found herself cradling a large mug of Earl Grey in her hands, and starting to feel a bit more human again. She didn't dare open one of the huge patio doors to go out onto the balcony, fearing that some complicated alarm system was in place, but she did risk opening one of the windows at the kitchen end, and sitting on the heavily cushioned bench seat beneath it.

With what passed for fresh air in London wafting in, and the sound of birds in the trees down in the garden reminding her of walks in the country, she felt her head beginning to clear a bit more. Yet one thing was really intriguing her. Who was Gabriele's father? Angelo had hinted that he could guess, but hadn't said anything so far, and Fleur wondered whether he might now rethink that in light of what had happened in the last couple of days.

She'd referred to 'Gabriele Vance' to the police, primarily because even after all these years, his mother still called herself Mrs Vance. So wherever she'd been when she gave birth to Gabriele, she would undoubtedly be recorded as Claudia Vance …unless, of course, she'd reverted to her maiden name for a while? Was he Gabriele Kingsford, perhaps? Yet whichever it was, or even a third surname she knew nothing about, dear old Jacko Vance was not his dad. So who was?

There was something very dark going on in that family, and whatever it was, it was bad enough for Angelo to have been desperate for it not to become public knowledge. But there really wasn't any option left now. And if Angelo wouldn't confide in her, then the only thing she could think of doing was going online and upping her subscription to *Ancestry* to include international records, and try and do some digging on the Italian family. Because it was clear that they were also heavily involved.

At that point, Angelo came tottering out of the master bedroom in search of coffee. And so for a while, time was taken up getting croissants and pain aux chocolate out of the freezer and cooked for a late breakfast. With the colour coming back into Angelo's face, and the midday turning warm and balmy, they ventured out onto the balcony, leading Fleur to dare to ask her first question.

"I'm so sorry that your family secret is going to have to come out in the open," she began, "but your brother is now a danger to others as well as himself. But how did your mother manage to keep him so invisible and for so long?"

Angelo stretched, and Fleur heard his shoulders creaking as he worked the knots out of them before answering.

"The 'how' is fairly easy. He was in Italy most of the time."

The penny dropped for Fleur. "Oh my God! It was him who that room you were imprisoned in was made for! *He* was the one who was originally kept in there!"

Angelo looked balefully at her. "Yes. And bloody cruel it was, too. Nobody should be kept imprisoned like that, and it surely didn't help him any." He took a deep breath. "I know you might find this hard to believe, but until that point, I honestly never guessed that I had a brother."

"Good Lord! You had no inkling?"

Angelo shook his head. "None. Don't forget, I was only one when he was born, so I was little more than a baby myself. When I was of school age, I went initially as a day attender to a boarding school over there, then once I was seven, I was over here in proper boarding schools, though nowhere near the family homes as I later discovered. Mum clearly wanted me kept well clear of her father while I was young and impressionable. So there were only the school holidays when I might have encountered Gabriele."

"Okay, I get that. But even so, did you never get any hints of him? It just seems so bizarre! There you were, two boys of much the same age, living in the same house..."

"No! Not the same house, at all! You're forgetting that Great-uncle Antonio had a *castello*."

"Yes, but you said it wasn't that large. That once he married and started having a family, that there wasn't room for everyone... Oh! Of course! Your Grandmother Angelina had her own place in the grounds, didn't she!"

Angelo nodded. "But that wasn't even the place where they found me when Mum locked me up. That was yet another cottage out on the other side of the vineyards. Once upon a time, I suppose there were a lot of servants and workers at the *castello*, but by the time I remember it, pretty much all of the properties actually on the estate were deserted. The men who came in to tend the vines lived in the village and either walked or drove in. And Grandma and Great-aunt Sophia made do with cleaning women who came in several times a week. They didn't live in either."

"Goodness… So actually, your family were quite isolated on the estate, weren't they?"

"Very much so."

"So, there was your great-uncle and his family in the *castello.* What about his own parents? You said that your great-uncle Antonio took over the running of the estate, but I presume that his parents lived on beyond that point in time? Were they also living in the *castello*, and that's why it was congested there?"

Angelo grimaced. "They did for a while. But Antonio's father died within a couple of years – a lifetime of heavy smoking and sampling his own wines hadn't done his heart any favours. After that, his mother became quite a handful! Very much the Italian mamma who thought she could still dictate what her son should do. She made Great-aunt Sophia's life an utter misery, and in the end Great-uncle Antonio moved his mother out to be with his sister, my grandmother."

"Good Lord! That must have been quite a household! Your great-grandmother trying to tell your grandmother what to do, and she in her turn trying to tell your mother! I wouldn't have wanted to spend much time in that place. Please tell me that the oldest lady had gone by the time your own mum was back there regularly as a woman with you as a kid."

"Oh, I never met her. In fact, I have very little memory of my grandmother Angelina, and by then her mother was in a nursing home. …Indeed, it might even be that the push to send me to boarding school so young was because of Mum sharing with my grandmother, but I was so little my memories aren't that clear on that.

"I gather my great-grandmother hung on for decades, finally going in her late nineties, but no, she wasn't involved with the family for a very long time aside from people making the odd visit. And there wasn't a lot of incentive to do that, because she had no memory of who was who. Great-uncle Antonio could have been a total stranger, not her son, for all she knew."

"That's very sad, but I suppose it did relieve the pressure on living space." *But I still don't understand how a child was kept so secret,* Fleur fumed inwardly. *We're talking about the nineteen-eighties here, not bloody Dickensian London! You couldn't hide the family lunatic in the attic and somebody not notice!* "I know you said that when your mum was young, she lived with her mother, but what about later on, when she went back with you when you were tiny? Were you all under the same roof then?"

"Err, no, we had a different small place, then …I think."

"So there was you and your mum in one place, and I presume your grandmother and your Aunt Romana in the other?"

Yet Angelo shook his head. "No, Mum's sister was once again somebody I never really had contact with."

"Really?" Fleur found that hard to credit. "I know your mum told me that her sister had a difficult birth, and that she was mentally disabled, but we're talking about the sixties and seventies when she was growing up, surely? So I suppose she could have gone to a special school, but by the time you were there, she'd have long left that. Please don't tell me that they kept her locked up like they did your brother? That wasn't where they got the idea from, was it?"

"No, no!" But then he stopped and looked puzzled. "Damn, you've got me thinking now. …I always accepted what I was told as a kid, but you're right, my aunt ought to have been about the place. I was told that she didn't get out much because her health wasn't good, and I must admit that when I was back there for school holidays, I spent a lot of time down in the village, because at least I had other lads to play with there. If I thought about her at all, I think I presumed that she had her own cottage somewhere, or maybe even an apartment in the nearest town that was close to the hospital.

"I know that seems peculiar, but to be honest, she was hardly ever talked about, not by Mum, or Grandmother on the rare times I met her, and so I wasn't ever prompted to be curious. It's only now you've said it that I'm thinking just how odd it was. Mum always told me that Grandma Angelina didn't like having mucky little boys about her, that she was very much the *grande dame*, that her house was filled with things like beautiful porcelain, and that therefore I was never, under any circumstances, to go over there unaccompanied.

"And the rare times I met her she seemed so on edge. A very stiff lady compared to the lovely mums most of the lads I played with had. At the age of ten or twelve I'd have given anything to just be one of the village lads, with a proper dad who'd come and kick a football around with us for half an hour or so after work, while their mum's got the meal ready. Granted, that was only at times like Easter and in the summer, when I was back at home and the weather was good enough to do that, but it certainly *seemed* as if that was the norm for them. Now you've got me wondering whether Grandma Angelina was so tense because she was scared stiff that I might start asking awkward questions."

Fleur felt sorry for him. "It's weird how age suddenly gives you different perspectives on things, isn't it? And I do understand, honestly, I do. I accepted so much of what went on around me with my own sister. As a kid you get used to avoiding the things which you know will cause rows. You have this built in survival instinct that says, 'just don't go there, they'll only get mad at you,' and you don't."

"I think that's it," Angelo agreed. "Oh hell, this is going to bug me now."

"We could try digging into your ancestry now?" Fleur suggested. "I've got my laptop with me, because I was expecting to be answering some of your questions about the books and their owners.

But I think the more recent generations are a bit more pressing right now."

"Go grab it," Angelo enthused, and once she'd brought it through to the dining room, and he had insisted on paying for the upgrade to her membership, they sat down and began entering in names.

Yet the more they dug, the stranger things became. Too much information was coming up for Romana Kingsford to still be alive and protected by privacy laws, and then they found the record of her death.

"1999!" Angelo gasped. "How the hell did I not know she died then? That was immediately before I went back there when I was sixteen! When all the bad stuff happened!"

"Could it have been in part her sister's death that tipped your mum over the edge?" Fleur wondered. "You said your therapists said that it was unlikely to be just you. Well, this could have been a huge part of it."

"I suppose so," Angelo said dubiously, "but what I don't get is why it never cropped up in conversation. I mean, it's hardly Secret Service stuff, is it? Your sister dying. Happens to a lot of ordinary people. Why would that've had to be kept hidden?

"And it *was* hidden from me. There wasn't even a whiff of anyone going to a funeral …or having been to one …because I'm now seeing that she died on the first of February, and I didn't get out there until after my school exams in that summer. But by then the initial grief should surely have worn off? And you'd think that she would have been mentioned, even if it was only something along the lines of her life being cut off so short. I mean, forty is no age to die these days, is it?"

"No, it isn't," Fleur agreed, but hoping that he hadn't seen her jump when Grandma Rose's voice in her head said, '*ah, but it wasn't Romana who died!*'

Chapter 28

"Let's go backwards a bit, and see if we can put some dates on the rest of the Italian family," Fleur suggested, to cover her confusion.

Yet although they went back down the years, nothing leapt out at them. Angelina Montefiore, as she'd been, was born in 1920 and her younger brother Antonio in 1929. In between there were other children, but none of them survived to full adulthood, perhaps because of the deprivations many Italians suffered during the inter-war years, although the boy born in 1926 lived long enough to be drafted into the Italian army and to be killed at Monte Casino in 1944. The girl who came between him and Angelina had died as a toddler, and the two children who separated him from Antonio died together in the winter of 1957 from the terrible influenza epidemic which swept across the globe. It might not have reached quite the proportions of the one which killed millions in 1919, but when Fleur looked it up, British deaths ran at an average of six hundred a week while the virus ran its course, so there was nothing odd about the two children who were possibly malnourished dying, however tragic it might have been.

So in Angelina and Antonio's generation there seemed to be nothing amiss. Only when Angelina went to England and married Aleister Kingsford could they deduce that something started to go awry.

"I know Grandma Angelina wasn't happy with Grandfather," Angelo said, sitting back with a frustrated sigh, "but there's a hell of a difference between an unhappy marriage and keeping someone locked up! And given that Romana was born in 1960, they must have had some vestige of a marriage lingering on in those early years. She wasn't a virgin birth, for heaven's sake!"

"No," Fleur said distantly, and her distraction had Angelo sitting up and looking over her shoulder again.

"What on earth have you got there?"

"Ship's passenger lists," Fleur said, leaning away so that he could see. "You get these for people actually coming into the country to live, not just popping over for a holiday. So look at this! Angelina comes over on this ship to get married. Well that's as we knew. And then here she is going back to Italy, and that ties up with the birth of your mum in Italy in late 1957.

"…But then look here! September 1958 has them coming back into England, but then your Grandma Angelina going back alone in mid-February 1959. Wouldn't you have thought that she'd be more likely to go back earlier for Christmas to see her family? And that's it! That's the last time she sets foot in England ever again. Something must have happened in those six months to make her want to shake the dust of England off her feet and never return!"

"How odd," Angelo agreed. "And Romana is born in early April 1960, so Grandma wouldn't even have been pregnant with her at that point."

"And going by train all the way to Italy with your mum as a small child on your own? That's one exhausting journey, because if she's on this boat, then she wasn't flying, so she had to have caught a train at Calais and gone on from there. It's nothing like travelling there nowadays – it would literally have taken her *days*. What on earth prompted her to make such a journey with nobody to help her? She must have struggled off and on trains with your mum in a buggy and all of her suitcases, because there'd have been no direct train and she'd have to have changed three or four times at least. And she'd probably have had several cases if she'd originally packed thinking she was coming to England to stay."

"I wonder if the stress and strain of the separation, and then the arguments when Grandfather went over and tried to persuade her to come back was part of what made Romana's birth so difficult?" Angelo wondered.

"Possibly. I'll look on the manifests and see if I can see when Aleister went over and then returned. If he only stayed long enough to get your grandmother pregnant and then left, that would be pretty rough on her. Your mum did say that it was the difficult birth which made Romana the way she was," Fleur agreed. Then had to cover another twitch as Grandma Rose once again interrupted with, '*that wasn't what made her like she was!*'

Hurriedly excusing herself with a trip to the loo, Fleur locked herself into the en-suite and then hissed to the empty space, "For the love of God, Grandma! Stop doing that! I nearly peed myself then! And enough with the cryptic clues! Can't you give me something more to work with?"

She felt something like a ghostly sigh and the words, '*You know my hands are tied.*'

"Okay!" and Fleur flushed the loo and began washing her hands. "But can't you even give me a hint? I'm running in circles here. Is there anything dodgy with the Italian family at all?" Something ambiguous came back. "Okay, not in the family *per se*, but with Angelina, then?" Yet her grandma was still not definite. Making a wild guess Fleur asked, "Something happened to Angelina while she was in England?" and to her surprise got a definite sense of 'yes', but that whatever it was, it wasn't all of the story. "Oh heck."

Then she felt all of her skin prickling. Who was the one person she knew of who really was dodgy? Ignatius. Was *he* Romana's father? Then she tutted at herself. What was she thinking? She really was starting to chase her own tail if she could get that confused. Ignatius had had to die before Aleister and Angelina could get married, as far as anyone now knew, and had been dead a year even at the time of the wedding, so well before Claudia was conceived let alone Romana, meaning he certainly couldn't be blamed for this. Either that or he'd possessed skills no ghost before or since had had! And Romana had been conceived in Italy as well as born there, unless there was something hidden she hadn't found yet.

But then she'd not yet dug into those grimoires of Ignatius', let alone any Aleister might have had. So who knew how Ignatius might have warped his son, even if he'd done nothing in person to Angelina? However, she couldn't stay here, locked in the loo and talking to the wall! "Sorry, Gran, gotta go," she hissed, and let herself out.

When she got back into the big kitchen-diner, Angelo had got up and was in the kitchen part, starting to get pans down from the hooks over the work surface.

"Do you like risotto?" he asked. "I always find something soothing in cooking, and risotto is one of those things you have to watch, so it forces you to focus on it and not anything else that's running through your head."

"I've not had risotto that often, but when I have, I've enjoyed it."

"Great! One *risotto prima vera* coming up. Lots of green veg' and some nice parmesan," and he gave her one of those devastating smiles which had so disconcerted her back when they'd first met.

As she sat and watched him cook, Fleur thought that she could get used to this. A man who could find his way around the kitchen, and who didn't think it emasculating, made a pleasant change from what her married life had been like. Rather more disconcerting was realising just how strongly attracted she was to Angelo.

All of her instincts should have had her running like mad in the opposite direction, but every time she met him, she found herself unable to detach herself from him. Why had it mattered so much to her to prove his innocence? Why had she jumped to his defence when she could have as easily left it to his very competent solicitor?

Of course, there was that incredibly revealing tarot spread. That had done a great deal to convince Fleur that Angelo was the innocent victim in this, and not just because she was some gullible fool who twitched every time her horoscope said it would be a bad day. That sense of Grandma Rose watching over her was something that rarely came these days, and yet when doing that spread, she had been present in such a strong way.

However, that alone wasn't enough for Fleur to have dropped her guard so much as to be here, sitting in the metaphorical lion's den, and enjoying watching him cook for her. There was only one answer – the 'L' word – and Fleur wasn't sure she was ready for that. Wasn't sure she would ever be, if she was honest, but her heart seemed to be going in the opposite direction to her head.

"Just going to ring work before they all leave, and check on Mr H.," she said breezily, and managed a casual saunter out of the kitchen and across to the lounge before her imagination could take her any further. Watching Angelo's slim hips moving, as he shifted from hob to counter and back again, was doing her hormones no good at all!

This time it was Megan who answered the phone, and so Fleur found herself going over all the reasons why she believed beyond doubt that it wasn't Angelo Vance who had attacked Mr Harris.

"Lucy says that you've been sucked in by him," was Megan's last attempt to dissuade Fleur.

"Lucy is biased!" were words which came out of Fleur's lips before she could stop herself. Damn! She hadn't meant to let that slip. "She's Claire's friend, of course she's angry about what happened to her," Fleur managed to cover herself with. "But wouldn't she rather see the real culprit brought to justice?"

"Suppose so," she heard Megan sigh.

"So any word on Mr Harris yet?"

"No, but nobody's said that he's anywhere but at home, so I guess he's not too badly shaken or hurt."

"I sincerely hope not."

"Oh, and Denise left early today. Said something about her coat and then going to take Mr Harris some homemade soup."

"Great! Maybe now he'll take some notice of her and see what he's been missing," and Fleur heard Megan suddenly giggle. But she was thinking that Denise hadn't said anything to the others about what exactly she was going to do with the coat, and that maybe that might have something to do with Lucy getting very vocal at work. Fingers crossed, then, that Denise would go through with taking that coat to the police.

As she walked back into the kitchen, Angelo declared,

"Perfect timing, come and get it while it's at its best," and placed two bowls of steaming risotto on the table. "Help yourself to fresh parmesan," he added, placing a block with a grater on a plate in between them, then ground just a little black pepper over his from a large wooden pepper mill, which looked like it was regularly used and not just some poser's kitchen ornament.

Following his lead, Fleur added a touch of pepper, and then some shavings of parmesan. When she took her first mouthful, though, she couldn't help the gasp of delight.

"Oh! That's *so* good!"

"I'm glad you like it," and Angelo's smile was almost shy in his pleasure at her approval.

Why did the man have to be so bloody adorable when he was like that, Fleur wondered, as she did her best not to wolf the food down, but to savour it. A red wine that was way more expensive anything she would normally have drunk made it feel as though she was dining out at an exclusive restaurant, not having a meal with a friend. *Keep thinking 'friend'*, she told herself sternly. *'Friend', not a romantic meal.* But her pulse rate was taking no notice.

She was saved from making a fool of herself by the phone going. Oliver Walker, the solicitor whom Angelo had dragged out of bed the previous night, had news which Angelo went out of the room to discuss, leaving Fleur alone in the dining room, desperate for something to distract herself with. Feeling that it would be presumptuous to go into the lounge and put the TV on, or borrow one of his books, especially since she wasn't sure if Angelo had gone in there to take the call, her eyes wandered to her laptop, and she went down to that end of the table and nudged it back into life.

What was bugging her still was Gabriele. If he'd spent that much of his life in Italy, it explained why there were no obvious records of him over here in England. But how had he got here? Frustratingly, modern immigration records weren't something she had access to, so she couldn't check on that. But it bore thinking about, because if Gabriele was here legally, how come the police hadn't caught on to his presence back when Claire had been attacked? That was something she was going to have to ask Angelo about.

Idly scrolling through wider searches for any of the family names without really knowing why, Fleur's eyes suddenly caught something. It was a newspaper article with a photograph.

> **Only weeks after giving birth to their son, the grieving widow of rock star Jacko Vance leaves England for Italy with her sister**, it read. **'There are**

> **too many memories,' she told our reporter. 'Jacko is gone, and being here without him is too much for me right now.' Seen here with her sister, the glamorous former model manages to be stylish even in her grief.**

Well, if that was Romana with her, whatever had been wrong with her hadn't left a single visible mark. In fact, she looked more like Claudia's twin – elegant and epitomising Italian flair. In their matching black coats and hats, and handbags carried so that the Gucci labels were visible, they looked like two super-models of the time. Nobody would ever have singled her out for anything other than being a beautiful young woman.

"That was not what I was expecting," she breathed, leaning back and staring intently at the enlarged photo on her screen.

"What wasn't?" came Angelo's voice from behind her, and before she could remove the image, she heard him gasp. "Who's that with Mum?"

Inwardly wincing, Fleur gently said, "That's your Aunt Romana."

"Eh?" Angelo subsided onto the seat beside her. "Are you sure? Jeez! You can't tell them apart!"

"That's what the caption says. Look. 'Mrs Claudia Vance, and her sister Romana Kingsford at Heathrow.' And there's you, that little bundle all wrapped up in the buggy. That's the only way you can tell which one is your mum and which her sister. It's dated the thirtieth of September 1984, so how old would have been then?"

"Erm, about three months. My birthday is late June."

"So, about the right time for when it would first be considered safe to take you on a reasonably short haul flight."

"I suppose so. But why has Mum never mentioned that Romana was over here in England with her when Dad died?"

"Perhaps she came over as soon as the accident happened? That would be a fairly normal thing to do, wouldn't it? To rush to your sister's side in her hour of need. But I tell you one thing, Romana couldn't have been that badly disabled, could she? I mean, if you were Angelina, you wouldn't be allowing your disabled daughter to go alone halfway across Europe, even if it was to be with her sister, if it meant living in the same house as their father who you wished you'd never met.

"And there's no hint of Angelina here. No glamorous granny in the photo. And everything you and your mother have told me says that she wouldn't have gone within miles of *The Rookery*, and I presume, the Cheltenham house. But that's probably where the sisters were, don't you think?

"Now me, I wouldn't even entertain the idea of taking my sister abroad. She wouldn't begin to cope with the fact that people didn't speak English for a start. She'd be so distressed if she spoke to someone, and they answered but she couldn't understand them, because she's so friendly and chatty and she loves to talk to folks. Well, your aunt couldn't have been anything like that. Okay, I know there's no one-size-fits-all rule that applies to all mental disabilities, but there are still certain things that are close to universal, and one of those is keeping things familiar.

"Something about your aunt is very fishy. Who actually told you that Romana was mentally disabled? Only I'm thinking that if you hardly ever saw her, and that you didn't even know that you had a brother, there were an awful lot of secrets being kept from you. And by the way, when I asked you who was Gabriele's father, you told me you didn't know for certain, but suspected someone. Well who was that?"

Angelo went pale. "If I tell you, please promise me that you'll never tell anyone else."

Fleur was aghast. "Good grief, no. No, of course I won't!" And she meant it, because surely that had to be too far in the past for it to impact on the crisis now. "Who was it?"

Angelo took a deep breath. "I think it was Grandfather Aleister."

"Holy shit! You think your grandfather raped your mum? His own *daughter*? Bloody hell!"

Looking utterly miserable, Angelo nodded. "You see why this mustn't come out. On top of all the other crap that's floating around about me, the last thing my family needs is an accusation of incest."

Without thinking, Fleur's instinctive reaction was to lean over and wrap her arms around him.

"That's just horrible. Oh my God, no wonder your mum had such a troubled relationship with him, and tried to stay in Italy as much as possible. That explains so much. Why she wanted to be in whichever house he wasn't. …And oh, good grief, do you think that he'd raped her before that? That it wasn't the first time? Because that would seriously explain why she's such a mess now, and why your great-uncle was so reticent to get the authorities involved when she did what she did to you."

Angelo had leaned into her embrace, his head on her shoulder. And now his muffled voice said, "You see why I'm so trapped. I can't hold it against Mum, can I? She didn't do anything to deserve that."

"No, she didn't, because no kid who gets caught in that situation ever does," Fleur said, struggling to contain her anger. "And you've got me wondering whether he did the same to Romana, and that's why the death of her sister was the trigger for your mum's breakdown when you were sixteen. The loss of a sister who had gone through that with her, and who might have been the only person she *could* open up to about how she really felt, could have been catastrophic. Delayed PTSD is understood nowadays, but even back then it wasn't so much."

She felt Angelo's nod as he added, "So Gabriele is the product of an incestuous relationship. That's why he's never been right. How can I fault my mum for putting him first when his needs were so much greater than mine? I only lost a dad I never remembered. He got compromised even before he was born. That wasn't his fault. He didn't choose that life for himself."

"No, he didn't," Fleur said gently, stroking Angelo's hair and thinking how uncannily accurate that tarot spread had been. "That's what's had you in knots, hasn't it?"

"Oh, it's worse than that," Angelo said with a sniff, and pulling away from her to reach over to the box of tissues. "You see, Grandfather saw Gabriele as his own son. He wanted Gabriele to have *The Rookery*. But by 2010, when Grandfather remade his will, it was blindingly obvious that Gabriele would never be able to run *The Rookery* for himself. He's not stable enough to even be able to live independently. He's always been dependent on the family doing things for him. But of course, I knew nothing of this until I came back to Cheltenham for the reading of Grandfather's will.

"I tell you, Fleur, I felt physically sick when the solicitor read it out to us. Mum acted as though it was totally normal that the solicitor was talking about someone I'd never even heard of. And what could I say? Because Grandfather just referred to Gabriele as his son, and me as his grandson. So the solicitor assumed that Gabriele was someone of Mum's age, not mine. It was made clear that Gabriele had mental health problems, and so nobody official queried why he wasn't there.

"But the thing is, Fleur, he was. …Oh, not at the solicitors, but in Cheltenham, yes. A year or two before then I'd been in Italy to visit Great-uncle

Antonio, and Mum had been there part of the time. Well when I came to come back, I couldn't find my passport…"

"…Oh no! She didn't steal your passport and use that to get Gabriele into the country?"

Angelo nodded miserably. "And she played it clever. She took the passport weeks before I was due to return. So there I was, enjoying the sights of Rome and Florence and Bologna, never suspecting a thing, and of course then I had to linger longer while I wait for the consulate to sort me out a replacement. I thought I must have taken it with me to Rome and got it nicked – because pick-pockets were rife there back then – though I'd have sworn I'd left it at Uncle Antonio's. But with no other explanation making sense, I just accepted that I'd been unusually careless.

"So, by the time I went back in through customs at Heathrow, it was nearly four months since Gabriele had passed through with Mum, and nobody batted an eyelid, especially since I'd reported my old passport stolen. If it was anybody's job to investigate why 'Angelo Vance' had managed to enter England twice without leaving in between, I suppose that was a low priority compared to the number of illegal immigrants coming in. It just looked like a bureaucratic cock-up."

Fleur groaned. "But in reality, it was the way that Gabriele managed to be in England illegally – because I'm guessing that he never had an Italian passport – and nobody knew. …When did you find out? Was it at the will reading?"

"Immediately afterwards. I was still reeling from discovering about Gabriele, and then Mum comes to me at the Cheltenham house and says that Gabriele is *my* brother, not hers, and that it's my responsibility to look after him now. I remember saying how could that be when he was in Italy – because that was what the solicitor had implied – and she gave me this huge smile and said, no, he was here already. Then she went out of the room and came back in leading Gabriele by the hand!"

Chapter 29

"Good grief! You'd never laid eyes on him before then?" Fleur gasped.

"No. I knew nothing about him. I soon found out, though. There's something very twisted in Gabriele's mind. Something beyond just being genetically compromised. It came to me that night in a horrible nightmare, and I woke up and realised that that's where the imposter vlogs had come from. I hadn't had a clue up until then. To be frank, I'd been scared stiff that I was having some sort of mental breakdown where I didn't know what I was doing. That maybe, what had affected Mum and made her lock me up, was starting to come out in me."

"Oh my God, that's horrible," Fleur sympathised, taking his hand, and feeling her heart breaking for the suffering Angelo had been through, but also enormous anger at his mother for putting him through all of this. Disturbed Mrs Vance might be, but she'd been lucid enough at times that she could have tried to explain things to him.

"I'd left a laptop at what I thought was just Mum's place in Italy," Angelo carried on. "I had no worries about her using it. She hasn't the first clue about anything technological. So I never suspected that that was the machine which had been used with my saved log-in on it to get onto my vlog. But I woke up in a cold sweat that night, suddenly remembering where I'd seen that wild hair, and those crazy eyes before, and that they'd been staring back out at me from my own computer screen."

"That's dreadful." And Fleur could now understand why Angelo had been so distraught about everything. He'd known nothing of this brother, if indeed you could call him that with the double relationship, and so why would he have thought that that was who he was seeing on the other side of the laptop's camera?

"Thank you. I've been so trapped. It's in Grandfather's will that I can make use of *The Rookery*, but that it will only become mine after Gabriele dies, *and* if he has no sons of his own to pass it on to. There were some wild and rambling references which the solicitor said Grandfather insisted in having put into the will, about the property not being passed down through any female line. Something about it being tainted and wicked." He cuffed his eyes. "Personally, I couldn't imagine anything more tainted or wicked than what he'd done. It seemed hypocritical in the extreme for him to refer back to his mother, sister, and grandmother in that way."

Fleur was thinking furiously, and wondered, "Could this be anything to do with the whole thing about Aleister's sister Morwenna getting supposedly raped by her maternal uncle, Wantelo? I don't mean that I'm doubting that the poor girl got raped, but rather that doubt we had about who it was, and what they were doing at *The Rookery*?" Then she realised that, of course, it had been Lucy and Carrie-Ann who she'd had that conversation with, as she took in Angelo's horrified stare.

"Oh hell, I'm so sorry, Angelo. You didn't know about that, did you?"

His mute shake of the head made her feel even more rotten at having dropped that bombshell on him, and worse at having done it right now. Keeping it very simple, she told him about Carrie-Ann going digging, telling the white lie that it had been about finding a context for the notebooks, not that they'd been dishing the dirt on his mother. But added,

"Having now read up to and including his mother, Loretta's, notes, it's clear that poor Wantelo was what in those days would have been described as simple. Massive head trauma as a child had done irreparable damage, you see. Now it is possible that in some naïve way he just saw a pretty girl, had no idea who she was, and felt the need to satiate what would have been just a physical urge to him, without any concept of how much damage he was doing to Morwenna.

"But we all wondered – given the link via Ignatius to Aleister Crowley, and now my suspicions that at least at some point Annora along with her aunt, Starlina, was sucked into that cult – whether Ignatius had some creepy friend of his in one of the cottages? That newspaper report only referred to the man as the girl's 'uncle', but back in those days, it was perfectly normal to call a man who was a close friend of a parent as an uncle as a term of respect. These days, kids would possibly call someone like that by their first names, but not back then. That would have been considered unforgivably rude."

Angelo went over to a cabinet on the back wall of the dining room and opened it up to reveal a virtual bar full of spirits. "Malt whisky? Gin? Vodka? Rum? Only I'm having a bloody big malt, myself!"

Fleur could understand that. "I wouldn't mind a G&T."

He rattled off a string of names which meant nothing to Fleur, not being able to afford anything beyond supermarket prices, and seeing that, Angelo picked up a lovely dimpled bottle and said, "Kapriol. A gorgeous Italian gin. I think you'll like this, it's very smooth."

Used to long G&Ts, Fleur was surprised to see him drop just a couple of ice cubes in from the huge American style fried-freezer, then pour a generous amount of gin in, and just adding a splash of one of the premier tonics.

"Try that," he said with a grin, and when she took a sip and her eyes went wide in surprise, laughed. "Well, I have to get my own back on you somehow. You've been dropping surprises on me left, right and centre."

"That is the nicest gin I've ever tasted," Fleur said, taking another appreciative sip. "So smooth! I had no idea that the Italians made gin, but then why wouldn't they with all those wonderful Mediterranean herbs they have? …But to come back to surprises, I'm so sorry, Angelo. If things hadn't forced my hand so much, I'd been trying to think of ways to break so much of this news to you gently. Of course, I didn't know how much you already knew. I never dreamed that you'd been kept this much in the dark."

Angelo came and sat down, cradling a cut-glass tumbler in which swam a considerable amount of amber liquid. "I don't think it's so much dark as pitch-black," he said with wry humour. "But please don't feel guilty. It's such a relief to have someone here who's trying to help me piece all of this together. You haven't been blinded by people you care about telling you lies all of your life, so you're seeing everything far more clearly than me. So come on then, what's this about Wantelo, again?"

Fleur carefully repeated what they had found out about Morwenna being removed from the house because of the unwanted attentions of a man who never got named in the newspaper report.

"I suspect that the editor of a local newspaper in those days was very wary of being accused of slander," she expanded. "Ignatius was known as one of the local war heroes, and was a man of some substance. A local paper would think very carefully before getting into something which might lead to a court case, and an expensive settlement."

"So we only know that my grandfather's sister was removed from the family house for a time?"

"That's about it. She wasn't a child – as we first thought when we read it – but a young woman of approaching eighteen. Nonetheless still very much a minor by the laws of the time, mind you, hence her removal by the court. But then I think that was what made it stick, because she was able to speak out for herself. In those days they'd have probably thought a child was making it up, but a girl on the verge of adulthood accusing a man of trying to 'deflower' her against her will would have been seen in a different light.

"And even so, there must have been something in Ignatius' past that he didn't want to become public knowledge, because he didn't fight back over it. That suggests to me that he didn't want anyone digging into his own younger days, or perhaps what else was going on at *The Rookery*, and I now think that that included that grim Aleister Crowley link. Don't forget, this happened in 1937 and Crowley was still alive then. He didn't die until late in 1947, so some ten years after this. His notoriety would still have been very current."

Angelo took another sip while he thought, then asked, "You said 'mucky' practises when you referred to Crowley before. What do you think that meant in Ignatius' case?"

Fleur shrugged. "I can't be certain, you understand, but let's say that it wouldn't surprise me if Ignatius had a male lover, whom he kept on the estate alongside his wife and family. Someone who had been very involved alongside him in those 'sex magic' experiments."

She paused to sip her own drink and to give him a moment to consider that, before adding, "When I get back to work, I'm going to go straight up and start looking at Ignatius' notebooks. Because I have this strong feeling that although Annora was sucked into the cult as a young girl alongside her aunt, once she was married and had children of her own to consider, the shine rather wore off. What had probably seemed daring and exciting as a young woman barely into her twenties, had become something horribly degrading.

"Even in this day and age, it's pretty demeaning to have to admit that your husband would rather be with another man – makes you feel less of a woman, or so a lady who was going through her divorce at the same time as me told me. But in those days? Good grief! Homosexuality was illegal for a start off, so Ignatius and the other man would have gone to prison, but for Annora the shame would have been unbearable.

"It's probably why you read so much of her in the society pages of the day, or at least right up until the point when Morwenna is harmed. She was probably making sure she was very much known in case any of this stuff came out, but also to get herself as far away as possible from what might have been quite a dangerous situation for her. After that Annora seems to stay close to home to watch over her children, but at least that means that whoever it was wasn't a danger to them while they were small. At the time of the attack, Dulcibelle, the oldest, was already a young woman of twenty-three and had been married for two years to a chap called," and she had to do a quick refer back to her notes, "ah, yes, Harold Westcott. He dies in WW2, and she's not long after. But I think that there's a chance that Westcott might have been foisted off onto Dulcibelle by her father."

"Really? He could do that?"

"If she was under twenty-one at the time they married, yes, he could. If he went to the local registrar with some fiction of her being in the family way, as they would have put it, and that he was determined that the young man in question should do the 'decent thing', then nobody would have doubted him much. And of course, if anyone asked later, she would have conveniently miscarried. When I first heard the surname Westcott, it rang bells from being associated with Crowley. Now I'm wondering whether that man was Ignatius' secret lover, and Ignatius was keeping him close by marrying him off to his unfortunate daughter."

"God, that's cold!" Angelo shuddered. Then suddenly looked at Fleur in dismay. "If he could do that to his own daughter, could he have passed the blame for something this Westcott bloke did onto his harmless brother-in-law, Wantelo?"

"I wouldn't put it past him."

"But what you said about Wantelo claiming that his mother and sister were hexing him in some way, that's just rubbish, isn't it?"

However Fleur wasn't so quick to dismiss it. "If you mean that he died of something like poison which they administered, let alone some paranormal ritual, then no. The poor confused soul probably remembered them giving him medicinal herbs, and didn't really understand why. And I think we cannot discount the possibility that, because he was considered so feeble-minded by his family, they might have spoken unguardedly in front of him, never thinking for a minute that he'd remember what he'd heard. So I think that his story is a garbled mixture of a muddled memory of hearing about how his grandmother's sisters and their own mother got rid of Henrik, but with him not really knowing who Henrik was; coupled with him knowing that they were wise women in terms of herbs and spells, along with his own very genuine protestations of never having laid a finger on Morwenna, yet not being believed."

"Poor bugger!"

"I know. And of course, Wantelo would have been in his fifties by then, and may not have been a well man even before he went into prison. It could well be that the life inside only hastened an end that was coming anyway."

Angelo sighed. "I still feel so bloody sorry for him, though," and he clinked his glass against hers. "Here's to the memory of Wantelo, may he rest in peace."

"To Wantelo," Fleur echoed, and clinked her

glass back against his.

There was a moment of silence, then Angelo asked, "Do you think my grandfather would have known about all of this?"

Fleur glanced at the family tree she'd got sketched out. "I think it would be hard for him not to have. Morwenna was only four years older than him, so he'd have been a lad coming into his teens at the time she got molested. It's not like he was a toddler, whose memories would be blurred. My hope is, that when I get to Ignatius' notebooks, that there'll be something in there that'll shed some light on things. I have this odd feeling that Ignatius would have wanted to brag about what he'd done, and if he couldn't do it out loud, he'd have done it in a book which he instilled into his son should never be read by others."

Angelo leaned in so that he could see the family tree. "You haven't told me what happened to my great-grandmother's sisters. Looking at this, it surely ought to have been Kadilia who inherited, not Annora? In fact, Kadilia *and* Glorina are older than Annora. Can we find out when they died?"

Logging in again, Fleur put Kadilia's name in the search box and fairly quickly discovered that she had died in 1919. According to the 1911 census she'd been living in London by then, working a flower stall with her husband, Albert Buckland, and with Glorina living and working with them. Since all three of them died together, along with Kadilia's two small children, it wasn't hard to make the leap to them all perishing in that influenza epidemic. Searching for the brothers, Fleur found that the oldest, Muldobrai, perished in 1915 at Gallipoli, and Fennix only a year later at the Somme.

"Well so far it's tragic but not suspicious," Angelo said with some relief. "As a family they were abnormally unlucky but nothing more."

"Don't get too relieved," Fleur warned as she chased down another link. "Look at this. Paizeni dies in 1915 and Richenda in 1916, and they're both living at home as of the 1911 census. Paizeni was only seventeen in 1911 and Richenda thirteen. They might subsequently have gone into service, I suppose, because even Richenda was eighteen by the time she died and could have been in service for three or more years by that stage.

"Their mother, Loretta died back in 1913, so she wouldn't have had any say in what happened to them by the time they died, but if Annora was already off running around with her Aunt Starlina, it would have been reasonable to assume that one of these younger girls would have stayed at home to look after their father, especially if Loretta's health was already failing, though I've seen no trace of that. There was many a girl got trapped into lonely spinsterhood by the need for someone to look after an elderly parent. It was just your bad luck if you were the last girl to find a husband."

"Thank heavens for the modern health service!"

"Amen to that. But what I don't like is a pattern I've just noticed. …Look at this! It's 1913, and your great-grandparents, Annora and Ignatius, marry and presumably come to *The Rookery* to live – only months before Loretta died! Did *she* object to Ignatius, but William wasn't bothered? Because I don't like that coincidence.

"There are no obvious other candidates for occupants of the Dower House, so you'd expect the young couple to have that as their place, given that her father would still have occupied the main house. Her sister Kadilia has already married and gone, taking Glorina with her, presumably both of them having seen the writing on the wall, and Kadilia not wanting her favourite kid sister to get saddled with their rather useless father. But it's only months later that Loretta dies.

"Now that wouldn't be that suspicious given that she was in her early fifties by then, and people did die younger, but even so, fifty-two is a bit young for someone who wasn't ill. And I have to say that because I'm almost up to 1913 reading her own notebook, there's no hint of her trying to find remedies for something that was ailing her – and I think she would have, given her mother and grandmother's history. But what's really given me the shivers is seeing that it's only fifteen months later that Paizeni dies, and that's conveniently after they must have got the notice that Muldobrai had died in the War."

"You think that Ignatius was bumping off the competition to inherit?" Angelo asked, aghast.

"It's hard not to. Fennix was born mid-1887, so he was twenty-nine when he was killed. That means that if he signed up in the wave of patriotism at the start of the war, he would already have been old enough to send overseas as soon as possible. Many lads had to wait until they turned nineteen before they could 'do their bit', but he wouldn't have had to wait at all. He might even have already been in the army. So what were the chances that Ignatius thought that the male line would soon get wiped out? He'd have had to be totally out of touch not to start hearing about the massive casualties coming out of Flanders."

"But you said he served as well. That he was decorated for bravery?"

"I did. And at first, I thought he'd signed up right at the start. But no, according to the army record I've found, he was one of those who got forced to fight when conscription came in in 1916. I wonder if the claim of him signing up under age was a fiction he put about to make himself look more heroic? Okay, he *might* have volunteered even then, but given his age, it looks suspiciously as though he didn't."

And that makes more sense of Dulcibelle being born in 1915, and him being away for only three years, after which Morwenna was born, Fleur thought. *That three yar gap is far more like a family trying for an heir*, but not wanting to totally confuse Angelo, continued with the previous generation with,

"Yet even that wouldn't have looked dodgy if it wasn't for the fact that Richenda, the youngest of the sisters dies in the first quarter of 1916. In other words, just before Fennix gets sent off to fight, but was probably already in the army, if only here in England."

"Holy crap! Ignatius was clearing the way for himself to succeed, or at least for his kids to."

"Oh, I don't think there was much parental love, or at least not for his daughters. I think Ignatius wanted to be the lord of the manor with no contesters. Just look at it! He and Annora marry in 1913. The same year her mother dies. A little over a year later the oldest son is killed, and now Ignatius can really see the path opening out before him. He doesn't have to worry about Fennix – the war will take care of that for him. Kadilia and Glorina are for now out of his reach, so he goes for the easy targets, Paizeni and Richenda. I bet if we could get their death certificates it would be an open verdict."

"We can do that, can't we?" Angelo said eagerly. "We just have to order them online from the National Archive up the road."

With him already getting his platinum AmEx card out, Fleur found herself ordering a whole batch of death certificates online, and for speed opting for the PDF download, which would come through sooner. It would still take a while, and she could understand why Angelo was itching to find out what they said. Right now, the only thing which seemed to have saved Kadilia and Glorina was Ignatius himself being called up, and by the time he was fully demobbed, they were dead from the flu. Only ineffectual William and innocent Wantelo remained, and since Ignatius could rule the household without any opposition, he'd probably decided to bide his time. So far, he'd literally got away with murder, thanks to the cover of a world war and an epidemic, and since the owner of *The Rookery* in the form of William still lived, his motives for murder were hidden.

"I wonder if the reason why Annora was away so often during the Twenties was in part because she feared for her life?" Fleur mused. "She'd given Ignatius what he needed – a male heir – and so beyond that she was now surplus to requirements. Ignatius could have inherited on behalf of his children; he didn't need her for that."

"Christ!" Angelo muttered in disgust. "And following on from what you've picked out, I don't think we'd be being overly suspicious to think that after William dies of old age in 1930, that it's then that Ignatius starts pushing his oldest daughter into the arms of someone with his strange beliefs, and the middle one gets a nasty molesting at the hands of another of his cronies. You almost start thinking that the youngest daughter got off lightly by dying young, because at least she didn't have to go through any of that."

Now it was Fleur's turn to be horrified. How had she not seen how all of that fitted together?

"Angelo, I have to go back to Worcester anyway, tomorrow. I can't be away from work any longer without good reason. But I also think it's imperative that I get to the attic at work and get those notebooks to somewhere safe. If there's proof of even part of this in them, then they have to be kept out of Gabriele's hands. Because I've got this nasty feeling that what killed Paizeni and Richenda was a potion from the grimoires, and that Ignatius, at least, used others from those books. You said you don't know what your mother drugged you with? Well, I bet we'll find it in one of those books!"

Angelo looked horrified, and that suddenly triggered another memory for Fleur. "Look, I don't want to totally freak you out," she said gently, "but do you remember me talking to you about these books? I said about you helping your mum get them down out of the attic at the Dower House, and you saying that it hadn't been you?"

"Gabriele," Angelo said with a wince. "Of course! That's how he knew to go looking for the grimoires! He'd already looked at some of them with Mum."

And taking a deep breath, Fleur broke the news, "And I don't think that that was the first time she'd seen them. Where else would she have found the information on how to drug you up without her getting embroiled with drug pushers? She had to have known about those recipes long before you decided to get us involved."

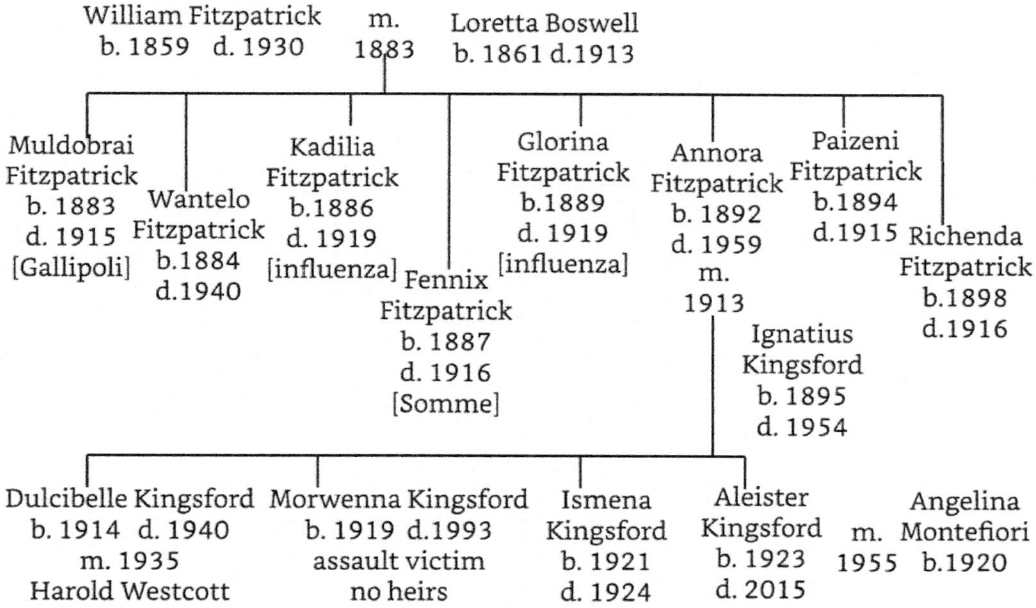
William Fitzpatrick
b. 1859 d. 1930
m.
1883
Loretta Boswell
b. 1861 d.1913
Muldobrai
Fitzpatrick
b. 1883
d. 1915
[Gallipoli]
Wantelo
Fitzpatrick
b.1884
d.1940
Kadilia
Fitzpatrick
b.1886
d. 1919
[influenza]
Fennix
Fitzpatrick
b. 1887
d. 1916
[Somme]
Glorina
Fitzpatrick
b.1889
d. 1919
[influenza]
Annora
Fitzpatrick
b. 1892
d. 1959
m.
1913
Paizeni
Fitzpatrick
b.1894
d.1915
Richenda
Fitzpatrick
b.1898
d.1916
Ignatius
Kingsford
b. 1895
d. 1954
Dulcibelle Kingsford
b. 1914 d. 1940
m. 1935
Harold Westcott
Morwenna Kingsford
b. 1919 d.1993
assault victim
no heirs
Ismena
Kingsford
b. 1921
d. 1924
Aleister
Kingsford
b. 1923
d. 2015
m.
1955
Angelina
Montefiori
b.1920

Chapter 30

Angelo looked stunned. "But she wouldn't have had the keys to the attic! We only got given them by the solicitor. That was years after she drugged me for the first time."

Fleur wagged a warning finger at him. "Then I think you need to get your smart Mr Walker to have a stern word with that solicitor. Because I'll bet that *he* only got those keys when your grandfather knew he was on his way out – better to let the family have the secret than a stranger, and all that. However, there'd have been absolutely nothing stopping your grandfather showing them to your mother long before then."

"But she hated him!"

"And? …Angelo, think about it. He could have shown her them as a threat, to prove to her that he could do with her as he wished. She didn't have to be complicit at that stage. She could have been very much the victim. …But then later on, when she's starting to come apart at the seams, she starts blurring you with Gabriele. Or maybe it was even before that?

"You've said yourself that there's something horribly wrong with him. Narcissistic personality disorder is one label that I could come up with, and I'm no expert. A total inability to relate to anyone other than himself. Well, if she was trapped between keeping Gabriele quiet, and therefore being able to stay with the family in Italy, or coming back here to the father who'd raped her, is it so outrageous to think of her returning to what she'd been told about? Maybe even to what had been used on her already?"

Angelo looked faintly relieved. "Put like that, I can see what you mean. Yes, she could still have been very much the innocent victim."

Fleur didn't want to say that she thought that while Claudia might be deeply disturbed, that innocent was something she'd not been in a very long time. There'd been far too much manipulation of Angelo which Claudia had been party to for that. How, for instance, had Gabriele got his hands on Angelo's laptop at her house if she hadn't allowed him to?

Once, you could put down to him escaping from her custody and doing it, but not multiple times. And she didn't believe that Claudia was like Mr Harris – completely at sea with anything technological – because again, if Gabriele had been kept away from the world for all that time, how on earth would he have known how to make a vlog? Fleur herself was no novice to technology, but she'd struggle to do that.

So the only thing that made sense was that Claudia had been allowing Gabriele to use Angelo's laptop for years, and had taught him at least the basics herself. From there he could have Googled how to do stuff, because it wasn't as if he'd had much of anything else to do with his time. Presumably Gabriele hadn't even been to school, but had been taught at home by Claudia, so he might be woefully ignorant in many areas, but not in others. Years of living cooped up in that cottage would have given him a lot of incentive to learn about the outside world electronically, and with all the time in the world to do so.

Unlike Angelo, who had at least tried to earn a living and learn how to invest his money, Gabriele had been a kept man right from the start. All of which worried Fleur, because Angelo was too fundamentally decent to be able to tell his mother to go to hell and break contact with her. If he could have done that, he would have years ago. Therefore she herself would need to be on her guard to make sure that he didn't get blinded by Claudia's excuses whenever they got to confront her.

However, for tonight Fleur thought they'd uncovered enough skeletons.

"I'm going to get an early night," she said with an apologetic smile. "I'm going to have to be on the earliest train I can get back to Worcester."

"And I'll be coming with you," Angelo shocked her by announcing, then as she gasped,

"Do you think it's safe to do that?" he said,

"Don't worry. Oliver is meeting us at Paddington, because we're going to go and speak to West Mercia Police. That's what the phone call was for. They've found the footage of the assault you told them about."

"Oh, thank heavens for that!"

"It's a bit more than that. Apparently on the footage you can see how bruised the assailant's face is, enough that even by now it won't have fully gone, and there are enough people who've seen me in the interim who can testify that I'm not knocked about like that. Oliver has persuaded me that I can no longer continue to protect my brother if he's going to be a danger to the general public, and thanks to you, we have proof in the form of him assaulting that poor guard. He'd done nothing to Gabriele to warrant that, and that rather makes our case for us.

"Mum can protest all she likes, but the place for Gabriele now is in a secure mental hospital. Oliver says that I'm still honouring the terms of Grandfather's will, because I'll be doing what's best for Gabriele, and it would hard to argue otherwise. The only thing I don't like is that his existence is bound to become public. I really wish I could spare Mum that."

Early the next morning the three of them stood on a freezing cold platform waiting for the Worcester train. Yet once on board, Angelo began dozing, and that gave Fleur an idea. Scribbling on a piece of spare paper, she showed Oliver Walker her email address, and so as Angelo snoozed, she and the solicitor carried on an intense conversation laptop to laptop.

By the time the train pulled in to Foregate Street Station, Oliver Walker was considerably better informed, and his last message told Fleur that he would be taking all of it into consideration when he advised Angelo. With a conspiratorial wink to her, he and Angelo left her at Castle Street to go into the central police station, and she walked on down the road and around the back street into work.

Mr Harris wasn't in, but then Fleur hadn't expected him to be, and before she got nabbed by anyone, she managed to stick her head around the door of Denise's office and got whispered confirmation that the coat was now with forensic scientists. As she was hanging her coat up in the cloakroom, however, Lucy stormed in and began haranguing her.

"You stupid fool! What the hell did you think you were doing going to London like that? You could have been killed! For fuck's sake, Fleur! Haven't I warned you enough about bloody Vance? He's a maniac! You can't trust him an inch!"

Her temper fraying, Fleur snapped, "Shut up!" All the tension and frustrations of the last week or so had been kept a lid on, but now they all began bubbling up inside her.

"Oh, it's like that is it?" said Lucy, descending into bitter sarcasm. "Fallen for the bad boy, have you? Well don't say I didn't warn you! You stupid girl! Did you learn nothing from your divorce? You can't trust men! None of them!"

Carrie-Ann had come in mid rant and was now staring at Lucy, dumbfounded. Fleur, however, had had enough.

"Stop it right now! I mean it, Lucy, shut up before I get really angry with you! …And don't you dare flounce out on me!" Fleur made it to the cloakroom door just in time, and leaned against it so that Lucy would have to physically shove her out of the way to leave.

"Move!" Lucy snapped, her green eyes flashing in real temper, but Fleur had a temper of her own, though she was far better at controlling it. And like most people who were slow to anger, when she did lose it, it was far more effective than Lucy's violent flare ups which burned out in minutes.

"Not a fucking chance, lady!" Fleur snarled back. "You're as much to blame for this god-awful mess as anyone! You and your guilty conscience over what happened to Claire – you bloody-well blinded everyone else with your prejudices so that they never spotted the truth!"

"Guilty conscience?" she heard Carrie-Ann gasping faintly, but Fleur had truly seen red this time, and although Lucy's temper had begun to fizzle out at the mention of 'guilty conscience', Fleur was far from done.

"You were already feeling like shit because you realised that you'd been driving Claire nuts while you stayed with her," Fleur ploughed on relentlessly.

"And so when she got so badly hurt, you couldn't forgive yourself. I get that. But what is bloody unforgivable is that you transferred all of that guilt onto Angelo Vance."

As she saw Lucy's face start to flush with temper again, Fleur snapped, "And don't you dare come all that bull with me now! *You* were the one who was telling everyone on our team that it had to be Angelo who had raped Claire. I've spoken to others who've confirmed that, even though I wasn't here then. *You* kept telling them that it *had* to be him who was leaving all the contradictory messages around the house when you were all working there, even when it was blindingly obvious that he couldn't have kept driving to and fro from London every night for weeks.

"It was *you* who kept on and on that the police weren't exploring every possible way that Angelo could have raped Claire, and then got away in time to have an alibi. Who the hell do you think you are that you would know more than the police? And because *we* all care for you, every bugger believed *you* over the evidence that was right in front of their eyes!"

She pulled herself right up to her full height, which still only came up to Lucy's nose, and glared up at her, eye to eye. "Because if you could have got past your own damned self-pity and self-righteousness, it should have been obvious what I have worked out. There are *two* men who look like that!"

"Oh fuck off!" Lucy snapped, turning and storming back to the hand-basin, folding her arms underneath her breasts as if holding in all that rage and guilt. "Absolute bollocks! Two Angelo Vances? I've never heard such nonsense!"

"Not two Angelo Vances, you sarcastic cow!" Fleur fumed back. "Jeez, Lucy! You can be such a pig-headed fool! Angelo has a brother who is just a year younger than him, and who is damned near his double. A brother who had been kept by the family over in Italy, because he was a danger to himself and anyone he took a like or dislike to. His name is Gabriele, and Mrs Vance actually stole Angelo's passport to get him over here."

Lucy gave a snort of disbelief.

"Stop it!" Fleur growled, waving a warning finger in her face. "You damned-well listen to me! Because it was Gabriele who raped Claire, and if you care about nothing else, surely to God you want the real rapist to do time for what he did to your friend?"

That took all of the wind out of Lucy's sails, and she visibly deflated whereas Fleur wasn't remotely done yet.

"Claudia Vance brought Gabriele over here because her father wanted *him* to inherit *The Rookery.* And you know why? Because that sick old bastard raped his own daughter when she was newly widowed, and got her pregnant. Gabriele is the product of incest!

"His father is also his grandfather, and that's why he has the mind and morals that would make a bloody corkscrew look straight. It's not his fault. He was born twisted. And Claudia has tried to keep him with her, even to the extent of shoving Angelo away to boarding school as soon as he could go.

"Angelo is as much a victim in this as Claire is, you bloody fool! He was kept at such arm's length, he didn't even know he *had* a brother until his grandfather's will got read. But then he found out that the old man had made him the custodian of *The Rookery*, because by then even that old pervert realised that Gabriele wasn't sane. But Angelo can't inherit it while Gabriele – and here comes the real knife in the back – or Gabriele's son or sons live.

"Yes! The old man thought that even though he's mad, bad, and dangerous to know, that Gabriele might yet carry on the family line. Angelo apparently doesn't count because he's the son of a scruffy Brummy rock singer," and now Fleur became sarcastic, "Oh how fucking dreadful! Dearie me, can't have that in the family pedigree, can we? Except that the family pedigree is the biggest load of old tosh ever!"

She glared defiantly at Lucy. "So how does that all fit into your blame-shifting version, huh? If you'd kept your big gob shut. If you'd not positively relished going face to face with 'Angelo', because it gave you some warped sense of getting your own back on him since you could paint him as black as you liked to everyone else, and for them not to know the difference because of that… If you had stopped to wonder if the reeking, wild-eyed bloke in front of you could possibly transform at such notice into someone positively normal, instead of indulging in arguing with the lunatic because it fitted your version of events… If you hadn't shoved all of it down everyone's throats… calmer heads might have stopped to wonder who was where and when, but you kept muddying the waters. If all of that hadn't happened thanks to you, Gabriele Vance might have been caught years ago, and Mr Harris wouldn't have been assaulted, even if you think somehow that I deserved to be."

Carrie-Ann's shaky voice from over by the door asked, "You got assaulted too, Fleur? When was this?"

Her question calmed Fleur far more than Lucy's bristling anger, and she told her about her confrontation at the racecourse, but that that was the reason why she knew beyond doubt that the Angelo she'd met in London wasn't that man.

"For heaven's sake, I broke his damned finger in two places!" she said with an exasperated toss of her head. "I thumped him bloody hard *twice*, which was what gave him the bruises that Megan and Denise saw, and his split lip came from when I threw Mrs Vance when she attacked me from behind – her boot heel caught him right on the bottom lip and chin. The real Angelo Vance doesn't have a scratch on him!"

"Oh God, Fleur! I'm so sorry!" Carrie-Ann gulped. "We should have believed you."

"I sincerely wish Mr Harris had," Fleur said from the heart. "If he'd taken note of what I was telling him, he'd never have let Gabriele in. He should have yelled for Megan or Denise to call the police there and then. For heaven's sake, we're only a few hundred yards from the police station! It wouldn't have taken them long to get here, and that might have saved Mr Harris from the worst of the beating Gabriele gave him."

She turned to glare at Lucy again. "But he didn't believe me. He believed *you*! Believed that Angelo Vance is able to put on such an Oscar-winning act that he can be both as mad as a box of frogs, *and* pass as normal within hours of each of the two sides appearing."

"That is not *my* fault! It's *yours* for bringing him down on us!" Lucy snarled, and stormed out.

Carrie-Ann watched her go, wide-eyed. "Oh heck, Fleur, I don't think you'll ever be able to come back and work with us. Lucy won't forgive you for that, even though you're absolutely right."

Her words were like a dousing of cold water in Fleur's face. How had she not foreseen this? Standing up for Angelo was going to cost her her job, because regardless of who was right and who wrong, the company needed Lucy far more than they did her. And would Mr Harris forgive her? The odds weren't good on that, either.

Unexpectedly, Carrie-Ann's arms were suddenly around her, and Fleur found herself giving in to tears.

"I'm so sorry, hon'," Carrie-Ann said as they hugged one another. "Promise me we'll still stay friends? Because I don't think I'll be staying long after you go. I was close to leaving right before you came, because Lucy bullied the hell out of your predecessor, and it was a horrible atmosphere to work in. But then you came, and it was clear that you wouldn't stand for her pushing you around, and it became fun to come into work again." She shook her head as they both went in search of tissues. "But this is the old Lucy. I thought she'd gone, but it seems she's only been buried."

"Then I'm really sorry this has blown up in your face too," Fleur apologised. "Look, I'm going upstairs to do some hurried packing of those things I was working on. Angelo Vance travelled here on the same train as me with his solicitor, and I think they'll be here later. I want him to be able to take some of those things away with him right away, even if it'll have to be in a taxi to whichever hotel they're staying at, or to the train. I don't want Lucy to get some weird idea of taking revenge on him by burning half of them, or throwing them through a shredder."

"Fleur! She wouldn't do that! Not to a book!"

"Not to a proper printed book she wouldn't. But come on, you've heard her talking about her terribly religious upbringing, if only in terms of her parents never being able to accept that she's gay.

When she's running wholly on emotions, like now, can I take the risk that all that ingrained teaching about the Devil and stuff won't come to the fore?"

"Point taken," Carrie-Ann sighed. "Come on, I'll come and give you a hand with the packing. After all, I doubt that Mr Harris and the directors will want Sue to be doing any work on the fabrics after all this. It's all getting packed up and shipped out as fast as possible."

Fleur paused on the stairs and looked back at Carrie-Ann. "*Getting* packed up? What do you mean?"

"Oh, the word came down from the directors yesterday afternoon. They'd had a conference and decided that they no longer wish to work for a client who puts their staff at risk."

"So you and Lucy won't be carrying on with the ordinary library stuff today?"

"Nope. Already starting to put it all back into boxes – although at least with all the attached paperwork in each one. They're sending Mr Vance the bill for the work already done, so he has to have that, but we're not doing any more." Carrie-Ann sighed. "That's why I'm not in a hurry to get back down to the workshop. We were expecting to have at least enough work on that to last through next week, so there's no other job waiting. And I'm not sitting down there listening to Lucy calling you all the names under the sun all day."

Grateful for the company, Fleur showed Carrie-Ann the grimoires and notebooks, and set her to work parcelling each one back up in its cloth protector. Fleur had always been a methodical worker, but now more than ever she was glad that she'd tucked notes in the volumes which had the significant revelations in them. As a result, it was easy to separate those out from the rest, and Fleur began packing them up in a box of their own. Above all else, these were the ones she wanted Angelo to take with him now.

But then she turned to the later volumes. Could she identify those of Ignatius and Aleister fast enough to set them aside too? She glanced over her shoulder at Carrie-Ann, and saw that she was deeply engrossed in packing up the oldest books, and chronologically hadn't got as far as Starlina's endless scribbling yet. Great!

Trying to move nonchalantly to the far end of the bench, Fleur picked up the grimoire which she thought was the most recent one. Yes, this one had quite a bold hand, and when she leaned across and flipped open the one sixth back in line from it, it was a different, spikier handwriting in that one. Aleister and Ignatius, then – or at least she hoped so. A quick flip open of the ones in between showed that Aleister had only made entries in the last one, but the next one back was also a different hand, and Fleur quickly turned several pages to see if she could find a clue.

"Annora!" she breathed softly, as she saw the writer mention both Ignatius and Aleister by name. So this was a really important one, and she wrapped that straight up and slipped a piece of red card into the fabric folds to remind her which one it was. Ignatius had been more prolific, but at least he hadn't been like Starlina in terms of output, though many of his pages did seem to be covered in similar astrological charts and alchemical symbols. Altogether she had seven books of his to wade through later on, and with Loretta's – which she hadn't finished going through – Fleur had ten notebooks parcelled up to one side.

She'd just put the last one in when she heard feet hurrying up the stairs. Denise's head poked around the door to announce,

"Mr Vance has just come to see the directors with his solicitor and there's a policeman with them! I thought I'd better warn you, because Lucy is already pacing up and down the corridor outside the director's board room, and she's saying she's going to get you dismissed once they prove that she was right!"

Chapter 31

"Oh God, no!" Carrie-Ann cried, genuinely distressed at Lucy's vengeful behaviour, and even Denise was looking shaken, adding,

"We've always known Lucy's fiery, but this is totally unwarranted. She's saying that you threw books out, and that she can prove it because she took them home with her over the weekend for safe keeping."

"Oh no!" Fleur clapped a hand over her eyes. "No, no, no. Did she not believe me when I said that they were dangerous?"

"Dangerous?" Carrie-Ann queried, as Denise too looked askance. "What are you talking about?"

Fleur sighed. "Look, you can call me fanciful or whatever, but honestly guys, there are some books that have a real taint about them. And I'd already told Lucy about these ones. Are they going to summon the Devil himself into someone's front room? No, of course they aren't. Are they likely to invite in something more than you bargained for in the spirit sense? Almost certainly."

She saw Denise's sceptical expression and

added, "Do you think it's coincidence that all this upheaval, arguing, and violence has come about immediately after we've brought this stuff into here? People not listening to one another, and sniping at each other in a way that they've never done before?"

Denise gave a shiver. "Put like that, it is a bit spooky. Even Megan and I had a row yesterday afternoon, and we *never* disagree like that."

As if summoned by name, they suddenly heard Megan calling from the floor below,

"Lucy! Can you come downstairs? Bethany's here for you."

Hurrying past Denise and Carrie-Ann, Fleur ran out onto the landing in time to see an angry Lucy storming off down the stairs.

"Oh crap! I don't like the look of this at all," she muttered and hurried down after her, Denise and Carrie-Ann trotting in her wake.

As they got to the first-floor landing, they could see down into the hall below and hear what was being said.

"I'm sorry, Lucy, but I can't do this anymore," Bethany was saying. "You promised me that this was going to stop. That you would try and control this damned paranoia, and obsession with revenge for every little slight. But we're back to square-one again, aren't we? This last week you've been absolute hell to live with. It's like we're reliving Claire all over again, and it happens every time the company takes on a commission from Vance."

"Ha! Well, that won't be happening again!" Lucy

declared triumphantly. "He's had his marching orders from the directors!"

Yet if she thought that would sway Bethany she was mistaken. Instead, her partner just shook her head wearily. "To be frank, I really don't care. I don't give a damn what Mr Vance does. He can hold naked orgies with a troop of performing monkeys on his front lawn for all I care. It's when you drag it back home that it becomes my problem. I'm sick of you ranting at the top of your voice, and me then having to go around to the neighbours apologising afterwards. *You* never do."

She stepped to one side and suddenly the watchers on the landing saw three large suitcases.

"That's all of your clothes," Bethany said. "I've booked and paid for a week for you at the Premier Inn by the cricket ground. Since I'm the one who's paid for all the furniture in the house, I'll be taking that with me, but the flat went on the market this morning, and we've already had someone interested in it. I'll take the first reasonable offer and you can have your share as quickly as I can do it, but we're through. I can't take any more. I love you dearly, Lucy, but you're a nightmare to live with, with your eternal jealousy and accusations over wrongs only you ever see.

"I'm going back to mum and dad's for a while, and I've asked them not to answer the phone to you or let you in. I've also had a locksmith in to change the front door latch this morning, so when you want to go in and get your books and stuff, you'll have to liaise with the estate agents, because they've got the only other key. I've put their business card in your case fob. And anyway, all the furniture will be in storage within a couple of days. Goodbye, Lucy. I hope you conquer your demons one day, but I've run out of strength to try helping you." And with that, Bethany turned and walked out of the door, leaving Lucy rooted to the spot and white-faced.

Fleur, Carrie-Ann, Denise, and Megan, who had joined them, slunk silently back into the shadows, retreating hurriedly to the sanctity of Denise's office.

"Bloody hell! Poor Lucy!" Megan said as they closed the door. "But she's only got herself to blame."

That surprised Fleur, because it revealed that the rifts in Lucy's relationship had been more widely known, even if all of the details weren't.

"Denise," she said, "do you know if Lucy brought those books back into the building with her today?"

But it was Carrie-Ann who answered, "They're on her desk, I think. She didn't tell me that's what they were, but I saw a bundle of what looked like books there."

"Shit!" and Fleur took off, the others chasing after her, as she ran down and through to the workshop. Wherever Lucy was, it mercifully wasn't there, but only next door they could hear Alec and Tyler having a heated argument. That if nothing else convinced the others that maybe Fleur had a point, because Alec and Tyler were best mates and never argued over anything.

Seizing the bundle, Fleur turned around and ran out into the yard. Where the hell could she put these toxic things where they wouldn't cause any more harm? As she left the building, however, the shouting between the men abruptly stopped, and the other women heard a puzzled Alec saying,

"What was that all about?"

Fleur was still casting about her, looking for a spot, and then she saw the old rainwater butt in the corner. Years ago, it had probably served a purpose, but the only reason it was still there now was because nobody had got around to getting rid of it. Right now, though, it was at least half full of rather stagnant rain water from the run-off from the garage roof, and probably had a thick oily film of slime on top.

Burning the books would have been better, but consigning them to a watery grave would do. Hopefully, by the time anyone got around to draining the thing, the paper would be so much additional sludge in the bottom, let alone readable, and that would have to do. And so, running over to it, and tipping its heavy wooden lid off to fall with a clatter on the cobbles of the yard, Fleur reached up and launched the package into it. A muffled splash announced the consignment of the books and tarot deck to the murky depths, and a sudden peace descended on the place.

"I felt that go," a very shaken Megan said, as Fleur returned to them.

"Me too," agreed Carrie-Ann, giving Denise a worried look, and saw the secretary nodding in agreement. "Good grief, Fleur, it's a good job we've got you here, or heaven knows what would have happened."

Fleur wasn't keen on dwelling on that, but at least it was nice to feel vindicated in the eyes of some of her colleagues. Right now, though, she was worried about how the polluted atmosphere had affected what was going on in the board room, and she hurried back inside and up the stairs. As she reached the top floor landing, she saw an unfamiliar burly man in a heavy jacket standing in the open doorway of the board room, looking about him as if he too had felt the removal of the tarot deck. This had to be the policeman Denise had mentioned. As his eyes met hers he smiled, and then Angelo's voice came from behind him calling her into the room as the policeman left.

For the next half hour Fleur got a grilling off her bosses, but by the end of I,t even they had to admit that there was nothing she could have done to prevent Mr Harris' assault. They were also now convinced that Angelo had never intentionally put anyone in danger, and were prepared to wait over sending the books back to see if the police could apprehend Gabriele. Right now, officers should be driving up to *The Rookery* prepared to make an arrest, Angelo bringing Fleur up to speed on the fact that he'd given them a full set of keys to both houses and with his full permission to search everywhere.

As they departed the board room, he said softly to her,

"I hated doing that, but I just couldn't take the chance on Mum not letting them in, and telling them that they had to come back with a search warrant. They're going into the Cheltenham house with keys as well, just in case she's moved him over to there."

In turn, Fleur told him of her packing up the grimoires and her desire for him to take as many packing cases of them away with him as possible, if only because Gabriele might return here if not caught, and the last thing anyone needed was him getting his hands on a poison recipe. Oliver departed to go and have strong words with the solicitor in Cheltenham who had acted for Aleister Kingsford, saying that he was determined to get to the bottom of this strange relationship now. Carrie-Ann said that she would take the time in lieu and went home since there was nothing for her to do at the moment, and nobody had seen Lucy since Bethany had left. All of which left Fleur and Angelo rather in limbo.

"Why don't we go and carry on looking at the notebooks?" Fleur suggested. "At least it looks like I'm not going to get thrown out on my ear today, at least."

Angelo turned to her horrified. "What do you mean?"

And so Fleur had to explain that, even though she'd been proven right, it didn't mean that Mr

Harris and Lucy would be any too keen to continue working with her. "They can't afford to lose either Mr Harris or Lucy," she said with a resigned shrug. "I'm the cheap one to let go, because I haven't been here long enough to cost much in severance, and I'm the easiest to get a replacement for."

"Oh Fleur, I'm so sorry," Angelo said from the heart. "I never for one moment thought this would cost you your job."

"Well it'll be more than my job if I can't find another one fast," Fleur admitted, suddenly feeling more than a little wobbly again now that the adrenaline had gone. "I've got a mortgage payment to find in a week or so's time, and while I've got enough to cover this month, I don't earn enough to have sufficient savings to cover beyond next month's. I could be homeless again by mid-summer and back in my mum's spare room."

"No!" The force of Angelo's refusal surprised her. "Absolutely not! I will not have you lose everything on my account. I will pay your mortgage for as long as it takes."

"That's very kind of you, but I…"

"No 'but's! I insist, truly I do." And Fleur could see that he meant it. Not that she was exactly in a position to refuse, but she also saw the way he was looking at her, and thought it was more than common decency driving him to make the offer. He was feeling the same spark between them that she was. That was confirmed by the way he placed a hand on her shoulder as they walked up to the attic and pulled her into him for a hug. Maybe a passionate kiss on the stairs of her workplace was a bit much to hope for, but this at least seemed to hint that she hadn't been wholly wrong about him.

Back in the attic, she swiftly finished off what Carrie-Ann had been doing, and with the majority of the grimoires in boxes and taped shut, she felt she could return once more to Loretta's volume. With Angelo sitting beside her she turned to where she had left her marker and began leafing through. It didn't take long.

I cannot believe that Annora has brought such a man into our home. Loretta wrote. *I totally blame my sister for this. What was she thinking introducing my lovely girl to such a depraved set of men? This Ignatius is pure evil!*

I have felt Aunt Loverin and Grandma's spirits so close to me since he arrived, as if they are both trying to warn me and watch over me. Only the other day I found him pouring over their old notebooks with an evil gleam in his eye. Part of me wants to take them all out and burn them, for I know what some of them contain, yet they are one of the few things that I have left of my beloved aunt and grandma's, for William ordered so much to be thrown out when Aunt Loverin died, and I was in such grief that I did not know until it was too late. William does not have a sentimental bone in his body, but then he cares so little for anything other than his own pleasure these days, why would he understand why I was so desperate to keep hold of my keepsakes?

"Poor Loretta," Angelo said sympathetically. "I don't know a great deal about the history of the times she was living in – my interests tend to run to earlier stuff – but I'm guessing that as a woman, even if she was the lady of the household, she didn't have much authority to wield over who came into her house? If her husband invited them in, then there wasn't a fat lot she could do about it?"

Fleur nodded. "I think that's probably right. For all that she could see that there was something very wrong with Ignatius, if her husband didn't support her in turfing him out, then there wouldn't have been much she could do about it. I wonder why she didn't send her remaining daughters away? Was it a lack of somewhere to send them? I doubt that they'd made many friends amongst the local gentry, which would have made it possible to ask another fine lady to take one of the girls into her home for a while."

The answer wasn't long in coming, being dated only a few weeks later on.

Kadilia says she would take Richenda or Paizeni on their own, but Paizeni will not leave me, and Richenda will not leave Annora. She tells me that something very bad went on while they were at Boleskine House.

"Bloody hell!" Fleur gulped. "So not only Ignatius went there but the two sisters as well! That's not good, Angelo, it's really not good."

"Didn't you say that Starlina was the one into all that stuff? Where's she in all this?"

"Good point. …We're up to the twentieth century by now, so Starlina would have been a woman potentially heading for forty at the time this happened in …oh! Late 1912! That's ominous." She grimaced. "I know Crowley was unkind to his lovers who got older, ditching them for younger models, so to speak. Did that happen to Starlina, I wonder?"

"When did Starlina die? Do we know?"

Fleur went across to her laptop and did another rapid search. "Blimey! Starlina's record of death is up in Inverness in 1912! Jeez, that's too close to Boleskine House for comfort, isn't it? I'd better get that death record as well!"

"That's a bit convenient when Ignatius marries Annora the year after, as well," Angelo said, looking even more worried. "Does Loretta say anything about it?" and they turned to the grimoire once more.

The evil man himself was not there that time, thank the Lord, Loretta continued, *but Richenda tells me that terrible noises are heard in the neighbourhood, and local people avoid it at all costs. My poor deluded sister took her own life at that time, unable to take the rejection by the man she obsessed over. What a waste of a life when she could have married Albert Lee and travelled with his family, having children of her own, instead of such a loveless existence buried in rituals and rites.*

Richenda had to beg Annora to bring her away that last time she went, even though Ignatius lingered nearby. She swears she cannot put a name to this faceless evil she felt, but says that since then, although Annora plays the part of the dutiful wife in front of us all at meal times, which is the only time they join us, that when Annora and Ignatius are alone, she is truly frightened of him. Why oh why did my girl not say something before she was wed? She could have left with our families and got far away from him, whereas now she is trapped.

I do not know what to do about all of this. Dare I go back to Aunt Loverin and Grandma's old notebooks and try to see what they made to deal with Henrik? And would it be possible to do that again? We live in such a different world nowadays, and I fear that for all that they did what they had to in self-defence, that these days it would not be possible to do that without dreadful repercussions. I have no desire to end my days from the end of a rope, or mouldering in a prison where I can't keep an eye on my dear ones.

The next entry came not long after, and Loretta's handwriting was suddenly not as clear and strong.

Oh how I wish I had paid more mind to Aunt trying to tell me about administering poisons! I was repelled by the idea, never grasping that she was trying to prepare me for the worst. But then Aunt was stronger in the Sight than I will ever be. She foresaw something evil coming, and I mistakenly thought it would be something as simple as William losing the house and estate in a gambling game, the same way as our family got a hold of it.

Yet in these last few days I have begun to feel so ill, and I do not believe it is natural causes. I am terrified. I have the dread belief that Ignatius is trying to get me out of the way. He has already wormed his way into William's good graces by the simple expediency of taking over much of the running of the estate – or at least what is not being done by the manager. William is so idle that anything which allows him to do even less is a blessing in his eyes, and I see the crafty way that Ignatius sometimes looks at him when we are all at dinner.

He has already got the measure of his father-in-law, and knows that he is so much dough in his hands. Far worse is that he is clever enough to have realised that I am the one he has most to fear from, for dear Wantelo is now as a child in his mind. He wanders the estate, talking to the animals and birds, and is never happier than when he is helping in the garden.

How I wish that my Uncle Shadrach was still at the home farm. At least I would feel that I still had an ally there, and a place of refuge. Yet Shadrach has passed over and his dear wife also, and their sons never took to William, meaning that they left to find a better life in America years ago. The man who runs the farm now is a stranger to me aside from exchanging pleasantries in the lane as we pass. I do not feel that I could turn to him in my hour of need without him promptly sending someone to William – and what good would that do?

I have written to my dear Kadilia, and she begs me to come and stay with her and Glorina. They have only a small house, and it would mean Glorina and me sharing a bedroom, but that seems little privation to be amongst those I love and trust once more. Yet this last week my strength is failing me. I stagger some times when I try to rise from my chair or bed, and I fear that I now cannot make as much as the journey to the station, let alone the train journey to London. I am writing again to Kadilia to warn her never to let Ignatius into their house, and though it breaks my heart, to warn her against Annora whilst she is still under the spell of this monster.

"And that's it for Loretta," Fleur said, turning

over the leaf and seeing a blank page. "The date matches with being just before she died as well."

Angelo leaned back with a frown. "Then I don't think that there's any doubt that Ignatius murdered his mother-in-law because she was suspicious of him."

Chapter 32

"Poor Loretta. To know that you're being poisoned to death and to not know how to prevent it," Fleur said with a despairing shake of her head.

She carefully wrapped the book back up and placed it in the box, taking out the first of Ignatius'. Yet if they'd expected to jump straight into a confession of murder, they were disappointed. Someone, and presumably that had to have been Starlina, had taught him about keeping their own grimoire, and so these were his early writings. They made for unpleasant reading, because it was clear that Ignatius had long planned to become a man of leisure beyond the limited means his parents could give him, even if they were quite affluent by the standards of the day. However initially, there was no record of ill-doing, beyond confirming that he had kept in touch with two other young men whom he'd met at Boleskine House.

We believe in the power of three, he wrote. *And since I am the one who has control of his own estate, Harold and Walter have joined me. These fools here have enough spare cottages on the estate for me to have had two of them done up for them, and since my idiot father-in-law never checks his bank account, it was easy to take the money for that from him. The manager has been put firmly in his place, and now knows not to cross me. I wish I could get rid of him, but unless I want to do the work myself, he is unfortunately useful. Let him deal with bushels of grain and hogsheads of cider, I have higher matters to contemplate!*

"Hell's teeth! The arrogance of the man!" Fleur declared in disgust. "Sitting there in luxury and yet still looking down his nose at those who were working to keep him there. I'm amazed that manager didn't walk out."

"What year is this again," Angelo asked, reaching over and turning a page back so that he could see the date when it had been written. "Ah, June 1920. So he'd been through the war and was back home. Doesn't seem to have traumatised him any, does it?"

"No," Fleur agreed with a sigh. "They say the Devil looks after his own, and I think this is a prime example."

The next entry had them both disgusted.

I have made The Dower House my own. I will not allow Wife to enter it, nor Girl. This is for Walter, Harold, and myself only. A place where we can experiment in privacy. It disgusts me to do so, but I must occasionally return to Wife's room and bed her, for the last time she whelped it was another useless girl, and we agree it must be a son who inherits. Such knowledge as we have is wasted on weak women. I need a son whom I can induct into our circle as soon as he is old enough.

"I feel quite sick," Angelo said, getting up and going to the window, which he threw open and leaned out of to suck in deep breaths.

Fleur came and joined him. "Well, that confirms what a misogynist Ignatius was, but I didn't expect to see that Harold Westcott, and whoever this Walter was, were so involved. Mind you, it does rather sound as though Ignatius is the ring leader. They may have been just dissolute young men who were easily led, and willing to go along with him if it meant they could live as kept men."

Angelo sniffed. "That all sounded suspiciously like they were having threesomes, though. Not something the gay men I've known have ever wanted, I have to say. And there's a part of me that's wondering whether, if Ignatius was charismatic enough to draw Starlina in enough to hand over her nieces to him, he might not have latched onto two gullible young men?"

Fleur gave a shiver. "That's a worrying thought, isn't it? Because if Harold Westcott was of an age to be handed Ignatius' daughter, was he substantially younger than Ignatius? In 1920 Ignatius would have been twenty-five years old, but the others could have barely been out of their teens. They might have been doing nothing more than experimenting with their sexuality – although to do that in those days was really courting danger, given that being convicted of homosexuality could land you in jail. It wasn't without real dangers back then.

"…On the other hand, looking at the dates, maybe poor Dulcibelle got landed with an old man? If she married in 1935 just before she turned twenty-one, a guy who was eighteen in 1920 would have been thirty-three by then. Hardly love's young dream, eh? Especially if she already knew that he was her father's lover."

"Christ, that's enough to traumatise anyone," Angelo said glumly. "Poor girl. I know people might ask, why didn't she rebel? But I know from my own experience that it's not that easy. When you've had it drummed into you to do or not do something from the moment you can walk and talk, you can be frighteningly accepting of what someone else has decided will be your 'normal'."

Fleur squeezed his arm reassuringly. "Well we're straightening things out now, aren't we? Come on, let's flip through the rest of Ignatius' ramblings. We don't have to pollute our eyeballs reading every word, just keeping a watch for anything truly significant."

With that in mind they hoped they would sail through the journals, but at the recording of Ismena's birth there was a dreadful confirmation of Fleur's fears.

Another useless girl! Ignatius fumed, and they could see how his pen had dug into the paper in his fury. *I get rid of the aunt, the mother and two of the squawking wenches, then praise him, Baphomet got rid of the other two by plague, only for me to get stuck with a new generation of the creatures!*

"Charming," said Angelo, wrinkling his nose in disgust. "That sounds worryingly as if he pushed Starlina over the edge mentally, even if not physically. And who on earth is Baphomet?"

Fleur rolled her eyes. "A demon the Templars were purported to have worshipped, if you buy into the propaganda used to blacken their name so that the king of France could seize all their land and wealth. Crowley took the name for himself. Baphomet is part man part goat, and get this, Crowley preached that Baphomet was a divine androgyne – in other words, being both male and female at the same time – but also the representation of the spiritual nature of sperm, and symbolic of the divine child which had been born as a product of 'sex magic'." Then she couldn't help but snort with laughter because Angelo's face was a picture.

"The divine androgyne?" he spluttered. "Spiritual sperm? What a load of bollocks!" but that only reduced Fleur to further giggles as she said,

"Well fairly literally, if you're going by anatomical proximity!"

For a second Angelo looked at her even more astounded, then he too collapsed with laughter. "Bloody hell, Fleur! This Crowley bloke was a right conman! There are hellfire and brimstone preachers in the States who could learn a trick or two from him for when they hand around the collection plate."

"Oh yes, Crowley was infamous with good reason. The tragedy here, though, is that it's had such a terrible knock-on effect down the generations of your family. And your pal Oliver Walker is going to need to see this, I reckon, because it's as good as a confession that Ignatius murdered Loretta, Paizeni and Richenda, and could be convicted of assisting Starlina's death."

Angelo's humour evaporated. "Christ, it is, isn't it? And I'm wondering now whether little Ismena died of natural causes. A man like Ignatius would have had no compunction over smothering a sickly toddler, even if there was nothing more wrong with her than a bit of a bug." He gave a shudder. "I'm really not liking what I'm finding out about my family."

"It's only one side of your family, though," Fleur consoled him with. "Jacko Vance's lot might not have been posh, but they were perfectly ordinary working-class folks, with a fully functioning set of moral standards. And from what you've said, the Italian lot for the most part were completely normal too. It's only on your mum's paternal side that it gets this blackened.

"Hold on to that thought. You're not condemned to follow in your ancestor's footstep by genetics alone – and remind me to show you a chart which explains really well how diluted the gene pool gets. You only have one eighth of Ignatius in you, that's scientific fact, nothing less, and that eighth might be leaning heavily towards physical characteristics rather than personality."

"It's an eighth too much," Angelo said gloomily. "I may never be able to look at myself in the mirror ever again."

"Have you got any photographs of Ignatius?" Fleur wondered, keeping everything crossed that Angelo would look nothing like this monster.

"I think that one of the framed photographs in the Dower House is him, but Mum would know better than me." He sighed and ruffled his hair, as if shaking the nasty residue away. "Come on, let's get through this."

For three more notebook's-worth there was plenty which was disgusting, but nothing that they felt they had to dredge through in detail. Aleister's birth was greeted with huge celebrations, and Fleur had the feeling that that was probably shared by Annora, if it meant that she didn't have to suffer Ignatius' attentions anymore. When they reached 1935, they went more slowly through the pages, and finally they found Ignatius' version of events surrounding Dulcibelle's marriage.

The traitor! Ignatius fumed. *I give him the girl to play with and get another heir upon, just in case we need one, and he decides to keep her for himself! I know he has not joined Walter and me in our celebrations for many years, but we thought he had just become jaded with the limitations on our sex with there only being three of us.*

Wife declines to spend time with us, which I do not mind as she is prudish and will not experiment. But she takes herself away from the house, and the children with her, and that limits what I can offer my boys. Walter has never wanted a woman, but I saw the way Harold looked at the local females in the past, and thought to liven things up for him.

What an ingrate! Now they are living in Edinburgh, of all places, and the traitor writes that he only stayed so that he could one day free Dulcibelle from me. Free her? How dare he say such a thing! She has always been mine to do with as I please, for that is a father's right. But he will not bring her back, and so Walter and I must bide our time and make what use we can of the middle one, for dear Aleister caught a dreadful chill the last time we took him out to the grove at midnight. It made me realise that we cannot leave it to chance that he will father us the child we need.

"Blimey," Fleur groaned, "that sounds as though they were trying to induct Aleister into their foul world when he was barely into his teens. He may not have been a likeable man, Angelo, but you have to grant that he would hardly have had chance to be normal if that was going on."

Angelo buried his face in his hands as he shook his head. "Bloody hell! It just keeps getting worse and worse! Is there more?"

"I'm afraid so," and Fleur read aloud,

This is not good, though, for Middle Girl has been listening to Wife, and she is poisoned against us. Worse, I have found old books of Wife's family which reveal her mother's family to be witches of the worst kind, and that they have thought naught of disposing of a man who stood in their way to be mistresses of this house. I will not let that happen again. It is an abomination to think of something in a skirt ruling here!

"Flaming hell" Fleur said, turning to look at Angelo in horror. "He found the confessions to killing Henrik! But instead of seeing it for what it was, which was self-defence, he's so filled with loathing for women that he's making them out to be some nest of vipers just waiting to bump off any man who crossed them."

"I really hate him," Angelo said with disgust. "This way he refers to Annora as 'Wife'. The poor woman doesn't even warrant a proper name to him. And have you noticed, he never names his daughters except that once. He really is totally warped."

Fleur nodded. "But I'm rather heartened to hear that Harold Westcott wasn't the creep we thought he was. It's fairly obvious that he got pulled into Ignatius' orbit when still young and naïve, and then spent years trying to wriggle out of it. And yet he hung on on the periphery just to be able to save Dulcibelle. So it looks like on his part at least, it was a love match."

"No other children, though, apart from the one she died having," Angelo observed. "I wonder if she was seriously traumatised and had been badly groped, if not specifically raped, by her father and Walter?"

"If she was terrified of sex, then that would surely account for it," Fleur agreed, "And going on what we now know, I'm seriously wondering whether Harold was an absolute gent about things, and gave her years to get to the point where she wasn't scared witless if he touched her?"

"If so, then it's truly tragic that they both died when their lives were just starting to settle into something like normality. But hang on, we're only a couple of years away from when Morwenna brings those accusations, aren't we?"

They hurried on through and found the entries.

Curse the viperous wench! Ignatius scrawled. *She has left the house and caught the train to Worcester where she went to the police! Walter is distraught. He swears he cannot survive in prison, and I will not be without him. He may not be as pretty as he once was, but we are all we each have left nowadays.*

A week later came the next entry.

There is nothing for it, Wantelo must go in Walter's place. He does not have long to live anyway, for the fool has lumps growing all over him, which I tell him are the result of his witch of a sister putting a hex upon him. He is so witless that he believes me, and he has started shouting in fear every time he sees her. Walter and I laugh so to watch when that happens.

"Evil bastards!" Angelo breathed, with Fleur agreeing with a terse nod.

I have managed to convince the local bobby that my foolish daughter is so upset by what happened to her that she has the name wrong. My Walter has never gone into the village, and we only ever drive through to catch the train to Cheltenham or Bath, where we are not bothered by locals sticking their noses into our affairs. Therefore I told the bobby, 'we have nobody called Walter here,' and he believed me.

Idiot! I tried to say it must have been some vagrant passing through, but the bobby says that she is adamant that it is a man living here. I locked Wife in her room when she tried to speak to the bobby. I will not have Her interfering in this! So I put on my most distraught expression and with huge regret handed over my brother-in-law.

When he had been taken away, Walter and I cracked open the last of the champagne that William laid down. It is a bitter celebration, for just as I get rid of the last heir, the death of his father has meant that I cannot afford to live here anymore. Death duties! What wicked irony! Despite fighting it all the way for years now, we have had to sell off the home farm and acres of land, but if I am to have anything to live on in a proper manner, then I shall need more income, and the only way is to let out the house or sell it, and I will not do that.

Walter wants to go to Italy or Greece, and frolic naked in the sun for the rest of his days, but I have had to tell him that this is not possible. War is coming – I can feel it, and the Witch says she has foreseen it, and in that respect her foul blood has its uses. I must remain here to ensure that the Dear Boy does not come to harm. I will do whatever it takes to ensure that he does not fight.

The Second World War came around, and there was considerable fear that Aleister might perish. Annora and Morwenna moved into a cottage in the grounds, taking refuge, Angelo and Fleur guessed, in the fact that there were always people about now that the house was a hotel, which meant that Ignatius and Walter moved to London until the Blitz started. But it was clear that Ignatius was starting to weary of Walter. To Fleur and Angelo, there were clear hints that while Ignatius was just sex obsessed, as revealed by his occasional mentions of going to find prostitutes in London who would cater to his more 'exotic' tastes, Walter was genuinely gay and, poor soul, genuinely in love with Ignatius.

Later brief entries implied that he had had to be forced to do what he did to Morwenna, which was why she had got of more lightly than she might have. Walter could not face having actual sex with her, it seemed, and if his groping and fumbling had been unnecessarily rough, it also sounded as though he had been beside himself in distress at that time, and had barely known what he was doing – or trying to do.

"What a thoroughly evil man my great-grandfather was," Angelo said as they broke off and went out in search of coffee. "I don't like the way that Walter came to grief in that air raid."

"No, reading between the lines I was wondering whether Ignatius wouldn't let him into the air-raid shelter," Fleur admitted. "It sounded very much as if Walter was getting too clingy as he got older, and Ignatius wasn't having any of that."

"Have we got much more to get through?" Angelo asked, as they walked back armed with takeout cappuccinos and baguettes.

"Thank heavens, no! Only one more of Ignatius' and that's not complete. Then we've just got Annora's own journal and Aleister's."

The bits they read of Ignatius' implied that Aleister had proven to be disinterested in what his father had to offer, and had spent as little time with his father as possible.

That damned Italian witch has him by the balls! Ignatius ranted in 1953. *Why did the Dear Boy have to stay on in the army? Could he not have come home? Though it makes me spit in fury to have to say this, even coming home to his damned mother would have been better than this! At least at The Rookery I would have had chance to speak to him alone, but as it stands, I only ever see him to have lunch with him at The Ritz, or his club, before he dashes off to some business meeting or other. I cannot get him to understand that he has a Great Fate awaiting him if he would only begin his apprenticeship in our arts with some passion.*

"Sounds like Aleister was running like mad in the opposite direction," Fleur observed, and saw how relieved Angelo looked at that. She didn't want to burst that bubble by saying what he'd clearly forgotten for the moment, which was that Aleister had raped his own daughter later on. Talk about bad blood will out!

And then there came an entry which had them staring at one another in horror.

We had a new arrival at The Rookery while I was there at Christmas, he wrote. Aleister came to stay at the hotel with the Italian Witch and a man who swears he is his cousin. I was not sure at first, but Wife tells me that he knows things that only a member of the family could know. It seems that Gabriel Angelo Fitzpatrick – if we can truly call him a Fitzpatrick – is the illegitimate son of Muldobrai by some Greek wench he fell for.

"Gabriel Angelo?" His namesake choked on the words. "Dear God, please let me not have been called after him!"

Fleur could only hold his hand tightly as they read on,

There he was in the hotel dining room, eating Christmas dinner with Wife and Daughter, and dear Aleister and the Witch. Such a pretty man, even though he is approaching forty now, and as we looked at one another we recognised something familiar. That night we entertained one another to great mutual satisfaction in my rooms in the Dower House. The others declared that they would not spend time in my company, and returned to Wife's cottage, but Gabe is not so prudish.

By the time we went down to breakfast in the morning he was my man through and through. He is not as Walter was, and only interested in men, nor as crippled by morals as Harold was. He wants what he sees should be his, which is nothing less than the inheritance his father ought to have had, and though I have no intention of letting him have that over me, it serves my purpose to let him think that I support him. Even better, he has the Levantine man's superior attitude towards women, and agrees that the Italian Witch is ruining Aleister, and must go.

I have been trying to find a way to get rid of her, but reluctantly concede that I cannot do to her as I did to the sisters. It would be too easily found out in these modern times. But Gabe has a plan. He believes that Aleister will not want the Witch if she is spoiled goods, so spoiled she must be! And he is willing to do the job. I have lost my appetite for women, especially when as rebellious as she is. That attitude quenches my ardour faster than anything. Why should I work so hard to have to prove my superiority when they should recognise it as a matter of course? But that is modern women for you. No sense of their place.

A couple of weeks went by and then Ignatius was ranting again.

Curse that damned woman! She has taken Aleister back to Italy after Gabe tried his best to get her alone. The hotel staff heard her calling for help, and may they be damned, they came and pulled Gabe away. I did suggest that Gabe follow them to Italy, but he is not sufficiently biddable that he would leave the comforts of the hotel, though the manager is far from happy about him staying.

The damned man had the effrontery to tell me that owner or not, he would not bow to my demands to keep on a guest such as that! There is only one blessing, and that is that Wife and Daughter still believe that Gabe is as repulsed by me as they are. Because of that I have sent Gabe to the Cheltenham house, but also because I do not want him letting it slip that he and I are close. I must try to intercept any messages that come for Wife from Aleister, which might tell all of what I got Gabe to do. It would not do for them and Aleister and the Witch to start plotting against me in unison!

An oddly long gap appeared in the dates, and then a much more scrawled entry,

Curse them to eternity! Wife and Daughter have done for me! What ignominy, to have done to me what I did to her mother! Why have my gods not protected me? I do not have long, and I must make arrangements, for I must ensure the females do not get their hands on what I have worked so hard for. It <u>must</u> go to Aleister! And the only one I can trust to ensure that happens is Gabe. It means leaving him a *substantial bequest in the form of him being allowed to remain as a guest in perpetuity at the hotel, albeit in* Her *mother's cottage, but the condition is that he makes sure that my son is not emasculated by his mother, sister, and his witch – for the fool declares that he is as in love with her as ever.*

Chapter 33

"Emasculated by her?" Angelo re-read aloud. "Christ! What a monster he was!"

Fleur was rubbing his back soothingly, trying to show whatever solidarity she could with him. "Does it help to say that Ignatius married into the family owning *The Rookery*? That the other line isn't tainted at all?"

Angelo turned to look at her mournfully. "Not really. He's still my damned great-grandfather, isn't he?"

"Unfortunately, yes." What else could she say? And yet her heart went out to him, because Ignatius Kingsford was a monster of grand proportions. Then a thought came to her. "Why don't we skip over and look at Annora's book and see if we can find an entry for the same period? It could prove really interesting to see things from her side – not least why, at this late stage, she felt impelled to do something about Ignatius? This is the woman who had stood for God-knows-what for decades. So why now? Why decide to get rid of him now? Surely she would have wanted him gone long ago, when he was a threat to her children when they were younger?"

Angelo's bleak expression faded. "Now that's a really interesting thought, isn't it? Okay, let's see what Annora has to say."

They didn't have far to go to find the first entry, for after a couple of updates to old family recipes, in 1920 she wrote,

I find I must use this book as my mother and her aunt before her did, because I must tell someone for my own sanity's sake. I cannot believe my Aunt Starlina dragged me into this unholy mess – for unholy it is. The man I am wed to is a monster on a scale I had not dreamt could exist within an Englishman. I thought such lewd and unsavoury practices only existed in exotic places far from here.

He has brought two men to our home, and I am under no illusions as to what he does with them under the cover of darkness. I am so isolated here that I cannot refuse him my bed. To do so would risk him tying me down and then forgetting about me afterwards. But I give thanks to whatever goddess is watching over me that he does not attend to me often. Only three times this year so far, Goddess be praised, and if I am left sore and bruised afterwards, at least he does not seek my company for many months afterwards. I have heard of women with more normal husbands who demand more of them and more frequently, even though they loath those husbands as much as I do mine. And it is little to put up with to have my lovely girls. They are my blessings and my joy.

As for the men, the one called Harold, I pity. He is a naïve and impressionable boy, little more. He has no malice in him at all, and the other day I found him weeping in the stables. He was so embarrassed he could not fully tell me what was wrong, but I swiftly gathered that Ignatius had been as

rough in bed with him as he is with me. I gave Harold some of the salve I use myself, and later gave him some of the scented oil I use to ease Ignatius forcing himself upon me.

Poor young lad, he was so pathetically grateful, and told me that he would run away except that he has nowhere to go. His parents disowned him last year, and told him never to darken their door. What a wicked thing to do to your own son for nothing more than falling in love with the wrong person when little more than a child.

"Wow!" Angelo gasped. "She was pretty forward thinking for a woman of her time! There must have been many who would have just shoved Harold aside having already labelled him a pervert, his parents amongst them."

"Yes, huge kudos to Annora there," Fleur agreed. "I wonder if it was because she realised from her own experience how easy it was to be drawn into something you didn't expect, or understand, in your teens? She must have had such a rude awakening when she finally grasped what her aunt had let her in for. Yet she turned it to a positive thing by becoming so much more understanding of other people. You see, Angelo, your great-grandmother is the good counter-balancing your great-grandfather, and that has to be worth holding on to."

Angelo gave a faint smile. "Yes, it is. Thank you, that is worth remembering. …So what's the next entry?"

Fleur turned the page.

I pity Walter too, now, for he is in love with Ignatius in a way that that monster will never love anyone but himself. He is as careless with Walter as he is with me, and though Walter is not a likable young man in the way that Harold is, he still does not deserve the treatment he gets from Ignatius. I will not call that evil creature my husband, for husband implies a level of care for at least one's physical condition, if not actual consideration, yet I get nothing like either from him. I am pregnant once more, and I pray nightly that it might be the son he craves so that I may be spared his attentions.

"Poor Annora. That's dated Christmas 1920," Fleur told Angelo. "She'd had Morwenna back in December 1919, and must have got pregnant almost as soon as she could, because Ismena was born in the April of 1921 – a year and four months on from Morwenna."

"When was Aleister born?" Angelo asked, clearly struggling to remember the date in amongst this sea of ancestors.

"October 1923, so two years and six months on from Ismena. I wonder whether she just had trouble conceiving as quickly that time around? Because there's no hint here that she suffered a miscarriage in between the two."

"I do hope so, because Annora suffered enough as it was."

They read on, with another significant entry coming in the November of 1923.

I have a son, but whether he will ever be allowed to be mine is another matter, wrote Annora, the page stained with her tears, which made the ink bleed in places. *My worst fears have been confirmed in that he insists that the child must be named after his hero, Aleister. What a name to give him! Why would anyone wish for their son to be given the name of such a notorious man? It will brand him forever with that peculiar spelling. If he had to call him after the one who perverted him, why could he at least not have acquiesced to my plea to spell it the Scottish way? Alistair, not Aleister. Such is the selfishness of the Monster. I will call him nothing else from this day onwards.*

"Good grief!" Angelo gasped. "She really hates him by this time, doesn't she?"

Fleur nodded. "And with good reason, you have to admit. She's watching him and knowing that her only son will be dragged into darkness unless she can find a way to prevent it. And given that she can't even get free of him herself, what chance can she have had to free her son?

"Annora wasn't stupid. She had to know how she was trapped by the mores of the time. It's hard to remember how much closer to Victorian morals people were between the two world wars than after them. We just see it as a continuous flow of progress, but it wasn't like that for those living it. The Second World War did so much for emancipation for women. In those six years everything changed, and Annora hasn't got there yet."

Annora's writing continued with many heartfelt comments on how Ignatius mistreated everyone around them. Yet there was also hope. Ignatius was often absent with Walter, while the faithful Harold stayed at *The Rookery*, and in those times while Ignatius' malevolent influence was gone, did what he could to help Annora give the children as normal an upbringing as possible.

By the time Dulcibelle was into her late teens, Annora was expressing her wishes that Harry, as she now called him, would be able to get Dulcibelle away from *The Rookery*. There was even one point when they wondered whether Annora and Harry had done some mutual consoling of one another, in a way that would have had Ignatius incandescent with anger, but which never seemed to come to anything.

Yet, it left Fleur and Angelo in no doubt that Dulcibelle's escape to Edinburgh had been jointly arranged between Harry and Annora, with the agreement of Dulcibelle herself, who was far less frightened of Harry than she was of her father. However, the molesting of Morwenna changed everything for Annora. Whereas she had been openly writing that she was visiting whatever contacts she could presume upon, to get her and the children away from the house as frequently as she could, the arrest of her brother shook her to the core.

I cannot believe that even one as wicked as Ignatius could be so utterly evil as to send poor Wantelo to prison, she wrote in a page near illegible for tear blots. *My poor, sweet brother. Oh how I weep for what has become of him. He is eight years older than me, yet for all of my life I have felt the need to protect him like a big sister. But I have failed him abysmally. They dragged him away screaming his innocence, and I was locked away up on the top floor of the Dower House, unable to protest or do a thing.*

I later found out that although the Dower House is often used as spare bedrooms for the hotel, that Ignatius has never allowed them the keys to the attic where I was kept. And here I found my grandmother and her mother's tarot decks and their books. Luckily Ignatius was so pleased with himself that he never noticed that I slipped a little cloth into the lock as he freed me, and now I have access to the attic.

"Go, Annora!" Fleur breathed in admiration as they read on.

I now know the truth of what happened to Henrik, and I totally understand why. They had no choice, and neither do I. All that remains is for me to find the right time. Morwenna and Dulcibelle must never come under suspicion. My dear, sweet Ismena is beyond her evil father's reach now, and will remain unsullied; therefore I must ensure that my other two girls remain the same.

I have gone to the woods and met with the rest of the travelling family. For too long I resisted the connection that is there, tainted by the twisted versions of what they believe fed to me by Starlina. But now she is dead, may God forgive her her wickedness, and my Aunt Pomona comes with them, though she is now of a great age and only travels as far as us and back to her home in Hereford.

She has set so many things right in my mind, about both the Roma and our immediate family, and I can no longer disregard my heritage. We sat around the camp fire, Aunt Pomona, Morwenna and I, along with the other women of the family, and we discussed what must be done at length. A gypsies' curse is not to be taken lightly, but we are all agreed that Ignatius deserves it in every way possible.

Therefore with the three of us still living who are related to him as the active participants, the deed was done, and with three wise women from the wider family and their daughters present too. Three times three is a potent combination, and may everything that Ignatius has brought down upon the innocent be returned upon him and unto the third generation of his male heirs, for I cannot discount the possibility that he has already corrupted my son beyond his redemption. I do not wish evil upon my sweet boy, but I fear that he is no longer mine to influence.

"Bloody hell!" Angelo gasped. "She really believed this!"

Fleur nodded. "I think she did. By this time there can't have been any doubt in her mind that Ignatius would corrupt Aleister if he could. And notice that she said his *male* heirs. She knows, Angelo! She knows what a misogynist Ignatius is, and that he discounts his daughters as useless. But *she* doesn't! She's setting things up as best she can so that if not her daughters, then her granddaughters can inherit."

By this time the Second World War was almost upon them, and as with Ignatius' entries, Fleur and Angelo skipped through them as fast as possible. Out in the western counties there were no accounts of air raids which might have endangered lives, and apart from Aleister, no other men of the family went away to fight. Many of the travelling family went to Ireland to avoid conscription, and though Fleur was not approving of that, as she said to Angelo,

"It's only with hindsight that we know how many gypsies were sent to the concentration camps by the Nazis. For them it was far simpler. They were just avoiding fighting for a country which had never treated them kindly. That other nations were doing far worse to their distant kin might have been something they knew next to nothing about. It probably never occurred to them that fighting for England was helping to guarantee their long-term safety."

However, after the war, things at *The Rookery* began to change.

I have managed to persuade Aleister to remain in the army, Annora wrote. *With the worst of the fighting over and done with, he is not in great danger anymore, and the last time he was here on leave, he confessed to me that his father's fanaticism frightens him. He says that the few true Nazis he encountered were just such men as him – so convinced of their own inherent right to dominate that they saw no other path. I would not wish war upon anyone, but if experiencing that has finally made Aleister see his father in his true light, then I cannot help but be glad.*

Even better, Aleister has met a lovely girl over in Italy, and seems truly in love with her. He told his father, and was shocked when the Monster told him that if he should marry against his wishes, that he would both disown him and throw Morwenna and I out of the cottage and leave us destitute. This is beyond tolerable! I will not have Morwenna go through the terrible experience she had with Walter – even if he was as frightened of Ignatius as she was – only for her to be made homeless forever.

As it is, she cannot bear the thought of the touch of a man, so she will never marry and as a consequence will never be provided for in that way. And Aleister deserves to be able to be happy with a wife who is normal and who genuinely loves him – not some perverted harridan the Monster has scraped off the streets, who will do as he tells her for the right price! Therefore I must make this right. I have stood for the Monster for too long. I must gather my courage and do what must be done. I have the recipe the family gave me in the woods that night, and also the one my grandmother used. May they serve me just as well.

"Bloody hell!" Angelo exclaimed. "So that's what made her act! She foresaw Ignatius going on and blighting both of her remaining children's lives for as long as he continued to live."

Fleur nodded thoughtfully. "What I find just as interesting is that she's forgiving of Walter for what happened to Morwenna, even if she didn't particularly like him. She doesn't hold him to blame, does she? She gets that he's terrified of what Ignatius would have done in his fury, if he hadn't gone ahead with what he did with Morwenna. In fact, it sounds as if Walter was in fear of his life at that point, which makes me wonder how often he'd heard Ignatius ranting about what he'd do to Harold if he got his hands on him?"

She thought for a second, then added, "Do you think that Walter's desire to go to Greece or Italy was his way of trying to get free of Ignatius? Did he know that Ignatius would never properly settle in the Med', but that if he could get that far away, then if

Ignatius decided to return to England, that he might stay behind?"

Angelo was momentarily startled, but then thought about what she'd said and couldn't help but agree. "Poor old Walter. He really was trapped, wasn't he? And maybe, by the time he had to traipse after Ignatius to London, he was really wishing he could stay behind at *The Rookery*? Because even facing Annora's maternal wrath, and his own guilt over Morwenna, was better than having to follow a man whom he thought would kill him with no more compunction than crushing a fly?"

"I think so. Ignatius must have convinced Walter that he had some terrible hold over him to keep him trapped for all of those years. And from the little we know of Walter, it probably wasn't true, but something which Ignatius told him would be believed of him. …My guess would be that it was something even worse than being imprisoned for being a homosexual, and God knows, that was bad enough back in those days."

Angelo shuddered. "Poor soul, what a life he must have led. You wouldn't wish that on your worst enemy, would you? …So come on, then. What's next?"

Fleur turned the pages, and soon they were confronted with her confession.

I have used the herbs my great-grandmother used, she wrote. *May the goddess forgive me for this terrible thing that I do, but I have no choice. I have tried every way I can think of to get Morwenna and myself away from the Monster's grasp, but he is too powerful, too good at playing the country gentleman to those who scarcely know him. Were we to come before a judge, and him making accusations against us, he would be the one believed. The Devil surely watches over the Monster!*

Therefore it should be slow and carefully done. The doctor has told me that he fears Ignatius' heart is no longer strong because of what he smokes in such quantity, which gives me hope that I might not be discovered. But no sudden death for him! Why should I give him that? Why should he not know what it is like to live in the shadow of the fear of one's own death?

For a year now, I have crept up to the Dower House when he is there, watching him through the windows from beneath the cover of the great rhododendron bushes; watching and observing his habits for the one I might use without fear of discovery. And now his arrogance has played into my hands. The wine he drinks with such relish every evening comes from the general stock of the hotel, so if he sickens from it, the health of the other guests should surely quash any doubts in that direction? But in his posturing, he has it decanted for him every time. Ha! As if he could tell the difference between one wine and another!

I have seen him finish one decanter-full and have it topped up straightaway, though the wine waiter who brings the bottles looks at him with such disgust for just sloshing the wine in instead of taking his time with it or having a clean decanter brought. So, whatever is in the decanter that is not absorbed in the first bottleful is surely absorbed by the second. What worked for Mezelly will surely work for me!

And it is rare that he makes do with only one bottle per meal these days. If there is a half or quarter bottle left from the previous night, he downs it with speed and then commences on the next, regardless of whether he last had a French wine and now an Italian, or a Merlot and now a Pinot Noir. And he dares to call me a peasant!

She continued, *I followed great-grandmother's recipe to the letter, allowing the brew to steep for several days before I strained it through muslin. And on consideration, added an ingredient of my own which ought to act on his already weakened heart, though I will not say which here for fear of it being found. Indeed I strained my brew twice to make sure that it would not cloud the wine. Morwenna and I tried a little on the tips of our tongues, and thought it a trifle bitter, so we added just enough sugar to it to take the harsh edge off it. I then sent dear Morwenna off to visit with our travelling folk for a while, to ensure that she is not at the house when this thing happens. Under no circumstances can she be around to take any of the blame should I fail, and I have made Aunt Pomona's folk promise to keep her with them if I should be caught and end up in jail.*

"God, she really was covering all her options, wasn't she?" Fleur said in awe. "I'm not sure I could be that calm in the face of possible defeat. And she must have known that it was nothing like a certainty that she'd succeed. All it would have taken was a curious washer-up wondering what that deposit was in the decanter." And suddenly Grandma Rose's voice was in her head again saying, *Ah! But she'd made it into a solution already! She let it stand and strained it off any residue that might give it away.*

Fleur just about covered her shock in a cough, as Angelo said,

"Good grief, it really was premeditated murder, then, wasn't it? Though it's hard not to see it as self-defence just as Mezelly's act was."

Fleur nodded, clearing her throat before saying, "I think that's right. But if I were you, this is one notebook I wouldn't be showing to Oliver Walker. We don't want him thinking that you come from a multi-generational set of murderers! Especially not if Gabriele comes to trial!"

Chapter 34

Angelo turned to her in shock. "Lord, I hadn't thought about it like that, but you're right! We can't have anyone doubting whether I'm any saner than Gabriele is. If we do create that doubt, then he's conniving enough to try passing the blame back to me, and telling people he's like he is because I kept him a prisoner. And he can be so bloody convincing, as your colleagues found when they genuinely believed he was me."

Fleur agreed. "We have to keep the impression rooted in people's minds that Gabriele is truly the sick one. …Which he is, of course! I just meant that they can't start looking sideways at you at the same time."

Angelo smiled faintly at her, then gestured at the notebook. "So what's next? Turn the page, Fleur. The suspense is killing me!"

It is done! Annora wrote triumphantly a couple of weeks later. *I have been slipping in and dosing the decanter on a daily basis. Not too much. Just enough for the poison to gradually start building up inside him. I can scarcely believe that I am getting away with this, but the wine waiter from the hotel is now so disgusted with its foul owner that he only brings the opened bottle into the Dower House and leaves it on the dinner table. The Monster has one of the young locals who waits at table come across and pour it for him when his food arrives.*

And it is a different young lad each time, although limited by the number of them working for the hotel. But from my point of view the important thing is that no single one of them has come several nights in a row, and therefore will never come under suspicion (I could not bear for an innocent to suffer for what I do). Maybe it is because they are afraid of what the Monster might do to an attractive lad alone in that place? I do not know, for I venture so rarely into the village these days I do not hear the local gossip. It is easier for Morwenna and I to drive into Worcester or Hereford to shop for ourselves – somewhere where we are not tainted by the Monster's notoriety – and now she is away, I swallow my pride and catch the bus like any other housewife.

Strangely, I have been welcomed into the community of ordinary women in a way that I never have amongst the set the Monster wishes to ingratiate himself with. All it took was being polite and not having airs and graces, and sharing the odd complaint with them. And since he keeps me so short of funds, and I would not risk any other young woman coming to our house and falling into the Monster's clutches, I wash and cook like any other wife of the county. Praise the Goddess, then, for the kindness of women towards one another in a world ruled by men; for if the Suffragettes won the vote for ladies of means, for those of us with husbands who allow them nothing, or those still dependent upon a landlord, the world has changed little. We can only help one another when we can.

"And that's still true today," Fleur said bitterly.

"No! Come on," Angelo protested, "you vote, you can own property, you can hold down high-powered jobs; it's a world away from the downtrodden housewives of the thirties or fifties!"

"You think?" Fleur said with a sniff of disgust. "You try standing in a courtroom in front of a male judge, and try telling him that your husband is so off his face on pills, that he's trying to knock three shades of shit out of you whenever he comes home. That you're not the bitch trying to bleed him white, like his rabble of testosterone-filled friends are all standing up and swearing to, with scant regard for telling the truth under oath. You don't see much female emancipation then, I can tell you from bitter experience!"

Angelo looked at her in horror. "Oh my God, Fleur! Is that what happened to you?"

Realising that she hadn't ever told him about this, Fleur blushed. "Sorry. Didn't mean to wear my wounds on my sleeve quite so openly."

"You don't need to apologise," Angelo protested. "Good God, that's enough to have you loathing men for life. I'm just grateful that you've given me a chance to prove myself. To show that I'm not some manic rapist, and that I'm at least reasonably sane."

"I think you're more than 'reasonably sane'," Fleur said with a faint smile. "In fact, I think it's amazing that you're as normal as you are. What you've been through would have broken many a tough guy."

"Back at you," Angelo quipped, but with empathy in every word.

Fleur gave a weak laugh. "Quite the pair, aren't we?"

"That we are." Angelo put his arm around her shoulders. "And if I had to go through this nightmare with anyone, I'm so bloody glad that it was with a woman like you, who could see the wood for the trees. I wouldn't wish your experience on anyone, but if that's what's made you able to see what I've been through, then I can only say that I'm humbly grateful. Because you're the first person I've met who I've thought might come even close to understanding my nightmares."

That gave Fleur a warm feeling inside, even if she wished she'd never had to stand in that court room for her divorce. If no other positive thing had come out of it, it was worth it to know that it had made her capable of seeing the real Angelo from Gabriele, and that she might yet be able to help him clear his name. The gentle kiss which followed it from Angelo was less expected, but no less welcome.

When they broke apart, Fleur turned the page of the notebook. Straightaway she could see from the date that they were months on from the last entry.

I cannot believe it, Annora wrote, *but nobody has expressed the slightest misgivings about Ignatius' death, nor any grief. How can that be if not for the guiding hand of the Goddess and the gypsies' curse upon him holding? How can such a perceived war hero die choking on his own vomit in the mid-afternoon, and nobody question how he came to be so weak as to not be able to even roll over? I confess that I am greatly relieved that his death was taken at face value as that of a weakened drunkard, and that nobody demanded an inquest, for if they had, they would surely have discovered what I had been dosing him with these last months? Yet no inquest was held, the attending doctor's word being good enough since he knew him of old.*

Within the year came the declaration that Aleister intended to wed Angelina now that his father wasn't there to object, and also entries declaring Annora and Morwenna's pleasure at seeing their son and brother so happily married. The subsequent announcement of a pregnancy was greeted with great delight, yet with a hint that things were still not wholly right.

Angelina is much distressed, yet I cannot get it out of her why. The language barrier does not help, for her English is not good, and my Italian non-existent. I do not need words, though, to see that she is not happy here. Much as I would wish to be present when my grandson or -daughter gets born, if it will keep both baby and mother safe, then I will not protest over her returning to Italy for the birth.

And then a few months on came,

Blessed be! A baby girl who Aleister and Angelina are going to call Claudia. What a lovely name. I am so looking forward to meeting her when she is old enough for them to bring over here.

"Woah! Hang on a moment!" Fleur gasped. "That doesn't match up!"

Angelo looked perplexed. "What doesn't?"

"Well, when I first met your mum, she was telling me about the family. And she said that her mother miscarried her first pregnancy." She flipped the pages back and forth. "There's no mention of that here. And given the way that Annora is so delighted at the news, I think she'd have mentioned it, don't you?" She looked at the dates again. "And there isn't really time for another child, or at least a reasonably advanced pregnancy, in this timing. How odd."

"Maybe Mum's just got confused?" Angelo suggested, but then the next discrepancy hit Fleur hard, and she shook her head.

"No, Angelo, something's really wrong here. Your mum told me that Annora was already *dead* when she was born. But Annora doesn't die until two years after Claudia was born – that's official records, not somebody's memory. I'll grant you that she wouldn't have many strong memories of her grandmother at that age, but if it was…" Fleur's throat constricted and she couldn't get the words, 'her sister' out, let alone the rest of what had pounded into her mind.

"Fleur! …Fleur, are you alright?" The urgency in Angelo's voice brought her back to reality. "You've gone white. What's the matter?"

Taking a deep breath, Fleur asked, "Where are you staying tonight?"

"We've booked in at *The Talbot* out at Knightwick."

"Then let's get these packed up and get you into a taxi with all of these."

"Fleur, for the love of God, what's wrong?"

She turned to him with a baleful expression. "If my suspicions are right, a lot. A huge amount. Epic! The kind that will have you wanting a stiff drink in your hand all the way. And I think you'll want to have Oliver present when we do work this out, because I'm already feeling sick at the legal implications."

He kept on asking, but Fleur was resolute – not here, and not now. Even so, her head was still spinning at what she feared. It had been *Romana* who had been born in Italy after Annora had died. Romana who was the double of her sister as a young woman. So who exactly had been sat in that room at the Dower House with Fleur? And which sister had died? Because the suspicions, which wouldn't leave Fleur be, just kept making connection after connection, and they weren't good.

A hurried phone call to Oliver found that he was already on his way back with unpleasant news of his own, and so rather than fight his way back into Worcester with the late afternoon traffic starting to build, he too would go to the hotel.

They met up in a quiet corner of the lounge area of the lovely old inn, leaving the few others in there to cluster around the huge open fire with its log smouldering gently in it. With it being between lunch and dinner, there were no diners around, and most of the few people in for drinks were enjoying a remarkably warm day for the time of year, and taking them outside to the garden.

"Now for God's sake, will you tell me what's got you in such a flap?" Angelo demanded, as Oliver put the three wine glasses and the bottle of red down on the table, and began pouring.

Fleur took a deep breath and braced herself. "Okay. So you know that when I arrived at *The Rookery* I met Claudia. At that time, she told me her version of your family history, and of course, with nothing to tell me otherwise, I believed what I was told. But the thing is, now that we're reading these first-hand accounts from the time when things actually happened, her story just doesn't add up."

She gave Oliver a watery smile. "You won't know this, but Claudia told me that her parents married in 1955, which is perfectly true. But she then told me that her mother – that's Angelina who married Aleister Kingsford – had a miscarriage first, and that that's supposedly why she went back to Italy to have her, Claudia I mean. According to her, it was all to do with Angelina hating *The Rookery* and the stress of living there."

Now she tapped the notebook, which she'd kept a hold of. "But this is Annora's *contemporary* account of what went on, and Annora is certainly clear and lucid. There's no mention of any miscarriage at all, and given Annora's interest in healing and herbs, I think she would have taken note of that, even if it hadn't been her first potentially living grandchild she was talking about."

She saw the scepticism in the two men's faces, and added firmly, "This is the account by the woman whose oldest daughter had already died in childbirth, guys! Dulcibelle and what ought to have been the first grandchild died together in a difficult birth *years* before this. So don't you think that Annora, of all people, would have been watching her daughter-in-law like a hawk to make sure nothing went wrong this time? Before, she wasn't able to get to her daughter, because it was in the middle of World War Two, and Dulcibelle and Harold were in Edinburgh, far, far from here. But now, Angelina was living in the same place as her.

"And that makes another point. This is already post-Ignatius' death, but Claudia told me that her mother didn't like the main house, yet it can't possibly have been because of his presence, can it? And the main house was *already* a hotel from decades before that because of the death duties for William Fitzpatrick. It was the *Dower* House that Aleister and Angelina moved in to when they married, not *The Rookery* itself; and Annora and Morwenna had moved into the coach house cottage, because the cottage they had been in had had to be sold in the second round of death duties from Ignatius. They weren't living across the estate from Angelina, they were just across the *yard*! So who do you think Aleister would have called upon if his wife started to miscarry, eh? His mum! But does she say a word of that here? No."

Angelo was still looking puzzled, but Oliver was already starting to wear a worried frown as he weighed up what Fleur was saying. And so Fleur opened her laptop and showed him the photograph of Claudia and Romana leaving England after Jacko's death, and instantly his eyes flew wide open and he stared at her in horror.

"What?" demanded Angelo. "What the fuck have you two seen?"

Fleur reached across and took his hands in hers. "Okay, take a deep breath. …I don't think that's your mum out at *The Rookery*. I think it's her sister. The sister who is physically her double, but a very different woman inside."

"*Noooo!*" Angelo was stunned.

"It's the one thing which makes sense of all this," Fleur said gently. "Claudia, your mum, was born in 1957 when Annora was still alive. But by the time *Romana* was born in 1960, her grandmother Annora really *was* dead, so that memory is true to the woman who told it to me. It explains why it's so out of step with what we know for Claudia, though. Claudia wasn't Angelina's second pregnancy, but Romana *was*. Or potentially her third if there was one between the real Claudia and Romana. Can you see, Angelo? She's blurring the lines between her own childhood and your mother's."

Angelo was shaking his head mutely, unable to take it in.

"I'm not saying that Claudia wasn't your mum," Fleur continued, knowing that she had to tell him the rest of what she suspected now. "I think she was most definitely that. But I suspect that, had there been notebooks for her generation here, we'd find that the reason why she sent you off to school so soon had a double edge, the first being that she and her family finally realised just how unstable Romana was.

"That's why she was so very loving with you when you were at home, and yet could still send you far away from her. Far away from her *sister*! Your real mum, Claudia, was trying to keep you safe and away from a sister who was potentially dangerous. But also, a sister whose son – born while you were still little more than a babe yourself – was even worse. …I think Gabriele isn't your brother, he's your *cousin*. Gabriele is *Romana's* son, not Claudia's. It was *Romana* who left England pregnant and had her child in Italy, not your mum!"

"Holy shit!" Oliver gasped, taking a swig of his wine. "That really puts the cat amongst the pigeons!"

"I'm sorry," Fleur apologised, "and although it does, it also makes sense of the garbled things the woman at *The Rookery* said to me. Do you remember us telling you about that whole bizarre conversation we had on the stairs with Mr Harris and the other guys present? She kept referring to her 'son', but when we said Angelo's name, she kept on about 'not him'.

"It was so bloody weird to us then, but I think in that moment of stress she was telling us the absolute truth. The man who had some weird fixation with me was *her* son, Gabriele, not you, Angelo. And that's also why your *real* mum never mentioned to you about you having a brother when you were younger, because you truly didn't!

"It's only when you came back from school when you were sixteen, and you were around for longer, that you walked into the time and place where those two lives collide." She felt dreadful for having to tell him like this, but said gently. "I'm so sorry, Angelo, but I think the woman who died wasn't Romana. It was your mum, Claudia. So that also makes sense of why at that time she never mentioned Romana dying, because *she* wasn't dead!

"And I think Oliver is going to have to have words with their lawyers over there, because I think there can be only one of two possibilities going on there. The one is that Romana was having one of her more stable moments, and so she actually convinced your great-uncle and -aunt that she *was* Claudia at that point. And that it wasn't until later that they realised that they'd been duped.

"Or alternatively, that Romana killed your mum, and the family were so distraught that they helped her cover up that crime, rather than Angelina effectively lose both of her daughters – because of course, Angelina didn't die until 1999, and we're talking about events …oh holy crap! The year *after* that!

"Shit, shit, *shit*! I thought Angelina was still alive at that point in 2000, but of course she wasn't! Was her mum dying the moment when Romana thought she could finally steal Claudia's life – in every way? Oh, flaming hell!" and she clapped a hand to her forehead in disbelief at the collision of events that they hadn't seen before.

Angelo was so white Fleur thought he might faint, and even Oliver had gone pale at the international legal implications.

"If it helps," she added, and mentally keeping her fingers crossed that it would, even if she was still holding one of Angelo's hands while he held his glass shakily in the other, "I think your Italian family got duped, at least for several months. I have a gut feeling that it was Romana imprisoning you, and letting Gabriele free, that gave things away. Possibly she tried to con them into thinking he was you. But even then, he was so unstable that that was never going to work. And that's why when your great-uncle freed you, he also sent Romana and Gabriele away to a mental facility for a long while.

"I think only he, or whoever is still alive over there, can answer this, but I suspect the money ran out to keep them *both* there, and so Romana came out, and then Gabriele some time later. And with you now believing that Romana was your mum, they were trapped. To tell you the truth was to admit to something which could get them all imprisoned. Whereas you were now nearly an adult, and presumably they hoped that you would be living more independently anyway, so you'd be less vulnerable to Romana's psychotic episodes.

"But can you see that all of those enforced absences while you were growing up, meant that you didn't know your mum well enough to tell her apart from a sister who was damned near her double? Look at that photo. There's barely an inch difference in height.

"Well, if you'd had a growth spurt in between seeing her from one time to the next, you'd put that disorientation down to you being taller, not her, wouldn't you? And Romana's a touch slighter in build. But again, if you'd grown a couple of inches and filled out a bit, you might just put that down to your perspective shifting and her saying she'd been on a diet. A sixteen-year-old lad wouldn't question that! And earlier on, when you were around your real mum, you've said yourself you were more likely to be down in the village with the other kids than sitting around with her."

Oliver shook his head. "How damnably clever. How damnably bloody clever. But you're right, Fleur, it does all make sense of what was such a muddle."

"Did you find out anything useful from the solicitors?" Fleur wondered.

"Some," said Oliver cagily. "The old man – that's Ignatius Kingsford – certainly tied his son Aleister up in knots, and pretty unbreakably too. Aleister really had no options. He had to pay to keep the man who called himself Gabriele Angelo

Fitzpatrick at least serviced in the cottage by the hotel part of *The Rookery,* or he himself would be disinherited, and the whole property would be put into trust for Fitzpatrick. I don't think it was much consolation that in reality Ignatius didn't want Fitzpatrick to inherit, nor that Fitzpatrick would only have been allowed to live off the income of the estate until such time as Aleister, or his descendant, produced an heir who *was* willing to jump through Ignatius' hoops.

"And what hoops they were! He insisted that the heir be named after Fitzpatrick, though Lord alone knows why. That, I was told, came in in the last iteration of the will, and it might be that Ignatius wasn't entirely *compos mentis* at that point. Certainly, it was only a month or so before he died."

"Oh dear," Fleur groaned, and with a resigned glance to Angelo, showed him Annora's confession.

When he sat back after reading that, and Angelo had gone for another much-needed bottle of wine, he declared, "I think you're right, Fleur, in that Annora had suffered so much abuse at the hands of Ignatius, that if this were to come to light in a modern case, she would have good grounds for trying to claim self-defence, or at least diminished responsibility as a result of prolonged abuse. And that bit about the Fitzpatrick inheritance looks very much as if Ignatius knows what's happening to himself, and is doing this to spite her as much as anyone. What a vicious old bastard he was!"

Fleur thought for a moment and then asked, "Could that be why Claudia gave our Angelo here that name? That she knew that if he was to stand an earthly chance of inheriting her father's estate, then she had very little choice but to pick one of Fitzpatrick's names, but went for the one with the least associations with him?"

Angelo gave a sigh of relief. "Put like that it doesn't feel half as bad. Better by far than her thinking it was some great name to give me."

Fleur shook her head. "Oh I don't think for one second she thought it was just a lovely name based on a pack of lies someone had told her about it being a family name. I think she probably did it through gritted teeth. And I have a strong sense that it was her deliberately picking that son of Muldobrai's *second* name as the least objectionable choice."

She paused then looked to Oliver. "Is there any way we can check to see if this bloke really was Muldobrai's illegitimate son? I'm thinking that if he stayed in the area, if he was buried, could we ask for an exhumation for a DNA test? There's hardly going to be anyone alive to object to him being dug up is there? And if he was maybe brought up Orthodox Greek, he might have wanted a burial rather than a cremation?"

Oliver pulled out a note book and frantically scribbled down some notes. "That's a really good thought, Fleur. It might answer a lot of questions, not least about whether our Angelo has inherited the fruits of a tainted tree, so to speak. You can't benefit from a murder, but if we can prove that it was Romana and Gabriele who were planning to do that, then it might ease things if it ever comes to court about whether Angelo has the right to inherit *The Rookery* in his own right."

Fleur gasped. "Do you mean he might not? That if Gabriele or his mother died, that Angelo would be disinherited?"

Chapter 35

Oliver shrugged. "Sadly it might. I can't tell you exactly, because in all the years I've practiced, I've never had a case even remotely like this to refer back to. But at some point, I think we're going to have to go to court over this, if only to break old man Aleister's will over Gabriele, or his descendants, being the only ones able to inherit his property. We can't just transfer ownership and hope nobody will notice. And sadly, the one thing I have discovered is that technically, although Angelo has every right to run *The Rookery* and make whatever improvements he sees fit, at the end of the day he has still been denied actual ownership of the place. So unless Gabriele willingly signs it over to him – which in the light of what you've told me is about as likely as a cold day in Hell – then Angelo is not the rightful owner, and couldn't sell it even if he wanted to."

To Fleur that suddenly made sense of Angelo's caginess when she'd referred to the possibility of him selling up. If he'd been present at the will reading, then he already knew this. It must have been a bitter pill to swallow, and explained why she'd had the feeling that he wasn't telling her the full truth at times. It wasn't that he was a liar by inclination, but that his hands were so tied and yet had to keep up a pretence to the outside world.

"Did your grandfather make any conditions about not revealing Gabriele's infirmities to the outside world?" she thought to ask, but it was Oliver who nodded, and replied,

"Oh yes. By then, Aleister Kingsford was as bad as his father for tying everyone in legal knots. There are conditions of care written into the will, including protecting Gabriele from outside censure based on his mental infirmities. But the good thing, if you can call it that, is that this time Gabriele has unquestionably broken the law, and that will override any conditions in the will. That CCTV you put us on to, Fleur, is in the public domain. It won't matter a jot what Angelo says or wants. This is a case of assault being brought in a court of law, not just protecting Gabriele from scandal and gossip. We're into a whole other area now."

"Good!" Fleur said with feeling, but before they could talk more, Oliver's phone went and they heard him say,

"Yes, sergeant. …What? At neither?" and he got up and walked away to hear more clearly, a noisy party having just come into the bar area.

"God, what a mess," Angelo groaned, getting up and heading for the gents' loos.

Left on her own, Fleur realised that they'd never fully finished Annora's notebook, and picked it up from off the bench seat beside her. There was a delighted entry over Aleister and Angelina bringing baby Claudia over to visit, but then only a couple of days after their arrival a more frantic entry appeared.

We have been harbouring a viper! Gaby turns out to have been in the Monster's grip all along! Angelina's English is improved enough that she came to me while Aleister went away on business. She tells me that the reason she could not bear to live here was because of Gaby. The damned man tried to rape her before she was married, and then again when they came back to visit us after they were married. One day she was out in the grounds and he found her again – and this time he succeeded.

I can only think that Gabriel has been so terrified by Ignatius' threats of haunting him that, even though the Monster is gone, his dire influence has lingered for Gabriel. But that is not the worst of it. Angelina tells me in confidence that while she loves Aleister dearly, he is not what could be described as an attentive lover. Something to do with his experiences during the war, she believes. And so, the paper suddenly became blotted with tears, and the next words were written in deep scratches into the page, *she fears that baby Claudia is not his. This is why she could not bear to be here for the birth! She feared she would not be able to welcome this child into the world in a way that we would expect.*

Oh how we hugged and wept as she told me. She says that now, baby Claudia is as precious to her as any child could be. I told her that I understand, and of how I can love my children regardless of the monster their father was. A new bond has developed between us, and between her and

Morwenna, and we have promised to write regularly even if we cannot meet often.

With bated breath Fleur turned the page to the next entry, which was written with the same force and passion.

We have implored Aleister to send Gaby away, but he tells us that his hands are tied and that he cannot. Oh how I hate the Monster all over again! Even from the grave that foul excuse for a man is blighting our lives. I have asked Aleister to at least determine once and for all whether Gaby is truly my brother's son, for he owes his wife that much explanation of why he must stay, if not us.

There were a couple of other entries covering Aleister and Angelina's return to Italy, and the announcement of the pregnancy which would result in Romana's birth. Fleur didn't know whether to be glad or sad that Angelina was delighted that there could be no doubt that Aleister was the father this time.

Yet the final entry was in a different hand.

My fool of a brother has killed my poor mother, Morwenna wrote. *Gaby is indeed Uncle Muldobrai's son. Aleister has come back to England to tell us that he has had word from lawyers in Greece confirming it, and for some reason now proclaims Gaby as his dear cousin. But what caused dear Mamma's heart attack was walking in and discovering Aleister and Gaby giggling like school boys in his cottage with a Ouija board. Fools! Idiots! They thought it some joke to try and communicate with Ignatius.*

I heard Mamma's scream and ran in only to catch her in my arms as she fell by the door. I could still hear Gaby and

Aleister laughing upstairs, may they be damned forever. When the doctor came, he said that there was nothing anyone could have done, she barely had chance to gasp to me what they were doing and then she was gone. The only blessing is that she did not linger to suffer what has followed.

Mamma did her best to undo the harm done by the Monster, and everything deemed to be hers she has left to me alone so that I am not at Aleister's mercy. Her jewellery and other bits will not fetch much, but I am resolved to leave and go as far from this place as I can. There is nothing here for me now, especially since following that night, Aleister is much changed. Nobody but our travelling kin will believe me, but in these last weeks, I catch him looking at me sometimes, and though it is Aleister's face, it is the Monster's eyes looking out of it at me. I fear on that night that something happened to allow the Monster through, and that it was Mamma's passing, for she was the one who moved for the gypsies' curse, and maybe that was weakened by her death?

Worse, I believe it to be something older and fouler that lurked within the Monster that keeps coming back. How else to explain how the curse of Henrik keeps haunting us? That man was truly a demon incarnate, and only the strength of the women around him kept him from killing everyone in our family. And it has been the women who have had the strength to resist him. William Fitzpatrick was a fool, yet such a fool that the ghost of Henrik had poor clay to mould to his will. But when my monstrous father arrived in this house, already primed by his own foolish experiments in his youth, that evil spirit found a ready vessel to inhabit, and a bad man was made even worse. How such a haunting could linger for so long

I do not know, and in truth I do not wish to go back to our wandering kin and ask if they know either.

All I know is that I went down into the kitchen of the hotel that night, when it was all shut up. That was where my courageous great-great-grandmother Mezelly and her daughters first brewed their poison and endowed it with a witch's curse, if witches they truly were as well as Romany. *And so I sat there, holding their books in my hand, and I prayed with all my might for them to lend their strength to a curse of my own. My brother as I knew him is gone. In his place is something I refuse to acknowledge as kin to me.*

And now the next words were again gouged so deep into the page that they had roughed up the surface.

I curse my brother and the soul of my father. May they rot in Hell for the evil they have brought upon this family. May the Goddess and the spirits of the witches in my family watch over and preserve Angelina and her babies, and keep that vile thing that inhabits my brother far from them. I will soon be gone, far over the sea and away from his reach, for they are too close. And may Fitzpatrick feel the weight of the curse of understanding fully what his greed and stupidity have done. I curse you, Aleister, and I curse you, Gaby!

She was still sitting open-mouthed staring at the page when both Angelo and Oliver returned.

"They've given the police the slip," Oliver said angrily, as Angelo suddenly took in Fleur's expression and asked,

"What's wrong?"

With a shaky hand she turned the open book

around so that they could read the entries for themselves.

"Bloody hell!" Oliver breathed as he looked up. "Well, that makes sense of the other piece of news I got out of the solicitors in Cheltenham today. Only weeks after Annora died, Gaby Fitzpatrick – as she calls him – went to the top floor of *The Rookery* and hung himself from one of the beams."

"Jeez!" Angelo gasped, while Fleur was too shaken for words.

"Apparently he left a note saying that he regretted everything that he'd done, including a confession to the rape of Angelina." He turned to Angelo and said sympathetically, "I didn't say anything earlier, because I spent the entire drive over here wondering how on earth I could tell you that your grandfather wasn't your grandfather, and that your mother was born from an act of rape. But given what we've uncovered this afternoon, I'm now less sure whether that's the bad news you might think it is?"

Angelo grabbed his glass of wine and downed it in one. "Well at least the Monster isn't my grandfather, I suppose. That's one blessing."

"But then Annora isn't your grandmother either," Oliver said, glancing at the family tree Fleur had drawn to explain the various people to him.

However, Fleur now saw a brighter side to things. "Hold on, though. If you allow Gaby Fitzpatrick the leeway of being utterly taken over by first Ignatius, and then to some extent Aleister, he's not the fully evil creature that Ignatius was. Okay, an attempted rape and an actual one don't make him a nice guy, but he was being coerced, and we have to give him some leeway for that, if not a lot; especially given how many other people we know that Ignatius managed to befuddle into doing as he wanted. And if Gaby *is* Muldobrai's son, then Muldobrai – as the oldest son of William and Loretta Fitzpatrick – *ought* to have been their legitimate heir, had he not died in the war. And it means that through Muldobrai, you are still related to the family all the way back to the Petulengros. It's just that it's through a different line.

"William and Loretta are still your great-great-grandparents. It's just that you skip that wicked line that comes in with Ignatius marrying unfortunate Annora. But on top of that, it means that your mum, the real Claudia, was also not tainted by Ignatius' genes. But Romana was! And if this twisted version of Aleister who appeared after the episode with the Ouija board – and who knows, he might have been daft enough to go back and mess with that more times after that – then raped the young woman who really *was* his daughter, by which I mean Romana, then that still makes Gabriele a child born out of incest.

"Do you see the implications as Aleister would have? He *knew* that Claudia wasn't his! That's what this tangle about inheritance goes back to, Angelo. It's less about you not being his son than your mum not being his daughter!"

Angelo and Oliver looked at her, stunned.

"I have no idea how I'm going to unravel this mess legally," Oliver said with a groan, and the expression of one with a massive headache brewing. "But that mention of Gabriele brings us back to the news from the police. Claudia Vance – or rather Romana Kingsford, as we should now call her – and her son Gabriele, are both missing. They're not at the Cheltenham house, and they're not at *The Rookery*. The police have put out a 'be on the lookout' for them, and have taken the registration numbers of any of the cars they might be in. But can either of you think of anywhere they might have gone? Would they try to get back to Italy?"

Angelo could only shrug helplessly, but then given the shocks he'd had this afternoon, neither Fleur nor Oliver was expecting him to be thinking clearly. However, something did come to Fleur.

"Oliver, I presume that you've now seen some sort of documents relating to *The Rookery's* estate as it is nowadays?" He nodded. "Well, I'm wondering about the place where Gaby Fitzpatrick stayed – the place where that Ouija board session took place. It had to be somewhere accessible for Annora to have walked in on them – I hardly imagine her trekking right across the estate unless she had something really important to say to him.

"In the notebooks we hear about the cottage which the women first stayed in having to be sold when Ignatius died, and that was why they had to come to the coach house cottage right by the house. But if that was the case, which cottage did

Fitzpatrick live in until his death? It can't have been the one Annora and Morwenna shared previous to that, and it can't have been the coach house cottage if it was vacant for them to move in to – not to mention its proximity to the hotel and its guests. But it has to be somewhere else on the estate. Somewhere close enough for Fitzpatrick to walk across for his meals, and for the housekeepers to go across and sort out things like changing beds. So where is it?"

"The lodge!" Angelo yelped. "Bloody hell, it's the lodge! When I was sorting out the restoration, those sodding solicitors in Cheltenham wrote to me, and told me that there was some kind of notice on it that it could only be let out very short-term, not to a long-term tenant, and that it always had to be held available for other members of the family to use. Well nobody would want to live in that place as it is! It's damp and old-fashioned and needs completely gutting, but that was something I was going to get you to fight them over, Oliver, once I'd got the main house sorted."

"I'll drive!" Fleur volunteered. "I've had only one large glass of wine all afternoon, whereas neither of you two ought to get behind a wheel. If we get to the lodge, we can direct the police to it when they arrive."

"I'll stay and wait for the police," Oliver volunteered. "If I ring them now, some can go on ahead while others grab me from here, because I think we'll need a couple of cars – after all we're talking about catching a murderess in Romana, aren't we? We'll probably catch up with you two anyway if they put on the blues and twos. Take mine!" and he handed Fleur the keys to the car he'd hired in Worcester to go to Cheltenham with.

Running out to Oliver's car, Fleur slid in behind the wheel and moved the driver's seat forward to fit her. She'd never driven a car as big and powerful as this top of the range Ford, and at first, she was cautious pulling out onto the twisting road which followed the River Teme. But urgency lent her confidence, and soon she was pushing it as close to the speed limit as the bends in the road would allow.

It still felt like far too long before they slid to a halt outside the old lodge, set well off to the side of the new entrance to *The Rookery*.

"The hotel had the entrance moved away from that nasty blind bend that's up ahead," Angelo explained as they got out, leaving the hire-car where the police would see the flashing hazard lights, which they left on. "Too many guests even in the early days had near misses trying to pull out. I'm glad they did, because it would be a death trap with the speed of modern traffic on this road, but that's why the old lodge is so far from the gates."

In fact, it lay so far back behind a tangle of undergrowth that Fleur had never noticed it before. The original stone piers of what had once been an imposing gateway were smothered in ivy, and couple of large sliver birches had self-seeded in the intervening years and blocked the old gateway itself.

As they walked up what was meant to be the newer narrow side-drive just to the lodge, they saw that it had weeds and small bushes sprouting up through the tarmac. No wonder the police hadn't thought to look there. If you did know about the place, even so it would seem derelict, and that air of complete abandonment prompted Fleur and Angelo to look closer.

Where they stepped out onto what had once been the road end of the main drive, however, it was clear that a car had fairly recently been up and down here. And so moving cautiously, Angelo and Fleur crept around the building, avoiding the windows. By the back door they found black bin bags of refuse, indicating that somebody had spent some time here. Most looked as though they'd been outside for a while, but one's black plastic was still shiny, as if it had only just come off the roll. It immediately brought to Fleur's mind what Debbie the landlady had said to her about the local girls feeling as if someone was lurking in the undergrowth watching them this close to the road. They hadn't been wrong; it had just been Gabriele while he was here, not Angelo.

"Bugger! They were here," Angelo sighed, and reached out to turn the back door's knob.

"Be careful," Fleur urged him. "If they're in there, they won't be pleased to see you. We should wait for the police."

Yet Angelo shook his head. "I don't think they're here. Gabriele has no restraint. If he heard the car he'd have been out here ranting and raving at us." Inside they found newly washed mugs on the draining board, which were still damp. "Well I think there's no doubt that they hid from the police down here. They must have gone out the back way, because there's an old path that eventually loops around to here that follows the perimeter of the estate almost all the way around. But there's also a cut through from some of the ornamental gardens. From the house it just looks like it loops around those big rhododendron bushes you see as you drive in, and comes back out on the lawn, but right at the back there's a way through to the other path. I bet that's the way they've come and gone."

"Then let's not try and follow them that way," Fleur urged. "We don't want to cover their footsteps with ours if it'll help the police prove how they eluded them."

Getting back into the car, Fleur now drove with much more caution up to the main house. She parked out on the drive a way back from the courtyard, and turned the car around so that it was facing the right way to leave, but also so that any police cars could get past.

"I don't want us to get trapped in that courtyard," she told Angelo with feeling. "If they've both totally lost the plot, we don't try and deal with them, okay?"

She saw the sadness in his eyes as he nodded. This was going to be so hard for him, because even if he did now know that this woman was his deranged aunt, not his mother, she was still the person he'd been acting as a son towards for so many years now.

"Which house do you want to tackle first?" Angelo asked, and remembering that locked door in *The Rookery* itself, and the whole floor that she'd never seen, Fleur gestured to the *Dower House.*

"This one," she said firmly. "Fewer rooms, and you never know, we might find more evidence in the attic." But then as they let themselves in through the French window at the front, her memory was jogged of a conversation heard back here. "Angelo, when I first met you, I remember overhearing you saying to the woman I thought was Mrs Vance, 'Please tell me you haven't? …Oh no, please, not *again*!' What was that about? What was 'not again'?"

And Angelo went pale.

Chapter 36

Fleur got a nasty sinking feeling as she looked at the dread written across his face. "Come on, tell me. We've got this far, surely you know you can trust me."

Angelo went and grabbed a glass and ran it full of cold water, which he guzzled at speed, then splashed some cold water from the tap onto his face. Leaning with his elbows on the sink, he looked up at Fleur through dripping curls. "Gabriele. At first, I merely knew he wasn't quite right. You couldn't try to talk to him and not notice that. But it wasn't for a month or two until I realised just how bad he was. I asked Mum," and Fleur noticed how easy it was for him to fall back into calling Romana that, "to take him back to Italy. But she said she couldn't.

"At first I thought it was to do with him not having a passport …almost offered to let him use mine again if it would have got him away from me. But then I got it out of her. Gabriele is wanted by the police in Italy. He killed a girl a few years ago, only about six months before she brought him here, in a hit and run when he got hold of Mum's car keys."

He scrubbed a hand over his face. "They don't know it's Gabriele they're after. Mum covered it up for him by saying that her car had been stolen, and since he crashed and burned it not much further on, there was no DNA from the driver surviving for them to take as evidence.

"I was so shocked, Fleur. I didn't know what to do. I tried talking to the solicitors in Cheltenham – after all, they were the ones pushing me into this intolerable situation of being responsible for him. But they said that handing him over to the Italian police was breaking the terms of the will."

He saw her frown and hurriedly added. "It wasn't that I was that bothered about losing *The Rookery*. I've got money of my own. But Mum was absolutely beside herself. She was practically coming apart before my eyes. She kept on about how could I do that to her and to my own brother? Robbing her of her home – because if it went back into trust for Gabriele or his kids, then they would have to let it out, and she'd have nowhere to go. And breaking 'the law' – as she kept referring to the will as – by denying Gabriele somewhere 'safe' to live, as well."

Fleur gave a snort of disgust. "God, she really tied you in knots, didn't she?"

He nodded. "So I said that I'd get the coach house cottage done up first, and that he could stay there until the *Dower House* was finished. She said she'd watch over Gabriele, and like a fool, I believed her. But then the next thing I know she'd taken him to the Cheltenham house, telling me that I couldn't keep him cooped up in that tiny place after all the freedom he'd had in Italy."

"But he hadn't, had he?" Fleur sighed. "She told you a pack of lies there, because although you didn't know it back then, you yourself had been kept prisoner in the room she must have used for him."

Angelo shot upright. "Good God!" And once again Fleur thought that he'd been so entangled with dealing with the present that he'd had no chance to make the connections to the past.

"So did you let him stay there?" she asked.

Angelo sighed and gave a shrug. "He was already there, so there wasn't a lot I *could* do about it. I could hardly get the bailiffs in, could I? And to be fair, for the first six months she made sure that he took his medication – though now I've no idea whether that was a prescription from a proper doctor, or some street drugs which she could get her hands on, but which kept him doped up – and he seemed to be calm enough.

"But then Claire came to work there, and he just became obsessed with her. …Christ, Fleur, one day I went up into one of the rooms we never used – or so I thought – and there was this shrine to her! …Photos taken, as if he had been stalking her for weeks, and scrawled 'love' messages on bits of paper stuck up on the walls.

"I was horrified! That was the first time I went and talked to Oliver about it all. I'd used another partner in his firm for things like buying my London homes, but I asked for someone who knew about family law, and they put me on to him.

"I took all the photos and notes with me to show him, which was why they weren't on the walls when Claire's rape was investigated." He shook his head. "I had no idea I'd be destroying evidence which would have helped convict him. But once I'd taken them down, of course, any defence lawyer could say that I'd just made it up that they'd been in that room without my knowledge.

"Heaven knows, nobody else had ever seen it there, so it was my word alone. And I was in such a muddle because of the accusations being thrown straight at *me*. *I* knew I hadn't done it, but it was taking me all of my time to stay on the right side of the law in my own right, let alone Gabriele's."

"I can understand that," and she could. What a nightmare to find yourself in – accused of a violent assault and rape, and at the same time having to try and sort out a brother you had no emotional ties to, and who was out-and-out certifiable.

"I made Mum promise to take him to a cottage I rented for them out in the Welsh hills, far from anywhere. She didn't like it, but I pointed out that both the *Dower House* and *The Rookery* were swathed in scaffolding and builders, and that if Gabriele stayed in Cheltenham, then sooner or later some passer-by was bound to recognise him as the man who'd been at the house and then he would be locked up. I'm afraid I painted a very bleak picture of what Gabriele could expect in an English prison as a foreigner and a rapist, and she was so distraught and determined that he would retain some freedom, that she accepted it. They went off in a right huff, and I didn't see anything of them in person for nearly a year, a year in which everything stayed quiet.

"So once the builders were out of the *Dower House*, I let Mum pick the decorative scheme to placate her, and with the promise that she could come back as long as she'd allow Gabriele to go into a care home. I hoped that the rampant emotions had calmed down a bit, you see, and that the strain of looking after him had convinced her that she needed help. I set aside a huge chunk of money for his care, and told her to pick wherever she wanted. I wanted her to choose, because I knew that wherever I picked wouldn't be good enough, and at least that way, she couldn't blame me.

"The money went out of her bank account monthly to another bank, and so I presumed – stupidly – that he was somewhere safe. It was only when you came here that I got the suspicion that she'd been keeping him a lot closer than that. When I got back to London, I asked Oliver to look into just which account the money had been paid into, and it turned out to be just another account in Mum's …Oh crap!"

"What?"

"The bank account was in the name of Romana Kingsford. I thought then that Mum was just using that name to make sure that she got the money away from me. That she thought it was Grandfather's money paying for Gabriele, which he and she were entitled to in her mind. But it wasn't, it was my own money. Oliver said he'd try and sort it out, but that it would be difficult when she'd used all of what I presumed, up until today, were her sister's legal documents to set the account up. You know, birth certificate and stuff. Never in a million years did I think that they were actually her own."

Fleur had to feel sorry for him, especially as she now understood that he'd been in London a lot of the time, and not on hand to see the deceptions.

"When did the lock go on the door up to the second floor?" she asked, and saw Angelo's genuine surprise.

"What door, what lock?"

"You know that the main staircase doesn't go on up to the top floor of *The Rookery*?"

"Yes, you have to go to what were the servants' stairs, but which had previously been the main stairs of the first phase of the house. Quite a nice Jacobean oak staircase, actually, up on that floor. I wanted the builders to reveal it on the ground and first floors, but they said it would involve taking too many walls out now."

"Well, those servants' stairs now have a very stout door on them and a padlock. Have you never been up there?"

Angelo shook his head. "Not in a long while – probably a couple of years ago. I just left instructions with the builders as to what I wanted done, and told them to paint everything up there magnolia. After all, I was only ever intending to use them as spare bedrooms if I was entertaining there. And by then, what I knew of my grandfather meant that I never, ever intended to live in the house myself.

"*The Rookery* was going to be the show house for business functions only. An acquaintance of mine asked me if her could use the place to launch his new products, which was the event your colleagues saw being set up when they were here in the marquee. Quite separate to that, Mum was going to have the *Dower House* – I didn't ever expect her to have Gabriele there!"

From behind them there came a manic laugh. "Stupid boy! Did you really think I'd leave *mio prezioso ragazzo* behind? *Stupido imbecille*!"

"He's not a stupid imbecile, Romana!" Fleur snapped back at her, and at the sound of her real name, the woman reeled back from them. "Yes, you are Romana, aren't you! We worked it out. You've not been clever enough by far."

"*Vipera malvagia!*" Romana snarled back, making the gesture to ward off the Devil at Fleur. "It's all you! You should never have come here! *Mio povero ragazzo*. What did he see in you, that he should have wanted you here?"

And then the voice that they had all dreaded, came from beside her, and Gabriele stepped into view, saying, "You remind me of them! Of the witches who lived here!" and he laughed crazily. "I see them! I see them now, lining up behind you. You're one of them. One of those *women*," and he invested that word with such scorn that Fleur actually flinched, "who thought they could rob my father and grandfather of what was rightfully theirs. And they weren't the first, were they? Other men died so that they could prosper. *Vili streghe*! Well you'll die now, and all of them with you!"

"Christ! You're totally insane," Fleur heard Angelo's choked whisper from beside her, but she was too focused on Gabriele to do or say anything to him. For her, the temperature in the kitchen had plummented, and she didn't need to look at Gabriele's flickering eyes to know that he was seeing the shades of all the women who'd live here in a semi-circle behind her – she could feel them for herself. Grandma Rose was here now as well, standing on Fleur's right, and then a small grey-haired ghost who barely came up to her shoulder, stepped forward on her left.

'You'm had your chance, Henrik,' she felt rather than heard Mezelly say. *'You infected every man who came here after you in your evil desire for revenge upon us. Well it stops now. No more.'*

"Henrik? Who's Henrik?" Gabriele shrieked, and both Romana and Angelo looked at him aghast, having not heard what he and Fleur had. "I'm Gabriele!"

'You'm Henrik's shade, then you lurked 'round here until Ignatius, and then you went into Aleister, you evil swine. And from him you went into this poor twisted thing of a child when you raped this daughter of yours, leaving your taint behind you in Aleister.'

"He didn't rape her!" Gabriele screamed. "She loved him! She told me that! He told her she was special! His special girl, and nobody else was ever to touch her!"

He flung an accusing arm towards Fleur, screaming, "You fucking evil witch! Don't you throw accusations at her!" making Angelo step forward to come between him and Fleur with the riposte of,

"Don't you dare speak to her like that!"

"I'm not speaking to just her!" Gabriele yelled back. "I'm talking to all of *them*!" and his hand made a sweeping gesture to include all of the shades behind and beside Fleur, but which only they could see.

"You're mad! Completely and utterly bonkers," Angelo said with withering contempt. "You can't work out what's real and what's in your twisted mind." He turned to the woman he had been calling 'Mum' up until only a day ago. "And you. What did you do with my real mother? What did you do to your sister?"

Yet Romana didn't answer him, but instead jabbed an accusing finger at him, snarling, "*You* weren't supposed to live! *You* weren't supposed to escape from the cage they put *mio caro ragazzo*, my darling boy, in."

She turned and spat furiously. "Great-uncle Antonio and his vile bitch of a wife, Sophia! They were the ones who imprisoned my boy! They told me they'd take care of him. Liars! *Bastardi*, all of them! They said the money had run out. They said that if I didn't want him committed to a state asylum, then I must look after him as they said. That he must never be free to harm another girl ever again.

"What life was that for him? What right did they have to decide that he should never have another woman beneath him? He's a man with a man's needs!"

And she spun to jab the finger of blame at Fleur now. "You should have been grateful that he noticed you! Should have been glad to have a man like him wanting *you*! All this," and she waved her hand wildly to encompass the house and beyond, "could have been yours! It's *his*! Not this one's." And she flicked Angelo away as if he was nothing more than an old spider's web in her way.

Yet if she expected Fleur to bite at her taunts, she was much mistaken. "Grateful? I don't think so," she replied coldly. "I've already had experience of what it's like to be married to a man who thinks nothing of you."

"Marriage?" screamed Romana. "He wouldn't marry you! You're not good enough for *that*! You were only ever there to provide a spare heir in case he didn't find someone *better*! You're *una puttana frivola*!"

"Don't you dare call Fleur a filthy whore!" Angelo fought back with, and suddenly Romana seemed to realise that even if Angelo wouldn't defend himself, he would Fleur.

"Oh! So it's like that, is it?" she laughed nastily, and lunged forward to snatch at Fleur. "Take her, Gabriele! He won't hurt you while you've got her!"

As Gabriele lurched at Fleur, she easily broke Romana's grip, but as Angelo aimed a punch at Gabriele, Gabriele ducked sideways, caught a hold of his mother's arm, and spun her around. Even as both Fleur and Angelo tried to grab him, he was spinning again, and before they knew it, he was out of the French window and throwing Romana over his shoulder.

"I've got her, Mamma!" he yelled, breaking into a run with the screaming Romana thrashing in his grip, and yet unable to free herself. "We've got her! We've got our sacrifice at last! Come on!"

Chapter 37

Angelo and Fleur were almost tripping over one another trying to follow, but Gabriele's last words stopped them in their tracks.

"Did he just say 'sacrifice'?" Angelo gasped in horror.

Fleur could only nod in mute horror, then they were both tearing out and around into the courtyard. Ahead of them, Gabriele had already made it to the kitchen door, and to their growing panic, they heard him slam the door and the bolt being shot across too.

"I've got you now!" they heard his fading voice crowing as he headed deeper inside. "You can't get away from me now."

And Romana's desperate cries of, "It's me! Your mamma! Put me down! Gabriele, stop it! Put me down!"

At the kitchen door, Angelo tried putting his shoulder to it, but it was no use. The door was too stout and the lock too good. "Christ, I'm locked out by my own security," Angelo groaned.

"And he's totally lost it," Fleur said sadly. "Dear God, if he can't even recognise his own mother anymore, there's going to be no reasoning with him." She didn't want to add that she didn't give much for Romana's chances of surviving whatever the madman had planned for her, and right now it was little consolation that it was Romana in there and not her. Nobody deserved this.

They walked back out to the front lawn, hoping to catch a glimpse or hear something. For a few moments there was nothing, and then Angelo grabbed Fleur's arm, pointing up to the top floor. "There they are!"

Gabriele had obviously put Romana down, and now she was beating on the window, calling for help. Yet the secondary double glazing that Angelo had had put in up there was muffling her.

"Oh God!" Angelo moaned. "I couldn't have ordinary double glazing put in because of the Grade II listing, so I asked for secondary, but for windows that could be properly locked in a way that the original ones can't. She's trapped! Oliver said that the police went through and made sure that every window and door was fully locked to stop Gabriele getting in. He must have had a key at least to the kitchen door, but without the other keys, she can't open the inner windows!"

Fleur frowned. "I thought secondary glazing had to be removable in places like this?"

"It is! But there's one hell of a difference between having it taken out by professionals, and my mu… Romana being able to lift it out. Taken out properly, there'll hardly be a mark to say that it was ever there, but it's heavy when it's in windows as big as these, and if only for safety's sake they have to be properly fixed in. You can't have a big pane of glass like that tipping out on someone."

He sounded stressed and a bit annoyed at having to explain this even as he was going around to the French windows and trying to rattle them loose.

"I'm sorry, Angelo, I was only wondering if there was anything we could shout to her to do that would help her."

He lifted his foot and kicked the French window door hard, but it didn't move at all.

"What have I done?" he moaned in a voice choked with tears. "I've killed her, that's what I've done."

"Angelo Vance, you stop that right now!" Fleur said sharply. "*You've* done nothing!" She went up to him and pulled him around by both arms so that he was facing her. "Now you listen to me! That's Romana Kingsford in there. Whatever good memories you have of your mum as a child, that *is not* the woman that's in there. That's her *murderer*!

"What's more, she's brought all of this down on herself. *You* didn't do this, *she* did. If she'd done as you asked and found a secure unit for Gabriele, he'd be safe and sound being looked after by professionals, who might just have helped him. He wouldn't be running wild out here. And you certainly gave her enough money to pick a top institution, didn't you?"

Angelo nodded miserably, making Fleur pull him in closer so that she could hug him. "I know this is so bloody hard for you. Your memories must be all over the place right now, and I'm sure you've got some long therapy sessions ahead of you to sort your feelings out. But the one thing you have *got* to get your head around right now is that this *isn't* your fault."

"Thank you," he said thickly, his face buried in her hair, and she felt his hold on her tighten.

Then both of them smelled it at the same time.

"What's that?" Fleur asked, as Angelo said,

"Petrol! …Oh no! No, no, *no*!" and together they ran back enough to be able to see the other floors' windows. On this side there wasn't much of the top floor visible, only one large window, but even in that they saw the start of flickers of orange starting to be reflected in the glass.

Pulling out her phone, Fleur dialled 999 and asked for the fire service. The sooner they got called, the sooner they might get here before the fire took too much of hold to save anyone. What she didn't want to say to Angelo was that the response time to get out here wasn't likely to be good. Rural fire services tended to be run by volunteer fire fighters, and that meant that they had to get to the station before they could even roll out.

By the time she'd given them all of the information, Angelo had gone back around to the front of the house and was standing back on the drive, staring up at the top windows, his hands clasped to his mouth in horror. As Fleur joined him and looked up, she saw Romana run into the smaller front bedroom and hammer on that window too. Then at the main front window up there, they saw Gabriele dance past, laughing maniacally and waving his arms around. He was clearly shouting something, but whatever it was was indistinguishable from below.

As Angelo ran to the hire car and grabbed the tyre wrench from the boot, then ran back to the front door and began hammering at one of the side panes of glass nearest to where the latch was on the inside, Fleur felt someone beside her.

'You must not let Angelo be near him when he dies,' Grandma Rose said sadly. *'If it can, the thing that's inside of Gabriele will transfer itself to Angelo. There's enough of a blood connection between them for that to happen.'*

"Does he have to die?" Fleur asked softly, glad that Angelo was so busy beating the glass that he wasn't noticing her seeming to talk to thin air.

'I'm afraid he does. Gabriele embraced the darkness – the evil entity – too fully to ever be free of it. As long as he lives, he's a danger to Angelo and any others of his family he comes near. Even if he was put into a secure hospital, if the nurses called the family in because he was dying, that thing would still slide from him to whoever was nearest. And besides, Gabriele has never been fully sane, not even as a small child. Angelo doesn't know this, but the cruelty Gabriele inflicted on animals when he was barely a toddler marked him as severely warped. Some people get like that because of what

they have inflicted on them, but a rare few seem to have it built into their very DNA.'

"Then can we save Romana? Poor Angelo has such mixed emotions over her."

Yet Grandma Rose shook her ghostly head. '*I am not party to all that she has done, but her family will not allow it. They tell me that despite her mother's best efforts that she was drawn to Aleister and what he knew.*

Claudia wouldn't have him near her, but Romana chose a darker path for herself. At first she was very much the abused child, but there came a point when she was so jealous of Claudia having Jacko, who loved her for who she was, whereas the one person who could make her feel special was her father and his dreadful rituals. She knew it wasn't real love, but she chose to keep returning to him anyway, and that was how Gabriele came to be born. She could have left like Claudia did, but she thought staying gave her power over her family. Sadly, the time has now come for her to answer to a higher authority than us for what she has done.'

Fleur didn't like the sound of that, and then she saw what Angelo couldn't. Within the rising smoke up on the top floor there was something else moving. Female shapes were swirling around Romana, driving her back from the window. In the distance she suddenly heard faint echoes of sirens, but they sounded like police cars, not fire engines, and the police would be no more able to get in than they could. They might get the doors open, but the smoke was starting to billow down into the first-floor bedrooms now. There was no way that anyone was getting to the top floor and Romana without breathing apparatus.

Then the first flames licked out through the tiles on the roof in the far corner, where it swept down to first floor level, with only a sloping attic space beneath not rooms. As the air got sucked in through the break in the tiles, it fed the flames, and suddenly there was a *whoosh* as the fire intensified. But above the main stairwell, and providing light down through the glass floor that Fleur had seen on her first visit, there was an area of flat, glazed roof, and suddenly Gabriele appeared up there.

Fleur's scream of shock brought Angelo back to her side, and together in horror they watched him capering about up there.

"It's mine! All mine!" they heard him yelling hysterically. "Baphomet be praised forever! Nobody's taking it from me now! …You sharn't have it! …Hahaha! Fools! Witches! …You can't stop me now!"

"Who the hell is he shouting at?" Angelo demanded despairingly, though Fleur could see them.

And then they saw her. Crawling along the flat roof towards the edge was Romana. The fake fur on the coat she had been wearing was already smouldering with the heat, wreathing her in tendrils of smoke, and they saw her momentarily double over with a wracking cough. But then she hauled herself back up onto her hands and knees and move another few feet towards the sloping roof.

"No!" Angelo screamed. "Mum! Stay there! The

fire engine's on its way! They'll get you down! …No, Mum! Stop! …You're right by the edge! …Mum, *please* stop! *Stop!*"

In the instant that they saw Romana topple over onto the sloping roof and begin to tumble down it, Fleur grabbed Angelo's arm and hauled at him with all of her might. As he overbalanced and stumbled towards Fleur, he missed seeing Romana go over the edge, and though Fleur saw that, Angelo then mercifully blocked her view of the spot where Romana hit the ground.

"No! Don't go to her," Fleur said, pulling him to her and holding him tight. "She couldn't possibly have survived that fall. You don't need to see her like that. Say your goodbyes when the undertakers have done their best. Remember her as she was. You don't need to see this, Angelo, you really don't."

Only moments later two police cars came screeching to a halt beside them and officers piled out along with Oliver, who came straight to Fleur and Angelo.

"Bloody hell, what happened?" he asked, staring aghast at the flames now rising through the roof of *The Rookery* in multiple places.

"Gabriele set fire to it," Fleur said shakily. "Something about some ritual, though God knows what." She hugged Angelo a bit tighter as she added. "Romana fell off the roof. She's on the ground around to the left on the patio."

"Is she dead?"

"Oliver, nobody could survive that fall, and

anyway, by then her lungs must have been full of smoke. If the fall didn't kill her, the fire did."

She saw him take in Angelo's distraught state and came to take his arm. "Come on. Let's go and sit in my car. You don't need to deal with this right now." Fleur handed him the keys back, and together they got Angelo to the car and sat him down in the back.

It took nearly twenty minutes before the fire engines came roaring up the drive, and by then the whole of *The Rookery* was alight. Fleur took it upon herself to go with Oliver and bring the police up to speed on what had happened, and so once they recognised that the two suspects had to be dead, even if they only had one body so far, there was no point in all of them staying when nobody could get into the building, and one car drove off.

At some stage the leading fireman came over and said that they would be able to save the *Dower House* and the stables, but that there was little hope for the rest of the place. A detective turned up to take initial statements about Romana's death, but after he'd gone to look at the body and come back looking pale and shaken, Oliver was allowed to drive Fleur and Angelo back to *The Talbot*. A doctor was called for Angelo, and he was given a strong sedative which had him asleep in no time.

For a while Fleur sat by his bedside, holding his hand, but as the evening wore on, Oliver came and fetched her downstairs to have something to eat.

"Angelo won't wake up until the morning," he

said kindly, "and you've had as much of a stressful day as he has. You need to eat something, Fleur. You won't be able to help him if you're passing out on him for lack of food before breakfast."

She couldn't face anything meaty, but there was a lovely homemade quiche on the menu, and it wasn't until it arrived and she started nibbling at it that she realised that she was starving. To her own amazement she polished off every crumb, and then felt substantially better afterwards.

"Thank you for making me come and have that," she said gratefully to Oliver, who had also bought a bottle of nice wine for them to share.

"My pleasure," he replied with a smile, then became more serious. "We're going to have to keep a close eye on Angelo, you know. I know he's just my client, but we've become pretty good friends in the last couple of years. I feel so bloody sorry for him. What a messed-up childhood he had. I've never been so grateful for my ordinary mum and dad since I've heard about his family."

Fleur took another sip of her wine and said, "I know just what you mean. My family was a bit messed up, but only in the normal way of things. At the last, when we could see Romana getting closer and closer to the edge of the roof, he just went back to calling her 'mum'. The changes have come too recently for him to have got his head around the fact that she wasn't his mum and for him to think otherwise in that horribly stressful moment. God, what a couple of days it's been for him," and her thoughts went back to that tarot reading and the image of the crumbling Tower.

Angelo's world had changed in shockingly dramatic fashion, with everything he knew falling apart around him. And yet she could see that in this cauterising set of domino events, his life had actually changed for the better. At some point in the future, he would be able to come clean about the late cousin who had stolen his identity and put that part of his life straight.

The terms of his grandfather's will would no longer hang over him like some cursed sword of Damocles, for not only would Oliver be able to break that now, there was also nobody left to stand in the way of Angelo having everything that was due to him. Not that he would want it, Fleur suspected, but with the right gentle nudging, he might be persuaded to turn it to good use. He would never want to live in the *Dower House*, let alone any resurrected version of *The Rookery*, but he might feel that a form of reparation might be to turn it into something which could benefit the village.

"I think you and I should stay in close contact," Oliver was saying. "Without you I would have still been wading through this mess for years to come. You found the right bits of information just at the right time, and I think you care about what happens to Angelo?"

Fleur blushed but had to admit that she did. Whether anything long-term would come out of that, or they would simply stay good friends remained to be seen, but she had the feeling that Angelo was going to be in her life for a long time.

In the morning Fleur chose to return to London with Angelo and Oliver, and to stay with Angelo. They collected a large suitcase of clothes for her from her flat and by the evening she was settled into his spare room. They both skirted around any questions of how long this would go on for, with Angelo genuinely glad that she was there, and Fleur knowing that she would have been worried sick for him if she'd thought he was going to be there on his own.

They had to return to Worcester several times over the following weeks to answer questions by the police. Neither was a suspect in any way, but there was a lot of background information which needed to be passed on. In this they were lucky in that it was the big detective who Fleur had seen at work who led the case. DI Scathlock was all sympathy and understanding, and more than happy to walk around the corner from the central station to speak to them at Fleur's flat.

So by his second visit, Fleur felt able to ask him something which had been worrying her.

"Have you managed to unravel whether Romana was wholly her father's victim, or was she willingly going along with him?" she asked Scathlock as Angelo left them to go and top up their coffees.

Scathlock leaned back in his seat and gave a nod. "I can see why you'd be worried. Obviously we can't interview Romana now, but what I'll say is this: if we were, we'd be treating her as a vulnerable adult. And that's because where someone has been abused for a long time, going back into childhood, they are almost programmed to do what pleases their abuser."

"But she hardly ever met him," Angelo said, coming in at the tail end of what he was saying.

"Ah, that's more tangled than you thought," Scathlock said, and Fleur could see that he was trying to put this gently to Angelo. "You see we've dug deeper into who came into the country and when, and it's clear that when his daughters were young children, he went to Italy quite a lot.

"Now I can't give you absolute answers on this, but my assumption would be that that was when the abuse presumably started, and it probably started with your real mum, Claudia. But then when Romana reached an age when she triggered his interests, for want of a better word, he abused her too. As to why Claudia refused to go near him, and Romana was drawn to him …all I can say is that I've known families of abused kids down the years, and no two ever react the same. But your mum and aunt do fall within a recognisable spectrum of reactions – some sadly do go on to become abusers themselves, she's not unique in that."

"That's weirdly reassuring," Angelo said. "You know, that Romana wasn't a total freak."

"And it probably explains why your mum was a bit of a wild child when she came to school over here," Fleur added sympathetically. "It's just that she got it out of her system then, and then went on to meet your dad and be happy with him."

"Ah," Scathlock said pointedly. "Erm… that's not quite all. Yes, Claudia did get booted out of a couple of schools for being the wild girl. But, while we were filling in her background in Birmingham with your dad, we found an anomaly. Possibly because she couldn't stand being close to her father – even the distance between Cheltenham and *The Rookery* – she ran away when she was coming up fifteen.

"You see we traced her by going backwards from when we knew she was with your dad, and we found her at a hostel for homeless kids in the city and her subsequent attendance at a local college up there until she turned sixteen. At that stage, she was calling herself Claudia Montefiore – a name she used right up until she had to sign her marriage certificate, I might add – and eventually she gave her mum's address in Italy, but it's on record that she was adamant that she didn't want to go back there. Something I think we might now put down to her not wanting to be near her sister.

"Yet at the same time, we have her going to a new school down near Cheltenham. And that's when the really appalling behaviour kicks in."

"Bloody hell!" Angelo gasped. "Grandfather brought Romana over and passed her off as Claudia!"

"Yes, we think he did. Possibly so that he didn't

have to account for where she had been at school previously, because she was so bad that she has records with the local authority, and they say that she was barely literate! Whereas the real Claudia, at previous schools, was quite an academic high-flyer. So we're thinking that Romana was possibly so disruptive that she hardly went to school in Italy beyond her first year or two."

"Oh, my God!" Fleur groaned. "Of course! *That's* how she knew there were boxes of grimoires in the attic at the *Dower House*! The wrappings weren't disturbed enough for her an Gabriele to have gone through them all, and that started to bug me when I was looking at them. But of course, then we got into all the drama, and I didn't think about it for a while.

"It makes sense of things, though. Even in the middle of everything, it kept nudging me to wonder why she was so obsessed with the grimoires. But if her father had told her about them, of course she would know that there were boxes full of them, even if she'd never been let into the locked attic to see them for herself. And if she was as uneducated as you think – and I'd agree with you on that – then even though she was far from stupid, she may well have been sucked into Aleister's fantasies that they contained magical powers, or the ability to control people. And *that*, I think, would have really appealed to someone who had had so little control over what happened in her life."

"But why did she hate my mum enough to want

to kill her?" Angelo asked, looking pleadingly at Fleur and Scathlock. "I mean, I'm assuming from what I know now that mum's death wasn't natural."

"I think you're right, and I would guess jealousy," Scathlock said sadly. "And I think that Fleur's right. Romana got brought over here, and once in her father's company, mistook his warped attention for love – something again which, sadly, I've seen before. She was probably worried that if Claudia came back, then she would have to share Aleister with her. But then Claudia did something worse, she went and found a man who loved only her – Jacko Vance. And however illogical it might seem to us, with her mind already in such a state, that probably felt like the final straw.

"Did she think that if she had a child by Aleister, then that would ensure she was always one step higher in his affections than your mother. You can't dismiss how outraged she might have felt when your mum had you, and Aleister finally had a male heir. It might have been enough for her to submit to her father's sexual attentions willingly, even if the reality was so dreadful that she fled to Italy with her sister and you after the event."

All those questions, however, continued to plague Angleo.

A couple of months went by with Angelo going back to see his therapist as a matter of some urgency, with Fleur gradually finding her way around the London neighbourhood, since she was technically suspended from her job pending an enquiry. As the third month came around, though, Fleur thought it was about time that they addressed the loose threads still left. She wanted Angelo to deal with this mess now, not be having to cope with bits and pieces coming out of the woodwork years from now. He needed to heal properly this time, though she wasn't foolish enough not to think he wouldn't have some terrible mental scars.

"Ask your therapist what he thinks," she said encouragingly on the morning of Angelo's next appointment, "but I think you need to get in touch with the Italians. There must be somebody left over there who knew about Romana. She only brought Gabriele over here a handful of years ago, so before she left, there has to have been somebody living at the *castello* who had some idea of what had happened. Go talk to Vince," his therapist, "and see what he advises."

Vince, it seemed, was all in favour of tying up the loose ends, and if possible, in person.

"Vince says that I'll feel better about it if I can see their faces and know whether they're lying about what they're telling me," Angelo said as he packed a travel bag. "Please come with me Fleur, I need your insight."

And so having gone back to Worcester to get her passport, Fleur found herself on a flight from London to Pisa, and then being chauffeured to the family *castello* in the Tuscan countryside.

Chapter 38

To Fleur's amazement, both Great-uncle Antonio and Great-aunt Sophia were still alive, although very old and very frail. However, it was their son, Giuseppe – Claudia and Romana's cousin – who ran the vineyards and estate nowadays, and with his daughter, Ilaria, and her husband Matteo in their turn gradually taking over from him. As soon as they knew why Angelo had come, Giuseppe sent Ilaria and Matteo away under the pretext of it being old family stuff which they couldn't help with.

"I do not want them to know anything about this English business," he said firmly and with some distaste, as if it was something which Angelo had brought down upon them. "If the law gets involved, I want them to be able to swear that they knew nothing of it, and to be obviously telling the truth."

Fleur thought that was a bit rich, given that it was this side of the family who had failed to get Gabriele committed in the first place, but also realised that it wasn't her place to comment, however irritating Giuseppe's attitude was. However, for the two old people, there seemed to be huge relief that they could finally tell the truth. As they sat down in the beautiful central courtyard of the *castello*, with glasses of their own wine, and Italian coffee wafting its scent around, Fleur thought how incongruous it was that they should be in such a glorious setting talking about something so dark.

"You have to understand," Antonio began in his quavering voice, as dusty as autumn leaves these days, "that we never, ever intended for things to get as out of hand as they did."

Fleur immediately reassured him with, "Nobody is here to shove blame onto anyone. Angelo just needs to know the truth so that he can put this all behind him," and she saw Sophia nodding sympathetically. *Yes*, Fleur thought, *you get it. How this has been such a dreadful trial for him.* She wasn't sure that Giuseppe had any such empathy, and felt a quiet satisfaction knowing that even he was in for some dreadful revelations.

"We knew that something was wrong with Romana right from the early days," Antonio continued. "She was such a strange little girl. Nothing like Claudia. Claudia had friends down in the village. Romana only ever went to someone's house once and was never invited again. We didn't hear why at the time, but my poor sister was clearly becoming more and more distraught. Finally, she took us into her confidence, asking us what on earth she should do about Romana. It turned out that when she'd gone to other children's homes, family pets had suddenly become desperately ill, some even dying, and then one toddler became very sick – bad enough to be hospitalised. At that point, my poor sister realised that she needed to keep Romana away from the world, that she was very wrong somehow."

"And that would have been the mid-sixties," Fleur said gently, glad that she'd done some rapid brushing up on her Italian before coming out here, and could therefore follow what was being said for the most part. "So for all of the love and peace and freedom of the era being bandied about, child psychology was still woefully inadequate to deal with someone like her. I'm guessing that a lot of the blame would have been thrown Angelina's way for being a bad mother?"

Sophia sighed with relief. "You see it! Blessed Madonna, you understand."

"She does," Angelo replied, "and so do I."

With more confidence, Antonio continued, "We put it about that Romana was mentally disabled, and thankfully nobody questioned that we were therefore keeping her on the estate, and that Angelina was schooling her at home. We made out that she would never keep up with a normal class of children. Sadly that was far from true. Claudia was a bright child, but Romana sucked up what she wanted to learn like a sponge, but if she wasn't interested, then nothing you could do would persuade her to sit down and learn."

Sophia was nodding in agreement. "I've never known such a child for being wilful and stubborn at such an early age," she confessed. "She had been here before, no doubt about that," and remembering what her grandmother's ghost had told her about spiritual transference, Fleur shivered, thinking of Starlina who couldn't make a break from Ignatius.

But Sophia noticed. "You know," she said pointedly to Fleur. "You understand. She wasn't just an old soul. There was something wicked within that child. We got the local priest in to pray over her, and you'd have thought he was pouring boiling water over her instead of saying prayers for her soul. He told us to put her far away from us for our own sakes. I wish we had listened."

Antonio nodded. "We do. Everyone in this house suffered because of Romana. While she was a child, we managed to persuade her mother to keep her closeted on the estate, away from anyone's view, but that got harder as she got older. Even visits from her father didn't help. In fact, they seemed to make her worse."

Fleur and Angelo exchanged a covert glance at that. No point in upsetting these two old people even more by telling them what they suspected, but it was all adding up.

"And she hated Claudia with a passion," Antonio was continuing. "Claudia got to go out, she didn't. Claudia had friends, she didn't. But then as they reached their teens, Romana's hatred of Claudia rose to a whole new level, and in the end, Angelina thought it best to send Claudia back to England to the father who'd virtually become estranged, for her own safety."

"Can I ask something?" Fleur interjected. "I heard from the woman I thought was Claudia that her father was very cruel to her. That she was something of a wild child, and that he was very heavy-handed in his attempts to control her. Was that true? Was that really *Claudia's* experience of him? Or did Romana ever visit England, and Aleister finally realise what his wife had been coping with on her own for all those years."

There was a sob from Sophia, who had to be given a brandy to restore her as she almost fainted with relief at finally being understood.

"You hold onto this lady," Antonio told Angelo firmly, as he poured Fleur another coffee. "She is one in a million!"

Angelo smiled. "I've worked that out already, thank you, Uncle. And yes, she is!"

"So what happened?" Fleur asked when they were all calmer again, but taking a quiet pleasure in seeing how disconcerted Giuseppe was with these revelations. Clearly it had been all too easy for him to shove all the blame onto the English family when he'd known so little of what had gone on.

Antonio sighed and shook his head despairingly. "She was so exhausted – my sister Angelina I mean. So many years of watching Romana around the clock was taking its toll. And her husband had turned out to be not the man she thought she was marrying. Oh, he wasn't cruel to her. But he wasn't loving, either. When he met her during the war, he was a very different man, she told us."

"I don't know if this helps you or not," Fleur said gently, "but I found some old notebooks from other members of the Kingsford family. Wise women, they would have been called in the old days, or even witches." She used the Italian word for 'witch', *stregha,* and saw the immediate understanding on their faces.

"Aleister's mother and sister say in them that around the time Romana was born, he attempted to contact his father in the beyond. A very evil man," and she saw them start and then understanding dawning. They were much more open to grasping the way that Aleister had tapped into the evil which had consumed his father, having been brought up with the acceptance of the mysteries of the Catholic Church. "I'm not surprised the exorcism didn't work on Romana," she added. "I fear that the evil was too deeply imbedded."

"It was," Antonio said sadly. "In the end I wrote to Aleister and told him that he must step up and become a proper father to his daughters for his wife's sake." There was another despairing shake of his head. "I think he saw it as some failing on Angelina's part, not on his. He soon felt differently when he had to deal with his younger daughter."

"Poor Claudia," Sophia added. "It was too easy for Romana to pretend to be her to get out of trouble."

"Ah! The party where the drug taking took place!" Fleur guessed.

"Exactly," Antonio sighed. "Claudia herself was nowhere near the place. She had already taken herself off to secretarial college up in Birmingham, and was living up there, albeit at only sixteen years' old. That was where she got spotted and went into modelling, giving her enough money to be fully independent. She'd already had enough of Aleister and his strange ideas. She was determined to get as far away from him and her sister as possible. She was repulsed by his ideas, whereas she told us that Romana lapped them up even in the short time she was around him."

Sophia sniffed into a tissue. "Claudia was so happy when she met your father, Angelo. So glad to have met a normal man who loved her for who she was. Whereas her father was beside himself over who she had chosen. And Romana was so jealous it was terrifying. To this day we are not sure whether she knew enough to damage the brakes on his car. She was certainly in England at the time."

"Bloody hell!" Angelo gulped. This was a new twist nobody had expected.

"I am so sorry, Angelo," his great-uncle Antonio said regretfully. "I wish we could have been honest with you. But by the time we began to suspect what Romana had done, Claudia had already fled from your grandfather back here, though we wished Romana hadn't come too, even though we soon found out she was pregnant. We became fearful of what Romana might do to her sister if we ever raised doubts about your father's death, you see. And since nothing we could do would bring him back, we let matters lie.

"I must apologise to you for that now. If we'd had any inkling of what would come in the future, we might have acted differently. As it was, Angelina decided that she must once more shoulder the burden of her younger daughter, if only for the sake of her older one. Romana was kept well away from you when you were a baby, and then of course we swiftly discovered that Romana was pregnant. At first, we thought that since she had been so promiscuous in England, that it was the child of some young boy she had had a brief moment with. Please believe me that it took years before we understood why she kept giving us those sly smiles when we asked about Gabriele's father."

"I do," Angelo answered with a sigh. "She could be so damned convincing when she wanted to be, couldn't she? …And in truth, you all did a very good job of keeping her and Gabriele away from me when I was a child. I'm still very grateful for that. I dread to think what my childhood would have been like if I'd had him around for all of it."

His words drew thin smiles from his great-aunt and –uncle.

However, Fleur felt compelled to ask, "What changed? Something clearly did around the time that the girls' mother Angelina died."

The smiles vanished to be replaced with looks of bleak despair.

"Claudia tried to warn us," Antonio said, as

Sophia held onto his hand for reassurance now. "She said that her sister was getting more and more resentful of the way their mother was keeping her and Gabriele confined." He stopped and seemed to struggle to get the next bit out. "Claudia said that Romana had threatened to kill their mother if she didn't allow her and Gabriele to live as normal people.

"...I'm so terribly sorry, Angelo. We didn't really believe her. We were used to Romana's histrionics, you see. A lot of temper, and throwing things, but nothing more than that. ...It was only when Angelina was found at the foot of the stairs in her house, with her neck broken, that we realised that the threat was real."

"Did nobody here question her death?" Angelo asked, aghast.

Sophia dabbed at her eyes with a lace handkerchief but managed to answer, "No they didn't. It was an old cottage. The stairs were very steep. And Angelina had been complaining about feeling dizzy of late."

"Bloody hell!" Fleur gasped in English. "The witches' brew! Did Romana know about that from her father? And did she use it on her mother?"

The Italians were looking at her puzzled, but by the way Angelo went white they guessed that Fleur had made another connection. It took a few minutes for Angelo to explain what they had found in the old grimoires and notebooks, and why it had been used in the distant past, but once he was done, the two elderly Italians were nodding along with what Fleur had guessed.

"I think you are right," Antonio said grimly. "Romana established such a strong bond with Aleister that it carried on even after she was far away from him. Every so often a letter would appear from England for Romana – never for Claudia or Angelina, I may add. Of course, being written in English we had no idea what was said in them…"

"…but I know a recipe when I see one," Great-aunt Sophia said, openly weeping now, "and I saw more than one. I think you are right, Fleur. She must have asked her father for a way to get rid of her mother, and he – evil man that he was – supplied it for her. Sadly, those letters no longer survive to prove it, but I'm sure that you are right."

It was scant satisfaction to Fleur that Giuseppe had become paler and paler through this revelation. *Yes,* she thought grimly, *you get it now. The English family suffered every bit as much as you. People died there as well as over here.*

And that also explained something she had worried over, which was how Romana could have known the details of the recipes if she had never handled the grimoires until around the time that she herself had gone to catalogue them. That not knowing what exactly was inside them had been genuine – which was why she had been so taken in by her. Romana hadn't needed to open the grimoires to get the recipes, because Aleister had copied them out for her.

Indeed, Fleur had a suspicion that, given how long some of those parcels had been bundled up, Aleister himself might not have looked at all of the grimoires, but had been given the salient recipes by the dreadful Ignatius. Nor did she doubt that Ignatius would have given them to Aleister in case he needed to use them to secure that the 'right' heir, in his eyes, got to inherit. By the time of his death, Aleister had become so warped it was possible that he had left the grim things to Romana, because who at the solicitors would have seen anything suspicious in being asked to hand on what were presumed to be just a bundle of family letters?

Angelo was asking his great-uncle in horrified tones, "Are you seriously telling me that Romana killed her own mother?"

Antonio gave the very Italian shrug. "We couldn't prove it. But did we think it? Yes, we did! And the worst of it was, that your dear mother had tried to warn us that it was going to happen, and we didn't believe her." Antonio choked up now. "Her death will be on my conscience until the day I die. …Claudia said that Romana would never forgive her for warning us, and she didn't!" He gave a sobbing, deep breath. "Only when Claudia was found out in the vineyards with a needle in her veins did we realise…" he choked up again, and this time couldn't continue.

But it was Giuseppe's horrified exclamation of, "Papa?" that told Fleur just how well the family had covered Romana's tracks.

"Papa… What have you done?" Giuseppe demanded, though with little force and a lot of shock.

Antonio emerged from the handkerchief he had resorted to and said, "What had to be done, my son. What had to be done. Who would have believed us, at that point, that we had known nothing of my sister's death? If we pointed the finger at Romana over Claudia, then how could we have answered any questions about my own sister? Because someone would surely have wondered about *two* deaths in quick succession once we'd said we had a murderer in the family.

"Do you see? Romana had us in a cleft stick. If we told the authorities what we suspected she'd done, then they would have asked an awful lot more questions. And at some point, *somebody* would have wondered whether the girls' mother's death was related? And why we hadn't said something at the time? We'd got as far as knowing something was very wrong with Gabriele, and had put him into a private hospital – because in those days we could still afford to pay for that – but Romana was an adult and not so easily dealt with.

"…You have to understand, Giuseppe. We'd lost Angelina barely six months before we lost Claudia. And her we loved dearly. The first time we were wrapped in grief and didn't think clearly. Only Claudia did that. And that was because, of all of us, she saw Romana clearly. She knew beyond a doubt what her sister was capable of. Whereas we had told the lie of her being mentally disabled for so many years we had come to believe it ourselves."

Fleur nodded. "And of course, once you realised that, you were trapped. You couldn't come clean without condemning yourselves for a crime you hadn't even known you were committing."

Sophia smiled gratefully at her. "That's exactly it. By then we had our own Giuseppe and his sisters to think about. What would have happened to them if we'd been taken to prison? Who would have looked after my babies? And in truth, we had done nothing. All we were guilty of was not believing the worst of our niece. Yet she used that against us time and again to get her own way."

"Well not all her own way," Antonio clarified. "When you came home that summer, Angelo, you hadn't seen any of us in over six months. You'd spent Christmas revising for your exams at the home of a friend, because we didn't want you home that year because there was a nasty flu epidemic going around, and you could have only come for a couple of weeks anyway. If, for one second, we had thought that that Christmas would be the last time you saw your dear mamma alive, then of course, we would have insisted that you come back. But we couldn't, and therefore we didn't, and it has been on our consciences ever since."

Angelo got up and went and hugged first his great-aunt and then his great-uncle. "I don't hold either of you responsible for any of this," he told them. "Good God, she was my mother, and yet I couldn't tell them apart!"

"And the same goes for you, Angelo," Fleur interjected. "I don't think Romana ever gave you the chance to tell her apart. How many times did you encounter her right after your real mother died? Not many. And so by the time you did meet more frequently, you were more of an adult, and seeing things through different eyes. And I think she knew that and played on it.

"But I have to ask you, Sophia and Antonio, what the hell happened when Angelo was sixteen and Romana kept him imprisoned? I know it was only months after Claudia had been killed, and you must have been in shock, but by then you had to know which of the sisters had survived and which one had died. So what did you do?"

Antonio groaned and threw his hands in the air in exasperation. "We didn't know that Angelo *had* come back. I know that sounds ridiculous said like this, but we didn't. His letters had gone to his mother, and Romana had opened them and then destroyed them. So *she* knew which flight he was coming in on, when we didn't even know he was coming!"

He gestured to Giuseppe to fill the wine glasses up again, and Fleur noted that this time Giuseppe gave himself as big a glassful as anyone else.

"It was Gabriele getting free that did it," Antonio explained. "We would never have known anything otherwise – in fact we thought that

Gabriele was still being kept locked up at the house on the far side of the estate, because we'd already run out of money for the hospital. But then there came word that young girls were being accosted by a young man. And the description matched Gabriele too well for me to ignore. So I went into the village and nearby town and talked to the victims."

He shuddered. "By the time I'd finished I don't know how I kept going. It was so clear that it was Gabriele it was shocking. So I went to the house and opened the door to the locked room. I found you, Angelo, and in that moment, I knew what had happened. If I'd opened the door on Gabriele, he would have been at me like a wild beast. But you just lay there weeping." Now Antonio himself was weeping. "I carried you outside and then went to get my car. I drove you to the hospital straightaway. I can't tell you how sorry I am that you had to go through that.

"But then I went in search of Romana. I was so angry! So furious at her for doing that to you! Yet she still had a card left to play. She agreed that she would allow Gabriele to be taken to a hospital, paid for out of Claudia's money this time, as long as you never heard a word about him, and continued to think of her as Claudia.

"…What could I do? Risk him attacking another girl, and maybe another, before he was caught? She had him so well hidden from us, you see, and refused to tell me where he was. So I said yes, and we picked Gabriele up that night from a spot out in the countryside which she had insisted upon, though clearly not wherever he had been, and I took him to a sanatorium.

"It was the one and only time I won against Romana, for as soon as Gabriele had been led away, I called the nurses and handed over Romana as well. How she cursed me that night! I have never heard language like that from anyone, let alone a woman. And she meant it! But the one good thing was that the nursing staff saw her at her worst and understood why I needed her to be locked away. We nursed you back to health, Angelo, and swore that you would never see Romana again. I wish we'd told you the truth then, but we were so deep in the lie by then that it just didn't occur to us."

Angelo heaved a heavy sigh. "But of course, I did. You weren't rich enough to keep her in there forever. At some point the money ran out, didn't it?"

His great-uncle nodded. "I reached a point where I either had to sell up to fund her care, and leave nothing to Giuseppe and his family, or let her out. And I couldn't tap into Claudia's money in the way Romana had because I couldn't pretend to be her! By then Romana seemed to have improved – or according to the nursing staff she had. We were told that as long as she continued to take her medication that there was nothing to fear from her."

"But they didn't know that she was a double murderess, did they?" Fleur sighed. "That was the one thing you didn't dare tell them."

"No, we didn't," admitted Sophia. "And once again we were fooled. We thought that she'd done what she did because she was so mentally unwell. Therefore now that she'd had years of treatment, and the hospital thought that she was fit enough to come home, that she'd done what she did out of sickness, not malice."

Antonio squeezed his wife's hand comfortingly. "And in truth, for the first couple of years, she was a different person. She was actually so much more like Claudia that we were lulled into a false sense of security. There were no outbursts. No screaming fits. Nothing to alert us to the fact that she was someone who would never be fully cured of her insanity. She behaved incredibly normally."

"When did that change?" Angelo wondered.

Yet his great-uncle could only shrug again. "I can't tell you exactly when, because from our point of view, nothing *did* change. Money for Gabriele's care again became an issue because she'd drained Claudia's accounts, but this time Romana was all understanding and compliance. Yes, she agreed, she would have him home, and yes, she would keep him under restraint. We didn't want him imprisoned, we told her, just kept away from ordinary people so that he did them no harm. And she gave every impression of understanding that."

"So it kind of crept up on you?" Fleur guessed.

Antonio nodded. "It did. I think the first time I became seriously worried was when Angelo was over here telling us about the terrible time he had had with his videos online. Of course, he couldn't imagine how such a thing could happen, but I think that was the point when I looked at him and remembered how Gabriele had looked the last time I had seen him, and at that point I think in my heart of hearts I knew that Gabriele had impersonated Angelo."

Angelo ducked his head to hide what Fleur knew would be the hurt in his eyes that his great-uncle hadn't been straight with him. Yet he said, "You couldn't tell me, could you? Romana was still holding you to that promise that she would behave if I carried on thinking she was my mum."

"Of course!" Fleur saw the catch. "Romana was still behaving! Gabriele wasn't, but *she* was. But by this time, I bet she was starting to threaten you with letting him loose!"

Sophia sighed. "That was exactly how it was. And she was crafty enough to know that we hadn't told the police anything of her involvement with either Angelina's death, or Claudia's. So she had that hold over us too."

"The evil bitch," Fleur breathed without thinking, but then saw Sophia nodding in agreement. After all they'd been through, there wasn't much family love left for Romana.

Angelo leaned back and gave them all a baleful stare. "And then the word came about my grandfather being in his last illness, didn't it? I get that to you it must have been a heaven-sent opportunity to get her out of your lives once and for all. Send her and her lunatic son over to England and never see them again."

Surprisingly it was Giuseppe who answered this time. "I'm the one who has to take the blame for that. Papa and Mamma had never told me the full story of the hold Romana had over them. In fact, like you, I thought it was Claudia who I was seeing and hearing, that's how much I was out of the loop. And so, when she said she needed me to go and get your passport to get you out of the country – because she said you were the one who'd crashed her car and was in hiding – I was the one who got your passport to her."

"Bloody hell" Angelo gasped.

Giuseppe looked deeply contrite. "If I had known that she'd killed twice already, I might have been more inclined to go to the police here and tell them of how she had been blackmailing my parents. Instead, I just saw a spoilt cousin who was eternally making my beloved parents miserable, and that there was a way to get rid of her forever without any pain to us, even though I always liked you."

"I don't think anyone can blame you for that," Fleur said, offering him the way out and keeping the peace. "If someone in the family had been tormenting my parents like that, I think I'd have been tempted to take the easiest way out, especially knowing only what you did at the time."

Giuseppe gave her a wan smile. "Thank you for that, but I'm realising now that it was too easy for me to shut my eyes to why my papa and mamma were so constrained. I should have thought more about it, and wondered why someone who could be such an astute businessman as Papa, and such a good reader of people, could be so taken in. I should have known that there was far more to it than that, and asked a lot more questions."

"We didn't want you to know," Sophia told her son sadly. "We didn't want you to be as burdened as we'd been. I for one hoped that once we were gone, that not knowing would mean that you could go to the police, and that that would be the way that Romana and Gabriele would be stopped. We've left letters with our wills telling you everything. You would have known once we were gone."

"Well, they're stopped now," Fleur said, unable to avoid thinking about the sight of Romana crawling her way to that smoke-wreathed abyss, her coat already starting to catch alight, and wondering whether the ghosts had been right all along. Romana had deserved every bit of pain she had suffered at the end. As for Gabriele, his charred remains had been found down in one of the rooms where the glass roof had cracked open and dropped him into the heart of the fire. There was a sense for her of it being fitting that he should have died alone and unable to pass on his dreadful spiritual passenger, but also in the cleansing effect of the fire, which nothing could have survived.

Epilogue

They remained in Italy for a week, during which time there were many more heart-searching conversations with various family members. But by the time Fleur and Angelo were waving them goodbye at Pisa airport, the ghosts of the past had been laid to rest, and Angelo was at peace with his family. He would be paying for the headstone on what he now knew was his mother's grave to be replaced, and there had been many tears all round when they had gone to lay flowers there. In contrast, Romana would be cremated in England at a non-attendant service. When Fleur had told them that there was such a thing, Angelo in particular breathed a huge sigh of relief. Maintaining the façade of a grieving son or nephew was something he had been dreading, especially if the press had got wind of it happening, and the paparazzi had been there with their snooping telephoto lenses.

"She gets cremated under her real name," Fleur reassured him, "so there's no reason why anyone would make the connection to you. But if you're still worried, why don't you ask the funeral directors to make the booking for the cremation in the name of

Romana Montefiore in order to retain some privacy. I can't imagine that there are any Montefiores in Cheltenham with the remotest connection to you."

Gabriele's few remains were to be further cremated at the same time, and then their combined ashes scattered by someone anonymous.

"I don't even want to know where they lie," Angelo told the family.

However, it was Oliver who came up with an even better solution when they got back to London and spoke to him.

"There's a Catholic cemetery in Sheffield," he told them. "I'm sure that for a generous donation towards its upkeep there wouldn't be a problem with having the ashes scattered there. After what you've told me of Romana's reaction to having the Italian priest praying over her, if anything is going to guarantee her and Gabriele lying quietly, it would be what little remains of them being on ground sanctified by the Roman Church."

They left the arrangements for that in his capable hands, Fleur remembering Grandma Rose's warning about not letting Angelo near the remains, and doing all she could to discourage his involvement.

With regard to her job, sadly Carrie-Ann's prediction came all too true. While Mr Harris and Lucy were off on their respective sick leaves – attributed to stress in Lucy's case – Fleur was deemed to be using up the holiday leave she had accumulated. But once they were back, it swiftly became clear that neither wanted to work with Fleur again.

In Mr Harris' case, she suspected that he couldn't come to terms with the way that she had told him what to do in those last phone calls. The fact that if he'd listened to her then he wouldn't have been so badly hurt seemingly didn't count in her favour, but rather against her. Lucy, however, blamed Fleur for Bethany breaking up with her – though how Fleur could have contributed to that nobody could work out. Yet the practicality of the firm needing Lucy more than they needed Fleur won out, and Fleur's contract was terminated, though with a generous settlement once Angelo had hinted that he would be getting Oliver's high-powered legal firm to fight an unfair dismissal case for her. Otherwise, she would have left without a penny in compensation.

Nor was the subsequent glowing reference they provided much consolation for her. It positively reeked of 'cover-up', to the extent that it was almost worse than no reference at all. For the first couple of weeks after that, Fleur had many a sleepless night, worried stiff about how she was going to earn her living now. But at that point Angelo began to make his feelings for her a lot clearer, and it gradually sank in that she was not going to need to worry about getting another job. And in a neat twist, Carrie-Ann applied to, and was immediately snapped up by, the company's nearest competitors, leaving Mr Harris and Lucy well and truly in the lurch since they would need to recruit not one but two capable people.

"Karma's a bitch!" Carrie-Ann told Fleur with glee, when she rang her to pass on the good news about her new job. "I think they'll have trouble getting replacements for *both* of us any time soon. And ever serve them right for backing Lucy, instead of disciplining her for the way she behaved towards you."

The oddest development, though, concerned *The Rookery*. Against the odds, the huge timbers of the original Jacobean stairwell had survived, and the fire had revealed a surprising amount of that original house. Certainly enough that pulling down what remained was out of the question. On the other hand, demolishing the old lodge posed no problems once Oliver's firm had finished with the firm Ignatius and Aleister had used, who were themselves facing some serious questions by the Law Society. That was going to be replaced as soon as possible with a purpose-built community centre for the village, and with the path to it being made into a nature walk for the locals.

The first night Fleur took Angelo into the *Fox & Hounds*, he felt very awkward, but the warmth of welcome and the sympathy he got from everyone soon won him around, though his paying for several rounds of drinks didn't hurt. And once he started asking the locals what they wanted and needed from a community centre, he soon got drawn into the details of village life. With his wallet considerably lighter, including a sizable donation to the church roof repair fund, by the time they left Fleur thought that another significant bridge had been crossed. Angelo might never want to live here permanently, but he would be accepted as a generous landlord in the area.

"Do you want to sell up once the work on *The Rookery* is done?" Fleur asked him, as they sat out on his balcony in London once they'd returned there.

"I never want to live in the *Dower House*, if that's what you mean," he answered with a shudder. "It's weird, isn't it, but it feels as if the fire wiped away a lot that was bad from the big house, whereas I still feel my skin crawling whenever I go in through the door of the *Dower*."

Fleur nodded. "Too much of Romana lurking there, I suspect, and of course it was where both your grandfather and great-grandfather spent a lot of time. I wasn't for one moment implying that you would ever want to live there. But it seems a shame to disregard the heritage side that comes with it from all of your female ancestors who worked so hard to make sure that the right people inherited it all."

Angelo sighed. "Put like, that, I see what you mean. It almost feels disrespectful to Mezelly, and Loverin, and Loretta, and Annora, to just stick it on the market and walk away."

"That's what I was thinking," though she didn't add that she'd not forgotten Henrik's skeleton out there somewhere in a barrel in a field. It wouldn't do for some property developer to snap the place up and decide that half a dozen executive houses would fit nicely out there, and for the bones to turn up with the first digger-full! Questions would definitely be asked if that happened.

"What about making it into a conference centre, though?" she asked instead. "A place where nobody would be staying for very long, so nobody getting very strange dreams or anything. There are lots of hotels making money out of small-scale meetings, and if you had some bright young architect design a modern building which showed off the best of what remains of the old Jacobean house, I suspect the planning permission people wouldn't object too hard. That way you'd be bringing work into the village, and not losing all control of the place, and yet not living there either."

"It's a thought," Angelo agreed enthusiastically. "I've already put the Cheltenham house on the market. That's hardly been in the family for generations, and I'll never use it. It'll be an easy sell, too, so the money I get from that can be used to help rebuild *The Rookery*." Then he turned and smiled at her. "But what about you, Fleur? Where do you want to live? I know you like this place, but you're not a big city girl. There's no way I'd want to keep you cooped up here for years on end. You need space and countryside. So where would you like to live?"

Fleur smiled. "I wouldn't mind being down in the village, or in one of the larger houses just on the edge of it. Oddly, I don't want to carry on living just up the road from where I was working – too many chances of walking into Lucy or Mr Harris there, and I don't know that I would be able to stop myself from speaking my mind now that I don't work with them."

"Oops!" Angelo chuckled. "Possibly not wise."

"No, I thought that. I thought I might rent my flat out for a while, though."

Angelo gave her a mock serious frown. "You can't help being so bloody independent, can you? Okay, rent your bijou flat out and keep the income, but you're not paying a penny towards anything while you live with me – I do have some pride left, you know."

Fleur blushed, but it felt good to have someone who wanted to look after her as much as she wanted to look after him. "And what about your vlogs, Mr Internet Superstar? Will you carry those on?"

Angelo rolled his eyes. "God, no! I think I've outgrown those. No, I think your idea of a conference centre is a good one, and learning how to make that work is something that grown-up Angelo could quite enjoy. Not half as much as being with you, though. Could you see your way to changing your name to Fleur Vance?"

Thank you for taking the time to read this book. I would like to invite you to join my mailing list. I promise I won't bombard you with endless emails, but I would like to be able to let you know when any new books come out, or of any special offers I have on the existing ones.

If you sign up, you will be able to download free material to read.

Also, if you've enjoyed this book you personally (yes, *you*) can make a big difference to what happens next.

Reviews are one of the best ways to get other people to discover my books. I'm an independent author, so I don't have a publisher paying big bucks to spread the word or arrange huge promos in bookstore chains, there's just me and my computer.

But I have something that's actually better than all that corporate money – it's you, my committed and loyal readers. Honest reviews help bring them to the attention of other readers (although if you think something needs fixing I would really like you to tell me first!). So if you've enjoyed this book, it would mean a great deal to me if you would spend a couple of minutes posting a review on the site where you purchased it.

Thank you so much.

Author's Notes

As ever with these houses I write about, there is no such place as *The Rookery*, though it is based on a real house that lies within the area. I find houses built over several phases fascinating, and always wonder what stories they hold. So for this outing I moved away from my beloved medieval era and wandered into a later, but still historical period, and I hope I have done the lovely houses from the late Jacobean and early Georgian period justice.

As for the gypsy names, it may surprise you to learn that they are names taken from records and newspaper articles of very real Romanies, and of the eras written about. There genuinely were gypsies called Wantelo, Muldobrai, Paizeni, Starlina and the others, all travelling around the Herefordshire/Worcestershire area or semi-settled in the counties. And it is not such a fictional stretch to think of one such family working initially with the horses at a local 'big house', and then gradually becoming more settled there, when so many Roma trade and work with horses even up to the present day – Smith is a gypsy occupational surname for a very good reason because many were itinerant farriers.

I have very deliberately not gone into great detail of the toxic extracts which can be made from plants. I did a good deal of research on this while I was writing this book, but decided that it would not be responsible to create some toxic cocktail which might be used in real life, because you never can tell who will pick up your book once it has flown out into the big wide world!

If you are really interested in this, then there are some very detailed books out there, and there are poison gardens still in existence. The most famous of these is the poison garden at Alnwick Castle, but for good reason it is kept under lock and key, and you cannot just wander into it. Deadly plants (if misused) include Foxgloves and Aconite, but in centuries past they also had medicinal uses – you just had to be very careful and know what you were doing.

I have known some folk who have ventured into the preservation and curation side of things, but any mistakes in describing Fleur and her colleagues' work are mine alone. And as with the house, there is no auction house/antique experts in the general area of Worcester as I've described who are like *Miller, Bronson & Carter*, and any similarity to any real company is totally coincidental. I do try to make sure that names don't match up but there's always an outside chance that I've missed a reference.

About the Author

L. J. Hutton lives in Worcestershire and writes history, mystery and fantasy novels. If you would like to know more about any of these books you are very welcome to come and visit my online home at www.ljhutton.com

Also by L. J. Hutton:

A Gate to Somewhen Else

Kat's boss has vanished, but they'll never find him where he's gone!

Interior designer Kat is broke and desperately needs this commission restoring the Edwardian mansion of Fownhope Priors, but her employer Scott's wife and mother-in-law are a nightmare. Yet when they are killed in suspicious circumstances, and she is the last person to see him, she can't help but be drawn in to the family's feuds. Where has Scott Hawkesmoor vanished to? Is it back to Yorkshire where his wife and mother-in-law died? Or is it somewhere far stranger? And how can she ever explain it to anyone – especially the police – let alone how she knows?

Enlisting the help of Scott's solicitor and friend, Drew, seems like a good idea, but is complicated by finding herself confusingly attracted to him. Could he be the fresh start she needs in a relationship? Then her own family's dark secret rears its ugly head and an over-eager detective jumps to the wrong conclusions. Can Kat convince Drew and the police that she's not a murderess? Why won't Drew trust her, and what is his own strange past that he's hiding?

Yet above all, once she discovers where Scott is trapped, can she find a way to send him a message that will show him the way back home, and can he go through the right gateway? Or will he end up somewhen else altogether? And will the experience of the portal reveal whether Scott or Drew is the man she's been looking for?

House of Lost Secrets

Some people keep secrets, this house hides them for generations. Can Cleo dig back in time to save lives in the present?

When genealogist Cleo is asked to investigate the family of Upper Moore Huse as a favour to her estate agent friend, it's a different commission to the ones she's used to. And right from the start she feels there's something not quite right about Mrs Darcy

D'Eath Wytcombe. What is Mrs Wytcome's real motive for digging so deep into her late husband's family? What secrets does she think Cleo will uncover? And is she prepared for what else might be revealed?

As Cleo discovers increasing numbers of old letters, some of which have been buried for over a century in hiding places within the house, a strange web of deceit begins to appear. What was the family's connection to Georgian and Victorian Croatia and Italy, and just how closely related to one another were some of the Wytcombes? More urgently, who have been the real heirs to the house down the generations, and have others been willing to resort to blackmail or even murder to keep it from them?

With Mrs Wytcombe pushing for a swift sale of the house, Cleo must work against the clock to find the true heirs to Upper Moore House and prevent a terrible miscarriage of justice.

Printed in Great Britain
by Amazon

56621828R00320